ABOUT THE AUTHOR

STEPHEN KING   Photograph © Dick Dickinson

There is a reason why Stephen King is one of the bestselling writers in the world, *ever*. As George Pelecanos says: 'King's gift of storytelling is unrivalled. His ferocious imagination is un-limited.' King knows how to write stories that draw you in and are *impossible to put down*.

King is the author of more than fifty books, all of them world-wide bestsellers, including the iconic, chilling classics *Cujo*, *The Dark Half*, *Doctor Sleep*, *Pet Sematary*, *'Salem's Lot* and *The Shining*. Many of his books and novellas have been turned into celebrated films, including *Cujo*, *Misery*, *The Shining* and *The Shawshank Redemption*.

King was the recipient of the 2003 National Book Foundation Medal for Distinguished Contribution to American Letters. He lives with his wife, novelist Tabitha King, in Maine.

By Stephen King and published by Hodder & Stoughton

NOVELS:

Carrie
'Salem's Lot
The Shining
The Stand
The Dead Zone
Firestarter
Cujo
Cycle of the Werewolf
Christine
Pet Sematary
IT
The Eyes of the Dragon
Misery
The Tommyknockers
The Dark Half
Needful Things
Gerald's Game
Dolores Claiborne
Insomnia
Rose Madder
Desperation
Bag of Bones
The Girl Who Loved Tom Gordon
Dreamcatcher
From a Buick 8
Cell
Lisey's Story
Duma Key
Under the Dome
11.22.63
Doctor Sleep
Mr Mercedes
Revival
Finders Keepers
End of Watch
Sleeping Beauties (with Owen King)
The Outsider

The Dark Tower I: The Gunslinger
The Dark Tower II:
The Drawing of the Three
The Dark Tower III: The Waste Lands
The Dark Tower IV: Wizard and Glass
The Dark Tower V: Wolves of the Calla
The Dark Tower VI: Song of Susannah
The Dark Tower VII: The Dark Tower
The Wind through the Keyhole:
A Dark Tower Novel

As Richard Bachman

Thinner
The Running Man
The Bachman Books
The Regulators
Blaze

STORY COLLECTIONS:

Night Shift
Different Seasons
Skeleton Crew
Four Past Midnight
Nightmares and Dreamscapes
Hearts in Atlantis
Everything's Eventual
Just After Sunset
Stephen King Goes to the Movies
Full Dark, No Stars
The Bazaar of Bad Dreams

NON-FICTION

Danse Macabre
On Writing (A Memoir of the Craft)

PRAISE FOR THE SHINING

'...ously a masterpiece, probably the best supernatural novel
...hundred years' – Peter Straub

'I recently picked up *The Shining* again, with a view to "having
... through". No chance of that – if you start it, you'll finish
... His characters are flesh and blood; his tone and technique
...ful' - Simon Lelic for *Love Reading*

'... and atmospheric' – James Smythe, *Guardian*

HAVE YOU READ . . . ?

CUJO

Cujo is a huge Saint Bernard dog, the family's best friend and protector. Then one day Cujo gets bitten by a rabid bat . . . and the gentle giant becomes a vortex of terror, trapping those around him.

THE DARK HALF

For years, Thad Beaumont has been writing books under the pseudonym George Stark. When a journalist threatens to expose Beaumont's pen name, the author decides to go public first, killing off his pseudonym. But Stark isn't content to be dispatched that easily . . .

PET SEMATARY

Dr Louis Creed and his family have just moved to rural Maine. Near their house, local children have created a cemetery for dogs and cats killed on the busy highway. But deeper in the woods lies another grave-yard, an ancient Indian burial ground whose sinister properties Dr Creed is about to discover . . .

'SALEM'S LOT

Author Ben Mears returns to 'Salem's Lot to write a book about a house that has haunted him since childhood, only to find his isolated hometown infested with vampires. Now Ben must gather the locals to combat the terrors before it is too late.

STEPHEN KING

THE SHINING

HODDER

Grateful acknowledgement is made for permission to
reprint excerpts from the following copyright material:

'Call Me' © 1973 by Jec Music Publishing Co. and Al Green
Music Inc. for the world. All rights for Canada controlled by Felsted Music
of Canada Ltd. All rights for the world except the United States and Canada
controlled by Burlington Music Co. Ltd, London

'Your Cheatin' Heart' by Hank Williams © 1952 by Fred Rose Music Inc.
Used by permission of the publisher, Fred Rose Music Inc., 2510 Franklin
Road, Nashville, Tennessee 37204. All right reserved.

Lyrics from 'Twenty Flight Rock' by Ned Fairchild © 1957 by
Hill and Range songs Inc., Noma Music Inc. and Elvis Presley Music,
International copyright secured. All rights reserved. Used by permission
of Unichappel Music, Inc. 'Bad Moon Rising' by John C. Fogerty ©
1969 Jondora Music, Berkeley, California. Used by permission. All
rights reserved. International copyright secured.

First published in Great Britain in © 1977 by New English Library,
a division of Hodder & Stoughton
An Hachette UK Company

This paperback edition published in 2011

A Hodder Paperback

33

A CIP catalogue record for this title is available from the British Library

ISBN 978 1 444 72072 3

Typeset in Bembo
Printed and bound in Great Britain by Clays Ltd, Elcograf S.p.A.

Hodder & Stoughton policy is to use papers that are natural,
renewable and recyclable products and made from wood grown in
sustainable forests. The logging and manufacturing processes are expected
to conform to the environmental regulations of the country of origin.

Hodder & Stoughton Ltd
Carmelite House
50 Victoria Embankment
London EC4Y 0DZ
www.hodder.co.uk

This is for Joe Hill King, who shines on

My editor on this book, as on the previous two, was Mr William G. Thompson, a man of wit and good sense. His contribution to this book has been large, and for it, my thanks.

S.K.

Some of the most beautiful resort hotels in the world are located in Colorado, but the hotel in these pages is based on none of them. The Overlook and the people associated with it exist wholly within the author's imagination.

It was in this apartment, also, that there stood ... a gigantic clock of ebony. Its pendulum swung to and fro with a dull, heavy, monotonous clang; and when ... the hour was to be stricken, there came from the brazen lungs of the clock a sound which was clear and loud and deep and exceedingly musical, but of so peculiar a note and emphasis that, at each lapse of an hour, the musicians of the orchestra were constrained to pause ... to hearken to the sound; and thus the waltzers perforce ceased their evolutions; and there was a brief disconcert of the whole gay company; and, while the chimes of the clock yet rang, it was observed that the giddiest grew pale, and the more aged and sedate passed their hands over their brows as if in confused reverie or meditation. But when the echoes had fully ceased, a light laughter at once pervaded the assembly ... and [they] smiled as if at their own nervousness ... and made whispering vows, each to the other, that the next chiming of the clock should produce in them no similar emotion; and then, after the lapse of sixty minutes ... there came yet another chiming of the clock, and then were the same disconcert and tremulousness and meditation as before.

But in spite of these things, it was a gay and magnificent revel ...

E. A. Poe
'The Masque of the Red Death'

The sleep of reason breeds monsters.
Goya

It'll shine when it shines.
Folk saying

INTRODUCTION

STEPHEN KING

I think that in every writer's career – usually early in it – there comes a 'crossroads novel,' where the writer is presented with a choice: either doing what you have done before, or try to reach a little higher. What you only realize in retrospect is how important that choice is. Sometimes the moment only comes once. For me, the crossroads novel was *The Shining*, and I did decide to reach. I can even remember the exact moment the choice came: it was when Jack Torrance, *The Shining*'s flawed protagonist, is remembering his father, a drunken brute who abused his son mentally, physically and emotionally . . . all the ways it can be done, in other words.

Part of me wanted to describe the father's brutality and leave it at that. Surely, I thought, the book's readers would make the connection between Jack's relationship with his father and Jack's relationship with his own son, Danny, who is of course *The Shining*'s psychic focal point.

Another part of me wanted to go deeper – to admit Jack's love of his father in spite of (perhaps even *because* of) his father's unpredictable and often brutal nature. That was the part I listened to, and it made a big difference to the novel as a whole. Instead of changing from a relatively nice guy into a two-dimensional villain driven by supernatural forces to kill his wife and son, Jack Torrance became a more realistic (and therefore more frightening) figure. A killer motivated to his crimes by supernatural forces was, it seemed to me, almost comforting once you got below the surface thrills provided by any halfway competent ghost story. A killer that might be doing it because of childhood abuse *as well as* those ghostly forces . . . ah, that seemed genuinely disturbing. Furthermore, it offered a chance to blur the line between the supernatural and the psychotic, to take my story into that I-hope-this-is-only-a-dream territory where the merely scary becomes outright horrifying. My single conversation with the late Stanley Kubrick, about six months before he commenced filming on his version of *The Shining*, suggested that it was this quality about the story that appealed to him: what, exactly, is impelling Jack Torrance toward murder in the winter-isolated rooms and hallways of the Overlook Hotel? Is it undead people, or undead memories? Mr. Kubrick and I came to different conclusions (I *always* thought there were malevolent ghosts in The Overlook, driving Jack to the precipice), but perhaps those different conclusions are, in fact, the same. For aren't memories the true ghosts of our lives? Do they not drive all of us to words and acts we regret from time to time?

The decision I made to try and make Jack's father a real person, one who was loved as well as hated by his flawed son, took me a long way down the road to my current beliefs concerning what is so blithely dismissed as 'the horror novel.' I believe these stories exist because we sometimes need to create unreal monsters and bogies to stand in for all the things we fear in our real lives: the parent who punches instead of kissing, the auto accident that takes a loved one, the cancer we one day discover living in our own bodies. If such terrible occurrences were acts of darkness, they might actually be easier to cope with. But instead of being dark, they have their own terrible brilliance, it seems to me, and none shine so bright as the acts of cruelty we sometimes perpetrate in our own families. To look directly at such brilliance is to be blinded, and so we create any number of filters. The ghost story, the horror story, the uncanny tale – all of these are such filters. The man or woman who insists there are no ghosts is only ignoring the whispers of his or her own heart, and how cruel that seems to me. Surely even the most malignant ghost is a lonely thing, left out in the dark, desperate to be heard.

None of these things occurred to me in coherent or even semi-coherent form when I was writing *The Shining* in my little study looking out toward the Flatirons; I had a story to write, my daily goal of 3,000 words to meet (I'm lucky if I can manage 1,800 a day in my sixth decade). All I knew was that I had a choice, either to make little Jacky's father a flat-out bad guy (which I could do in my sleep) or to try for something a little more difficult and complex: in a word, reality.

If I had been less well-fixed financially, I might well have opted for choice number one. But my first two books, *Carrie* and *'Salem's Lot*, had been successful, and we Kings were doing okay in that regard. And I didn't want to settle for less when I sensed I could up the book's emotional ante considerably by making Jack Torrance a real character instead of just The Overlook's boogeyman.

The result wasn't perfect, and there is a cocky quality to some of *The Shining*'s prose that has come to grate on me in later years, but I still like the book enormously, and recognize the importance of the choice it forced on me: between the safe unreality of the amusement park funhouse and the much more dangerous truths that lurk between the lines of the fantasy genre's more successful works. That truth is that monsters are real, and ghosts are real, too. They live inside us, and sometimes they win.

That our better angels sometimes – often! – win instead, in spite of all odds, is another truth of *The Shining*. And thank God it is.

New York City
February 8, 2001

PART ONE
PREFATORY MATTERS

CHAPTER ONE
JOB INTERVIEW

Jack Torrance thought: *Officious little prick.*

Ullman stood five-five, and when he moved, it was with the prissy speed that seems to be the exclusive domain of all small plump men. The part in his hair was exact, and his dark suit was sober but comforting. I am a man you can bring your problems to, that suit said to the paying customer. To the hired help it spoke more curtly: This had better be good, you. There was a red carnation in the lapel, perhaps so that no one on the street would mistake Stuart Ullman for the local undertaker.

As he listened to Ullman speak, Jack admitted to himself that he probably could not have liked any man on that side of the desk – under the circumstances.

Ullman had asked a question he hadn't caught. That was bad; Ullman was the type of man who would file such lapses away in a mental Rolodex for later consideration.

'I'm sorry?'

'I asked if your wife fully understands what you would be taking on here. And there's your son, of course.' He glanced down at the application in front of him. 'Daniel. Your wife isn't a bit intimidated by the idea?'

'Wendy is an extraordinary woman.'

'And your son is also extraordinary?'

Jack smiled, a big wide PR smile. 'We like to think so, I suppose. He's quite self-reliant for a five-year-old.'

No returning smile from Ullman. He slipped Jack's application back into a file. The file went into a drawer. The desk top was now completely bare except for a blotter, a telephone, a Tensor lamp, and an in/out basket. Both sides of the in/out were empty, too.

Ullman stood up and went to the file cabinet in the corner.

'Step around the desk, if you will, Mr Torrance. We'll look at the hotel floor plans.'

He brought back five large sheets and set them down on the glossy walnut plain of the desk. Jack stood by his shoulder, very much aware of the scent of Ullman's cologne. *All my men wear English Leather or they wear nothing at all* came into his mind for no reason at all, and he had to clamp his tongue between his teeth to keep in a bray of laughter. Beyond the wall, faintly, came the sounds of the Overlook Hotel's kitchen, gearing down from lunch.

'Top floor,' Ullman said briskly. 'The attic. Absolutely nothing up there now but bric-a-brac. The Overlook has changed hands several times since World War II and it seems that each successive manager has put everything they don't want up in the attic. I want rattraps and poison bait sowed around in it. Some of the third-floor chambermaids say they have heard rustling noises. I don't believe it, not for a moment, but there mustn't even be that one-in-a-hundred chance that a single rat inhabits the Overlook Hotel.'

Jack, who suspected that every hotel in the world had a rat or two, held his tongue.

'Of course you wouldn't allow your son up in the attic under any circumstances.'

'No,' Jack said, and flashed the big PR smile again. Humiliating situation. Did this officious little prick actually think he would allow his son to goof around in a rattrap attic full of junk furniture and God knew what else?

Ullman whisked away the attic floor plan and put it on the bottom of the pile.

'The Overlook has one hundred and ten guest quarters,' he said in a scholarly voice. 'Thirty of them, all suites, are here on the third floor. Ten in the west wing (including the Presidential Suite), ten in the center, ten more in the east wing. All of them command magnificent views.'

Could you at least spare the salestalk?

But he kept quiet. He needed the job.

Ullman put the third floor on the bottom of the pile and they studied the second floor.

THE SHINING

'Forty rooms,' Ullman said, 'thirty doubles and ten singles. And on the first floor, twenty of each. Plus three linen closets on each floor, and a storeroom which is at the extreme east end of the hotel on the second floor and the extreme west end on the first. Questions?'

Jack shook his head. Ullman whisked the second and first floors away.

'Now. Lobby level. Here in the center is the registration desk. Behind it are the offices. The lobby runs for eighty feet in either direction from the desk. Over here in the west wing is the Overlook Dining Room and the Colorado Lounge. The banquet and ballroom facility is in the east wing. Questions?'

'Only about the basement,' Jack said. 'For the winter care-taker, that's the most important level of all. Where the action is, so to speak.'

'Watson will show you all that. The basement floor plan is on the boiler room wall.' He frowned impressively, perhaps to show that as manager, he did not concern himself with such mundane aspects of the Overlook's operation as the boiler and the plumbing. 'Might not be a bad idea to put some traps down there too. Just a minute . . .'

He scrawled a note on a pad he took from his inner coat pocket (each sheet bore the legend *From the Desk of Stuart Ullman* in bold black script), tore it off, and dropped it into the out basket. It sat there looking lonesome. The pad disappeared back into Ullman's jacket pocket like the conclusion of a magician's trick. Now you see it, Jacky-boy, now you don't. This guy is a real heavyweight.

They had resumed their original positions, Ullman behind the desk and Jack in front of it, interviewer and interviewee, supplicant and reluctant patron. Ullman folded his neat little hands on the desk blotter and looked directly at Jack, a small, balding man in a banker's suit and a quiet gray tie. The flower in his lapel was balanced off by a small lapel pin on the other side. It read simply STAFF in small gold letters.

'I'll be perfectly frank with you, Mr Torrance. Albert Shock-ley is a powerful man with a large interest in the Overlook, which showed a profit this season for the first time in its history.

5

Mr Shockley also sits on the Board of Directors, but he is not a hotel man and he would be the first to admit this. But he has made his wishes in this caretaking matter quite obvious. He wants you hired. I will do so. But if I had been given a free hand in this matter, I would not have taken you on.'

Jack's hands were clenched tightly in his lap, working against each other, sweating. *Officious little prick, officious little prick, officious—*

'I don't believe you care much for me, Mr Torrance. I don't care. Certainly your feelings toward me play no part in my own belief that you are not right for the job. During the season that runs from May fifteenth to September thirtieth, the Overlook employs one hundred and ten people full-time; one for every room in the hotel, you might say. I don't think many of them like me and I suspect that some of them think I'm a bit of a bastard. They would be correct in their judgment of my character. I have to be a bit of a bastard to run this hotel in the manner it deserves.'

He looked at Jack for comment, and Jack flashed the PR smile again, large and insultingly toothy.

Ullman said: 'The Overlook was built in the years 1907 to 1909. The closest town is Sidewinder, forty miles east of here over roads that are closed from sometime in late October or November until sometime in April. A man named Robert Townley Watson built it, the grandfather of our present maintenance man. Vanderbilts have stayed here, and Rockefellers, and Astors, and Du Ponts. Four Presidents have stayed in the Presidential Suite. Wilson, Harding, Roosevelt, and Nixon.'

'I wouldn't be too proud of Harding and Nixon,' Jack murmured.

Ullman frowned but went on regardless. 'It proved too much for Mr Watson, and he sold the hotel in 1915. It was sold again in 1922, in 1929, in 1936. It stood vacant until the end of World War II, when it was purchased and completely renovated by Horace Derwent, millionaire inventor, pilot, film producer, and entrepreneur.'

'I know the name,' Jack said.

'Yes. Everything he touched seemed to turn to gold . . .

except the Overlook. He funneled over a million dollars into it before the first postwar guest ever stepped through its doors, turning a decrepit relic into a showplace. It was Derwent who added the roque court I saw you admiring when you arrived.'

'Roque?'

'A British forebear of our croquet, Mr Torrance. Croquet is bastardized roque. According to legend, Derwent learned the game from his social secretary and fell completely in love with it. Ours may be the finest roque court in America.'

'I wouldn't doubt it,' Jack said gravely. A roque court, a topiary full of hedge animals out front, what next? A life-sized Uncle Wiggly game behind the equipment shed? He was getting very tired of Mr Stuart Ullman, but he could see that Ullman wasn't done. Ullman was going to have his say, every last word of it.

'When he had lost three million, Derwent sold it to a group of California investors. Their experience with the Overlook was equally bad. Just not hotel people.

'In 1970, Mr Shockley and a group of his associates bought the hotel and turned its management over to me. We have also run in the red for several years, but I'm happy to say that the trust of the present owners in me has never wavered. Last year we broke even. And this year the Overlook's accounts were written in black ink for the first time in almost seven decades.'

Jack supposed that this fussy little man's pride was justified, and then his original dislike washed over him again in a wave.

He said: 'I see no connection between the Overlook's admittedly colorful history and your feeling that I'm wrong for the post, Mr Ullman.'

'One reason that the Overlook has lost so much money lies in the depreciation that occurs each winter. It shortens the profit margin a great deal more than you might believe, Mr Torrance. The winters are fantastically cruel. In order to cope with the problem, I've installed a full-time winter caretaker to run the boiler and to heat different parts of the hotel on a daily rotating basis. To repair breakage as it occurs and to do repairs, so the elements can't get a foothold. To be constantly alert to any and every contingency. During our first winter I hired a family instead of a single man. There was a tragedy. A horrible tragedy.'

Ullman looked at Jack coolly and appraisingly.

'I made a mistake. I admit it freely. The man was a drunk.'

Jack felt a slow, hot grin – the total antithesis of the toothy PR grin – stretch across his mouth. 'Is that it? I'm surprised Al didn't tell you. I've retired.'

'Yes, Mr Shockley told me you no longer drink. He also told me about your last job . . . your last position of trust, shall we say? You were teaching English in a Vermont prep school. You lost your temper, I don't believe I need to be any more specific than that. But I do happen to believe that Grady's case has a bearing, and that is why I have brought the matter of your . . . uh, previous history into the conversation. During the winter of 1970–71, after we had refurbished the Overlook but before our first season, I hired this . . . this unfortunate named Delbert Grady. He moved into the quarters you and your wife and son will be sharing. He had a wife and two daughters. I had reservations, the main ones being the harshness of the winter season and the fact that the Gradys would be cut off from the outside world for five to six months.'

'But that's not really true, is it? There are telephones here, and probably a citizen's band radio as well. And the Rocky Mountain National Park is within helicopter range and surely a piece of ground that big must have a chopper or two.'

'I wouldn't know about that,' Ullman said. 'The hotel does have a two-way radio that Mr Watson will show you, along with a list of the correct frequencies to broadcast on if you need help. The telephone lines between here and Sidewinder are still aboveground, and they go down almost every winter at some point or other and are apt to stay down for three weeks to a month and a half. There is a snowmobile in the equipment shed also.'

'Then the place really isn't cut off.'

Mr Ullman looked pained. 'Suppose your son or your wife tripped on the stairs and fractured his or her skull, Mr Torrance. Would you think the place was cut off then?'

Jack saw the point. A snowmobile running at top speed could get you down to Sidewinder in an hour and a half . . . maybe.

THE SHINING

A helicopter from the Parks Rescue Service could get up here in three hours . . . under optimum conditions. In a blizzard it would never even be able to lift off and you couldn't hope to run a snowmobile at top speed, even if you dared take a seriously injured person out into temperatures that might be twenty-five below – or forty-five below, if you added in the wind chill factor.

'In the case of Grady,' Ullman said, 'I reasoned much as Mr Shockley seems to have done in your case. Solitude can be damaging in itself. Better for the man to have his family with him. If there was trouble, I thought, the odds were very high that it would be something less urgent than a fractured skull or an accident with one of the power tools or some sort of convulsion. A serious case of the flu, pneumonia, a broken arm, even appendicitis. Any of those things would have left enough time.

'I suspect that what happened came as a result of too much cheap whiskey, of which Grady had laid in a generous supply, unbeknownst to me, and a curious condition which the old-timers call cabin fever. Do you know the term?' Ullman offered a patronizing little smile, ready to explain as soon as Jack admitted his ignorance, and Jack was happy to respond quickly and crisply.

'It's a slang term for the claustrophobic reaction that can occur when people are shut in together over long periods of time. The feeling of claustrophobia is externalized as dislike for the people you happen to be shut in with. In extreme cases it can result in hallucinations and violence – murder has been done over such minor things as a burned meal or an argument about whose turn it is to do the dishes.'

Ullman looked rather nonplussed, which did Jack a world of good. He decided to press a little further, but silently promised Wendy he would stay cool.

'I suspect you did make a mistake at that. Did he hurt them?'

'He killed them, Mr Torrance, and then committed suicide. He murdered the little girls with a hatchet, his wife with a shotgun, and himself the same way. His leg was broken. Undoubtedly so drunk he fell downstairs.'

Ullman spread his hands and looked at Jack self-righteously. 'Was he a high school graduate?'

'As a matter of fact, he wasn't,' Ullman said a little stiffly. 'I thought a, shall we say, less imaginative individual would be less susceptible to the rigors, the loneliness—'

'That was your mistake,' Jack said. 'A stupid man is more prone to cabin fever just as he's more prone to shoot someone over a card game or commit a spur-of-the-moment robbery. He gets bored. When the snow comes, there's nothing to do but watch TV or play solitaire and cheat when he can't get all the aces out. Nothing to do but bitch at his wife and nag at the kids and drink. It gets hard to sleep because there's nothing to hear. So he drinks himself to sleep and wakes up with a hangover. He gets edgy. And maybe the telephone goes out and the TV aerial blows down and there's nothing to do but think and cheat at solitaire and get edgier and edgier. Finally . . . boom, boom, boom.'

'Whereas a more educated man, such as yourself?'

'My wife and I both like to read. I have a play to work on, as Al Shockley probably told you. Danny has his puzzles, his coloring books, and his crystal radio. I plan to teach him to read, and I also want to teach him to snowshoe. Wendy would like to learn how, too. Oh yes, I think we can keep busy and out of each other's hair if the TV goes on the fritz.' He paused. 'And Al was telling the truth when he told you I no longer drink. I did once, and it got to be serious. But I haven't had so much as a glass of beer in the last fourteen months. I don't intend to bring any alcohol up here, and I don't think there will be an opportunity to get any after the snow flies.'

'In that you would be quite correct,' Ullman said. 'But as long as the three of you are up here, the potential for problems is multiplied. I have told Mr Shockley this, and he told me he would take the responsibility. Now I've told you, and apparently you are also willing to take the responsibility—'

'I am.'

'All right. I'll accept that, since I have little choice. But I would still rather have an unattached college boy taking a year off. Well, perhaps you'll do. Now I'll turn you over to Mr

Watson, who will take you through the basement and around the grounds. Unless you have further questions?'

'No. None at all.'

Ullman stood. 'I hope there are no hard feelings, Mr Torrance. There is nothing personal in the things I have said to you. I only want what's best for the Overlook. It is a great hotel. I want it to stay that way.'

'No. No hard feelings.' Jack flashed the PR grin again, but he was glad Ullman didn't offer to shake hands. There were hard feelings. All kinds of them.

CHAPTER TWO
BOULDER

She looked out the kitchen window and saw him just sitting there on the curb, not playing with his trucks or the wagon or even the balsa glider that had pleased him so much all the last week since Jack had brought it home. He was just sitting there, watching for their shopworn VW, his elbows planted on his thighs and his chin propped in his hands, a five-year-old kid waiting for his daddy.

Wendy suddenly felt bad, almost crying bad.

She hung the dish towel over the bar by the sink and went downstairs, buttoning the top two buttons of her house dress. Jack and his pride! *Hey no. Al, I don't need an advance. I'm okay for a while.* The hallway walls were gouged and marked with crayons, grease pencil, spray paint. The stairs were steep and splintery. The whole building smelled of sour age, and what sort of place was this for Danny after the small neat brick house in Stovington? The people living above them on the third floor weren't married, and while that didn't bother her, their constant, rancorous fighting did. It scared her. The guy up there was Tom, and after the bars had closed and they had returned home, the fights would start in earnest – the rest of the week was just a prelim in comparison. The Friday Night Fights, Jack called them, but it wasn't funny. The woman – her name was Elaine – would at last be reduced to tears and to repeating over and over again: 'Don't, Tom. Please don't. Please don't.' And he would shout at her. Once they had even awakened Danny, and Danny slept like a corpse. The next morning Jack caught Tom going out and had spoken to him on the sidewalk at some length. Tom started to bluster and Jack had said something else to him, too quietly for Wendy to hear, and Tom had only shaken his head sullenly and walked away. That had been a week ago and for a few days things had been better, but since the weekend things had been working back to normal – excuse me, abnormal. It was bad for the boy.

Her sense of grief washed over her again but she was on the walk now and she smothered it. Sweeping her dress under her and sitting down on the curb beside him, she said: 'What's up, doc?'

He smiled at her but it was perfunctory. 'Hi, Mom.'

The glider was between his sneakered feet, and she saw that one of the wings had started to splinter.

'Want me to see what I can do with that, honey?'

Danny had gone back to staring up the street. 'No. Dad will fix it.'

'Your daddy may not be back until suppertime, doc. It's a long drive up into those mountains.'

'Do you think the bug will break down?'

'No, I don't think so.' But he had just given her something new to worry about. *Thanks, Danny. I needed that.*

'Dad said it might,' Danny said in a matter-of-fact, almost bored manner. 'He said the fuel pump was all shot to shit.'

'Don't say that, Danny.'

'Fuel pump?' he asked her with honest surprise.

She sighed. 'No, "All shot to shit." Don't say that.'

'Why?'

'It's vulgar.'

'What's vulgar, Mom?'

'Like when you pick your nose at the table or pee with the bathroom door open. Or saying things like "All shot to shit." Shit is a vulgar word. Nice people don't say it.'

'Dad says it. When he was looking at the bugmotor he said, "Christ this fuel pump's all shot to shit." Isn't Dad nice?'

How do you get into these things, Winnifred? Do you practice?

'He's nice, but he's also a grown-up. And he's very careful not to say things like that in front of people who wouldn't understand.'

'You mean like Uncle Al?'

'Yes, that's right.'

'Can I say it when I'm grown-up?'

'I suppose you will, whether I like it or not.'

'How old?'

'How does twenty sound, doc?'

'That's a long time to have to wait.'

'I guess it is, but will you try?'

'Hokay.'

He went back to staring up the street. He flexed a little, as if to rise, but the beetle coming was much newer, and much brighter red. He relaxed again. She wondered just how hard this move to Colorado had been on Danny. He was close-mouthed about it, but it bothered her to see him spending so much time by himself. In Vermont three of Jack's fellow faculty members had had children about Danny's age – and there had been the preschool – but in this neighborhood there was no one for him to play with. Most of the apartments were occupied by students attending CU, and of the few married couples here on Arapahoe Street, only a tiny percentage had children. She had spotted perhaps a dozen of high school or junior high school age, three infants, and that was all.

'Mommy, why did Daddy lose his job?'

She was jolted out of her reverie and floundering for an answer. She and Jack had discussed ways they might handle just such a question from Danny, ways that had varied from evasion to the plain truth with no varnish on it. But Danny had never asked. Not until now, when she was feeling low and least prepared for such a question. Yet he was looking at her, maybe reading the confusion on her face and forming his own ideas about that. She thought that to children adult motives and actions must seem as bulking and ominous as dangerous animals seen in the shadows of a dark forest. They were jerked about like puppets, having only the vaguest notions why. The thought brought her dangerously close to tears again, and while she fought them off she leaned over, picked up the disabled glider, and turned it over in her hands.

'Your daddy was coaching the debate team, Danny. Do you remember that?'

'Sure,' he said. 'Arguments for fun, right?'

'Right.' She turned the glider over and over, looking at the trade name (SPEEDOGLIDE) and the blue star decals on the wings, and found herself telling the exact truth to her son.

'There was a boy named George Hatfield that Daddy had to cut from the team. That means he wasn't as good as some of the others. George said your daddy cut him because he didn't like him and not because he wasn't good enough. Then George did a bad thing. I think you know about that.'

'Was he the one who put holes in our bug's tires?'

'Yes, he was. It was after school and your daddy caught him doing it.' Now she hesitated again, but there was no question of evasion now; it was reduced to tell the truth or tell a lie.

'Your daddy . . . sometimes he does things he's sorry for later. Sometimes he doesn't think the way he should. That doesn't happen very often, but sometimes it does.'

'Did he hurt George Hatfield like the time I spilled all his papers?'

Sometimes —

(Danny with his arm in a cast)

— he does things he's sorry for later.

Wendy blinked her eyes savagely hard, driving her tears all the way back.

'Something like that, honey. Your daddy hit George to make him stop cutting the tires and George hit his head. Then the men who are in charge of the school said that George couldn't go there anymore and your daddy couldn't teach there anymore.' She stopped, out of words, and waited in dread for the deluge of questions.

'Oh,' Danny said, and went back to looking up the street. Apparently the subject was closed. If only it could be closed that easily for her—

She stood up. 'I'm going upstairs for a cup of tea, doc. Want a couple of cookies and a glass of milk?'

'I think I'll watch for Dad.'

'I don't think he'll be home much before five.'

'Maybe he'll be early.'

'Maybe,' she agreed. 'Maybe he will.'

She was halfway up the walk when he called, 'Mommy?'

'What, Danny?'

'Do you want to go and live in that hotel for the winter?'

Now, which of five thousand answers should she give to that one? The way she had felt yesterday or last night or this morning? They were all different, they crossed the spectrum from rosy pink to dead black.

She said: 'If it's what your father wants, it's what I want.' She paused. 'What about you?'

'I guess I do,' he said finally. 'Nobody much to play with around here.'

'You miss your friends, don't you?'

'Sometimes I miss Scott and Andy. That's about all.'

She went back to him and kissed him, rumpled his light-colored hair that was just losing its baby-fineness. He was such a solemn little boy, and sometimes she wondered just how he was supposed to survive with her and Jack for parents. The high hopes they had begun with came down to this unpleasant apartment building in a city they didn't know. The image of Danny in his cast rose up before her again. Somebody in the Divine Placement Service had made a mistake, one she sometimes feared could never be corrected and which only the most innocent bystander could pay for.

'Stay out of the road, doc,' she said, and hugged him tight. 'Sure, Mom.'

She went upstairs and into the kitchen. She put on the teapot and laid a couple of Oreos on a plate for Danny in case he decided to come up while she was lying down. Sitting at the table with her big pottery cup in front of her, she looked out the window at him, still sitting on the curb in his bluejeans and his oversized dark green Stovington Prep sweatshirt, the glider now lying beside him. The tears which had threatened all day now came in a cloudburst and she leaned into the fragrant, curling steam of the tea and wept. In grief and loss for the past, and terror of the future.

CHAPTER THREE
WATSON

You lost your temper, Ullman had said.

'Okay, here's your furnace,' Watson said, turning on a light in the dark, musty-smelling room. He was a beefy man with fluffy popcorn hair, white shirt, and dark green chinos. He swung open a small square grating in the furnace's belly and he and Jack peered in together. 'This here's the pilot light.' A steady blue-white jet hissing steadily upward channeled destructive force, but the key word, Jack thought, was *destructive* and not *channeled*: if you stuck your hand in there, the barbecue would happen in three quick seconds.

Lost your temper.

(Danny, are you all right?)

The furnace filled the entire room, by far the biggest and oldest Jack had ever seen.

'The pilot's got a fail-safe,' Watson told him. 'Little sensor in there measures heat. If the heat falls below a certain point, it sets off a buzzer in your quarters. Boiler's on the other side of the wall. I'll take you around.' He slammed the grating shut and led Jack behind the iron bulk of the furnace toward another door. The iron radiated a stuporous heat at them, and for some reason Jack thought of a large, dozing cat. Watson jingled his keys and whistled.

Lost your—

(When he went back into his study and saw Danny standing there, wearing nothing but his training pants and a grin, a slow, red cloud of rage had eclipsed Jack's reason. It had seemed slow subjectively, inside his head, but it must have all happened in less than a minute. It only seemed slow the way some dreams seem slow. The bad ones. Every door and drawer in his study seemed to have been ransacked in the time he had been gone.

17

Closet, cupboards, the sliding bookcase. Every desk drawer yanked out to the stop. His manuscript, the three-act play he had been slowly developing from a novelette he had written seven years ago as an undergraduate, was scattered all over the floor. He had been drinking a beer and doing the Act II corrections when Wendy said the phone was for him, and Danny had poured the can of beer all over the pages. Probably to see it foam. *See it foam, see it foam*, the words played over and over in his mind like a single sick chord on an out-of-tune piano, completing the circuit of his rage. He stepped deliberately toward his three-year-old son, who was looking up at him with that pleased grin, his pleasure at the job of work so successfully and recently completed in Daddy's study; Danny began to say something and that was when he had grabbed Danny's hand and bent it to make him drop the typewriter eraser and the mechanical pencil he was clenching in it. Danny had cried out a little . . . no . . . no . . . tell the truth . . . he screamed. It was all hard to remember through the fog of anger, the sick single thump of that one Spike Jones chord. Wendy somewhere, asking what was wrong. Her voice faint, damped by the inner mist. This was between the two of them. He had whirled Danny around to spank him, his big adult fingers digging into the scant meat of the boy's forearm, meeting around it in a closed fist, and the snap of the breaking bone had not been loud, not loud but it had been *very* loud, *HUGE*, but not loud. Just enough of a sound to slit through the red fog like an arrow – but instead of letting in sunlight, that sound let in the dark clouds of shame and remorse, the terror, the agonizing convulsion of the spirit. A clean sound with the past on one side of it and all the future on the other, a sound like a breaking pencil lead or a small piece of kindling when you brought it down over your knee. A moment of utter silence on the other side, in respect to the beginning future maybe, all the rest of his life. Seeing Danny's face drain of color until it was like cheese, seeing his eyes, always large, grow larger still, and glassy, Jack sure the boy was going to faint dead away into the puddle of beer and papers; his own voice, weak and drunk, slurry, trying to take it all back, to find *a way* around that not too loud sound of bone cracking and into the past – is there a status quo in the house? – saying: *Danny, are you all right?* Danny's answering shriek, then Wendy's shocked gasp as she came around them and saw the peculiar angle Danny's forearm had to his elbow; no arm was meant to hang quite that way in a world of normal families. Her own scream as she swept him into her arms, and a nonsense babble: *Oh God Danny oh dear God oh sweet God your poor sweet arm*; and Jack was standing there, stunned and stupid, trying to understand how a thing like this could have happened. He was standing there and his eyes met the eyes of his wife and he saw that Wendy hated him. It did not occur to him what the hate might mean in practical terms; it was only later that he realized she might have left him that night, gone to a motel, gotten a divorce lawyer in the morning; or called the police. He saw only that his wife hated him and he felt staggered by it, all alone. He felt awful. This was what oncoming death felt like. Then she fled for the telephone and dialed the hospital with their screaming boy wedged in the crook of her arm, and Jack did not go after her, he only stood in the ruins of his office, smelling beer and thinking—)

You lost your temper.

He rubbed his hand harshly across his lips and followed Watson into the boiler room. It was humid in here, but it was more than the humidity that brought the sick and slimy sweat onto his brow and stomach and legs. The remembering did that, it was a total thing that made that night two years ago seem like two hours ago. There was no lag. It brought the shame and revulsion back, the sense of having no worth at all, and that feeling always made him want to have a drink, and the wanting of a drink brought still blacker despair – would he ever have an hour, not a week or even a day, mind you, but just one waking hour when the craving for a drink wouldn't surprise him like this?

'The boiler,' Watson announced. He pulled a red and blue bandanna from his back pocket, blew his nose with a decisive honk, and thrust it back out of sight after a short peek into it to see if he had gotten anything interesting.

The boiler stood on four cement blocks, a long and cylindrical metal tank, copper-jacketed and often patched. It squatted beneath a confusion of pipes and ducts which zigzagged upward into the high, cobweb-festooned basement ceiling. To Jack's right, two large heating pipes came through the wall from the furnace in the adjoining room.

'Pressure gauge is here.' Watson tapped it. 'Pounds per square inch, psi. I guess you'd know that. I got her up to a hundred now, and the rooms get a little chilly at night. Few guests complain, what the fuck. They're crazy to come up here in September anyway. Besides, this is an old baby. Got more patches on her than a pair of welfare overalls.' Out came the bandanna. A honk. A peek. Back it went.

'I got me a fuckin' cold,' Watson said conversationally. 'I get one every September. I be tinkering down here with this old whore, then I be out cuttin the grass or rakin that roque court. Get a chill and catch a cold, my old mum used to say. God bless her, she been dead six year. The cancer got her. Once the cancer gets you, you might as well make your will.

'You'll want to keep your press up to no more than fifty, maybe sixty. Mr Ullman, he says to heat the west wing one day, central wing the next, east wing the day after that. Ain't he a crazyman? I hate that little fucker. Yap-yap-yap, all the livelong day, he's just like one a those little dogs that bites you on the ankle then run around an pee all over the rug. If brains was black powder he couldn't blow his own nose. It's a pity the things you see when you ain't got a gun.

'Look here. You open an close these ducks by pullin these rings. I got em all marked for you. The blue tags all go to the rooms in the east wing. Red tags is the middle. Yellow is the west wing. When you go to heat the west wing, you got to remember that's the side of the hotel that really catches the weather. When it whoops, those rooms get as cold as a frigid woman with an ice cube up her works. You can run your press all the way to eighty on west wing days. I would, anyway.'

'The thermostats upstairs—' Jack began.

Watson shook his head vehemently, making his fluffy hair bounce on his skull. 'They ain't hooked up. They're just there for show. Some of these people from California, they don't think things is right unless they got it hot enough to grow a palm tree in their fuckin bedroom. All the heat comes from down here. Got to watch the press, though. See her creep?'

He tapped the main dial, which had crept from a hundred pounds per square inch to a hundred and two as Watson soliloquized. Jack felt a sudden shiver cross his back in a hurry and thought: *The goose just walked over my grave.* Then Watson gave the pressure wheel a spin and dumped the boiler off. There was a great hissing, and the needle dropped back to ninety-one. Watson twisted the valve shut and the hissing died reluctantly.

'She creeps,' Watson said. 'You tell that fat little peckerwood Ullman, he drags out the account books and spends three hours showing how we can't afford a new one until 1982. I tell you, this whole place is gonna go sky-high someday, and I just hope that fat fuck's here to ride the rocket. God, I wish I could be as charitable as my mother was. She could see the good in everyone. Me, I'm just as mean as a snake with the shingles. What the fuck, a man can't help his nature.

'Now you got to remember to come down here twice a day and once at night before you rack in. You got to check the press. If you forget, it'll just creep and creep and like as not you an your fambly'll wake up on the fuckin moon. You just dump her off a little and you'll have no trouble.'

'What's top end?'

'Oh, she's rated for two-fifty, but she'd blow long before that now. You couldn't get me to come down an stand next to her when that dial was up to one hundred and eighty.'

'There's no automatic shutdown?'

'No, there ain't. This was built before such things were required. Federal government's into everything these days, ain't it? FBI openin mail, CIA buggin the goddam phones . . . and look what happened to that Nixon. Wasn't that a sorry sight?

'But if you just come down here regular an check the press, you'll be fine. An remember to switch those ducks around like he wants. Won't none of the rooms get much above forty-five unless we have an amazin warm winter. And you'll have your own apartment just as warm as you like it.'

'What about the plumbing?'

'Okay, I was just getting to that. Over here through this arch.'

They walked into a long, rectangular room that seemed to stretch for miles. Watson pulled a cord and a single seventy-five-watt bulb cast a sickish, swinging glow over the area they were standing in. Straight ahead was the bottom of the elevator shaft, heavy greased cables descending to pulleys twenty feet in diameter and a huge, grease-clogged motor. Newspapers were everywhere, bundled and banded and boxed. Other cartons were marked *Records* or *Invoices* or *Receipts* – SAVE! The smell was yellow and moldy. Some of the cartons were falling apart, spilling yellow flimsy sheets that might have been twenty years old out onto the floor. Jack stared around, fascinated. The Overlook's entire history might be here, buried in these rotting cartons.

'That elevator's a bitch to keep runnin,' Watson said, jerking his thumb at it. 'I *know* Ullman's buying the state elevator inspector a few fancy dinners to keep the repairman away from that fucker.

'Now, here's your central plumbin core.' In front of them five large pipes, each of them wrapped in insulation and cinched with steel bands, rose into the shadows and out of sight.

Watson pointed to a cobwebby shelf beside the utility shaft. There were a number of greasy rags on it, and a loose-leaf binder. 'That there is all your plumbin schematics,' he said. 'I don't think you'll have any trouble with leaks – never has been – but sometimes the pipes freeze up. Only way to stop that is to run the faucets a little bit durin the nights, but there's over four hundred taps in this fuckin palace. That fat fairy upstairs would scream all the way to Denver when he saw the water bill. Ain't that right?'

'I'd say that's a remarkably astute analysis.'

Watson looked at him admiringly. 'Say, you really are a college fella, aren't you? Talk just like a book. I admire that, as long as the fella ain't one of those fairy-boys. Lots of em are. You know who stirred up all those college riots a few years ago? The hommasexshuls, that's who. They get frustrated an have to cut loose. Comin out of the closet, they call it. Holy shit, I don't know what the world's comin to.

'Now, if she freezes, she most likely gonna freeze right up in this shaft. No heat, you see. If it happens, use this.' He reached into a broken orange crate and produced a small gas torch.

'You just unstrap the insulation when you find the ice plug and put the heat right to her. Get it?'

'Yes. But what if a pipe freezes outside the utility core?'

That won't happen if you're doin your job and keepin the place heated. You can't get to the other pipes anyway. Don't you fret about it. You'll have no trouble. Beastly place down here. Cobwebby. Gives me the horrors, it does.'

'Ullman said the first winter caretaker killed his family and himself.'

'Yeah, that guy Grady. He was a bad actor, I knew that the minute I saw him. Always grinnin like an egg-suck dog. That was when they were just startin out here and that fat fuck Ullman, he woulda hired the Boston Strangler if he'd've worked for minimum wage. Was a ranger from the National Park that found em; the phone was out. All of em up in the west wing on the third floor, froze solid. Too bad about the little girls. Eight and six, they was. Cute as cut-buttons. Oh, that was a hell of a mess. That Ullman, he manages some honky-tonky resort place down in Florida in the off-season, and he caught a plane up to Denver and hired a sleigh to take him up here from Sidewinder because the roads were closed – a *sleigh*, can you believe that? He about split a gut tryin to keep it out of the papers. Did pretty well, I got to give him that. There was an item in the Denver *Post*, and of course the bituary in that pissant little rag they have down in Estes Park, but that was just about all. Pretty good, considerin the reputation this place has got. I expected some reporter would dig it all up again and just sorta put Grady in it as an excuse to rake over the scandals.'

'What scandals?'

Watson shrugged. 'Any big hotels have got scandals,' he said. 'Just like every big hotel has got a ghost. Why? Hell, people come and go. Sometimes one of em will pop off in his room, heart attack or stroke or something like that. Hotels are super-stitious places. No thirteenth floor or room thirteen, no mirrors on the back of the door you come in through, stuff like that. Why, we lost a lady just this last July. Ullman had to take care of that, and you can bet your ass he did. That's what they pay him twenty-two thousand bucks a season for, and as much as I dislike the little prick, he earns it. It's like some people just come here to throw up and they hire a guy like Ullman to clean up the messes. Here's this woman, must be sixty fuckin years old – my age! – and her hair's dyed just as red as a whore's stoplight, tits saggin just about down to her belly button on account of she ain't wearin no brassy-ear, big varycoarse veins all up and down her legs so they look like a couple of goddam roadmaps, the jools drippin off her neck and arms an hangin out her ears. And she's got this kid with her, he can't be no more than seventeen, with hair down to his asshole and his crotch bulgin like he stuffed it up with the funnypages. So they're here a week, ten days maybe, and every night it's the same drill. Down in the Colorado Lounge from five to seven, her suckin up singapore slings like they're gonna outlaw em tomorrow and him with just the one bottle of Olympia, suckin it, makin it last. And she'd be makin jokes and sayin all these witty things, and every time she said one he'd grin just like a fuckin ape, like she had strings tied to the corners of his mouth. Only after a few days you could see it was gettin harder an harder for him to grin, and God knows what he had to think about to get his pump primed by bedtime. Well, they'd go in for dinner, him walkin and her staggerin, drunk as a coot, you know, and he'd be pinchin the waitresses and grinnin at em when she wasn't lookin. Hell, we even had bets on how long he'd last.'

Watson shrugged.

'Then he comes down one night around ten, sayin his "wife" is "indisposed" – which meant she was passed out again like every other night they was there – and he's goin to get her some stomach medicine. So off he goes in the little Porsche they come in, and that's the last we see of him. Next morning she comes down and tries to put on this big act, but all day she's gettin paler an paler, and Mr Ullman asks her, sorta diplomatic-like, would she like him to notify the state cops, just in case maybe he had a little accident or something. She's on him like a cat. No-no-no, he's a fine driver, she isn't worried, everything's under control, he'll be back for dinner. So that afternoon she steps into the Colorado around three and never has no dinner at all. She goes up to her room around ten-thirty, and that's the last time anybody saw her alive.'

'What happened?'

'County coroner said she took about thirty sleepin pills on top of all the booze. Her husband showed up the next day, some big-shot lawyer from New York. He gave old Ullman four different shades of holy hell. I'll sue this an I'll sue that an when I'm through you won't even be able to find a clean pair of underwear, stuff like that. But Ullman's good, the sucker. Ullman got him quieted down. Probably asked that bigshot how he'd like to see his wife splashed all over the New York papers: Wife of Prominent New York Blah Blah Found Dead With Bellyful of Sleeping Pills. After playing hide-the-salami with a kid young enough to be her grandson.

'The state cops found the Porsche in back of this all-night burger joint down in Lyons, and Ullman pulled a few strings to get it released to that lawyer. Then both of them ganged up on old Archer Houghton, which is the county coroner, and got him to change the verdict to accidental death. Heart attack. Now ole Archer's driving a Chrysler. I don't begrudge him. A man's got to take it where he finds it, especially when he starts gettin along in years.'

Out came the bandanna. Honk. Peek. Out of sight.

'So what happens? About a week later this stupid cunt of a chambermaid, Delores Vickery by name, she gives out with a helluva shriek while she's makin up the room where those two stayed, and she faints dead away. When she comes to she says she seen the dead woman in the bathroom, layin naked in the tub. "Her face was all purple an puffy," she says, "an she was grinnin at me." So Ullman gave her two weeks' worth of walking papers and told her to get lost. I figure there's maybe forty-fifty people died in this hotel since my grandfather opened it for business in 1910.'

He looked shrewdly at Jack.

'You know how most of em go? Heart attack or stroke, while they're bangin the lady they're with. That's what these resorts get a lot of, old types that want one last fling. They come up here to the mountains to pretend they're twenty again. Sometimes somethin gives, and not all the guys who ran this place was as good as Ullman is at keepin it out of the papers. So the Overlook's got a reputation, yeah. I'll bet the fuckin Biltmore in New York City has got a reputation, if you ask the right people.'

'But no ghosts?'

'Mr Torrance, I've worked here all my life. I played here when I was a kid no older'n your boy in that wallet snapshot you showed me. I never seen a ghost yet. You want to come out back with me. I'll show you the equipment shed.'

'Fine.'

As Watson reached up to turn off the light, Jack said, 'There sure are a lot of papers down here.'

'Oh, you're not kiddin. Seems like they go back a thousand years. Newspapers and old invoices and bills of lading and Christ knows what else. My dad used to keep up with them pretty good when we had the old wood-burning furnace, but now they've got all out of hand. Some year I got to get a boy to haul them down to Sidewinder and burn em. If Ullman will stand the expense. I guess he will if I holler "rat" loud enough.'

'Then there are rats?'

'Yeah, I guess there's some. I got the traps and the poison Mr Ullman wants you to use up in the attic and down here. You keep a good eye on your boy, Mr Torrance. You wouldn't want nothing to happen to him.'

'No, I sure wouldn't.' Coming from Watson the advice didn't sting.

They went to the stairs and paused there for a moment while Watson blew his nose again.

'You'll find all the tools you need out there and some you don't, I guess. And there's the shingles. Did Ullman tell you about that?'

'Yes, he wants part of the west roof reshingled.'

THE SHINING

'He'll get all the for-free out of you that he can, the fat little prick, and then whine around in the spring about how you didn't do the job half right. I told him once right to his face, I said . . .'

Watson's words faded away to a comforting drone as they mounted the stairs. Jack Torrance looked over his shoulder once into the impenetrable, musty-smelling darkness and thought that if there was ever a place that should have ghosts, this was it. He thought of Grady, locked in by the soft, implacable snow, going quietly berserk and committing his atrocity. Did they scream? he wondered. Poor Grady, feeling it close in on him more every day, and knowing at last that for him spring would never come. He shouldn't have been here. And he shouldn't have lost his temper.

As he followed Watson through the door, the words echoed back to him like a knell, accompanied by a sharp snap – like a breaking pencil lead. Dear God, he could use a drink. Or a thousand of them.

CHAPTER FOUR
SHADOWLAND

Danny weakened and went up for his milk and cookies at quarter past four. He gobbled them while looking out the window, then went in to kiss his mother, who was lying down. She suggested that he stay in and watch 'Sesame Street' – the time would pass faster – but he shook his head firmly and went back to his place on the curb.

Now it was five o'clock, and although he didn't have a watch and couldn't tell time too well yet anyway, he was aware of passing time by the lengthening of the shadows, and by the golden cast that now tinged the afternoon light.

Turning the glider over in his hands, he sang under his breath:

'Skip to m Lou, n I don't care . . . skip to m Lou, n I don't care . . . my master's gone away . . . Lou, Lou, skip to m Lou . . .'

They had sung that song all together at the Jack and Jill Nursery School he had gone to back in Stovington. He didn't go to nursery school out here because Daddy couldn't afford to send him anymore. He knew his mother and father worried about that, worried that it was adding to his loneliness (and even more deeply, unspoken between them, that Danny blamed them), but he didn't really want to go to that old Jack and Jill anymore. It was for babies. He wasn't quite a big kid yet, but he wasn't a baby anymore. Big kids went to the big school and got a hot lunch. First grade. Next year. This year was someplace between being a baby and a real kid. It was all right. He did miss Scott and Andy – mostly Scott – but it was all right. It seemed best to wait alone for whatever might happen next.

He understood a great many things about his parents, and he knew that many times they didn't like his understandings and many other times refused to believe them. But someday they would have to believe. He was content to wait.

THE SHINING

It was too bad they could believe more, though, especially at times like now. Mommy was lying on her bed in the apartment, just about crying she was so worried about Daddy. Some of the things she was worried about were too grown-up for Danny to understand – vague things that had to do with security, with Daddy's *selfimage*, feelings of guilt and anger and the fear of what was to become of them – but the two main things on her mind right now were that Daddy had had a breakdown in the mountains (*then why doesn't he call?*) or that Daddy had gone off to do the Bad Thing. Danny knew perfectly well what the Bad Thing was since Scotty Aaronson, who was six months older, had explained it to him. Scotty knew because his daddy did the Bad Thing, too. Once, Scotty told him, his daddy had punched his mom right in the eye and knocked her down. Finally, Scotty's dad and mom had gotten a DIVORCE over the Bad Thing, and when Danny had known him, Scotty lived with his mother and only saw his daddy on weekends. The greatest terror of Danny's life was DIVORCE, a word that always appeared in his mind as a sign painted in red letters which were covered with hissing, poisonous snakes. In DIVORCE, your parents no longer lived together. They had a tug of war over you in a court (tennis court? badminton court? Danny wasn't sure which or if it was some other, but Mommy and Daddy had played both tennis and badminton at Stovington, so he assumed it could be either) and you had to go with one of them and you practically never saw the other one, and the one you were with could marry somebody you didn't even know if the urge came on them. The most terrifying thing about DIVORCE was that he had sensed the word – or concept, or whatever it was that came to him in his understandings – floating around in his own parents' heads, sometimes diffuse and relatively distant, sometimes as thick and obscuring and frightening as thunderheads. It had been that way after Daddy punished him for messing the papers up in his study and the doctor had to put his arm in a cast. That memory was already faded, but the memory of the DIVORCE thoughts was clear and terrifying. It had mostly been around his mommy that time, and he had been in constant terror that she would pluck the word from her brain and drag it out of her mouth, making it real. DIVORCE. It was a constant undercurrent in their thoughts, one of the few he could always pick up, like the beat of simple music. But like a beat, the central thought formed only the spine of more complex thoughts, thoughts he could not as yet even begin to interpret. They came to him only as colors and moods. Mommy's DIVORCE thoughts centered around what Daddy had done to his arm, and what had happened at Stovington when Daddy lost his job. That boy. That George Hatfield who got pissed off at Daddy and put the holes in their bug's feet. Daddy's DIVORCE thoughts were more complex, colored dark violet and shot through with frightening veins of pure black. He seemed to think they would be better off if he left. That things would stop hurting. His daddy hurt almost all the time, mostly about the Bad Thing. Danny could almost always pick that up too: Daddy's constant craving to go into a dark place and watch color TV and eat peanuts out of a bowl and do the Bad Thing until his brain would be quiet and leave him alone.

But this afternoon his mother had no need to worry and he wished he could go to her and tell her that. The bug had not broken down. Daddy was not off somewhere doing the Bad Thing. He was almost home now, put-putting along the highway between Lyons and Boulder. For the moment his daddy wasn't even thinking about the Bad Thing. He was thinking about . . . about . . .

Danny looked furtively behind him at the kitchen window. Sometimes thinking very hard made something happen to him. It made things – real things – go away, and then he saw things that weren't there. Once, not long after they put the cast on his arm, this had happened at the supper table. They weren't talking much to each other then. But they were thinking. Oh yes. The thoughts of DIVORCE hung over the kitchen table like a cloud full of black rain, pregnant, ready to burst. It was so bad he couldn't eat. The thought of eating with all that black DIVORCE around made him want to throw up. And because it had seemed desperately important, he had thrown himself fully into concentration and something had happened. When he came back to real things, he was lying on the floor with beans and mashed potatoes in his lap and his mommy holding him and crying and Daddy had been on the phone. He had been frightened, had tried to explain to them that there was nothing wrong, that this sometimes happened to him when he concentrated on understanding more than what normally came to him. He tried to explain about Tony, who they called his 'invisible playmate'.

His father had said: 'He's having a Ha Loo Sin Nation. He seems okay, but I want the doctor to look at him anyway.'

After the doctor left, Mommy had made him promise to never do that again, to *never* scare them that way, and Danny had agreed. He was frightened himself. Because when he had concentrated his mind, it had flown out to his daddy, and for just a moment, before Tony had appeared (far away, as he always did, calling distantly) and the strange things had blotted out their kitchen and the carved roast on the blue plate, for just a moment his own consciousness had plunged through his daddy's darkness to an incomprehensible word much more frightening than DIV-ORCE, and that word was SUICIDE. Danny had never come across it again in his daddy's mind, and he had certainly not gone looking for it. He didn't care if he never found out exactly what that word meant.

But he did like to concentrate, because sometimes Tony would come. Not every time. Sometimes things just got woozy and swimmy for a minute and then cleared – most times, in fact – but at other times Tony would appear at the very limit of his vision, calling distantly and beckoning . . .

It had happened twice since they moved to Boulder, and he remembered how surprised and pleased he had been to find Tony had followed him all the way from Vermont. So all his friends hadn't been left behind after all.

The first time he had been out in the back yard and nothing much had happened. Just Tony beckoning and then darkness and a few minutes later he had come back to real things with a few vague fragments of memory, like a jumbled dream. The second time, two weeks ago, had been more interesting. Tony, beckoning, calling from four yards over: '*Danny . . . come see . . .*' It seemed that he was getting up, then falling into a deep hole, like Alice in Wonderland. Then he had been in the basement of the apartment house and Tony had been beside him, pointing into the shadows at the trunk his daddy carried all his important papers in, especially 'THE PLAY'.

'See?' Tony had said in his distant, musical voice. 'It's under the stairs. Right under the stairs. The movers put it right . . . under . . . the stairs.'

Danny had stepped forward to look more closely at this marvel and then he was falling again, this time out of the back-yard swing, where he had been sitting all along. He had gotten the wind knocked out of himself, too.

Three or four days later his daddy had been stomping around, telling Mommy furiously that he had been all over the goddam basement and the trunk wasn't there and he was going to sue the goddam movers who had left it somewhere between Vermont and Colorado. How was he supposed to be able to finish 'THE PLAY' if things like this kept cropping up?

Danny said, 'No, Daddy. It's under the stairs. The movers put it right under the stairs.'

Daddy had given him a strange look and had gone down to see. The trunk had been there, just where Tony had shown him. Daddy had taken him aside, had sat him on his lap, and had asked Danny who let him down cellar. Had it been Tom from upstairs? The cellar was dangerous, Daddy said. That was why the landlord kept it locked. If someone was leaving it unlocked, Daddy wanted to know. He was glad to have his papers and his 'PLAY' but it wouldn't be worth it to him, he said, if Danny fell down the stairs and broke his . . . his leg. Danny told his father earnestly that he hadn't been down in the cellar. The door was always locked. And Mommy agreed. Danny never went down in the back hall, she said, because it was damp and dark and spidery. And he didn't tell lies.

'Then how did you know, doc?' Daddy asked.

'Tony showed me.'

His mother and father had exchanged a look over his head. This had happened before from time to time. Because it was frightening, they swept it quickly from their minds. But he knew they worried about Tony, Mommy especially, and he was careful about thinking the way that could make Tony come where she might see. But now he thought she was lying down, not moving about in the kitchen yet, and so he concentrated hard to see if he could understand what Daddy was thinking about.

His brow furrowed and his slightly grimy hands clenched into tight fists on his jeans. He did not close his eyes – that wasn't necessary – but he squinched them down to slits and imagined Daddy's voice, Jack's voice. John Daniel Torrance's voice, deep and steady, sometimes, quirking up with amusement or deepening even more with anger or just staying steady because he was thinking. Thinking of. Thinking about. Thinking . . .

(thinking)

Danny sighed quietly and his body slumped on the curb as if all the muscles had gone out of it. He was fully conscious; he saw the street and the girl and boy walking up the sidewalk on the other side, holding hands because they were

(?in love?)

so happy about the day and themselves together in the day. He saw autumn leaves blowing along the gutter, yellow cart-wheels of irregular shape. He saw the house they were passing and noticed how the roof was covered with

(shingles. i guess it'll be no problem if the flashing's ok yeah that'll be all right, watson. christ what a character. wish there was a place for him in 'THE PLAY' i'll end up with the whole fucking human race in it if i don't watch out. yeah. shingles. are there nails out there? oh shit forgot to ask him well they're simple to get. sidewinder hardware store. wasps, they're nesting this time of year. i might want to get one of those bug bombs in case they're there when i rip up the old shingles. new shingles. old)

shingles. So that's what he was thinking about. He had gotten the job and was thinking about shingles. Danny didn't know who Watson was, but everything else seemed clear enough. And he might get to see a wasps' nest. Just as sure as his name was

'*Danny . . . Dannee . . .*'

He looked up and there was Tony, far up the street, standing by a stop sign and waving. Danny, as always, felt a warm burst of pleasure at seeing his old friend, but this time he seemed to feel a prick of fear, too, as if Tony had come with some darkness hidden behind his back. A jar of wasps which when released would sting deeply.

But there was no question of not going.

He slumped further down on the curb, his hands sliding laxly from his thighs and dangling below the fork of his crotch. His chin sank onto his chest. Then there was a dim, painless tug as part of him got up and ran after Tony into the funneling darkness.

'*Dannee —*'

Now the darkness was shot with swirling whiteness. A coughing, whooping sound and bending, tortured shadows that resolved themselves into fir trees at night, being pushed by a screaming gale. Snow swirled and danced. Snow everywhere.

'Too deep,' Tony said from the darkness, and there was a sadness in his voice that terrified Danny. 'Too deep to get out.'

Another shape, looming, rearing. Huge and rectangular. A sloping roof. Whiteness that was blurred in the stormy darkness. Many windows. A long building with a shingled roof. Some of the shingles were greener, newer. His daddy put them on. With nails from the Sidewinder hardware store. Now the snow was covering the shingles. It was covering everything.

A green witchlight glowed into being on the front of the building, flickered, and became a giant, grinning skull over two crossed bones.

'Poison,' Tony said from the floating darkness. 'Poison.'

Other signs flickered past his eyes, some in green letters, some of them on boards stuck at leaning angles into the snowdrifts. **NO SWIMMING. DANGER! LIVE WIRES. THIS PROPERTY CONDEMNED. HIGH VOLTAGE. THIRD RAIL. DANGER OF DEATH. KEEP OFF. KEEP OUT. NO TRESPASSING. VIOLATORS WILL BE SHOT ON SIGHT.** He understood none of them completely – he couldn't read! – but got a sense of all, and a dreamy terror floated into the dark hollows of his body like light brown spores that would die in sunlight.

They faded. Now he was in a room filled with strange furniture, a room that was dark. Snow spattered against the windows like thrown sand. His mouth was dry, his eyes like hot marbles, his heart triphammering in his chest. Outside there was a hollow booming noise, like a dreadful door being thrown wide. Footfalls. Across the room was a mirror, and deep down in its silver bubble a single word appeared in green fire and that word was: REDRUM.

The room faded. Another room. He knew
(would know)
this one. An overturned chair. A broken window with snow swirling in; already it had frosted the edge of the rug. The drapes had been pulled free and hung on their broken rod at an angle. A low cabinet lying on its face.

More hollow booming noises, steady, rhythmic, horrible. Smashing glass. Approaching destruction. A hoarse voice, the voice of a madman, made the more terrible by its familiarity:

Come out! Come out, you little shit! Take your medicine!

Crash. Crash. Crash. Splintering wood. A bellow of rage and satisfaction. REDRUM. Coming.

Drifting across the room. Pictures torn off the walls. A record player.

(?Mommy's record player?)

overturned on the floor. Her records, Grieg, Handel, the Beatles, Art Garfunkel, Bach, Liszt, thrown everywhere. Broken into jagged black pie wedges. A shaft of light coming from another room, the bathroom, harsh white light and a word flickering on and off in the medicine cabinet mirror like a red eye, REDRUM, REDRUM, REDRUM—

'No,' he whispered. 'No, Tony please—'

And, dangling over the white porcelain lip of the bathtub, a hand. Limp. A slow trickle of blood (REDRUM) trickling down one of the fingers, the third, dripping onto the tile from the carefully shaped nail—

No oh no oh no—

(oh please, Tony, you're scaring me)

REDRUM REDRUM REDRUM

(stop it, Tony, stop it)

Fading.

In the darkness the booming noises grew louder, louder still, echoing, everywhere, all around.

And now he was crouched in a dark hallway, crouched on a blue rug with a riot of twisting black shapes woven into its pile, listening to the booming noises approach, and now a Shape turned the corner and began to come toward him, lurching, smelling of blood and doom. It had a mallet in one hand and it was swinging it (REDRUM) from side to side in vicious arcs, slamming it into the walls, cutting the silk wallpaper and knocking out ghostly bursts of plasterdust.

Come on and take your medicine! Take it like a man!

The Shape advancing on him, reeking of that sweet-sour odor, gigantic, the mallet head cutting across the air with a wicked hissing whisper, then the great hollow boom as it crashed into the wall, sending the dust out in a puff you could smell, dry and itchy. Tiny red eyes glowed in the dark. The monster was upon him, it had discovered him, cowering here with a blank wall at his back. And the trapdoor in the ceiling was locked.

Darkness. Drifting.

'Tony, please take me back, please, please—'

And he *was* back, sitting on the curb of Arapahoe Street, his shirt sticking damply to his back, his body bathed in sweat. In his ears he would still hear that huge, contrapuntal booming sound and smell his own urine as he voided himself in the extremity of his terror. He could see that limp hand dangling over the edge of the tub with blood running down one finger, the third, and that inexplicable word so much more horrible than any of the others: REDRUM.

And now sunshine. Real things. Except for Tony, now six blocks up, only a speck, standing on the corner, his voice faint and high and sweet. 'Be careful, doc . . .'

Then, in the next instant, Tony was gone and Daddy's battered red bug was turning the corner and chattering up the street, farting blue smoke behind it. Danny was off the curb in a second, waving, jiving from one foot to the other, yelling: 'Daddy! Hey, Dad! Hi! Hi!'

His daddy swung the VW into the curb, killed the engine,

and opened the door. Danny ran toward him and then froze, his eyes widening. His heart crawled up into the middle of his throat and froze solid. Beside his daddy, in the other front seat, was a short-handled mallet, its head clotted with blood and hair.

Then it was just a bag of groceries.

'Danny . . . you okay, doc?'

'Yeah. I'm okay.' He went to his daddy and buried his face in Daddy's sheepskin-lined denim jacket and hugged him tight tight tight. Jack hugged him back, slightly bewildered.

'Hey, you don't want to sit in the sun like that, doc. You're drippin sweat.'

'I guess I fell asleep a little. I love you, Daddy. I been waiting.'

'I love you too, Dan. I brought home some stuff. Think you're big enough to carry it upstairs?'

'Sure am!'

'Doc Torrance, the world's strongest man,' Jack said, and ruffled his hair. 'Whose hobby is falling asleep on street corners.'

Then they were walking up to the door and Mommy had come down to the porch to meet them and he stood on the second step and watched them kiss. They were glad to see each other. Love came out of them the way love had come out of the boy and girl walking up the street and holding hands. Danny was glad.

The bag of groceries – *just* a bag of groceries – crackled in his arms. Everything was all right. Daddy was home. Mommy was loving him. There were no bad things. And not everything Tony showed him always happened.

But fear had settled around his heart, deep and dreadful, around his heart and around that indecipherable word he had seen in his spirit's mirror.

CHAPTER FIVE
PHONEBOOTH

Jack parked the VW in front of the Rexall in the Table Mesa shopping center and let the engine die. He wondered again if he shouldn't go ahead and get the fuel pump replaced, and told himself again that they couldn't afford it. If the little car could keep running until November, it could retire with full honors anyway. By November the snow up there in the mountains would be higher than the beetle's roof . . . maybe higher than three beetles stacked on top of each other.

'Want you to stay in the car, doc. I'll bring you a candy bar.'

'Why can't I come in?'

'I have to make a phone call. It's private stuff.'

'Is that why you didn't make it at home?'

'Check.'

Wendy had insisted on a phone in spite of their unraveling finances. She had argued that with a small child – especially a boy like Danny, who sometimes suffered from fainting spells – they couldn't afford not to have one. So Jack had forked over the thirty-dollar installation fee, bad enough, and a ninety-dollar security deposit, which really hurt. And so far the phone had been mute except for two wrong numbers.

'Can I have a Baby Ruth, Daddy?'

'Yes. You sit still and don't play with the gearshift, right?'

'Right. I'll look at the maps.'

'You do that.'

As Jack got out, Danny opened the bug's glovebox and took out the five battered gas station maps: Colorado, Nebraska, Utah, Wyoming, New Mexico. He loved road maps, loved to trace where the roads went with his finger. As far as he was concerned new maps were the best part of moving West.

THE SHINING

Jack went to the drugstore counter, got Danny's candy bar, a newspaper, and a copy of the October *Writer's Digest*. He gave the girl a five and asked for his change in quarters. With the silver in his hand he walked over to the telephone booth by the keymaking machine and slipped inside. From here he could see Danny in the bug through three sets of glass. The boy's head was bent studiously over his maps. Jack felt a wave of nearly desperate love for the boy. The emotion showed on his face as a stony grimness.

He supposed he could have made this obligatory thank-you call to Al from home; he certainly wasn't going to say anything Wendy would object to. It was his pride that said no. These days he almost always listened to what his pride told him to do, because along with his wife and son, six hundred dollars in a checking account, and one weary 1968 Volkswagen, his pride was all that was left. The only thing that was his. Even the checking account was joint. A year ago he had been teaching English in one of the finest prep schools in New England. There had been friends – although not exactly the same ones he'd had before going on the wagon – some laughs, fellow faculty members who admired his deft touch in the classroom and his private dedication to writing. Things had been very good six months ago. All at once there was enough money left over at the end of each two-week pay period to start a little savings account. In his drinking days there had never been a penny left over, even though Al Shockley had stood a great many of the rounds. He and Wendy had begun to talk cautiously about finding a house and making a down payment in a year or so. A farmhouse in the country, take six or eight years to renovate it completely, what the hell, they were young, they had time.

Then he had lost his temper.

George Hatfield.

The smell of hope had turned to the smell of old leather in Crommert's office, the whole thing like some scene from his own play: the old prints of previous Stovington headmasters on the walls, steel engravings of the school as it had been in 1879, when it was first built, and in 1895, when Vanderbilt money had enabled them to build the field house that still stood at the west end of the soccer field, squat, immense, dressed in ivy. April ivy had been rustling outside Crommert's slit window and the drowsy sound of steam heat came from the radiator. It was no set, he remembered thinking. It was real. His life. How could he have fucked it up so badly?

'This is a serious situation, Jack. Terribly serious. The Board has asked me to convey its decision to you.'

The Board wanted Jack's resignation and Jack had given it to them. Under different circumstances, he would have gotten tenure that June.

What had followed that interview in Crommert's office had been the darkest, most dreadful night of his life. The wanting, the *needing* to get drunk had never been so bad. His hands shook. He knocked things over. And he kept wanting to take it out on Wendy and Danny. His temper was like a vicious animal on a frayed leash. He had left the house in terror that he might strike them. Had ended up outside a bar, and the only thing that had kept him from going in was the knowledge that if he did, Wendy would leave him at last, and take Danny with her. He would be dead from the day they left.

Instead of going into the bar, where dark shadows sat sampling the tasty waters of oblivion, he had gone to Al Shockley's house. The Board's vote had been six to one. Al had been the one.

Now he dialed the operator and she told him that for a dollar eighty-five he could be put in touch with Al two thousand miles away for three minutes. Time is relative, baby, he thought, and stuck in eight quarters. Faintly he could hear the electronic boops and beeps of his connection sniffing its way eastward.

Al's father had been Arthur Longley Shockley, the steel baron. He had left his only son, Albert, a fortune and a huge range of investments and directorships and chairs on various boards. One of these had been on the Board of Directors for Stovington Preparatory Academy, the old man's favorite charity. Both Arthur and Albert Shockley were alumni and Al lived in Barre, close enough to take a personal interest in the school's affairs. For several years Al had been Stovington's tennis coach.

THE SHINING

Jack and Al had become friends in a completely natural and uncoincidental way: at the many school and faculty functions they attended together, they were always the two drunkest people there. Shockley was separated from his wife, and Jack's own marriage was skidding slowly downhill, although he still loved Wendy and had promised sincerely (and frequently) to reform, for her sake and for baby Danny's.

The two of them went on from many faculty parties, hitting the bars until they closed, then stopping at some mom 'n' pop store for a case of beer they would drink parked at the end of some back road. There were mornings when Jack would stumble into their leased house with dawn seeping into the sky and find Wendy and the baby asleep on the couch, Danny always on the inside, a tiny fist curled under the shelf of Wendy's jaw. He would look at them and the self-loathing would back up his throat in a bitter wave, even stronger than the taste of beer and cigarettes and martinis – martians, as Al called them. Those were the times that his mind would turn thoughtfully and sanely to the gun or the rope or the razor blade.

If the bender had occurred on a weeknight, he would sleep for three hours, get up, dress, chew four Excedrins, and go off to teach his nine o'clock American Poets still drunk. Good morning, kids, today the Red-Eyed Wonder is going to tell you about how Longfellow lost his wife in the big fire.

He hadn't believed he was an alcoholic, Jack thought as Al's telephone began ringing in his ear. The classes he had missed or taught unshaven, still reeking of last night martians. Not me, I can stop anytime. The nights he and Wendy had passed in separate beds. Listen, I'm fine. Mashed fenders. Sure I'm okay to drive. The tears she always shed in the bathroom. Cautious looks from his colleagues at any party where alcohol was served, even wine. The slowly dawning realization that he was being talked about. The knowledge that he was producing nothing at his Underwood but balls of mostly blank paper that ended up in the wastebasket. He had been something of a catch for Stovington, a slowly blooming American writer perhaps, and certainly a man well qualified to teach that great mystery, creative writing. He had published two dozen short stories. He was

41

working on a play, and thought there might be a novel incubating in some mental back room. But now he was not producing and his teaching had become erratic.

It had finally ended one night less than a month after Jack had broken his son's arm. That, it seemed to him, had ended his marriage. All that remained was for Wendy to gather her will . . . if her mother hadn't been such a grade A bitch, he knew, Wendy would have taken a bus back to New Hampshire as soon as Danny had been okay to travel. It was over.

It had been a little past midnight. Jack and Al were coming into Barre on US 31, Al behind the wheel of his big Jag, shifting fancily on the curves, sometimes crossing the double yellow lines. They were both very drunk; the martians had landed that night in force. They came around the last curve before the bridge at seventy, and there was a kid's bike in the road, and then the sharp, hurt squealing as rubber shredded from the Jag's tires, and Jack remembered seeing Al's face looming over the steering wheel like a round white moon. Then the jingling crashing sound as they hit the bike at forty, and it had flown up like a bent and twisted bird, the handlebars striking the windshield, and then it was in the air again, leaving the starred safety glass in front of Jack's bulging eyes. A moment later he heard the final dreadful smash as it landed on the road behind them. Something thumped underneath them as the tires passed over it. The Jag drifted around broadside. Al still jockeying the wheel, and from far away Jack heard himself saying: 'Jesus, Al, We ran him down. I felt it.'

In his ear the phone kept ringing. *Come on, Al. Be home. Let me get this over with.*

Al had brought the car to a smoking halt not more than three feet from a bridge stanchion. Two of the Jag's tires were flat. They had left zigzagging loops of burned rubber for a hundred and thirty feet. They looked at each other for a moment and then ran back in the cold darkness.

The bike was completely ruined. One wheel was gone, and looking back over his shoulder Al had seen it lying in the middle of the road, half a dozen spokes sticking up like piano wire. Al had said hesitantly: 'I think that's what we ran over, Jacky-boy.'

'Then where's the kid?'

'Did you *see* a kid?'

Jack frowned. It had all happened with such crazy speed. Coming around the corner. The bike looming in the Jag's headlights. Al yelling something. Then the collision and the long skid.

They moved the bike to one shoulder of the road. Al went back to the Jag and put on its four-way flashers. For the next two hours they searched the sides of the road, using a powerful four-cell flashlight. Nothing. Although it was late, several cars passed the beached Jaguar and the two men with the bobbing flashlight. None of them stopped. Jack thought later that some queer providence, bent on giving them both a last chance, had kept the cops away, had kept any of the passers-by from calling them.

At a quarter past two they returned to the Jag, sober but queasy. 'If there was nobody riding it, what was it doing in the middle of the road?' Al demanded. 'It wasn't parked on the side; it was right out in the fucking *middle*!'

Jack could only shake his head.

'Your party does not answer,' the operator said. 'Would you like me to keep on trying?'

'A couple more rings, operator. Do you mind?'

'No, sir,' the voice said dutifully.

Come on, Al!

Al had hiked across the bridge to the nearest pay phone, called a bachelor friend and told him it would be worth fifty dollars if the friend would get the Jag's snow tires out of the garage and bring them down to the Highway 31 bridge outside of Barre. The friend showed up twenty minutes later, wearing a pair of jeans and his pajama top. He surveyed the scene.

'Kill anybody?' he asked.

Al was already jacking up the back of the car and Jack was loosening lug nuts. 'Providentially, no one,' Al said.

'I think I'll just head on back anyway. Pay me in the morning.'

'Fine,' Al said without looking up.

The two of them had gotten the tires on without incident,

and together they drove back to Al Shockley's house. Al put the Jag in the garage and killed the motor.

In the dark quiet he said: 'I'm off drinking, Jacky-boy. It's all over. I've slain my last martian.'

And now, sweating in this phonebooth, it occurred to Jack that he had never doubted Al's ability to carry through. He had driven back to his own house in the VW with the radio turned up, and some disco group chanted over and over again, talismanic in the house before dawn: *Do it anyway . . . you wanta do it . . . do it anyway you want . . .* No matter how loud he heard the squealing tires, the crash. When he blinked his eyes shut, he saw that single crushed wheel with its broken spokes pointing at the sky.

When he got in, Wendy was asleep on the couch. He looked in Danny's room and Danny was in his crib on his back, sleeping deeply, his arm still buried in the cast. In the softly filtered glow from the streetlight outside he could see the dark lines on its plastered whiteness where all the doctors and nurses in pediatrics had signed it.

It was an accident. He fell down the stairs.

(o you dirty liar)

It was an accident. I lost my temper.

(you fucking drunken waste god wiped snot out of his nose and that was you)

Listen, hey, come on, please, just an accident—

But the last plea was driven away by the image of that bobbing flashlight as they hunted through the dry late November weeds, looking for the sprawled body that by all good rights should have been there, waiting for the police. It didn't matter that Al had been driving. There had been other nights when he had been driving.

He pulled the covers up over Danny, went into their bedroom, and took the Spanish Llama .38 down from the top shelf of the closet. It was in a shoe box. He sat on the bed with it for nearly an hour, looking at it, fascinated by its deadly shine.

It was dawn when he put it back in the box and put the box back in the closet.

That morning he had called Bruckner, the department head, and told him to please post his classes. He had the flu. Bruckner agreed, with less good grace than was common. Jack Torrance had been extremely susceptible to the flu in the last year.

Wendy made him scrambled eggs and coffee. They ate in silence. The only sound came from the back yard, where Danny was gleefully running his trucks across the sand pile with his good hand.

She went to do the dishes. Her back to him, she said: 'Jack. I've been thinking.'

'Have you?' He lit a cigarette with trembling hands. No hangover this morning, oddly enough. Only the shakes. He blinked. In the instant's darkness the bike flew up against the windshield, starring the glass. The tires shrieked. The flashlight bobbed.

'I want to talk to you about . . . about what's best for me and Danny. For you too, maybe. I don't know. We should have talked about it before, I guess.'

'Would you do something for me?' he asked, looking at the wavering tip of his cigarette. 'Would you do me a favor?'

'What?' Her voice was dull and neutral. He looked at her back.

'Let's talk about it a week from today. If you still want to.'

Now she turned to him, her hands lacy with suds, her pretty face pale and disillusioned. 'Jack, promises don't work with you. You just go right on with—'

She stopped, looking in his eyes, fascinated, suddenly uncertain.

'In a week,' he said. His voice had lost all its strength and dropped to a whisper. 'Please. I'm not promising anything. If you still want to talk then, we'll talk. About anything you want.'

They looked across the sunny kitchen at each other for a long time, and when she turned back to the dishes without saying anything more, he began to shudder. God, he needed a drink. Just a little pick-me-up to put things in their true perspective—

'Danny said he dreamed you had a car accident,' she said

abruptly. 'He has funny dreams sometimes. He said it this morning, when I got him dressed. Did you, Jack? Did you have an accident?'

'No.'

By noon the craving for a drink had become a low-grade fever. He went to Al's.

'You dry?' Al asked before letting him in. Al looked horrible.

'Bone dry. You look like Lon Chaney in *Phantom of the Opera.*'

'Come on in.'

They played two-handed whist all afternoon. They didn't drink.

A week passed. He and Wendy didn't speak much. But he knew she was watching, not believing. He drank coffee black and endless cans of Coca-Cola. One night he drank a whole six-pack of Coke and then ran into the bathroom and vomited it up. The level of the bottles in the liquor cabinet did not go down. After his classes he went over to Al Shockley's – she hated Al Shockley worse than she had ever hated anyone – and when he came home she would swear she smelled scotch or gin on his breath, but he would talk lucidly to her before supper, drink coffee, play with Danny after supper, sharing a Coke with him, read a bedtime story, then sit and correct themes with cup after cup of black coffee by his hand, and she would have to admit to herself that she had been wrong.

Weeks passed and the unspoken word retreated further from the back of her lips. Jack sensed its retirement but knew it would never retire completely. Things began to get a little easier. Then George Hatfield. He had lost his temper again, this time stone sober.

'Sir, your party still doesn't—'

'Hello?' Al's voice, out of breath.

'Go ahead,' the operator said dourly.

'Al, this is Jack Torrance.'

'Jacky-boy!' Genuine pleasure. 'How are you?'

'Good. I just called to say thanks. I got the job. It's perfect. If I can't finish that goddam play snowed in all winter, I'll never finish it.'

'You'll finish.'

'How are things?' Jack asked hesitantly.

'Dry,' Al responded. 'You?'

'As a bone.'

'Miss it much?'

'Every day.'

Al laughed. 'I know that scene. But I don't know how you stayed dry after that Hatfield thing, Jack. That was above and beyond.'

'I really bitched things up for myself,' he said evenly.

'Oh, hell. I'll have the Board around by spring. Effinger's already saying they might have been too hasty. And if that play comes to something—'

'Yes. Listen, my boy's out in the car, Al. He looks like he might be getting restless—'

'Sure. Understand. You have a good winter up there, Jack. Glad to help.'

'Thanks again, Al.' He hung up, closed his eyes in the hot booth, and again saw the crashing bike, the bobbing flashlight. There had been a squib in the paper the next day, no more than a space-filler really, but the owner had not been named. Why it had been out there in the night would always be a mystery to them, and perhaps that was as it should be.

He went back out to the car and gave Danny his slightly melted Baby Ruth.

'Daddy?'

'What, doc?'

Danny hesitated, looking at his father's abstracted face.

'When I was waiting for you to come back from that hotel, I had a bad dream. Do you remember? When I fell asleep?'

'Um-hm.'

But it was no good. Daddy's mind was someplace else, not with him. Thinking about the Bad Thing again.

(I dreamed that you hurt me, Daddy)

'What was the dream, doc?'

'Nothing,' Danny said as they pulled out into the parking lot. He put the maps back into the glove compartment.

'You sure?'

'Yes.'

Jack gave his son a faint, troubled glance, and then his mind turned to his play.

CHAPTER SIX
NIGHT THOUGHTS

Love was over, and her man was sleeping beside her. *Her man.*

She smiled a little in the darkness, his seed still trickling with slow warmth from between her slightly parted thighs, and her smile was both rueful and pleased, because the phrase *her man* summoned up a hundred feelings. Each feeling examined alone was a bewilderment. Together, in this darkness floating to sleep, they were like a distant blues tune heard in an almost deserted night club, melancholy but pleasing.

Lovin' you baby, is just like rollin' off a log.
But if I can't be your woman, I sure ain't goin' to be your dog.

Had that been Billie Holiday? Or someone more prosaic like Peggy Lee? Didn't matter. It was low and torchy, and in the silence of her head it played mellowly, as if issuing from one of those old-fashioned jukeboxes, a Wurlitzer, perhaps, half an hour before closing.

Now, moving away from her consciousness, she wondered how many beds she had slept in with this man beside her. They had met in college and had first made love in his apartment . . . that had been less than three months after her mother drove her from the house, told her never to come back, that if she wanted to go somewhere she could go to her father since she had been responsible for the divorce. That had been in 1970. So long ago? A semester later they had moved in together, had found jobs for the summer, and had kept the apartment when their senior year began. She remembered that bed the most clearly, a big double that sagged in the middle. When they made love, the rusty box spring had counted the beats. That fall she had finally managed to break from her mother. Jack had helped her. She wants to keep beating you, Jack had said. The more times you phone her, the more times you crawl back begging forgiveness, the more she can beat you with your father. It's good for her, Wendy, because she can go on making believe it was your fault. But it's not good for you. They had talked it over again and again in that bed, that year.

(Jack sitting up with the covers pooled around his waist, a cigarette burning between his fingers, looking her in the eye – he had a half-humorous, half-scowling way of doing that – telling her: *She told you never to come back, right? Never to darken her door again, right? Then why doesn't she hang up the phone when she knows it's you? Why does she only tell you that you can't come in if I'm with you? Because she thinks I might cramp her style a little bit. She wants to keep putting the thumbscrews right to you, baby. You're a fool if you keep letting her do it. She told you never to come back, so why don't you take her at her word? Give it a rest.* And at last she'd seen it his way.)

It had been Jack's idea to separate for a while – to get perspective on the relationship, he said. She had been afraid he had become interested in someone else. Later she found it wasn't so. They were together again in the spring and he asked her if she had been to see her father. She had jumped as if he'd struck her with a quirt.

How did you know that?

The Shadow knows.

Have you been spying on me?

And his impatient laughter, which had always made her feel so awkward – as if she were eight and he was able to see her motivations more clearly than she.

You needed time, Wendy.

For what?

I guess . . . to see which one of us you wanted to marry.

Jack, what are you saying?

I think I'm proposing marriage.

The wedding. Her father had been there, her mother had not been. She discovered she could live with that, if she had Jack. Then Danny had come, her fine son.

That had been the best year, the best bed. After Danny was born, Jack had gotten her a job typing for half a dozen English

Department profs – quizzes, exams, class syllabi, study notes, reading lists. She ended up typing a novel for one of them, a novel that never got published . . . much to Jack's very irreverent and very private glee. The job was good for forty a week, and skyrocketed all the way up to sixty during the two months she spent typing the unsuccessful novel. They had their first car, a five-year-old Buick with a baby seat in the middle. Bright, upwardly mobile young marrieds. Danny forced a reconciliation between her and her mother, a reconciliation that was always tense and never happy, but a reconciliation all the same. When she took Danny to the house, she went without Jack. And she didn't tell Jack that her mother always remade Danny's diapers, frowned over his formula, could always spot the accusatory first signs of a rash on the baby's bottom or privates. Her mother never said anything overtly, but the message came through anyway: the price she had begun to pay (and maybe always would) for the reconciliation was the feeling that she was an inadequate mother. It was her mother's way of keeping the thumbscrews handy.

During the days Wendy would stay home and housewife, feeding Danny his bottles in the sunwashed kitchen of the four-room second-story apartment, playing her records on the battered portable stereo she had had since high school. Jack would come home at three (or at two if he felt he could cut his last class), and while Danny slept he would lead her into the bedroom and fears of inadequacy would be erased.

At night while she typed, he would do his writing and his assignments. In those days she sometimes came out of the bedroom where the typewriter was to find both of them asleep on the studio couch, Jack wearing nothing but his underpants, Danny sprawled comfortably on her husband's chest with his thumb in his mouth. She would put Danny in his crib, then read whatever Jack had written that night before waking him up enough to come to bed.

The best bed, the best year.

Sun gonna shine in my backyard someday . . .

In those days, Jack's drinking had still been well in hand. On Saturday nights a bunch of his fellow students would drop over and there would be a case of beer and discussions in which she seldom took part because her field had been sociology and his was English: arguments over whether Pepys's diaries were literature or history; discussions on Charles Olson's poetry; sometimes the reading of works in progress. Those and a hundred others. No, a thousand. She felt no real urge to take part; it was enough to sit in her rocking chair beside Jack, who sat cross-legged on the floor, one hand holding a beer, the other gently cupping her calf or braceleting her ankle.

The competition at UNH had been fierce, and Jack carried an extra burden in his writing. He put in at least an hour at it every night. It was his routine. The Saturday sessions were necessary therapy. They let something out of him that might otherwise have swelled and swelled until he burst.

At the end of his grad work he had landed the job at Stovington, mostly on the strength of his stories – four of them published at that time, one of them in *Esquire*. She remembered that day clearly enough; it would take more than three years to forget it. She had almost thrown the envelope away, thinking it was a subscription offer. Opening it, she had found instead that it was a letter saying that *Esquire* would like to use Jack's story 'Concerning the Black Holes' early the following year. They would pay nine hundred dollars, not on publication but on acceptance. That was nearly half a year's take typing papers and she had flown to the telephone, leaving Danny in his high chair to goggle comically after her, his face lathered with creamed peas and beef purée.

Jack had arrived from the university forty-five minutes later, the Buick weighted down with seven friends and a keg of beer. After a ceremonial toast (Wendy also had a glass, although she ordinarily had no taste for beer), Jack had signed the acceptance letter, put it in the return envelope, and went down the block to drop it in the letter box. When he came back he stood gravely in the door and said, '*Veni, vidi, vici.*' There were cheers and applause. When the keg was empty at eleven that night, Jack and the only two others who were still ambulatory went on to hit a few bars.

She had gotten him aside in the downstairs hallway. The other two were already out in the car, drunkenly singing the

New Hampshire fight song. Jack was down on one knee, owl-ishly fumbling with the lacings of his moccasins.

'Jack,' she said, 'you shouldn't. You can't even tie your shoes, let alone drive.'

He stood up and put his hands calmly on her shoulders. 'Tonight I could fly to the moon if I wanted to.'

'No,' she said. 'Not for all the *Esquire* stories in the world.'

'I'll be home early.'

But he hadn't been home until four in the morning, stumbling and mumbling his way up the stairs, waking Danny up when he came in. He had tried to soothe the baby and dropped him on the floor. Wendy had rushed out, thinking of what her mother would think if she saw the bruise before she thought of anything else – God help her, God help them both – and then picked Danny up, sat in the rocking chair with him, soothed him. She had been thinking of her mother for most of the five hours Jack had been gone, her mother's prophecy that Jack would never come to anything. *Big ideas*, her mother had said. *Sure. The welfare lines are full of educated fools with big ideas.* Did the *Esquire* story make her mother wrong or right? *Winnifred, you're not holding that baby right. Give him to me.* And was she not holding her husband right? Why else would he take his joy out of the house? A helpless kind of terror had risen up in her and it never occurred to her that he had gone out for reasons that had nothing to do with her.

'Congratulations,' she said, rocking Danny – he was almost asleep again. 'Maybe you gave him a concussion.'

'It's just a bruise.' He sounded sulky, wanting to be repentant: a little boy. For an instant she hated him.

'Maybe,' she said tightly. 'Maybe not.' She heard so much of her mother talking to her departed father in her own voice that she was sickened and afraid.

'Like mother like daughter,' Jack muttered.

'Go to bed!' she cried, her fear coming out sounding like anger. 'Go to bed, you're drunk!'

'Don't tell me what to do.'

'Jack . . . please, we shouldn't . . . it . . .' There were no words.

'Don't tell me what to do,' he repeated sullenly, and then went into the bedroom. She was left alone in the rocking chair with Danny, who was sleeping again. Five minutes later Jack's snores came floating out to the living room. That had been the first night she had slept on the couch.

Now she turned restlessly on the bed, already dozing. Her mind, freed of any linear order by encroaching sleep, floated past the first year at Stovington, past the steadily worsening times that had reached low ebb when her husband had broken Danny's arm, to that morning in the breakfast nook.

Danny outside playing trucks in the sandpile, his arm still in the cast. Jack sitting at the table, pallid and grizzled, a cigarette jittering between his fingers. She had decided to ask him for a divorce. She had pondered the question from a hundred different angles, had been pondering it in fact for the six months before the broken arm. She told herself she would have made the decision long ago if it hadn't been for Danny, but not even that was necessarily true. She dreamed on the long nights when Jack was out, and her dreams were always of her mother's face and of her own wedding.

(*Who giveth this woman?* Her father standing in his best suit which was none too good – he was a traveling salesman for a line of canned goods that even then was going broke – and his tired face, how old he looked, how pale: *I do.*)

Even after the accident – if you could call it an accident – she had not been able to bring it all the way out, to admit that her marriage was a lopsided defeat. She had waited, dumbly hoping that a miracle would occur and Jack would see what was happening, not only to him but to her. But there had been no slowdown. A drink before going off to the Academy. Two or three beers with lunch at the Stovington House. Three or four martinis before dinner. Five or six more while grading papers. The weekends were worse. The nights out with Al Shockley were worse still. She had never dreamed there could be so much pain in a life when there was nothing physically wrong. She hurt all the time. How much of it was her fault? That question haunted her. She felt like her mother. Like her father. Sometimes, when she felt like herself she wondered what it would be like for Danny, and she dreaded the day when he grew old enough to lay blame. And she wondered where they would go. She had no doubt her mother would take her in, and no doubt that after half a year of watching her diapers remade, Danny's meals recooked and/or redistributed, of coming home to find his clothes changed or his hair cut or the books her mother found unsuitable spirited away to some limbo in the attic ... after half a year of that, she would have a complete nervous breakdown. And her mother would pat her hand and say comfortingly, *Although it's not your fault, it's all your own fault. You were never ready. You showed your true colors when you came between your father and me.*

My father, Danny's father. Mine, his.

(*Who giveth this woman? I do.* Dead of a heart attack six months later.)

The night before that morning she had lain awake almost until he came in, thinking, coming to her decision.

The divorce was necessary, she told herself. Her mother and father didn't belong in the decision. Neither did her feelings of guilt over their marriage nor her feelings of inadequacy over her own. It was necessary for her son's sake, and for herself, if she was to salvage anything at all from her early adulthood. The handwriting on the wall was brutal but clear. Her husband was a lush. He had a bad temper, one he could no longer keep wholly under control now that he was drinking so heavily and his writing was going so badly. Accidentally or not accidentally, he had broken Danny's arm. He was going to lose his job, if not this year then the year after. Already she had noticed the sympathetic looks from the other faculty wives. She told herself that she had stuck with the messy job of her marriage for as long as she could. Now she would have to leave it. Jack could have full visitation rights, and she would want support from him only until she could find something and get on her feet – and that would have to be fairly rapidly because she didn't know how long Jack would be able to pay support money. She would do it with as little bitterness as possible. But it had to end.

So thinking, she had fallen off into her own thin and unrestful sleep, haunted by the faces of her own mother and father. *You're nothing but a home-wrecker,* her mother said. *Who giveth this woman?* the minister said. *I do,* her father said. But in the bright and sunny morning she felt the same. Her back to him, her hands plunged in warm dishwater up to the wrists, she had commenced with the unpleasantness.

'I want to talk to you about something that might be best for Danny and I. For you too, maybe. We should have talked about it before, I guess.'

And then he had said an odd thing. She had expected to discover his anger, to provoke the bitterness, the recriminations. She had expected a mad dash for the liquor cabinet. But not this soft, almost toneless reply that was so unlike him. It was almost as though the Jack she had lived with for six years had never come back last night – as if he had been replaced by some unearthly doppelgänger that she would never know or be quite sure of.

'Would you do something for me? A favor?'

'What?' She had to discipline her voice strictly to keep it from trembling.

'Let's talk about it in a week. If you still want to.'

And she had agreed. It remained unspoken between them. During that week he had seen Al Shockley more than ever, but he came home early and there was no liquor on his breath. She imagined she smelled it, but knew it wasn't so. Another week. And another.

Divorce went back to committee, unvoted on.

What had happened? She still wondered and still had not the slightest idea. The subject was taboo between them. He was like a man who had leaned around a corner and had seen an unexpected monster lying in wait, crouching among the dried bones of its old kills. The liquor remained in the cabinet, but he didn't touch it. She had considered throwing them out a dozen times but in the end always backed away from the idea, as if some unknown charm would be broken by the act.

And there was Danny's part in it to consider.

If she felt she didn't know her husband, then she was in awe of her child – awe in the strict meaning of that word: a kind of undefined superstitious dread.

Dozing lightly, the image of the instant of his birth was presented to her. She was again lying on the delivery table, bathed in sweat, her hair in strings, her feet splayed out in the stirrups.

(and a little high from the gas they kept giving her whiffs of; at one point she had muttered that she felt like an advertisement for gang rape, and the nurse, an old bird who had assisted at the births of enough children to populate a high school, found that extremely funny)

the doctor between her legs, the nurse off to one side, arranging instruments and humming. The sharp, glassy pains had been coming at steadily shortening intervals, and several times she had screamed in spite of her shame.

Then the doctor told her quite sternly that she must *PUSH*, and she did, and then she felt something being taken from her. It was a clear and distinct feeling, one she would never forget – the thing *taken*. Then the doctor held her son up by the legs – she had seen his tiny sex and known he was a boy immediately – and as the doctor groped for the airmask, she had seen something else, something so horrible that she found the strength to scream again after she had thought all screams were used up:

He has no face!

But of course there had been a face, Danny's own sweet face, and the caul that had covered it at birth now resided in a small jar which she had kept, almost shamefully. She did not hold with old superstition, but she had kept the caul nevertheless. She did not hold with wives' tales, but the boy had been unusual from the first. She did not believe in second sight but—

Did Daddy have an accident? I dreamed Daddy had an accident.

Something had changed him. She didn't believe it was just her getting ready to ask for a divorce that had done it. Something had happened before that morning. Something that had happened while she slept uneasily. Al Shockley said that nothing had happened, nothing at all, but he had averted his eyes when he said it, and if you believed faculty gossip, Al had also climbed aboard the fabled wagon.

Did Daddy have an accident?

Maybe a chance collision with fate, surely nothing much

more concrete. She had read that day's paper and the next day's with a closer eye than usual, but she saw nothing she could connect with Jack. God help her, she had been looking for a hit-and-run accident or a barroom brawl that had resulted in serious injuries or . . . who knew? Who wanted to? But no policeman came to call, either to ask questions or with a warrant empowering him to take paint scrapings from the VW's bumpers. Nothing. Only her husband's one hundred and eighty degree change and her son's sleepy question on waking:

Did Daddy have an accident? I dreamed . . .

She had stuck with Jack more for Danny's sake than she would admit in her waking hours, but now, sleeping lightly, she could admit it: Danny had been Jack's for the asking, almost from the first. Just as she had been her father's, almost from the first. She couldn't remember Danny ever spitting a bottle back on Jack's shirt. Jack could get him to eat after she had given up in disgust, even when Danny was teething and it gave him visible pain to chew. When Danny had a stomachache, she would rock him for an hour before he began to quiet, Jack had only to pick him up, walk twice around the room with him, and Danny would be asleep on Jack's shoulder, his thumb securely corked in his mouth.

He hadn't minded changing diapers, even those he called the special deliveries. He sat with Danny for hours on end, bouncing him on his lap, playing finger games with him, making faces at him while Danny poked at his nose and then collapsed with the giggles. He made formulas and administered them faultlessly, getting up every last burp afterward. He would take Danny with him in the car to get the paper or a bottle of milk or nails at the hardware store even when their son was still an infant. He had taken Danny to a Stovington-Keene soccer match when Danny was only six months old, and Danny had sat motionlessly on his father's lap through the whole game, wrapped in a blanket, a small Stovington pennant clutched in one chubby fist.

He loved his mother but he was his father's boy.

And hadn't she felt, time and time again, her son's wordless opposition to the whole idea of divorce? She would be thinking about it in the kitchen, turning it over in her mind as she turned the potatoes for supper over in her hands for the peeler's blade. And she would turn around to see him sitting cross-legged in a kitchen chair, looking at her with eyes that seemed both frightened and accusatory. Walking with him in the park, he would suddenly seize both her hands and say – almost demand: 'Do you love me? Do you love daddy?' And, confused, she would nod or say, 'Of course I do, honey.' Then he would run to the duck pond, sending them squawking and scared to the other end, flapping their wings in a panic before the small ferocity of his charge, leaving her to stare after him and wonder.

There were even times when it seemed that her determination to at least discuss the matter with Jack dissolved, not out of her own weakness, but under the determination of her son's will.

I don't believe such things.

But in sleep she did believe them, and in sleep, with her husband's seed still drying on her thighs, she felt that the three of them had been permanently welded together – that if their three/oneness was to be destroyed, it would not be destroyed by any of them but from outside.

Most of what she believed centered around her love for Jack. She had never stopped loving him, except maybe for that dark period immediately following Danny's 'accident'. And she loved her son. Most of all she loved them together, walking or riding or only sitting, Jack's large head and Danny's small one poised alertly over the fans of old maid hands, sharing a bottle of Coke, looking at the funnies. She loved having them with her, and she hoped to dear God that this hotel caretaking job Al had gotten for Jack would be the beginning of good times again.

> *And the wind gonna rise up, baby,*
> *and blow my blues away . . .*

Soft and sweet and mellow, the song came back and lingered, following her down into a deeper sleep where thought ceased and the faces that came in dreams went unremembered.

CHAPTER SEVEN
IN ANOTHER BEDROOM

Danny awoke with the booming still loud in his ears, and the drunk, savagely pettish voice crying hoarsely: *Come out here and take your medicine! I'll find you! I'll find you!*

But now the booming was only his racing heart, and the only voice in the night was the faraway sound of a police siren.

He lay in bed motionlessly, looking up at the wind-stirred shadows of the leaves on his bedroom ceiling. They twined sinuously together, making shapes like the vines and creepers in a jungle, like patterns woven into the nap of a thick carpet. He was clad in Doctor Denton pajamas, but between the pajama suit and his skin he had grown a more closely fitting singlet of perspiration.

'Tony?' he whispered. 'You there?'

No answer.

He slipped out of bed and padded silently across to the window and looked out on Arapahoe Street, now still and silent. It was two in the morning. There was nothing out there but empty sidewalks drifted with fallen leaves, parked cars, and the long-necked streetlight on the corner across from the Cliff Brice gas station. With its hooded top and motionless stance, the streetlight looked like a monster in a space show.

He looked up the street both ways, straining his eyes for Tony's slight, beckoning form, but there was no one there.

The wind sighed through the trees, and the fallen leaves rattled up the deserted walks and around the hubcaps of parked cars. It was a faint and sorrowful sound, and the boy thought that he might be the only one in Boulder awake enough to hear it. The only human being, at least. There was no way of knowing what else might be out in the night, slinking hungrily through the shadows, watching and scenting the breeze.

THE SHINING

I'll find you! I'll find you!

'Tony?' he whispered again, but without much hope.

Only the wind spoke back, gusting more strongly this time, scattering leaves across the sloping roof below his window. Some of them slipped into the raingutter and came to rest there like tired dancers.

Danny . . . Danneee . . .

He started at the sound of that familiar voice and craned out the window, his small hands on the sill. With the sound of Tony's voice the whole night seemed to have come silently and secretly alive, whispering even when the wind quieted again and the leaves were still and the shadows had stopped moving. He thought he saw a darker shadow standing by the bus stop a block down, but it was hard to tell if it was a real thing or an eyetrick.

Don't go, Danny . . .

Then the wind gusted again, making him squint, and the shadow by the bus stop was gone . . . if it had ever been there at all. He stood by his window for

(a minute? an hour?)

some time longer, but there was no more. At last he crept back into his bed and pulled the blankets up and watched the shadows thrown by the alien streetlight turn into a sinuous jungle filled with flesh-eating plants that wanted only to slip around him, squeeze the life out of him, and drag him down into a blackness where one sinister word flashed in red:

REDRUM.

PART TWO
CLOSING DAY

CHAPTER EIGHT
A VIEW OF THE OVERLOOK

Mommy was worried.

She was afraid the bug wouldn't make it up and down all these mountains and that they would get stranded by the side of the road where somebody might come ripping along and hit them. Danny himself was more sanguine; if Daddy thought the bug would make this one last trip, then probably it would.

'We're just about there,' Jack said.

Wendy brushed her hair back from her temples. 'Thank God.'

She was sitting in the right-hand bucket, a Victoria Holt paperback open but face down in her lap. She was wearing her blue dress, the one Danny thought was her prettiest. It had a sailor collar and made her look very young, like a girl just getting ready to graduate from high school. Daddy kept putting his hand high up on her leg and she kept laughing and brushing it off, saying Get away, fly.

Danny was impressed with the mountains. One day Daddy had taken them up in the ones near Boulder, the ones they called the Flatirons, but these were much bigger, and on the tallest of them you could see a fine dusting of snow, which Daddy said was often there year-round.

And they were actually *in* the mountains, no goofing around. Sheer rock faces rose all around them, so high you could barely see their tops even by craning your neck out the window. When they left Boulder, the temperature had been in the high seventies. Now, just after noon, the air up here felt crisp and cold like November back in Vermont and Daddy had the heater going . . . not that it worked all that well. They had passed several signs that said FALLING ROCK ZONE (Mommy read each one to him), and although Danny had waited anxiously to see some rock fall, none had. At least not yet.

Half an hour ago they had passed another sign that Daddy said was very important. This sign said ENTERING SIDEWINDER PASS, and Daddy said that sign was as far as the snowplows went in the wintertime. After that the road got too steep. In the winter the road was closed from the little town of Sidewinder, which they had gone through just before they got to that sign, all the way to Buckland, Utah.

Now they were passing another sign.

'What's that one, Mom?'

'That one says SLOWER VEHICLES USE RIGHT LANE. That means us.'

'The bug will make it,' Danny said.

'Please God,' Mommy said, and crossed her fingers. Danny looked down at the open-toed sandals and saw that she had crossed her toes as well. He giggled. She smiled back, but he knew that she was still worried.

The road wound up and up in a series of slow S curves, and Jack dropped the bug's stick shift from fourth gear to third, then into second. The bug wheezed and protested, and Wendy's eye fixed on the speedometer needle, which sank from forty to thirty to twenty, where it hovered reluctantly.

'The fuel pump . . .' she began timidly.

'The fuel pump will go another three miles,' Jack said shortly.

The rock wall fell away on their right, disclosing a slash valley that seemed to go down forever, lined a dark green with Rocky Mountain pine and spruce. The pines fell away to gray cliffs of rock that dropped for hundreds of feet before smoothing out. She saw a waterfall spilling over one of them, the early afternoon sun sparkling in it like a golden fish snared in a blue net. They were beautiful mountains but they were hard. She did not think they would forgive many mistakes. An unhappy foreboding rose in her throat. Further west in the Sierra Nevada the Donner Party had become snowbound and had resorted to cannibalism to stay alive. The mountains did not forgive many mistakes.

With a punch of the clutch and a jerk. Jack shifted down to first gear and they labored upward, the bug's engine thumping gamely.

'You know,' she said, 'I don't think we've seen five cars

since we came through Sidewinder. And one of them was the hotel limousine.'

Jack nodded. 'It goes right to Stapleton Airport in Denver. There's already some icy patches up beyond the hotel, Watson says, and they're forecasting more snow for tomorrow up higher. Anybody going through the mountains now wants to be on one of the main roads, just in case. That goddam Ullman better still be up there. I guess he will be.'

'You're sure the larder is fully stocked?' she asked, still thinking of the Donners.

'He said so. He wanted Hallorann to go over it with you. Hallorann's the cook.'

'Oh,' she said faintly, looking at the speedometer. It had dropped from fifteen to ten miles an hour.

'There's the top,' Jack said, pointing three hundred yards ahead. 'There's a scenic turnout and you can see the Overlook from there. I'm going to pull off the road and give the bug a chance to rest.' He craned over his shoulder at Danny, who was sitting on a pile of blankets. 'What do you think, doc? We might see some deer. Or caribou.'

'Sure, Dad.'

The VW labored up and up. The speedometer dropped to just above the five-mile-an-hour hashmark and was beginning to hitch when Jack pulled off the road.

('What's that sign, Mommy?' 'SCENIC TURNOUT', she read dutifully.)

and stepped on the emergency brake and let the VW run in neutral.

'Come on,' he said, and got out.

They walked to the guardrail together.

'That's it,' Jack said, and pointed at eleven o'clock.

For Wendy, it was discovering truth in a cliché: her breath was taken away. For a moment she was unable to breathe at all; the view had knocked the wind from her. They were standing near the top of one peak. Across from them – who knew how far? – an even taller mountain reared into the sky, its jagged tip only a silhouette that was now nimbused by the sun, which was beginning its decline. The whole valley floor was spread out below them, the slopes that they had climbed in the laboring bug falling away with such dizzying suddenness that she knew to look down there for too long would bring on nausea and eventual vomiting. The imagination seemed to spring to full life in the clear air, beyond the rein of reason, and to look was to helplessly see one's self plunging down and down and down, sky and slopes changing places in slow cartwheels, the scream drifting from your mouth like a lazy balloon as your hair and your dress billowed out . . .

She jerked her gaze away from the drop almost by force and followed Jack's finger. She could see the highway clinging to the side of this cathedral spire, switching back on itself but always tending northwest, still climbing but at a more gentle angle. Further up, seemingly set directly into the slope itself, she saw the grimly clinging pines give way to a wide square of green lawn and standing in the middle of it, overlooking all this, the hotel. The Overlook. Seeing it, she found breath and voice again.

'Oh, Jack, it's gorgeous!'

'Yes, it is,' he said. 'Ullman says he thinks it's the single most beautiful location in America. I don't care much for him, but I think he might be . . . Danny! Danny, are you all right?'

She looked around for him and her sudden fear for him blotted out everything else, stupendous or not. She darted toward him. He was holding onto the guardrail and looking up at the hotel, his face a pasty gray color. His eyes had the blank look of someone on the verge of fainting.

She knelt beside him and put steadying hands on his shoulders. 'Danny, what's—'

Jack was beside her. 'You okay, doc?' He gave Danny a brisk little shake and his eyes cleared.

'I'm okay, Daddy. I'm fine.'

'What was it. Danny?' she asked. 'Were you dizzy, honey?'

'No, I was just . . . thinking. I'm sorry. I didn't mean to scare you.' He looked at his parents, kneeling in front of him, and offered them a small puzzled smile. 'Maybe it was the sun. The sun got in my eyes.'

'We'll get you up to the hotel and give you a drink of water,' Daddy said.

'Okay.'

And in the bug, which moved upward more surely on the gentler grade, he kept looking out between them as the road unwound, affording occasional glimpses of the Overlook Hotel, its massive bank of westward–looking windows reflecting back the sun. It was the place he had seen in the midst of the blizzard, the dark and booming place where some hideously familiar figure sought him down long corridors carpeted with jungle. The place Tony had warned him against. It was here. It was here. Whatever Redrum was, it was here.

CHAPTER NINE
CHECKING IT OUT

Ullman was waiting for them just inside the wide, old-fashioned front doors. He shook hands with Jack and nodded coolly at Wendy, perhaps noticing the way heads turned when she came through into the lobby, her golden hair spilling across the shoulders of the simple navy dress. The hem of the dress stopped a modest two inches above the knee, but you didn't have to see more to know they were good legs.

Ullman seemed truly warm toward Danny only, but Wendy had experienced that before. Danny seemed to be a child for people who ordinarily held W. C. Fields' sentiments about children. He bent a little from the waist and offered Danny his hand. Danny shook it formally, without a smile.

'My son Danny,' Jack said. 'And my wife Winnifred.'

'I'm happy to meet you both,' Ullman said. 'How old are you, Danny?'

'Five, sir.'

'*Sir*, yet.' Ullman smiled and glanced at Jack. 'He's well mannered.'

'Of course he is,' Jack said.

'And Mrs Torrance.' He offered the same little bow, and for a bemused instant Wendy thought he would kiss her hand. She half-offered it and he did take it, but only for a moment, clasped in both of his. His hands were small and dry and smooth, and she guessed that he powdered them.

The lobby was a bustle of activity. Almost every one of the old-fashioned high-backed chairs was taken. Bellboys shuttled in and out with suitcases and there was a line at the desk, which was dominated by a huge brass cash register. The Bank-Americard and Master Charge decals on it seemed jarringly anachronistic.

To their right, down toward a pair of tall double doors that were pulled closed and roped off, there was an old-fashioned fireplace now blazing with birch logs. Three nuns sat on a sofa that was drawn up almost to the hearth itself. They were talking and smiling with their bags stacked up to either side, waiting for the check-out line to thin a little. As Wendy watched them they burst into a chord of tinkling, girlish laughter. She felt a smile touch her own lips; not one of them could be under sixty.

In the background was the constant hum of conversation, the muted *ding!* of the silver-plated bell beside the cash register as one of the two clerks on duty struck it, the slightly impatient call of 'Front, please!' It brought back strong, warm memories of her honeymoon in New York with Jack, at the Beekman Tower. For the first time she let herself believe that this might be exactly what the three of them needed: a season together away from the world, a sort of family honeymoon. She smiled affectionately down at Danny, who was goggling around frankly at everything. Another limo, as gray as a banker's vest, had pulled up out front.

'The last day of the season,' Ullman was saying. 'Closing day. Always hectic. I had expected you more around three, Mr Torrance.'

'I wanted to give the Volks time for a nervous breakdown if it decided to have one,' Jack said. 'It didn't.'

'How fortunate,' Ullman said. 'I'd like to take the three of you on a tour of the place a little later, and of course Dick Hallorann wants to show Mrs Torrance the Overlook's kitchen. But I'm afraid—'

One of the clerks came over and almost tugged his forelock.

'Excuse me, Mr Ullman—'

'Well? What is it?'

'It's Mrs Brant,' the clerk said uncomfortably. 'She refuses to pay her bill with anything but her American Express card. I told her we stopped taking American Express at the end of the season last year, but she won't . . .' His eyes shifted to the Torrance family, then back to Ullman. He shrugged.

'I'll take care of it.'

'Thank you, Mr Ullman.' The clerk crossed back to the desk,

where a dreadnought of a woman bundled into a long fur coat and what looked like a black feather boa was remonstrating loudly.

'I have been coming to the Overlook Hotel since 1955,' she was telling the smiling, shrugging clerk. 'I continued to come even after my second husband died of a stroke on that tiresome roque court – I told him the sun was too hot that day – and I have *never* . . . I repeat: *never* . . . paid with anything but my American Express credit card. Call the police if you like! Have them drag me away! I will still refuse to pay with anything but my American Express credit card. I repeat . . .'

'Excuse me,' Mr Ullman said.

They watched him cross the lobby, touch Mrs Brant's elbow deferentially, and spread his hands and nod when she turned her tirade on him. He listened sympathetically, nodded again, and said something in return. Mrs Brant smiled triumphantly, turned to the unhappy desk clerk, and said loudly: 'Thank God there is one employee of this hotel who hasn't become an utter Philistine!'

She allowed Ullman, who barely came to the bulky shoulder of her fur coat, to take her arm and lead her away, presumably to his inner office.

'Whooo!' Wendy said, smiling. 'There's a dude who earns his money.'

'But he didn't like that lady,' Danny said immediately. 'He was just pretending to like her.'

Jack grinned down at him. 'I'm sure that's true, doc. But flattery is the stuff that greases the wheels of the world.'

'What's flattery?'

'Flattery,' Wendy told him, 'is when your daddy says he likes my new yellow slacks even if he doesn't or when he says I don't need to take off five pounds.'

'Oh. Is it lying for fun?'

'Something very like that.'

He had been looking at her closely and now said: 'You're pretty, Mommy.' He frowned in confusion when they exchanged a glance and then burst into laughter.

'Ullman didn't waste much flattery on me,' Jack said. 'Come

on over by the window, you guys. I feel conspicuous standing out here in the middle with my denim jacket on. I honest to God didn't think there'd be anybody much here on closing day. Guess I was wrong.'

'You look very handsome,' she said, and then they laughed again, Wendy putting a hand over her mouth. Danny still didn't understand, but it was okay. They were loving each other. Danny thought this place reminded her of somewhere else

(the beak-man place)

where she had been happy. He wished he liked it as well as she did, but he kept telling himself over and over that the things Tony showed him didn't always come true. He would be careful. He would watch for something called Redrum. But he would not say anything unless he absolutely had to. Because they were happy, they had been laughing, and there were no bad thoughts.

'Look at this view,' Jack said.

'Oh, it's gorgeous! Danny, look!'

But Danny didn't think it was particularly gorgeous. He didn't like heights; they made him dizzy. Beyond the wide front porch, which ran the length of the hotel, a beautifully manicured lawn (there was a putting green on the right) sloped away to a long, rectangular swimming pool. A CLOSED sign stood on a little tripod at one end of the pool; *closed* was one sign he could read by himself, along with *Stop, Exit, Pizza*, and a few others.

Beyond the pool a graveled path wound off through baby pines and spruces and aspens. Here was a small sign he didn't know: ROQUE. There was an arrow below it.

'What's R-O-Q-U-E, Daddy?'

'A game,' Daddy said. 'It's a little bit like croquet, only you play it on a gravel court that has sides like a big billiard table instead of grass. It's a very old game, Danny. Sometimes they have tournaments here.'

'Do you play it with a croquet mallet?'

'Like that,' Jack agreed. 'Only the handle's a little shorter and the head has two sides. One side is hard rubber and the other side is wood.'

(*Come out, you little shit!*)

'It's pronounced *roke*,' Daddy was saying. 'I'll teach you how to play it, if you want.'

'Maybe,' Danny said in an odd colorless little voice that made his parents exchange a puzzled look over his head. 'I might not like it, though.'

'Well if you don't like it, doc, you don't have to play. All right?'

'Sure.'

'Do you like the animals?' Wendy asked. 'That's called a topiary.' Beyond the path leading to *roque* there were hedges clipped into the shapes of various animals. Danny, whose eyes were sharp, made out a rabbit, a dog, a horse, a cow, and a trio of bigger ones that looked like frolicking lions.

'Those animals were what made Uncle Al think of me for the job,' Jack told him. 'He knew that when I was in college I used to work for a landscaping company. That's a business that fixes people's lawns and bushes and hedges. I used to trim a lady's topiary.'

Wendy put a hand over her mouth and snickered. Looking at her, Jack said, 'Yes, I used to trim her topiary at least once a week.'

'Get away, fly,' Wendy said, and snickered again.

'Did she have nice hedges, Dad?' Danny asked, and at this they both stifled great bursts of laughter. Wendy laughed so hard that tears streamed down her cheeks and she had to get a Kleenex out of her handbag.

'They weren't animals, Danny,' Jack said when he had control of himself. 'They were playing cards. Spades and hearts and clubs and diamonds. But the hedges grow, you see—'

(*They creep*, Watson had said . . . no, not the hedges, the boiler. *You have to watch it all the time or you and your fambly will end up on the fuckin moon.*)

They looked at him, puzzled. The smile had faded off his face.

'Dad?' Danny asked.

He blinked at them, as if coming back from far away. 'They grow, Danny, and lose their shape. So I'll have to give them a haircut once or twice a week until it gets so cold they stop growing for the year.'

'And a playground, too,' Wendy said. 'My lucky boy.'

The playground was beyond the *topiary*. Two slides, a big swing set with half a dozen swings set at varying heights, a jungle gym, a tunnel made of cement rings, a sandbox, and a playhouse that was an exact replica of the Overlook itself.

'Do you like it, Danny?' Wendy asked.

'I sure do,' he said, hoping he sounded more enthused than he felt. 'It's neat.'

Beyond the playground there was an inconspicuous chain link security fence, beyond that the wide, macadamized drive that led up to the hotel, and beyond that the valley itself, dropping away into the bright blue haze of afternoon. Danny didn't know the word *isolation*, but if someone had explained it to him he would have seized on it. Far below, lying in the sun like a long black snake that had decided to snooze for a while, was the road that led back through Sidewinder Pass and eventually to Boulder. The road that would be closed all winter long. He felt a little suffocated at the thought, and almost jumped when Daddy dropped his hand on his shoulder.

'I'll get you that drink as soon as I can, doc. They're a little busy right now.'

'Sure. Dad.'

Mrs Brant came out of the inner office looking vindicated. A few moments later two bellboys, struggling with eight suitcases between them, followed her as best they could as she strode triumphantly out the door. Danny watched through the window as a man in a gray uniform and a hat like a captain in the Army brought her long silver car around to the door and got out. He tipped his cap to her and ran around to open the trunk.

And in one of those flashes that sometimes came, he got a complete thought from her, one that floated above the confused, low-pitched babble of emotions and colors that he usually got in crowded places.

(*i'd like to get into his pants*)

Danny's brow wrinkled as he watched the bellboys put her cases into the trunk. She was looking rather sharply at the man in the gray uniform, who was supervising the loading. Why would she want to get that man's pants? Was she cold, even

75

with that long fur coat on? And if she was that cold, why hadn't she just put on some pants of her own? His mommy wore pants just about all winter.

The man in the gray uniform closed the trunk and walked back to help her into the car. Danny watched closely to see if she would say anything about his pants, but she only smiled and gave him a dollar bill – a tip. A moment later she was guiding the big silver car down the driveway.

He thought about asking his mother why Mrs Brant might want that car-man's pants, and decided against it. Sometimes questions could get you in a whole lot of trouble. It had happened to him before.

So instead he squeezed in between them on the small sofa they were sharing and watched all the people check out at the desk. He was glad his mommy and daddy were happy and loving each other, but he couldn't help being a little worried. He couldn't help it.

CHAPTER TEN
HALLORANN

The cook didn't conform to Wendy's image of the typical resort hotel kitchen personage at all. To begin with, such a personage was called a *chef*, nothing so mundane as a cook – cooking was what she did in her apartment kitchen when she threw all the leftovers into a greased Pyrex casserole dish and added noodles. Further, the culinary wizard of such a place as the Overlook, which advertised in the resort section of the New York Sunday *Times*, should be small, rotund, and pasty-faced (rather like the Pillsbury Dough-Boy); he should have a thin pencil mustache like a forties musical comedy star, dark eyes, a French accent, and a detestable personality.

Hallorann had the dark eyes and that was all. He was a tall black man with a modest afro that was beginning to powder white. He had a soft southern accent and he laughed a lot, disclosing teeth too white and too even to be anything but 1950-vintage Sears and Roebuck dentures. Her own father had had a pair, which he called Roebuckers, and from time to time he would push them out at her comically at the supper table ... always, Wendy remembered now, when her mother was out in the kitchen getting something else or on the telephone.

Danny had stared up at this black giant in blue serge, and then had smiled when Hallorann picked him up easily, set him in the crook of his elbow, and said: 'You ain't gonna stay up here all winter.'

'Yes I am,' Danny said with a shy grin.

'No, you're gonna come down to St Pete's with me and learn to cook right out on the beach every damn evenin watchin for crabs. Right?'

Danny giggled delightedly and shook his head no. Hallorann set him down.

'If you're gonna change your mind,' Hallorann said, bending over him gravely, 'you better do it quick. Thirty minutes from now and I'm in my car. Two and a half hours after that, I'm sitting at Gate 32, Concourse B, Stapleton International Airport, in the mile-high city of Denver, Colorado. Three hours after *that*, I'm rentin a car at the Miama Airport and on my way to sunny St Pete's, waiting to get inta my swimtrunks and just laaafin up my sleeve at anybody stuck and caught in the snow. Can you dig it, my boy?'

'Yes, sir,' Danny said, smiling.

Hallorann turned to Jack and Wendy. 'Looks like a fine boy there.'

'We think he'll do,' Jack said, and offered his hand. Hallorann took it. 'I'm Jack Torrance. My wife Winnifred. Danny you've met.'

'And a pleasure it was. Ma'am, are you a Winnie or a Freddie?'

'I'm a Wendy,' she said, smiling.

'Okay. That's better than the other two, I think. Right this way. Mr Ullman wants you to have the tour, the tour you'll get.' He shook his head and said under his breath: 'And won't I be glad to see the last of *him*.'

Hallorann commenced to tour them around the most immense kitchen Wendy had ever seen in her life. It was sparkling clean. Every surface was coaxed to a high gloss. It was more than just big; it was intimidating. She walked at Halloran's side while Jack, wholly out of his element, hung back a little with Danny. A long pegboard hung with cutting instruments which went all the way from paring knives to two-handed cleavers hung beside a four-basin sink. There was a breadboard as big as their Boulder apartment's kitchen table. An amazing array of stainless-steel pots and pans hung from floor to ceiling, covering one whole wall.

'I think I'll have to leave a trail of breadcrumbs every time I come in,' she said.

'Don't let it get you down,' Hallorann said. 'It's big, but it's still only a kitchen. Most of this stuff you'll never even have to touch. Keep it clean, that's all I ask. Here's the stove I'd be using, if I was you. There are three of them in all, but this is the smallest.'

Smallest, she thought dismally, looking at it. There were twelve burners, two regular ovens and a Dutch oven, a heated well on top in which you could simmer sauces or bake beans, a broiler, and a warmer – plus a million dials and temperature gauges.

'All gas,' Halloran said. 'You've cooked with gas before, Wendy?'

'Yes . . .'

'I love gas,' he said, and turned on one of the burners. Blue flame popped into life and he adjusted it down to a faint glow with a delicate touch. 'I like to be able to see the flame you're cookin with. You see where all the surface burner switches are?'

'Yes.'

'And the oven dials are all marked. Myself, I favor the middle one because it seems to heat the most even, but you use which-ever one you like – or all three, for that matter.'

'A TV dinner in each one,' Wendy said, and laughed weakly.

Halloran roared. 'Go right ahead, if you like. I left a list of everything edible over by the sink. You see it?'

'Here it is, Mommy!' Danny brought over two sheets of paper, written closely on both sides.

'Good boy,' Halloran said, taking it from him and ruffling his hair. 'You sure you don't want to come to Florida with me, my boy? Learn to cook the sweetest shrimp creole this side of paradise?'

Danny put his hands over his mouth and giggled and retreated to his father's side.

'You three folks could eat up here for a year, I guess,' Hallor-ann said. 'We got a cold-pantry, a walk-in freezer, all sorts of vegetable bins, and two refrigerators. Come on and let me show you.'

For the next ten minutes Halloran opened bins and doors, disclosing food in such amounts as Wendy had never seen before. The food supplies amazed her but did not reassure her as much as she might have thought: the Donner Party kept recurring to her, not with thoughts of cannibalism (with all this food it would indeed be a long time before they were reduced to such poor rations as each other), but with the reinforced idea that this was indeed a serious business: when snow fell, getting out of here would not be a matter of an hour's drive to Sidewinder but a major operation. They would sit up here in this deserted grand hotel, eating the food that had been left them like creatures in a fairy tale and listening to the bitter wind around their snowbound eaves. In Vermont, when Danny had broken his arm.

(when *Jack* broke Danny's arm)

she had called the emergency Medix squad, dialing the number from the little card attached to the phone. They had been at the house only ten minutes later. There were other numbers written on that little card. You could have a police car in five minutes and a fire truck in even less time than that, because the fire station was only three blocks away and one block over. There was a man to call if the lights went out, a man to call if the shower stopped up, a man to call if the TV went on the fritz. But what would happen up here if Danny had one of his fainting spells and swallowed his tongue?

(*oh God what a thought!*)

What if the place caught on fire? If Jack fell down the elevator shaft and fractured his skull? What if—?

(*what if we have a wonderful time now* stop *it, Winnifred!*)

Hallorann showed them into the walk-in freezer first, where their breath puffed out like comic strip balloons. In the freezer it was as if winter had already come.

Hamburger in big plastic bags, ten pounds in each bag, a dozen bags. Forty whole chickens hanging from a row of hooks in the wood-planked walls. Canned hams stacked up like poker chips, a dozen of them. Below the chickens, ten roasts of beef, ten roasts of pork, and a huge leg of lamb.

'You like lamb, doc?' Hallorann asked, grinning.

'I love it,' Danny said immediately. He had never had it.

'I knew you did. There's nothin like two good slices of lamb on a cold night, with some mint jelly on the side. You got the mint jelly here, too. Lamb eases the belly. It's a noncontentious sort of meat.'

From behind them Jack said curiously: 'How did you know we called him doc?'

Hallorann turned around. 'Pardon?'

'Danny. We call him doc sometimes. Like in the Bugs Bunny cartoons.'

'Looks sort of like a doc, doesn't he?' He wrinkled his nose at Danny, smacked his lips, and said, 'Ehhhh, what's up, doc?'

Danny giggled and then Hallorann said something

(*Sure you don't want to go to Florida, doc?*)

to him, very clearly. He heard every word. He looked at Hallorann, startled and a little scared. Hallorann winked solemnly and turned back to the food.

Wendy looked from the cook's broad, serge-clad back to her son. She had the oddest feeling that something had passed between them, something she could not quite follow.

'You got twelve packages of sausage, twelve packages of bacon,' Hallorann said. 'So much for the pig. In this drawer, twenty pounds of butter.'

'*Real* butter?' Jack asked.

'The A-number-one.'

'I don't think I've had real butter since I was a kid back in Berlin, New Hampshire.'

'Well, you'll eat it up here until oleo seems a treat,' Hallorann said, and laughed. 'Over in this bin you got your bread – thirty loaves of white, twenty of dark. We try to keep racial balance at the Overlook, don't you know. Now I know fifty loaves won't take you through, but there's plenty of makings and fresh is better than frozen any day of the week.

'Down here you got your fish. Brain food, right, doc?'

'Is it, Mom?'

'If Mr Hallorann says so, honey.' She smiled.

Danny wrinkled his nose. 'I don't like fish.'

'You're dead wrong,' Hallorann said. 'You just never had any fish that liked *you*. This fish here will like you fine. Five pounds of rainbow trout, ten pounds of turbot, fifteen cans of tuna fish—'

'Oh yeah, I like tuna.'

'and five pounds of the sweetest-tasting sole that ever swam in the sea. My boy, when next spring rolls around, you're gonna thank old . . .' He snapped his fingers as if he had forgotten something. 'What's my name, now? I guess it just slipped my mind.'

'Mr Hallorann,' Danny said, grinning. 'Dick, to your friends.'

'That's right! And you bein a friend, you make it Dick.'

As he led them into the far corner, Jack and Wendy exchanged a puzzled glance, both of them trying to remember if Hallorann had told them his first name.

'And this here I put in special,' Hallorann said. 'Hope you folks enjoy it.'

'Oh really, you shouldn't have,' Wendy said, touched. It was a twenty-pound turkey wrapped in a wide scarlet ribbon with a bow on top.

'You got to have your turkey on Thanksgiving, Wendy,' Hallorann said gravely. 'I believe there's a capon back here somewhere for Christmas. Doubtless you'll stumble on it. Let's come on out of here now before we all catch the pee-numonia. Right, doc?'

'Right!'

There were more wonders in the cold-pantry. A hundred boxes of dried milk (Hallorann advised her gravely to buy fresh milk for the boy in Sidewinder as long as it was feasible), five twelve-pound bags of sugar, a gallon jug of blackstrap molasses, cereals, glass jugs of rice, macaroni, spaghetti; ranked cans of fruit and fruit salad; a bushel of fresh apples that scented the whole room with autumn; dried raisins, prunes, and apricots ('You got to be regular if you want to be happy,' Hallorann said, and pealed laughter at the cold-pantry ceiling, where one old-fashioned light globe hung down on an iron chain); a deep bin filled with potatoes; and smaller caches of tomatoes, onions, turnips, squashes, and cabbages.

'My word,' Wendy said as they came out. But seeing all that fresh food after her thirty-dollar-a-week grocery budget so stunned her that she was unable to say just what her word was.

'I'm runnin a bit late,' Hallorann said, checking his watch, 'so I'll just let you go through the cabinets and fridges as you get settled in. There's cheeses, canned milk, sweetened condensed milk, yeast, bakin soda, a whole bagful of those Table Talk pies, a few bunches of bananas that ain't even near to ripe yet—'

'Stop,' she said, holding up a hand and laughing. 'I'll never remember it all. It's super. And I promise to leave the place clean.'

'That's all I ask.' He turned to Jack. 'Did Mr Ullman give you the rundown on the rats in his belfry?'

Jack grinned. 'He said there were possibly some in the attic, and Mr Watson said there might be some more down in the basement. There must be two tons of paper down there, but I didn't see any shredded, as if they'd been using it to make nests.'

'That Watson,' Hallorann said, shaking his head in mock sorrow. 'Ain't he the foulest-talking man you ever ran on?'

'He's quite a character,' Jack agreed. His own father had been the foulest-talking man Jack had ever run on.

'It's a sort of a pity,' Hallorann said, leading them back toward the wide swinging doors that gave on the Overlook dining room. 'There was money in that family, long ago. It was Watson's granddad or great-granddad – I can't remember which – that built this place.'

'So I was told,' Jack said.

'What happened?' Wendy asked.

'Well, they couldn't make it go,' Hallorann said. 'Watson will tell you the whole story – twice a day, if you let him. The old man got a bee in his bonnet about the place. He let it drag him down, I guess. He had two boys and one of them was killed in a riding accident on the grounds while the hotel was still a-building. That would have been 1908 or '09. The old man's wife died of the flu, and then it was just the old man and his youngest son. They ended up getting took on as caretakers in the same hotel the old man had built.'

'It is sort of a pity,' Wendy said.

'What happened to him? The old man?' Jack asked.

'He plugged his finger into a light socket by mistake and that was the end of him,' Hallorann said. 'Sometime in the early thirties before the Depression closed this place down for ten years.

'Anyway, Jack, I'd appreciate it if you and your wife would keep an eye out for rats in the kitchen, as well. If you should see them . . . traps, not poison.'

Jack blinked. 'Of course. Who'd want to put rat poison in the kitchen?'

Hallorann laughed derisively. 'Mr Ullman, that's who. That was his bright idea last fall. I put it to him, I said: "What if we all get up here next May, Mr Ullman, and I serve the traditional opening night dinner" – which just happens to be salmon in a very nice sauce – "and everybody gits sick and the doctor comes and says to you, 'Ullman, what have you been doing up here? You've got eighty of the richest folks in America suffering from rat poison!'"'

Jack threw his head back and bellowed laughter. 'What did Ullman say?'

Hallorann tucked his tongue into his cheek as if feeling for a bit of food in there. 'He said: "Get some traps, Hallorann."'

This time they all laughed, even Danny, although he was not completely sure what the joke was, except it had something to do with Mr Ullman, who didn't know everything after all.

The four of them passed through the dining room, empty and silent now, with its fabulous western exposure on the snow-dusted peaks. Each of the white linen tablecloths had been covered with a sheet of tough clear plastic. The rug, now rolled up for the season, stood in one corner like a sentinel on guard duty.

Across the wide room was a double set of batwing doors, and over them an old-fashioned sign lettered in gilt script: *The Colorado Lounge*.

Following his gaze, Hallorann said, 'If you're a drinkin man, I hope you brought your own supplies. That place is picked clean. Employees' party last night, you know. Every maid and bellhop in the place is goin' around with a headache today, me included.'

'I don't drink,' Jack said shortly. They went back to the lobby.

It had cleared greatly during the half hour they'd spent in the kitchen. The long main room was beginning to take on the quiet, deserted look that Jack supposed they would become familiar with soon enough. The high-backed chairs were empty. The nuns who had been sitting by the fire were gone, and the fire itself was down to a bed of comfortably glowing coals. Wendy glanced out into the parking lot and saw that all but a dozen cars had disappeared.

She found herself wishing they could get back in the VW and go back to Boulder . . . or anywhere else.

Jack was looking around for Ullman, but he wasn't in the lobby.

A young maid with her ash-blond hair pinned up on her neck came over. 'Your luggage is out on the porch, Dick.'

'Thank you, Sally.' He gave her a peck on the forehead. 'You have yourself a good winter. Getting married, I hear.'

He turned to the Torrances as she strolled away, backside twitching pertly. 'I've got to hurry along if I'm going to make that plane. I want to wish you all the best. Know you'll have it.'

'Thanks,' Jack said. 'You've been very kind.'

'I'll take good care of your kitchen,' Wendy promised again. 'Enjoy Florida.'

'I always do,' Halloran said. He put his hands on his knees and bent down to Danny. 'Last chance, guy. Want to come to Florida?'

'I guess not,' Danny said, smiling.

'Okay. Like to give me a hand out to my car with my bags?'

'If my mommy says I can.'

'You can,' Wendy said, 'but you'll have to have that jacket buttoned.' She leaned forward to do it but Halloran was ahead of her, his large brown fingers moving with smooth dexterity.

'I'll send him right back in,' Halloran said.

'Fine,' Wendy said, and followed them to the door. Jack was still looking around for Ullman. The last of the Overlook's guests were checking out at the desk.

CHAPTER ELEVEN
THE SHINING

There were four bags in a pile just outside the door. Three of them were giant, battered old suitcases covered with black imitation alligator hide. The last was an oversized zipper bag with a faded tartan skin.

'Guess you can handle that one, can't you?' Hallorann asked him. He picked up two of the big cases in one hand and hoisted the other under his arm.

'Sure,' Danny said. He got a grip on it with both hands and followed the cook down the porch steps, trying manfully not to grunt and give away how heavy it was.

A sharp and cutting fall wind had come up since they had arrived; it whistled across the parking lot, making Danny wince his eyes down to slits as he carried the zipper bag in front of him, bumping on his knees. A few errant aspen leaves rattled and turned across the now mostly deserted asphalt, making Danny think momentarily of that night last week when he had wakened out of his nightmare and had heard – or thought he heard, at least – Tony telling him not to go.

Hallorann set his bags down by the trunk of a beige Plymouth Fury. 'This ain't much car,' he confided to Danny, 'just a rental job. My Bessie's on the other end. She's a car. 1950 Cadillac, and does she run sweet? I'll tell the world. I keep her in Florida because she's too old for all this mountain climbing. You need a hand with that?'

'No, sir,' Danny said. He managed to carry it the last ten or twelve steps without grunting and set it down with a large sigh of relief.

'Good boy,' Hallorann said. He produced a large key ring from the pocket of his blue serge jacket and unlocked the trunk. As he lifted the bags in he said: 'You shine on, boy. Harder than anyone I ever met in my life. And I'm sixty years old this January.'

'Huh?'

'You got a knack,' Hallorann said, turning to him. 'Me, I've always called it shining. That's what my grandmother called it, too. She had it. We used to sit in the kitchen when I was a boy no older than you and have long talks without even openin our mouths.'

'Really?'

Hallorann smiled at Danny's openmouthed, almost hungry expression and said, 'Come on up and sit in the car with me for a few minutes. Want to talk to you.' He slammed the trunk.

In the lobby of the Overlook, Wendy Torrance saw her son get into the passenger side of Hallorann's car as the big black cook slid in behind the wheel. A sharp pang of fear struck her and she opened her mouth to tell Jack that Hallorann had not been lying about taking their son to Florida – there was a kidnaping afoot. But they were only sitting there. She could barely see the small silhouette of her son's head, turned attentively toward Hallorann's big one. Even at this distance that small head had a set to it that she recognized – it was the way her son looked when there was something on the TV that particularly fascinated him, or when he and his father were playing old maid or idiot cribbage. Jack, who was still looking around for Ullman, hadn't noticed. Wendy kept silent, watching Hallorann's car nervously, wondering what they could possibly be talking about that would make Danny cock his head that way.

In the car Hallorann was saying: 'Get you kinda lonely, thinkin you were the only one?'

Danny, who had been frightened as well as lonely sometimes, nodded. 'Am I the only one you ever met?' he asked.

Hallorann laughed and shook his head. 'No, child, no. But you shine the hardest.'

'Are there lots, then?'

'No,' Hallorann said, 'but you do run across them. A lot of folks, they got a little bit of shine to them. They don't even know it. But they always seem to show up with flowers when their wives are feelin blue with the monthlies, they do good on school tests they don't even study for, they got a good idea how people are feelin as soon as they walk into a room. I come across fifty or sixty like that. But maybe only a dozen, countin my gram, that *knew* they was shinin.'

'Wow,' Danny said, and thought about it. Then: 'Do you know Mrs Brant?'

'Her?' Hallorann asked scornfully. 'She don't shine. Just sends her supper back two-three times every night.'

'I know she doesn't,' Danny said earnestly. 'But do you know the man in the gray uniform that gets the cars?'

'Mike? Sure, I know Mike. What about him?'

'Mr Hallorann, why would she want his pants?'

'What are you talking about, boy?'

'Well, when she was watching him, she was thinking she would sure like to get into his pants and I just wondered why —'

But he got no further. Hallorann had thrown his head back, and rich, dark laughter issued from his chest, rolling around in the car like cannonfire. The seat shook with the force of it. Danny smiled, puzzled, and at last the storm subsided by fits and starts. Hallorann produced a large silk handkerchief from his breast pocket like a white flag of surrender and wiped his streaming eyes.

'Boy,' he said, still snorting a little, 'you are gonna know everything there is to know about the human condition before you make ten. I dunno if to envy you or not.'

'But Mrs Brant —'

'You never mind her,' he said. 'And don't go askin your mom, either. You'd only upset her, dig what I'm sayin?'

'Yes, sir,' Danny said. He dug it perfectly well. He had upset his mother that way in the past.

'That Mrs Brant is just a dirty old woman with an itch, that's all you have to know.' He looked at Danny speculatively. 'How hard can you hit, doc?'

'Huh?'

'Give me a blast. Think at me. I want to know if you got as much as I think you do.'

'What do you want me to think?'

'Anything. Just think it *hard*.'

'Okay,' Danny said. He considered it for a moment, then gathered his concentration and flung it out at Hallorann. He had never done anything precisely like this before, and at the last instant some instinctive part of him rose up and blunted some of the thought's raw force – he didn't want to hurt Mr Hallorann. Still the thought arrowed out of him with a force he never would have believed. It went like a Nolan Ryan fastball with a little extra on it.

(Gee I hope I don't hurt him)

And the thought was:

(*!!! HI, DICK !!!*)

Hallorann winced and jerked backward on the seat. His teeth came together with a hard click, drawing blood from his lower lip in a thin trickle. His hands flew up involuntarily from his lap to the level of his chest and then settled back again. For a moment his eyelids fluttered limply, with no conscious control, and Danny was frightened.

'Mr Hallorann? Dick? Are you okay?'

'I don't know,' Hallorann said, and laughed weakly. 'I honest to God don't. My God, boy, you're a pistol.'

'I'm sorry,' Danny said, more alarmed. 'Should I get my daddy? I'll run and get him.'

'No, here I come. I'm okay, Danny. You just sit right there. I feel a little scrambled, that's all.'

'I didn't go as hard as I could,' Danny confessed. 'I was scared to, at the last minute.'

'Probably my good luck you did . . . my brains would be leakin out my ears.' He saw the alarm on Danny's face and smiled. 'No harm done. What did it feel like to you?'

'Like I was Nolan Ryan throwing a fastball,' he replied promptly.

'You like baseball, do you?' Hallorann was rubbing his temples gingerly.

'Daddy and me like the Angels,' Danny said. 'The Red Sox in the American League East and the Angels in the West. We saw the Red Sox against Cincinnati in the World Series. I was a lot littler then. And Daddy was . . .' Danny's face went dark and troubled.

'Was what, Dan?'

'I forget,' Danny said. He started to put his thumb in his mouth to suck it, but that was a baby trick. He put his hand back in his lap.

'Can you tell what your mom and dad are thinking, Danny?' Hallorann was watching him closely.

'Most times, if I want to. But usually I don't try.'

'Why not?'

'Well . . .' he paused a moment, troubled. 'It would be like peeking into the bedroom and watching while they're doing the thing that makes babies. Do you know that thing?'

'I have had acquaintance with it,' Hallorann said gravely.

'They wouldn't like that. And they wouldn't like me peeking at their thinks. It would be dirty.'

'I see.'

'But I know how they're feeling,' Danny said. 'I can't help that. I know how you're feeling, too. I hurt you. I'm sorry.'

'It's just a headache. I've had hangovers that were worse. Can you read other people, Danny?'

'I can't read yet at all,' Danny said, 'except a few words. But Daddy's going to teach me this winter. My daddy used to teach reading and writing in a big school. Mostly writing, but he knows reading, too.'

'I mean, can you tell what anybody is thinking?'

Danny thought about it.

'I can if it's *loud*,' he said finally. 'Like Mrs Brant and the pants. Or like once, when me and Mommy were in this big store to get me some shoes, there was this big kid looking at radios, and he was thinking about taking one without buying it. Then he'd think, what if I get caught? Then he'd think, I really want it. Then he'd think about getting caught again. He was making himself sick about it, and he was making *me* sick. Mommy was talking to the man who sells the shoes so I went over and said, "Kid, don't take that radio. Go away." And he got really scared. He went away fast.'

Hallorann was grinning broadly. 'I bet he did. Can you do anything else, Danny? Is it only thoughts and feelings, or is there more?'

THE SHINING

Cautiously: 'Is there more for you?'

'Sometimes,' Hallorann said. 'Not often. Sometimes ... sometimes there are dreams. Do you dream, Danny?'

'Sometimes,' Danny said, 'I dream when I'm awake. After Tony comes.' His thumb wanted to go into his mouth again. He had never told anyone but Mommy and Daddy about Tony. He made his thumb-sucking hand go back into his lap.

'Who's Tony?'

And suddenly Danny had one of those flashes of understanding that frightened him most of all; it was like a sudden glimpse of some incomprehensible machine that might be safe or might be deadly dangerous. He was too young to know which. He was too young to understand.

'What's wrong?' he cried. 'You're asking me all this because you're worried, aren't you? Why are you worried about me? Why are you worried about *us*?'

Hallorann put his large dark hands on the small boy's shoulders. 'Stop,' he said. 'It's probably nothin. But if it is somethin ... well, you've got a large thing in your head, Danny. You'll have to do a lot of growin yet before you catch up to it, I guess. You got to be brave about it.'

'But I don't *understand* things!' Danny burst out. 'I *do* but I *don't*! People ... they feel things and I feel them, but I don't know what I'm feeling!' He looked down at his lap wretchedly. 'I wish I could read. Sometimes Tony shows me signs and I can hardly read any of them.'

'Who's Tony?' Hallorann asked again.

'Mommy and Daddy call him my "invisible playmate",' Danny said, reciting the words carefully. 'But he's really real. At least, I think he is. Sometimes, when I try real hard to understand things, he comes. He says, "Danny, I want to show you something." And it's like I pass out. Only ... there are dreams, like you said.' He looked at Hallorann and swallowed. 'They used to be nice. But now ... I can't remember the word for dreams that scare you and make you cry.'

'Nightmares?' Hallorann asked.

'Yes. That's right. Nightmares.'

'About this place? About the Overlook?'

Danny looked down at his thumb-sucking hand again. 'Yes,' he whispered. Then he spoke shrilly, looking up into Hallorann's face: 'But I can't tell my daddy, and you can't, either! He has to have this job because it's the only one Uncle Al could get for him and he has to finish his play or he might start doing the Bad Thing again and I know what that is, it's getting *drunk*, that's what it is, it's when he used to always be *drunk* and that was a Bad Thing to do!' He stopped, on the verge of tears.

'Shh,' Hallorann said, and pulled Danny's face against the rough serge of his jacket. It smelled faintly of mothballs. 'That's all right, son. And if that thumb likes your mouth, let it go where it wants.' But his face was troubled.

He said: 'What you got, son, I call it shinin on, the Bible calls it having visions, and there's scientists that call it precognition. I've read up on it, son. I've studied on it. They all mean seeing the future. Do you understand that?'

Danny nodded against Hallorann's coat.

'I remember the strongest shine I ever had that way . . . I'm not liable to forget. It was 1955. I was still in the Army then, stationed overseas in West Germany. It was an hour before supper, and I was standin by the sink, givin one of the KPs hell for takin too much of the potato along with the peel. I says, "Here, lemme show you how that's done." He held out the potato and the peeler and then the whole kitchen was gone. Bang, just like that. You say you see this guy Tony before . . . before you have dreams?'

Danny nodded.

Hallorann put an arm around him. 'With me it's smellin oranges. All that afternoon I'd been smellin them and thinkin nothin of it, because they were on the menu for that night – we had thirty crates of Valencias. Everybody in the damn kitchen was smellin oranges that night.

'For a minute it was like I had just passed out. And then I heard an explosion and saw flames. There were people screaming. Sirens. And I heard this hissin noise that could only be steam. Then it seemed like I got a little closer to whatever it was and I saw a railroad car off the tracks and laying on its side with *Georgia and South Carolina Railroad* written on it, and I knew like a flash that my brother Carl was on that train and it jumped the tracks and Carl was dead. Just like that. Then it was gone and here's this scared, stupid little KP in front of me, still holdin out that potato and the peeler. He says, "Are you okay, Sarge?" And I says, "No. My brother's just been killed down in Georgia." And when I finally got my momma on the overseas telephone, she told me how it was.

'But see, boy, I already knew how it was.'

He shook his head slowly, as if dismissing the memory, and looked down at the wide-eyed boy.

'But the thing you got to remember, my boy, is this: *Those things don't always come true*. I remember just four years ago I had a job cookin at a boys' camp up in Maine on Long Lake. So I am sittin by the boarding gate at Logan Airport in Boston, just waiting to get on my flight, and I start to smell oranges. For the first time in maybe five years. So I say to myself, "My God, what's comin on this crazy late show now?" and I got down to the bathroom and sat on one of the toilets to be private. I never did black out, but I started to get this feelin, stronger and stronger, that my plane was gonna crash. Then the feeling went away, and the smell of oranges, and I knew it was over. I went back to the Delta Airlines desk and changed my flight to one three hours later. And do you know what happened?'

'What?' Danny whispered.

'*Nothin!*' Hallorann said, and laughed. He was relieved to see the boy smile a little, too. 'Not one single thing! That old plane landed right on time and without a single bump or bruise. So you see . . . sometimes those feelins don't come to anything.'

'Oh,' Danny said.

'Or you take the race track. I go a lot, and I usually do pretty well. I stand by the rail when they go by the starting gate, and sometimes I get a little shine about this horse or that one. Usually those feelins help me get real well. I always tell myself that someday I'm gonna get three at once on three long shots and make enough on the trifecta to retire early. It ain't happened yet. But there's plenty of times I've come home from the track on shank's mare instead of in a taxicab with my wallet swollen up. Nobody shines on all the time, except maybe for God up in heaven.'

'Yes, sir,' Danny said, thinking of the time almost a year ago when Tony had showed him a new baby lying in a crib at their house in Stovington. He had been very excited about that, and had waited, knowing that it took time, but there had been no new baby.

'Now you listen,' Hallorann said, and took both of Danny's hands in his own. 'I've had some bad dreams here, and I've had some bad feelins. I've worked here two season now and maybe a dozen times I've had . . . well, nightmares. And maybe half a dozen times I've thought I've seen things. No, I won't say what. It ain't for a little boy like you. Just nasty things. Once it had something to do with those damn hedges clipped to look like animals. Another time there was a maid, Delores Vickery her name was, and she had a little shine to her, but I don't think she knew it. Mr Ullman fired her . . . do you know what that is, doc?'

'Yes, sir,' Danny said candidly, 'my daddy got fired from his teaching job and that's why we're in Colorado, I guess.'

'Well, Ullman fired her on account of her saying she'd seen something in one of the rooms where . . . well, where a bad thing happened. That was in Room 217, and I want you to promise me you won't go in there, Danny. Not all winter. Steer right clear.'

'All right,' Danny said. 'Did the lady – the maiden – did she ask you to go look?'

'Yes, she did. And there was a bad thing there. But . . . I don't think it was a bad thing that could *hurt* anyone, Danny, that's what I'm tryin to say. People who shine can sometimes see things that are *gonna* happen, and I think sometimes they can see things that *did* happen. But they're just like pictures in a book. Did you ever see a picture in a book that scared you, Danny?'

'Yes,' he said, thinking of the story of *Bluebeard* and the picture where *Bluebeard*'s new wife opens the door and sees all the heads.

'But you knew it couldn't hurt you, didn't you?'

'Ye – ess . . .' Danny said, a little dubious.

'Well, that's how it is in this hotel. I don't know why, but it seems that all the bad things that ever happened here, there's little pieces of those things still layin around like fingernail clippins or the boogers that somebody nasty just wiped under a chair. I don't know why it should just be here, there's bad goings-on in just about every hotel in the world, I guess, and I've worked in a lot of them and had no trouble. Only here. But Danny, I don't think those things can hurt anybody.' He emphasized each word in the sentence with a mild shake of the boy's shoulders. 'So if you should see something, in a hallway or a room or outside by those hedges . . . just look the other way and when you look back, it'll be gone. Are you diggin me?'

'Yes,' Danny said. He felt much better, soothed. He got up on his knees, kissed Hallorann's cheek, and gave him a big hard hug. Hallorann hugged him back.

When he released the boy he asked: 'Your folks, they don't shine, do they?'

'No, I don't think so.'

'I tried them like I did you,' Hallorann said. 'Your momma jumped the tiniest bit. I think all mothers shine a little, you know, at least until their kids grow up enough to watch out for themselves. Your dad . . .'

Hallorann paused momentarily. He had probed at the boy's father and he just didn't know. It wasn't like meeting someone who had the shine, or someone who definitely did not. Poking at Danny's father had been . . . strange, as if Jack Torrance had something – *something* – that he was hiding. Or something he was holding in so deeply submerged in himself that it was impossible to get to.

'I don't think he shines at all,' Hallorann finished. 'So you don't worry about them. You just take care of you. *I don't think there's anything here that can hurt you.* So just be cool, okay?'

'Okay.'

'*Danny! Hey, doc!*'

Danny looked around. 'That's Mom. She wants me. I have to go.'

'I know you do,' Hallorann said. 'You have a good time here, Danny. Best you can, anyway.'

'I will. Thanks, Mr Hallorann. I feel a lot better.'

The smiling thought came in his mind:

(Dick, to my friends)

(Yes, Dick, okay)

Their eyes met, and Dick Hallorann winked.

Danny scrambled across the seat of the car and opened the passenger side door. As he was getting out, Hallorann said, 'Danny?'

'What?'

'If there *is* trouble . . . you give a call. A big loud holler like the one you gave a few minutes ago. I might hear you even way down in Florida. And if I do, I'll come on the run.'

'Okay,' Danny said, and smiled.

'You take care, big boy.'

'I will.'

Danny slammed the door and ran across the parking lot toward the porch, where Wendy stood holding her elbows against the chill wind. Hallorann watched, the big grin slowly fading.

I don't think there's anything here that can hurt you.

I don't *think*.

But what if he was wrong? He had known that this was his last season at the Overlook ever since he had seen that thing in the bathtub of Room 217. It had been worse than any picture in any book, and from here the boy running to his mother looked so *small* . . .

I don't *think*—

His eyes drifted down to the topiary animals.

Abruptly he started the car and put it in gear and drove away, trying not to look back. And of course he did, and of course the porch was empty. They had gone back inside. It was as if the Overlook had swallowed them.

CHAPTER TWELVE
THE GRAND TOUR

'What were you talking about, hon?' Wendy asked him as they went back inside.

'Oh, nothing much.'

'For nothing much it sure was a long talk.'

He shrugged and Wendy saw Danny's paternity in the gesture; Jack could hardly have done it better himself. She would get no more out of Danny. She felt strong exasperation mixed with an even stronger love: the love was helpless, the exasperation came from a feeling that she was deliberately being excluded. With the two of them around she sometimes felt like an outsider, a bit player who had accidentally wandered back onstage while the main action was taking place. Well, they wouldn't be able to exclude her this winter, her two exasperating males; quarters were going to be a little too close for that. She suddenly realized she was feeling jealous of the closeness between her husband and her son, and felt ashamed. That was too close to the way her own mother might have felt . . . too close for comfort.

The lobby was now empty except for Ullman and the head desk clerk (they were at the register, cashing up), a couple of maids who had changed to warm slacks and sweaters, standing by the front door and looking out with their luggage pooled around them, and Watson, the maintenance man. He caught her looking at him and gave her a wink . . . a decidedly lecherous one. She looked away hurriedly. Jack was over by the window just outside the restaurant, studying the view. He looked rapt and dreamy.

The cash register apparently checked out, because now Ullman ran it shut with an authoritative snap. He initialed the tape and put it in a small zipper case. Wendy silently applauded the

97

head clerk, who looked greatly relieved. Ullman looked like the type of man who might take any shortage out of the head clerk's hide . . . without ever spilling a drop of blood. Wendy didn't much care for Ullman or his officious, ostentatiously bustling manner. He was like every boss she'd ever had, male or female. He would be saccharin sweet with the guests, a petty tyrant when he was backstage with the help. But now school was out and the head clerk's pleasure was written large on his face. It was out for everyone but she and Jack and Danny, anyway.

'Mr Torrance,' Ullman called peremptorily. 'Would you come over here, please?'

Jack walked over, nodding to Wendy and Danny that they were to come too.

The clerk, who had gone into the back, now came out again wearing an overcoat. 'Have a pleasant winter, Mr Ullman.'

'I doubt it,' Ullman said distantly. 'May twelfth, Braddock. Not a day earlier. Not a day later.'

'Yes, sir.'

Braddock walked around the desk, his face sober and dignified, as befitted his position, but when his back was entirely to Ullman, he grinned like a schoolboy. He spoke briefly to the two girls still waiting by the door for their ride, and he was followed out by a brief burst of stifled laughter.

Now Wendy began to notice the silence of the place. It had fallen over the hotel like a heavy blanket muffling everything but the faint pulse of the afternoon wind outside. From where she stood she could look through the inner office, now neat to the point of sterility with its two bare desks and two sets of gray filing cabinets. Beyond that she could see Hallorann's spotless kitchen, the big portholed double doors propped open by rubber wedges.

'I thought I would take a few extra minutes and show you through the Hotel,' Ullman said, and Wendy reflected that you could always hear that capital *H* in Ullman's voice. You were supposed to hear it. 'I'm sure your husband will get to know the ins and outs of the Overlook quite well, Mrs Torrance, but you and your son will doubtless keep more to the lobby level and the first floor, where your quarters are.'

'Doubtless,' Wendy murmured demurely, and Jack shot her a private glance.

'It's a beautiful place,' Ullman said expansively. 'I rather enjoy showing it off.'

I'll bet you do, Wendy thought.

'Let's go up to third and work our way down,' Ullman said. He sounded positively enthused.

'If we're keeping you—' Jack began.

'Not at all,' Ullman said. 'The shop is shut. *Tout fini*, for this season, at least. And I plan to overnight in Boulder – at the Boulderado, of course. Only decent hotel this side of Denver . . . except for the Overlook itself, of course. This way.'

They stepped into the elevator together. It was ornately scrolled in copper and brass, but it settled appreciably before Ullman pulled the gate across. Danny stirred a little uneasily, and Ullman smiled down at him. Danny tried to smile back without notable success.

'Don't you worry, little man,' Ullman said. 'Safe as houses.'

'So was the *Titanic*,' Jack said, looking up at the cut-glass globe in the center of the elevator ceiling. Wendy bit the inside of her cheek to keep the smile away.

Ullman was not amused. He slid the inner gate across with a rattle and a bang. 'The *Titanic* made only one voyage, Mr Torrance. This elevator has made thousands of them since it was installed in 1926.'

'That's reassuring,' Jack said. He ruffled Danny's hair. 'The plane ain't gonna crash, doc.'

Ullman threw the lever over, and for a moment there was nothing but a shuddering beneath their feet and the tortured whine of the motor below them. Wendy had a vision of the four of them being trapped between floors like flies in a bottle and found in the spring . . . with little bits and pieces gone . . . like the Donner Party . . .

(*Stop it!*)

The elevator began to rise, with some vibration and clashing and banging from below at first. Then the ride smoothed out. At the third floor Ullman brought them to a bumpy stop, retracted the gate, and opened the door. The elevator car was still six inches below floor level. Danny gazed at the difference in height between the third-floor hall and the elevator floor as if he had just sensed the universe was not as sane as he had been told. Ullman cleared his throat and raised the car a little, brought it to a stop with a jerk (still two inches low), and they all climbed out. With their weight gone the car rebounded almost to floor level, something Wendy did not find reassuring at all. Safe as houses or not, she resolved to take the stairs when she had to go up or down in this place. And under no conditions would she allow the three of them to get into the rickety thing together.

'What are you looking at doc?' Jack inquired humorously. 'See any spots there?'

'Of course not,' Ullman said, nettled. 'All the rugs were shampooed just two days ago.'

Wendy glanced down at the hall runner herself. Pretty, but definitely not anything she would choose for her own home, if the day ever came when she had one. Deep blue pile, it was entwined with what seemed to be a surrealistic jungle scene full of ropes and vines and trees filled with exotic birds. It was hard to tell just what sort of birds, because all the interweaving was done in unshaded black, giving only silhouettes.

'Do you like the rug?' Wendy asked Danny.

'Yes, Mom,' he said colorlessly.

They walked down the hall, which was comfortably wide. The wallpaper was silk, a lighter blue to go against the rug. Electric flambeaux stood at ten-foot intervals at a height of about seven feet. Fashioned to look like London gas lamps, the bulbs were masked behind cloudy, cream-hued glass that was bound with crisscrossing iron strips.

'I like those very much,' she said.

Ullman nodded, pleased. 'Mr Derwent had those installed throughout the Hotel after the war – number Two, I mean. In fact most – although not all – of the third-floor decorating scheme was his idea. This is 300, the Presidential Suite.'

He twisted his key in the lock of the mahogany double doors and swung them wide. The sitting room's wide western exposure made them all gasp, which had probably been Ullman's intention. He smiled. 'Quite a view, isn't it?'

'It sure is,' Jack said.

The window ran nearly the length of the sitting room, and beyond it the sun was poised directly between two sawtoothed peaks, casting golden light across the rock faces and the sugared snow on the high tips. The clouds around and behind this picture-postcard view were also tinted gold, and a sunbeam glinted duskily down into the darkly pooled firs below the timberline.

Jack and Wendy were so absorbed in the view that they didn't look down at Danny, who was staring not out the window but at the red-and-white-striped silk wallpaper to the left, where a door opened into an interior bedroom. And his gasp, which had been mingled with theirs, had nothing to do with beauty.

Great splashes of dried blood, flecked with tiny bits of grayish-white tissue, clotted the wallpaper. It made Danny feel sick. It was like a crazy picture drawn in blood, a surrealistic etching of a man's face drawn back in terror and pain, the mouth yawning and half the head pulverized—

(*So if you should see something . . . just look the other way and when you look back, it'll be gone. Are you diggin me?*)

He deliberately looked out the window, being careful to show no expression on his face, and when his mommy's hand closed over his own he took it, being careful not to squeeze it or give her a signal of any kind.

The manager was saying something to his daddy about making sure to shutter that big window so a strong wind didn't blow it in. Jack was nodding. Danny looked cautiously back at the wall. The big dry bloodstain was gone. Those little gray-white flecks that had been scattered all through it, they were gone, too.

Then Ullman was leading them out. Mommy asked him if he thought the mountains were pretty. Danny said he did, although he didn't really care for the mountains, one way or the other. As Ullman was closing the door behind them, Danny looked back over his shoulder. The bloodstain had returned, only now it was fresh. It was running. Ullman, looking directly at it, went on with his running commentary about the famous men who had stayed here. Danny discovered that he had bitten his lip hard enough to make it bleed, and he had never even felt it. As they walked on down the corridor, he fell a little behind the others and wiped the blood away with the back of his hand and thought about

(blood)

(Did Mr Hallorann see blood or was it something worse?)

(*I don't think those things can hurt you.*)

There was an iron scream behind his lips, but he would not let it out. His mommy and daddy could not see such things; they never had. He would keep quiet. His mommy and daddy were loving each other, and that was a real thing. The other things were just like pictures in a book. Some pictures were scary, but they couldn't hurt you. *They . . . couldn't . . . hurt you.*

Mr Ullman showed them some other rooms on the third floor, leading them through corridors that twisted and turned like a maze. They were all sweets up here, Mr Ullman said, although Danny didn't see any candy. He showed them some rooms where a lady named Marilyn Monroe once stayed when she was married to a man named Arthur Miller (Danny got a vague understanding that Marilyn and Arthur had gotten a DIVORCE not long after they were in the Overlook Hotel).

'Mommy?'

'What, honey?'

'If they were married, why did they have different names? You and Daddy have the same names.'

'Yes, but we're not famous, Danny,' Jack said. 'Famous women keep their names even after they get married because their names are their bread and butter.'

'Bread and butter,' Danny said, completely mystified.

'What Daddy means is that people used to like to go to the movies and see Marilyn Monroe,' Wendy said, 'but they might not like to go to see Marilyn Miller.'

'Why not? She'd still be the same lady. Wouldn't everyone know that?'

'Yes, but—' She looked at Jack helplessly.

'Truman Capote once stayed in this room,' Ullman interrupted impatiently. He opened the door. 'That was in my time. An awfully nice man. Continental manners.'

There was nothing remarkable in any of these rooms (except for the absence of sweets, which Mr Ullman kept calling them), nothing that Danny was afraid of. In fact, there was only one other thing on the third floor that bothered Danny, and he could not have said why. It was the fire extinguisher on the wall just before they turned the corner and went back to the elevator, which stood open and waiting like a mouthful of gold teeth.

It was an old-fashioned extinguisher, a flat hose folded back a dozen times upon itself, one end attached to a large red valve, the other ending in a brass nozzle. The folds of the hose were secured with a red steel slat on a hinge. In case of a fire you could knock the steel slat up and out of the way with one hard push and the hose was yours. Danny could see that much; he was good at seeing how things worked. By the time he was two and a half he had been unlocking the protective gate his father had installed at the top of the stairs in the Stovington house. He had seen how the lock worked. His daddy said it was a NACK. Some people had the NACK and some people didn't.

This fire extinguisher was a little older than others he had seen – the one in the nursery school, for instance – but that was not so unusual. Nonetheless it filled him with faint unease, curled up there against the light blue wallpaper like a sleeping snake. And he was glad when it was out of sight around the corner.

'Of course all the windows have to be shuttered,' Mr Ullman said as they stepped back into the elevator. Once again the car sank queasily beneath their feet. 'But I'm particularly concerned about the one in the Presidential Suite. The original bill on that window was four hundred and twenty dollars, and that was over thirty years ago. It would cost eight times that to replace today.'

'I'll shutter it,' Jack said.

They went down to the second floor where there were more rooms and even more twists and turns in the corridor. The light from the windows had begun to fade appreciably now as the sun went behind the mountains. Mr Ullman showed them one or two rooms and that was all. He walked past 217, the one

Dick Hallorann had warned him about, without slowing. Danny looked at the bland number-plate on the door with uneasy fascination.

Then down to the first floor. Mr Ullman didn't show them into any rooms here until they had almost reached the thickly carpeted staircase that led down into the lobby again. 'Here are your quarters,' he said. 'I think you'll find them adequate.'

They went in. Danny was braced for whatever might be there. There was nothing.

Wendy Torrance felt a strong surge of relief. The Presidential Suite, with its cold elegance, had made her feel awkward and clumsy – it was all very well to visit some restored historical building with a bedroom plaque that announced Abraham Lincoln or Franklin D. Roosevelt had slept there, but another thing entirely to imagine you and your husband lying beneath acreages of linen and perhaps making love where the greatest men in the world had once lain (the most powerful, anyway, she amended). But this apartment was simpler, homier, almost inviting. She thought she could abide this place for a season with no great difficulty.

'It's very pleasant,' she said to Ullman, and heard the gratitude in her voice.

Ullman nodded. 'Simple but adequate. During the season, this suite quarters the cook and his wife, or the cook and his apprentice.'

'Mr Hallorann lived here?' Danny broke in.

Mr Ullman inclined his head to Danny condescendingly. 'Quite so. He and Mr Nevers.' He turned back to Jack and Wendy. 'This is the sitting room.'

There were several chairs that looked comfortable but not expensive, a coffee table that had once been expensive but now had a long chip gone from the side, two bookcases (stuffed full of Reader's Digest Condensed Books and Detective Book Club trilogies from the forties, Wendy saw with some amusement), and an anonymous hotel TV that looked much less elegant than the buffed wood consoles in the rooms.

'No kitchen, of course,' Ullman said, 'but there is a dumbwaiter. This apartment is directly over the kitchen.' He slid aside a square of paneling and disclosed a wide, square tray. He gave it a push and it disappeared, trailing rope behind it.

'It's a secret passage!' Danny said excitedly to his mother, momentarily forgetting all fears in favor of that intoxicating shaft behind the wall. 'Just like in *Abbott and Costello Meet the Monsters*!'

Mr Ullman frowned but Wendy smiled indulgently. Danny ran over to the dumb-waiter and peered down the shaft.

'This way, please.'

He opened the door on the far side of the living room. It gave on the bedroom, which was spacious and airy. There were twin beds. Wendy looked at her husband, smiled, shrugged.

'No problem,' Jack said. 'We'll push them together.'

Mr Ullman looked over his shoulder, honestly puzzled. 'Beg pardon?'

'The beds,' Jack said pleasantly. 'We can push them together.'

'Oh, quite,' Ullman said, momentarily confused. Then his face cleared and a red flush began to creep up to the collar of his shirt. 'Whatever you like.'

He led them back into the sitting room, where a second door opened on a second bedroom, this one equipped with bunk beds. A radiator clanked in one corner, and the rug on the floor was a hideous embroidery of western sage and cactus – Danny had already fallen in love with it, Wendy saw. The walls of this smaller room were paneled in real pine.

'Think you can stand it in here, doc?' Jack asked.

'Sure I can. I'm going to sleep in the top bunk. Okay?'

'If that's what you want.'

'I like the rug, too. Mr Ullman, why don't you have all the rugs like that?'

Mr Ullman looked for a moment as if he had sunk his teeth into a lemon. Then he smiled and patted Danny's head. 'Those are your quarters,' he said, 'except for the bath, which opens off the main bedroom. It's not a huge apartment, but of course you'll have the rest of the hotel to spread out in. The lobby fireplace is in good working order, or so Watson tells me, and you must feel free to eat in the dining room if the spirit moves you to do so.' He spoke in the tone of a man conferring a great favor.

'All right,' Jack said.

'Shall we go down?' Mr Ullman asked.

'Fine,' Wendy said.

They went downstairs in the elevator, and now the lobby was wholly deserted except for Watson, who was leaning against the main doors in a rawhide jacket, a toothpick between his lips.

'I would have thought you'd be miles from here by now,' Mr Ullman said, his voice slightly chill.

'Just stuck around to remind Mr Torrance here about the boiler,' Watson said, straightening up. 'Keep your good weather eye on her, fella, and she'll be fine. Knock the press down a couple of times a day. She creeps.'

She creeps, Danny thought, and the words echoed down a long and silent corridor in his mind, a corridor lined with mirrors where people seldom looked.

'I will,' his daddy said.

'You'll be fine,' Watson said, and offered Jack his hand. Jack shook it. Watson turned to Wendy and inclined his head. 'Ma'am,' he said.

'I'm pleased,' Wendy said, and thought it would sound absurd. It didn't. She had come out here from New England, where she had spent her life, and it seemed to her that in a few short sentences this man Watson, with his fluffy fringe of hair, had epitomized what the West was supposed to be all about. And never mind the lecherous wink earlier.

'Young master Torrance,' Watson said gravely, and put out his hand. Danny, who had known all about handshaking for almost a year now, put his own hand out gingerly and felt it swallowed up. 'You take good care of em, Dan.'

'Yes, sir.'

Watson let go of Danny's hand and straightened up fully. He looked at Ullman. 'Until next year, I guess,' he said, and held his hand out.

Ullman touched it bloodlessly. His pinky ring caught the lobby's electric lights in a baleful sort of wink.

'May twelfth, Watson,' he said. 'Not a day earlier or later.'

'Yes, sir,' Watson said, and Jack could almost read the codicil in Watson's mind: . . . *you fucking little faggot*.

'Have a good winter, Mr Ullman.'

'Oh, I doubt it,' Ullman said remotely.

Watson opened one of the two big main doors; the wind whined louder and began to flutter the collar of his jacket. 'You folks take care now,' he said.

It was Danny who answered. 'Yes, sir, we will.'

Watson, whose not-so-distant ancestor had owned this place, slipped humbly through the door. It closed behind him, muffling the wind. Together they watched him clop down the porch's broad front steps in his battered black cowboy boots. Brittle yellow aspen leaves tumbled around his heels as he crossed the lot to his International Harvester pickup and climbed in. Blue smoke jetted from the rusted exhaust pipe as he started it up. The spell of silence held among them as he backed, then pulled out of the parking lot. His truck disappeared over the brow of the hill and then reappeared, smaller, on the main road, heading west.

For a moment Danny felt more lonely than he ever had in his life.

CHAPTER THIRTEEN
THE FRONT PORCH

The Torrance family stood together on the long front porch of the Overlook Hotel as if posing for a family portrait. Danny in the middle, zippered into last year's fall jacket which was now too small and starting to come out at the elbow, Wendy behind him with one hand on his shoulder, and Jack to his left, his own hand resting lightly on his son's head.

Mr Ullman was a step below them, buttoned into an expensive-looking brown mohair overcoat. The sun was entirely behind the mountains now, edging them with gold fire, making the shadows around things look long and purple. The only three vehicles left in the parking lots were the hotel truck, Ullman's Lincoln Continental, and the battered Torrance VW.

'You've got your keys, then,' Ullman said to Jack, 'and you understand fully about the furnace and the boiler?'

Jack nodded, feeling some real sympathy for Ullman. Everything was done for the season, the ball of string was neatly wrapped up until next May 12 – not a day earlier or later – and Ullman, who was responsible for all of it and who referred to the hotel in the unmistakable tones of infatuation, could not help looking for loose ends.

'I think everything is well in hand,' Jack said.

'Good. I'll be in touch.' But he still lingered for a moment, as if waiting for the wind to take a hand and perhaps gust him down to his car. He sighed. 'All right. Have a good winter, Mr Torrance, Mrs Torrance. You too, Danny.'

'Thank you, sir,' Danny said. 'I hope you do, too.'

'I doubt it,' Ullman repeated, and he sounded sad. 'The place in Florida is a dump, if the out-and-out truth is to be spoken. Busywork. The Overlook is my real job. Take good care of it for me, Mr Torrance.'

'I think it will be here when you get back next spring,' Jack said, and a thought flashed through Danny's mind.

(but will we?)

and was gone.

'Of course. Of course it will.'

Ullman looked out toward the playground where the hedge animals were clattering in the wind. Then he nodded once more in a businesslike way.

'Good-by, then.'

He walked quickly and prissily across to his car – a ridiculously big one for such a little man – and tucked himself into it. The Lincoln's motor purred into life and the taillights flashed as he pulled out of his parking stall. As the car moved away, Jack could read the small sign at the head of the stall: RESERVED FOR MR ULLMAN, MGR.

'Right,' Jack said softly.

They watched until the car was out of sight, headed down the eastern slope. When it was gone, the three of them looked at each other for a silent, almost frightened moment. They were alone. Aspen leaves whirled and skittered in aimless packs across the lawn that was now neatly mowed and tended for no guest's eyes. There was no one to see the autumn leaves steal across the grass but the three of them. It gave Jack a curious shrinking feeling, as if his life force had dwindled to a mere spark while the hotel and the grounds had suddenly doubled in size and become sinister, dwarfing them with sullen, inanimate power.

Then Wendy said: 'Look at you, doc. Your nose is running like a fire hose. Let's get inside.'

And they did, closing the door firmly behind them against the restless whine of the wind.

PART THREE

THE WASPS' NEST

CHAPTER FOURTEEN
UP ON THE ROOF

'Oh you goddam fucking son of a bitch!'

Jack Torrance cried these words out in both surprise and agony as he slapped his right hand against his blue chambray workshirt, dislodging the big, slow-moving wasp that had stung him. Then he was scrambling up the roof as fast as he could, looking back over his shoulder to see if the wasp's brothers and sisters were rising from the nest he had uncovered to do battle. If they were, it could be bad; the nest was between him and his ladder, and the trap door leading down into the attic was locked from the inside. The drop was seventy feet from the roof to the cement patio between the hotel and the lawn.

The clear air above the nest was still and undisturbed.

Jack whistled disgustedly between his teeth, sat straddling the peak of the roof, and examined his right index finger. It was swelling already, and he supposed he would have to try to creep past that nest to his ladder so he could go down and put some ice on it.

It was October 20. Wendy and Danny had gone down to Sidewinder in the hotel truck (an elderly, rattling Dodge that was still more trustworthy than the VW, which was now wheezing gravely and seemed terminal) to get three gallons of milk and do some Christmas shopping. It was early to shop, but there was no telling when the snow would come to stay. There had already been flurries, and in some places the road down from the Overlook was slick with patch ice.

So far the fall had been almost preternaturally beautiful. In the three weeks they had been here, golden day had followed golden day. Crisp, thirty-degree mornings gave way to afternoon temperatures in the low sixties, the perfect temperature for climbing around on the Overlook's gently sloping western roof and doing the shingling. Jack had admitted freely to Wendy that he could have finished the job four days ago, but he felt no real urge to hurry. The view from up here was spectacular, even putting the vista from the Presidential Suite in the shade. More important, the work itself was soothing. On the roof he felt himself healing from the troubled wounds of the last three years. On the roof he felt at peace. Those three years began to seem like a turbulent nightmare.

The shingles had been badly rotted, some of them blown entirely away by last winter's storms. He had ripped them all up, yelling 'Bombs away!' as he dropped them over the side, not wanting Danny to get hit in case he had wandered over. He had been pulling out bad flashing when the wasp had gotten him.

The ironic part was that he warned himself each time he climbed onto the roof to keep an eye out for nests; he had gotten that bug bomb just in case. But this morning the stillness and peace had been so complete that his watchfulness had lapsed. He had been back in the world of the play he was slowly creating, roughing out whatever scene he would be working on that evening in his head. The play was going very well, and although Wendy had said little, he knew she was pleased. He had been roadblocked on the crucial scene between Denker, the sadistic headmaster, and Gary Benson, his young hero, during the last unhappy six months at Stovington, months when the craving for a drink had been so bad that he could barely concentrate on his in-class lectures, let alone his extracurricular literary ambitions.

But in the last twelve evenings, as he actually sat down in front of the office-model Underwood he had borrowed from the main office downstairs, the roadblock had disappeared under his fingers as magically as cotton candy dissolves on the lips. He had come up almost effortlessly with the insights into Denker's character that had always been lacking, and he had rewritten most of the second act accordingly, making it revolve around the new scene. And the progress of the third act, which he had been turning over in his mind when the wasp put an end to cogitation, was coming clearer all the time. He thought he could rough it out in two weeks, and have a clean copy of the whole damned play by New Year's.

He had an agent in New York, a tough red-headed woman named Phyllis Sandler who smoked Herbert Tareytons, drank Jim Beam from a paper cup, and thought the literary sun rose and set on Sean O'Casey. She had marketed three of Jack's short stories, including the *Esquire* piece. He had written her about the play, which was called *The Little School*, describing the basic conflict between Denker, a gifted student who had failed into becoming the brutal and brutalizing headmaster of a turn-of-the-century New England prep school, and Gary Benson, the student he sees as a younger version of himself. Phyllis had written back expressing interest and admonishing him to read O'Casey before sitting down to it. She had written again earlier that year asking where the hell was the play? He had written back wryly that *The Little School* had been indefinitely – and perhaps infinitely – delayed between hand and page 'in that interesting intellectual Gobi known as the writer's block.' Now it looked as if she might actually get the play. Whether or not it was any good or if it would ever see actual production was another matter. And he didn't seem to care a great deal about those things. He felt in a way that the play itself, the whole thing, was the roadblock, a colossal symbol of the bad years at Stovington Prep, the marriage he had almost totaled like a nutty kid behind the wheel of an old jalopy, the monstrous assault on his son, the incident in the parking lot with George Hatfield, an incident he could no longer view as just another sudden and destructive flare of temper. He now thought that part of his drinking problem had stemmed from an unconscious desire to be free of Stovington and the security he felt was stifling whatever creative urge he had. He had stopped drinking, but the need to be free had been just as great. Hence George Hatfield. Now all that remained of those days was the play on the desk in his and Wendy's bedroom, and when it was done and sent off to Phyllis's hole-in-the-wall New York agency, he could turn to other things. Not a novel, he was not ready to stumble into the swamp of another three-year undertaking, but surely more short stories. Perhaps a book of them.

Moving warily, he scrambled back down the slope of the roof on his hands and knees past the line of demarcation where the fresh green Bird shingles gave way to the section of roof he had just finished clearing. He came to the edge on the left of the wasps' nest he had uncovered and moved gingerly toward it, ready to backtrack and bolt down his ladder to the ground if things looked too hot.

He leaned over the section of pulled-out flashing and looked in.

The nest was in there, tucked into the space between the old flashing and the final roof undercoating of three-by-fives. It was a damn big one. The grayish paper ball looked to Jack as if it might be nearly two feet through the center. Its shape was not perfect because the space between the flashing and the boards was too narrow, but he thought the little buggers had still done a pretty respectable job. The surface of the nest was acrawl with the lumbering, slow-moving insects. They were the big mean ones, not yellow jackets, which are smaller and calmer, but wall wasps. They had been rendered sludgy and stupid by the fall temperatures, but Jack, who knew about wasps from his childhood, counted himself lucky that he had been stung only once. And, he thought, if Ullman had hired the job done in the height of summer, the workman who tore up that particular section of the flashing would have gotten one hell of a surprise. Yes indeedy. When a dozen wall wasps land on you all at once and start stinging your face and hands and arms, stinging your legs right through your pants, it would be entirely possible to forget you were seventy feet up. You might just charge right off the edge of the roof while you were trying to get away from them. All from those little things, the biggest of them only half the length of a pencil stub.

He had read someplace – in a Sunday supplement piece or a back-of-the-book newsmagazine article – that 7 per cent of all automobile fatalities go unexplained. No mechanical failure, no excessive speed, no booze, no bad weather. Simply one-car crashes on deserted sections of road, one dead occupant, the driver, unable to explain what happened to him. The article had included an interview with a state trooper who theorized that many of these so-called 'foo crashes' resulted from insects in the car. Wasps, a bee, possibly even a spider or moth. The driver gets panicky, tries to swat it or unroll a window to let it out. Possibly the insect stings him. Maybe the driver just loses control. Either way it's bang! . . . all over. And the insect, usually completely unharmed, would buzz merrily out of the smoking wreck, looking for greener pastures. The trooper had been in favor of having pathologists look for insect venom while autopsying such victims, Jack recalled.

Now, looking down into the nest, it seemed to him that it could serve as both a workable symbol for what he had been through (and what he had dragged his hostages to fortune through) and an omen for a better future. How else could you explain the things that had happened to him? For he still felt that the whole range of unhappy Stovington experiences had to be looked at with Jack Torrance in the passive mode. He had not done things; things had been done to him. He had known plenty of people on the Stovington faculty, two of them right in the English Department, who were hard drinkers. Zack Tunney was in the habit of picking up a full keg of beer on Saturday afternoon, plonking it in a backyard snowbank overnight, and then killing damn near all of it on Sunday watching football games and old movies. Yet through the week Zack was as sober as a judge – a weak cocktail with lunch was an occasion.

He and Al Shockley had been alcoholics. They had sought each other out like two castoffs who were still social enough to prefer drowning together to doing it alone. The sea had been whole-grain instead of salt, that was all. Looking down at the wasps, as they slowly went about their instinctual business before winter closed down to kill all but their hibernating queen, he would go further. He was *still* an alcoholic, always would be, perhaps had been since Sophomore Class Night in high school when he had taken his first drink. It had nothing to do with willpower, or the morality of drinking, or the weakness or strength of his own character. There was a broken switch somewhere inside, or a circuit breaker that didn't work, and he had been propelled down the chute willynilly, slowly at first, then accelerating as Stovington applied its pressures on him. A big greased slide and at the bottom had been a shattered, ownerless bicycle and a son with a broken arm. Jack Torrance in the passive mode. And his temper, same thing. All his life he had been trying unsuccessfully to control it. He could remember himself at seven, spanked by a neighbor lady for playing with matches. He had gone out and hurled a rock at a passing car. His father had seen that, and he had descended on little Jacky, roaring. He had reddened Jack's behind . . . and then blacked his eye. And when his father had gone into the house, muttering, to see what was on television, Jack had come upon a stray dog and kicked it into the gutter. There had been two dozen fights in grammar school, even more of them in high school, warranting two suspensions and uncounted detentions in spite of his good grades. Football had provided a partial safety valve, although he remembered perfectly well that he had spent almost every minute of every game in a state of high piss-off, taking every opposing block and tackle personally. He had been a fine player, making All-Conference in his junior and senior years, and he knew perfectly well that he had his own bad temper to thank . . . or to blame. He had not enjoyed football. Every game was a grudge match.

And yet, through it all, he hadn't *felt* like a son of a bitch. He hadn't felt mean. He had always regarded himself as Jack Torrance, a really nice guy who was just going to have to learn how to cope with his temper someday before it got him in trouble. The same way he was going to have to learn how to cope with his drinking. But he had been an emotional alcoholic just as surely as he had been a physical one – the two of them were no doubt tied together somewhere deep inside him, where you'd just as soon not look. But it didn't much matter to him if the root causes were interrelated or separate, sociological or psychological or physiological. He had had to deal with the results: the spankings, the beatings from his old man, the suspensions, with trying to explain the school clothes torn in playground brawls, and later the hangovers, the slowly dissolving glue of his marriage, the single bicycle wheel with its bent spokes pointing into the sky, Danny's broken arm. And George Hatfield, of course.

He felt that he had unwittingly stuck his hand into The Great

Wasps' Nest of Life. As an image it stank. As a cameo of reality, he felt it was serviceable. He had stuck his hand through some rotted flashing in high summer and that hand and his whole arm had been consumed in holy, righteous fire, destroying conscious thought, making the concept of civilized behavior obsolete. Could you be expected to behave as a thinking human being when your hand was being impaled on red-hot darning needles? Could you be expected to live in the love of your nearest and dearest when the brown, furious cloud rose out of the hole in the fabric of things (the fabric you thought was so innocent) and arrowed straight at you? Could you be held responsible for your own actions as you ran crazily about on the sloping roof seventy feet above the ground, not knowing where you were going, not remembering that your panicky, stumbling feet could lead you crashing and blundering right over the rain gutter and down to your death on the concrete seventy feet below? Jack didn't think you could. When you unwittingly stuck your hand into the wasps' nest, you hadn't made a covenant with the devil to give up your civilized self with its trappings of love and respect and honor. It just happened to you. Passively, with no say, you ceased to be a creature of the mind and became a creature of the nerve endings; from college-educated man to wailing ape in five easy seconds.

He thought about George Hatfield.

Tall and shaggily blond, George had been an almost insolently beautiful boy. In his tight faded jeans and Stovington sweatshirt with the sleeves carelessly pushed up to the elbows to disclose his tanned forearms, he had reminded Jack of a young Robert Redford, and he doubted that George had much trouble scoring – no more than that young football-playing devil Jack Torrance had it ten years earlier. He could say that he honestly didn't feel jealous of George, or envy him his good looks; in fact, he had almost unconsciously begun to visualize George as the physical incarnation of his play hero, Gary Benson – the perfect foil for the dark, slumped, and aging Denker, who grew to hate Gary so much. But he, Jack Torrance, had never felt that way about George. If he had, he would have known it. He was quite sure of that.

George had floated through his classes at Stovington. A soccer and baseball star, his academic program had been fairly undemanding and he had been content with Cs and an occasional B in history or botany. He was a fierce field contender but a lackadaisical, amused sort of student in the classroom. Jack was familiar with the type, more from his own days as a high school and college student than from his teaching experience, which was at second hand. George Hatfield was a jock. He could be a calm, undemanding figure in the classroom, but when the right set of competitive stimuli was applied (like electrodes to the temples of Frankenstein's monster, Jack thought wryly), he could become a juggernaut.

In January, George had tried out with two dozen others for the debate team. He had been quite frank with Jack. His father was a corporation lawyer, and he wanted his son to follow in his footsteps. George, who felt no burning call to do anything else, was willing. His grades were not top end, but this was, after all, only prep school and it was still early times. If should be came to must be, his father could pull some strings. George's own athletic ability would open still other doors. But Brian Hatfield thought his son should get on the debate team. It was good practice, and it was something that law-school admissions boards always looked for. So George went out for debate, and in late March Jack cut him from the team.

The late winter inter-squad debates had fired George Hatfield's competitive soul. He became a grimly determined debater, prepping his pro or con position fiercely. It didn't matter if the subject was legalization of marijuana, reinstating the death penalty, or the oil-depletion allowance. George became conversant, and he was just jingoist enough to honestly not care which side he was on — a rare and valuable trait even in high-level debaters, Jack knew. The souls of a true carpetbagger and a true debater were not far removed from each other; they were both passionately interested in the main chance. So far, so good.

But George Hatfield stuttered.

This was not a handicap that had even shown up in the classroom, where George was always cool and collected (whether he had done his homework or not), and certainly not on the Stovington playing fields, where talk was not a virtue and they sometimes even threw you out of the game for too much discussion.

When George got tightly wound up in a debate, the stutter would come out. The more eager he became, the worse it was. And when he felt he had an opponent dead in his sights, an intellectual sort of buck fever seemed to take place between his speech centers and his mouth and he would freeze solid while the clock ran out. It was painful to watch.

'S-S-So I th-th-ink we have to say that the fuh-fuh-facts in the c-case Mr D-D-D-Dorsky cites are ren-ren-rendered obsolete by the ruh-recent duh-duh-decision handed down in-in-in . . .'

The buzzer would go off and George would whirl around to stare furiously at Jack, who sat beside it. George's face at those moments would be flushed, his notes crumpled spasmodically in one hand.

Jack had held on to George long after he had cut most of the obvious flat tires, hoping George would work out. He remembered one late afternoon about a week before he had reluctantly dropped the ax. George had stayed after the others had filed out, and then had confronted Jack angrily.

'You s-set the timer ahead.'

Jack looked up from the papers he was putting back into his briefcase.

'George, what are you talking about?'

'I d-didn't get my whole five mih-minutes. You set it ahead. I was wuh-watching the clock.'

'The clock and the timer may keep slightly different times, George, but I never touched the dial on the damned thing. Scout's honor.'

'Yuh-yuh-you *did*!'

The belligerent, I'm-sticking-up-for-my-rights way George was looking at him had sparked Jack's own temper. He had been off the sauce for two months, two months too long, and he was ragged. He made one last effort to hold himself in. 'I assure you I did not, George. It's your stutter. Do you have any idea what causes it? You don't stutter in class.'

'I duh-duh-don't s-s-st-st-stutter!'

'Lower your voice.'

'You w-want to g-get me! You duh-don't w-want me on your g-g-goddam team!'

'Lower your voice, I said. Let's discuss this rationally.'

'F-fuh-fuck th-that!'

'George, if you can control your stutter, I'd be glad to have you. You're well prepped for every practice and you're good at the background stuff, which means you're rarely surprised. But all that doesn't mean much if you can't control that—'

'I've neh-neh-never stuttered!' He cried out. 'It's yuh-you! I-I-if sub-someone else had the d-d-deb-debate t-team, I could—'

Jack's temper slipped another notch.

'George, you're never going to make much of a lawyer, corporation or otherwise, if you can't control that. Law isn't like soccer. Two hours of practice every night won't cut it. What are you going to do, stand up in front of a board meeting and say, "Nuh-nuh-now, g-gentlemen, about this t-t-tort"?'

He suddenly flushed, not with anger but with shame at his own cruelty. This was not a man in front of him but a seventeen-year-old boy who was facing the first major defeat of his life, and maybe asking in the only way he could for Jack to help him find a way to cope with it.

George gave him a final, furious glance, his lips twisting and bucking as the words bottled up behind them struggled to find their way out.

'Yuh-yuh-you s-s-set it ahead! You huh-hate me b-because you nuh-nuh-nuh-know . . . you know . . . nuh-nuh—'

With an inarticulate cry he had rushed out of the classroom, slamming the door hard enough to make the wire-reinforced glass rattle in its frame. Jack had stood there, feeling, rather than hearing, the echo of George's Adidas in the empty hall. Still in the grip of his temper and his shame at mocking George's stutter, his first thought had been a sick sort of exultation: For the first time in his life George Hatfield had wanted something he could not have. For the first time there was something wrong that all of Daddy's money could not fix. You couldn't bribe a speech center. You couldn't offer a tongue an extra fifty a week and a bonus at Christmas if it would agree to stop flapping like a record needle in a defective groove. Then the exultation was simply buried in shame, and he felt the way he had after he had broken Danny's arm.

Dear God, I am not a son of a bitch. Please.

That sick happiness at George's retreat was more typical of Denker in the play than of Jack Torrance the playwright.

You hate me because you know . . .

Because he knew what?

What could he possibly know about George Hatfield that would make him hate him? That his whole future lay ahead of him? That he looked a little bit like Robert Redford and all conversation among the girls stopped when he did a double gainer from the pool diving board? That he played soccer and baseball with a natural, unlearned grace?

Ridiculous. Absolutely absurd. He envied George Hatfield nothing. If the truth was known, he felt worse about George's unfortunate stutter than George himself, because George really would have made an excellent debater. And if Jack had set the timer ahead – and of course he hadn't – it would have been because both he and the other members of the squad were embarrassed for George's struggle, they had agonized over it the way you agonize when the Class Night speaker forgets some of his lines. If he had set the timer ahead, it would have been just to . . . to put George out of his misery.

But he hadn't set the timer ahead. He was quite sure of it.

A week later he had cut him, and that time he had kept his temper. The shouts and the threats had all been on George's side. A week later after that he had gone out to the parking lot halfway through practice to get a pile of sourcebooks that he had left in the trunk of the VW and there had been George, down on one knee with his long blond hair swinging in his face, a hunting knife in one hand. He was sawing through the VW's right front tire. The back tires were already shredded, and the bug sat on the flats like a small, tired dog.

Jack had seen red, and remembered very little of the encounter that followed. He remembered a thick growl that seemed to issue from his own throat: 'All right, George. If that's how you want it, just come here and take your medicine.'

He remembered George looking up, startled and fearful. He had said: 'Mr Torrance— ' as if to explain how all this was just a mistake, the tires had been flat when he got there and he was just cleaning dirt out of the front treads with the tip of this gutting knife he just happened to have with him and—

Jack had waded in, his fists held up in front of him, and it seemed that he had been grinning. But he wasn't sure of that.

The last thing he remembered was George holding up the knife and saying: 'You better not come any closer—'

And the next thing was Miss Strong, the French teacher, holding Jack's arms, crying, screaming: 'Stop it, Jack! Stop it! You're going to kill him!'

He had blinked around stupidly. There was the hunting knife, glittering harmlessly on the parking lot asphalt four yards away. There was his Volkswagen, his poor old battered bug, veteran of many wild midnight drunken rides, sitting on three flat shoes. There was a new dent in the right front fender, he saw, and there was something in the middle of the dent that was either red paint or blood. For a moment he had been confused, his thoughts

(jesus christ al we hit him after all)

of that other night. Then his eyes had shifted to George, George lying dazed and blinking on the asphalt. His debate group had come out and they were huddled together by the door, staring at George. There was blood on his face from a scalp laceration that looked minor, but there was also blood running out of one of George's ears and that probably meant a concussion. When George tried to get up, Jack shook free of Miss Strong and went to him. George cringed.

Jack put his hands on George's chest and pushed him back down. 'Lie still,' he said. 'Don't try to move.' He turned to Miss Strong, who was staring at them both with horror.

'Please go call the school doctor, Miss Strong,' he told her. She turned and fled toward the office. He looked at his debate class then, looked them right in the eye because he was in charge again, fully himself, and when he was himself there wasn't a nicer guy in the whole state of Vermont. Surely they knew that.

'You can go home now,' he told them quietly. 'We'll meet again tomorrow.'

But by the end of that week six of the debaters had dropped out, two of them the class of the act, but of course it didn't matter much because he had been informed by then that he would be dropping out himself.

Yet somehow he had stayed off the bottle, and he supposed that was something.

And he had not hated George Hatfield. He was sure of that. He had not acted but had been acted upon.

You hate me because you know . . .

But he had known nothing. *Nothing.* He would swear that before the Throne of Almighty God, just as he would swear that he had set the timer ahead no more than a minute. And not out of hate but out of pity.

Two wasps were crawling sluggishly about on the roof beside the hole in the flashing.

He watched them until they spread their aerodynamically unsound but strangely efficient wings and lumbered off into the October sunshine, perchance to sting someone else. God had seen fit to give them stingers and Jack supposed they had to use them on somebody.

How long had he been sitting here, looking at that hole with its unpleasant surprise down inside, raking over old coals? He looked at his watch. Almost half an hour.

He let himself down to the edge of the roof, dropped one leg over, and felt around until his foot found the top rung of the ladder just below the overhang. He would go down to the equipment shed where he had stored the bug bomb on a high shelf out of Danny's reach. He would get it, come back up, and then they would be the ones surprised. You could be stung, but you could also sting back. He believed that sincerely. Two hours from now the nest would be just so much chewed paper and Danny could have it in his room if he wanted to – Jack had had one in his room when he was just a kid, it had always smelled faintly of woodsmoke and gasoline. He could have it right by the head of his bed. It wouldn't hurt him.

'I'm getting better.'

The sound of his own voice, confident in the silent afternoon, reassured him even though he hadn't meant to speak aloud. He *was* getting better. It was possible to graduate from passive to active, to take the thing that had once driven you nearly to madness as a neutral prize of no more than occasional academic interest. And if there was a place where the thing could be done, this was surely it.

He went down the ladder to get the bug bomb. They would pay. They would pay for stinging him.

CHAPTER FIFTEEN
DOWN IN THE FRONT YARD

Jack had found a huge white-painted wicker chair in the back of the equipment shed two weeks ago, and had dragged it around to the porch over Wendy's objections that it was really the ugliest thing she had ever seen in her whole life. He was sitting in it now, amusing himself with a copy of E. L. Doctorow's *Welcome to Hard Times*, when his wife and son rattled up the driveway in the hotel truck.

Wendy parked in the turn-around, raced the engine sportily, and then turned it off. The truck's single taillight died. The engine rumbled grumpily with post-ignition and finally stopped. Jack got out of his chair and ambled down to meet her.

'Hi, Dad!' Danny called, and raced up the hill. He had a box in one hand. 'Look what Mommy bought me!'

Jack picked his son up, swung him around twice, and kissed him heartily on the mouth.

'Jack Torrance, the Eugene O'Neill of his generation, the American Shakespeare!' Wendy said, smiling. 'Fancy meeting you here, so far up the mountains.'

'The common ruck became too much for me, dear lady,' he said, and slipped his arms around her. They kissed. 'How was your trip?'

'Very good. Danny complains that I keep jerking him but I didn't stall the truck once and . . . oh, Jack, you finished it!'

She was looking at the roof, and Danny followed her gaze. A faint frown touched his face as he looked at the wide swatch of fresh shingles atop the Overlook's west wing, a lighter green than the rest of the roof. Then he looked down at the box in his hand and his face cleared again. At night the pictures Tony had showed him came back to haunt in all their original clarity, but in sunny daylight they were easier to disregard.

'Look, Daddy, look!'

Jack took the box from his son. It was a model car, one of the Big Daddy Roth caricatures that Danny had expressed an admiration for in the past. This one was the Violent Violet Volkswagen, and the picture on the box showed a huge purple VW with long '59 Cadillac Coupe de Ville taillights burning up a dirt track. The VW had a sunroof, and poking up through it, clawed hands on the wheel down below, was a gigantic warty monster with popping bloodshot eyes, a maniacal grin, and a gigantic English racing cap turned around backward.

Wendy was smiling at him, and Jack winked at her.

'That's what I like about you, doc,' Jack said, handing the box back. 'Your taste runs to the quiet, the sober, the introspective. You are definitely the child of my loins.'

'Mommy said you'd help me put it together as soon as I could read all of the first Dick and Jane.'

'That ought to be by the end of the week,' Jack said. 'What else have you got in that fine-looking truck, ma'am?'

'Uh-uh.' She grabbed his arm and pulled him back. 'No peeking. Some of that stuff is for you. Danny and I will take it in. You can get the milk. It's on the floor of the cab.'

'That's all I am to you,' Jack cried, clapping a hand to his forehead. 'Just a dray horse, a common beast of the field. Dray here, dray there, dray everywhere.'

'Just dray that milk right into the kitchen, mister.'

'It's too much!' he cried, and threw himself on the ground while Danny stood over him and giggled.

'Get up, you ox,' Wendy said, and prodded him with the toe of her sneaker.

'See?' he said to Danny. 'She called me an ox. You're a witness.'

'Witness, witness!' Danny concurred gleefully, and broad-jumped his prone father.

Jack sat up. 'That reminds me, chumly. I've got something for you, too. On the porch by my ashtray.'

'What is it?'

'Forgot. Go and see.'

Jack got up and the two of them stood together, watching

Danny charge up the lawn and then take the steps to the porch two by two. He put an arm around Wendy's waist.

'You happy, babe?'

She looked up at him solemnly. 'This is the happiest I've been since we were married.'

'Is that the truth?'

'God's honest.'

He squeezed her tightly. 'I love you.'

She squeezed him back, touched. Those had never been cheap words with John Torrance; she could count the number of times he had said them to her, both before and after marriage, on both her hands.

'I love you too.'

'Mommy! Mommy!' Danny was on the porch now, shrill and excited. 'Come and see! Wow! It's neat!'

'What is it?' Wendy asked him as they walked up from the parking lot, hand in hand.

'Forgot,' Jack said.

'Oh, you'll get yours,' she said, and elbowed him. 'See if you don't.'

'I was hoping I'd get it tonight,' he remarked, and she laughed. A moment later he asked, 'Is Danny happy, do you think?'

'You ought to know. You're the one who has a long talk with him every night before bed.'

'That's usually about what he wants to be when he grows up or if Santa Claus is really real. That's getting to be a big thing with him. I think his old buddy Scott let some pennies drop on that one. No, he hasn't said much of anything about the Overlook to me.'

'Me either,' she said. They were climbing the porch steps now. 'But he's very quiet a lot of the time. And I think he's lost weight, Jack, I really do.'

'He's just getting tall.'

Danny's back was to them. He was examining something on the table by Jack's chair, but Wendy couldn't see what it was.

'He's not eating as well, either. He used to be the original steam shovel. Remember last year?'

'They taper off,' he said vaguely. 'I think I read that in Spock. He'll be using two forks again by the time he's seven.'

They had stopped on the top step.

'He's pushing awfully hard on those readers, too,' she said. 'I know he wants to learn how, to please us . . . to please you,' she added reluctantly.

'To please himself most of all,' Jack said. 'I haven't been pushing him on that at all. In fact I do wish he wouldn't go quite so hard.'

'Would you think I was foolish if I made an appointment for him to have a physical? There's a GP in Sidewinder, a young man from what the checker in the market said—'

'You're a little nervous about the snow coming, aren't you?' She shrugged. 'I suppose. If you think it's foolish—'

'I don't. In fact, you can make appointments for all three of us. We'll get our clean bills of health and then we can sleep easy at night.'

'I'll make the appointments this afternoon,' she said.

'Mom! Look, Mommy!'

He came running to her with a large gray thing in his hands, and for one comic-horrible moment Wendy thought it was a brain. She saw what it really was and recoiled instinctively.

Jack put an arm around her. 'It's all right. The tenants who didn't fly away have been shaken out. I used a bug bomb.'

She looked at the large wasps' nest her son was holding but would not touch it. 'Are you sure it's safe?'

'Positive. I had one in my room when I was a kid. My dad gave it to me. Want to put it in your room, Danny?'

'Yeah! Right now!'

He turned around and raced through the double doors. They could hear his muffled, running feet on the main stairs.

'There *were* wasps up there,' she said. 'Did you get stung?'

'Where's my purple heart?' he asked, and displayed his finger. The swelling had already begun to go down, but she ooohed over it satisfyingly and gave it a small, gentle kiss.

'Did you pull the stinger out?'

'Wasps don't leave them in. That's bees. They have barbed

stingers. Wasp stingers are smooth. That's what makes them so dangerous. They can sting again and again.'

'Jack, are you sure that's safe for him to have?'

'I followed the directions on the bomb. The stuff is guaranteed to kill every single bug in two hours' time and dissipate with no residue.'

'I hate them,' she said.

'What . . . wasps?'

'Anything that stings,' she said. Her hands went to her elbows and cupped them, her arms crossed over her breasts.

'I do too,' he said, and hugged her.

CHAPTER SIXTEEN
DANNY

Down the hall, in the bedroom, Wendy could hear the type-writer Jack had carried up from downstairs burst into life for thirty seconds, fall silent for a minute or two, and then rattle briefly again. It was like listening to machine-gun fire from an isolated pillbox. The sound was music to her ears; Jack had not been writing so steadily since the second year of their marriage, when he wrote the story that *Esquire* had purchased. He said he thought the play would be done by the end of the year, for better or worse, and he would be moving on to something new. He said he didn't care if *The Little School* stirred any excitement when Phyllis showed it around, didn't care if it sank without a trace, and Wendy believed that, too. The actual act of his writing made her immensely hopeful, not because she expected great things from the play but because her husband seemed to be slowly closing a huge door on a roomful of monsters. He had had his shoulder to that door for a long time now, but at last it was swinging shut.

Every key typed closed it a little more.

'Look, Dick, look.'

Danny was hunched over the first of the five battered primers Jack had dug up by culling mercilessly through Boulder's myriad secondhand bookshops. They would take Danny right up to the second-grade reading level, a program she had told Jack she thought was much too ambitious. Their son was intelligent, they knew that, but it would be a mistake to push him too far too fast. Jack had agreed. There would be no pushing involved. But if the kid caught on fast, they would be prepared. And now she wondered if Jack hadn't been right about that, too.

Danny, prepared by four years of 'Sesame Street' and three years of 'Electric Company', seemed to be catching on with almost scary speed. It bothered her. He hunched over the innocuous little books, his crystal radio and balsa glider on the shelf above him, as though his life depended on learning to read. His small face was more tense and paler than she liked in the close and cozy glow of the gooseneckecd lamp they had put in his room. He was taking it very seriously, both the reading and the workbook pages his father had made up for him every afternoon. Picture of an apple and a peach. The word *apple* written beneath in Jack's large, neatly made printing. Circle the right picture, the one that went with the word. And their son would stare from the word to the picture, his lips moving, sounding out, actually *sweating* it out. And with his double-sized red pencil curled into his pudgy right fist, he could now write about three dozen words on his own.

His finger traced slowly under the words in the reader. Above them was a picture. Wendy half-remembered from her own grammar school days, nineteen years before. A laughing boy with brown curly hair. A girl in a short dress, her hair in blond ringlets, one hand holding a jump rope. A prancing dog running after a large red rubber ball. The first-grade trinity. Dick, Jane, and Jip.

'See Jip run,' Danny read slowly. 'Run, Jip, run. Run, run, run.' He paused, dropping his finger down a line. 'See the . . .' He bent closer, his nose almost touching the page now. 'See the . . .'

'Not so close, doc,' Wendy said quietly. 'You'll hurt your eyes. It's—'

'Don't tell me!' he said, sitting up with a jerk. His voice was alarmed. 'Don't tell me. Mommy, I can get it!'

'All right, honey,' she said. 'But it's not a big thing. Really it's not.'

Unheeding, Danny bent forward again. On his face was an expression that might be more commonly seen hovering over a graduate record exam in a college gym somewhere. She liked it less and less.

'See the . . . buh. Aw. El. El. See the buhaw-el-el? See the buhawl. *Ball!*' Suddenly triumphant. Fierce. The fierceness in his voice scared her. '*See the ball!*'

'That's right,' she said. 'Honey, I think that's enough for tonight.'

'A couple more pages, Mommy? Please?'

'No, doc.' She closed the red-bound book firmly. 'It's bed time.'

'Please?'

'Don't tease me about it, Danny. Mommy's tired.'

'Okay.' But he looked longingly at the primer.

'Go kiss your father and then wash up. Don't forget to brush.'

'Yeah.'

He slouched out, a small boy in pajama bottoms with feet and a large flannel top with a football on the front and NEW ENGLAND PATRIOTS written on the back.

Jack's typewriter stopped, and she heard Danny's hearty smack. 'Night, Daddy.'

'Goodnight, doc. How'd you do?'

'Okay, I guess. Mommy made me stop.'

'Mommy was right. It's past eight-thirty. Going to the bathroom?'

'Yeah.'

'Good. There's potatoes growing out of your ears. And onions and carrots and chives and—'

Danny's giggle, fading, then cut off by the firm click of the bathroom door. He was private about his bathroom functions, while both she and Jack were pretty much catch-as-catch-can. Another sign – and they were multiplying all the time – that there was another human being in the place, not just a carbon copy of one of them or a combination of both. It made her a little sad. Someday her child would be a stranger to her, and she would be strange to him . . . but not as strange as her own mother had become to her. Please don't let it be that way, God. Let him grow up and still love his mother.

Jack's typewriter began its irregular bursts again.

Still sitting in the chair beside Danny's reading table, she let her eyes wander around her son's room. The glider's wings had been neatly mended. His desk was piled high with picture books, coloring books, old Spiderman comic books with the covers half torn off, Crayolas, and an untidy pile of Lincoln Logs.

The VW model was neatly placed above these lesser things, its shrink-wrap still undisturbed. He and his father would be putting it together tomorrow night or the night after if Danny went on at this rate, and never mind the end of the week. His pictures of Pooh and Eeyore and Christopher Robin were tacked neatly to the wall, soon enough to be replaced with pin-ups and photographs of dope-smoking rock singers, she supposed. Innocence to experience. Human nature, baby. Grab it and growl. Still it made her sad. Next year he would be in school and she would lose at least half of him, maybe more, to his friends. She and Jack had tried to have another one for a while when things had seemed to be going well at Stovington, but she was on the pill again now. Things were too uncertain. God knew where they would be in nine months.

Her eyes fell on the wasps' nest.

It held the ultimate high place in Danny's room, resting on a large plastic plate on the table by his bed. She didn't like it, even if it was empty. She wondered vaguely if it might have germs, thought to ask Jack, then decided he would laugh at her. But she would ask the doctor tomorrow, if she could catch him with Jack out of the room. She didn't like the idea of that thing, constructed from the chewings and saliva of so many alien creatures, lying within a foot of her sleeping son's head.

The water in the bathroom was still running, and she got up and went into the big bedroom to make sure everything was okay. Jack didn't look up; he was lost in the world he was making, staring at the typewriter, a filter cigarette clamped in his teeth.

She knocked lightly on the closed bathroom door. 'You okay, doc? You awake?'

No answer.

'Danny?'

No answer. She tried the door. It was locked.

'Danny?' She was worried now. The lack of any sound beneath the steadily running water made her uneasy. 'Danny? Open the door, honey.'

No answer.

'Danny!'

'Jesus Christ, Wendy, I can't think if you're going to pound on the door all night.'

'Danny's locked himself in the bathroom and he doesn't answer me!'

Jack came around the desk, looking put out. He knocked on the door once, hard. 'Open up, Danny. No games.'

No answer.

Jack knocked harder. 'Stop fooling, doc. Bedtime's bedtime. Spanking if you don't open up.'

He's losing his temper, she thought, and was more afraid. He had not touched Danny in anger since that evening two years ago, but at this moment he sounded angry enough to do it.

'Danny, honey—' she began.

No answer. Only running water.

'Danny, if you make me break this lock I can guarantee you you'll spend the night sleeping on your belly,' Jack warned.

Nothing.

'Break it,' she said, and suddenly it was hard to talk. 'Quick.'

He raised one foot and brought it down hard against the door to the right of the knob. The lock was a poor thing; it gave immediately and the door shuddered open, banging the tiled bathroom wall and rebounding halfway.

'*Danny!*' she screamed.

The water was running full force in the basin. Beside it, a tube of Crest with the cap off. Danny was sitting on the rim of the bathtub across the room, his toothbrush clasped limply in his left hand, a thin foam of toothpaste around his mouth. He was staring, trancelike, into the mirror on the front of the medicine cabinet above the washbasin. The expression on his face was one of drugged horror, and her first thought was that he was having some sort of epileptic seizure, that he might have swallowed his tongue.

'*Danny!*'

Danny didn't answer. Guttural sounds came from his throat.

Then she was pushed aside so hard that she crashed into the towel rack, and Jack was kneeling in front of the boy.

'Danny,' he said. 'Danny, Danny!' He snapped his fingers in front of Danny's blank eyes.

'Ah–sure,' Danny said. 'Tournament play. Stroke. Nurrrrr . . .'

'Danny—'

'Roque!' Danny said his voice suddenly deep, almost manlike. 'Roque. Stroke. The roque mallet . . . has two sides. *Gaaaaaa*—'

'Oh Jack my God *what's wrong with him?*'

Jack grabbed the boy's elbows and shook him hard. Danny's head rolled limply backward and then snapped forward like a balloon on a stick.

'Roque. Stroke. Redrum.'

Jack shook him again, and Danny's eyes suddenly cleared. His toothbrush fell out of his hand and onto the tiled floor with a small click.

'What?' he asked, looking around. He saw his father kneeling before him, Wendy standing by the wall. 'What?' Danny asked again, with rising alarm. 'W-W-Wuh-What's wr-r-r—'

'*Don't stutter!*' Jack suddenly screamed into his face. Danny cried out in shock, his body going tense, trying to draw away from his father, and then he collapsed into tears. Stricken, Jack pulled him close. 'Oh, honey, I'm sorry. I'm sorry, doc. Please. Don't cry. I'm sorry. Everything's okay.'

The water ran ceaselessly in the basin, and Wendy felt that she had suddenly stepped into some grinding nightmare where time ran backward, backward to the time when her drunken husband had broken her son's arm and had then mewled over him in almost the exact same words.

(*Oh honey. I'm sorry. I'm sorry, doc. Please. So sorry.*)

She ran to them both, pried Danny out of Jack's arms somehow (she saw the look of angry reproach on his face but filed it away for later consideration), and lifted him up. She walked him back into the small bedroom, Danny's arms clasped around her neck, Jack trailing them.

She sat down on Danny's bed and rocked him back and forth, soothing him with nonsensical words repeated over and over. She looked up at Jack and there was only worry in his eyes now. He raised questioning eyebrows at her. She shook her head faintly.

'Danny,' she said. 'Danny, Danny, Danny. 'S okay, doc. 'S fine.'

At last Danny was quiet, only faintly trembling in her arms. Yet it was Jack he spoke to first, Jack who was now sitting beside them on the bed, and she felt the old faint pang

(It's him first and it's always been him first)

of jealousy. Jack had shouted at him, she had comforted him, yet it was to his father that Danny said,

'I'm sorry if I was bad.'

'Nothing to be sorry for, doc.' Jack ruffled his hair. 'What the hell happened in there?'

Danny shook his head slowly, dazedly. 'I . . . I don't know. Why did you tell me to stop stuttering, Daddy? I don't stutter.'

'Of course not,' Jack said heartily, but Wendy felt a cold finger touch her heart. Jack suddenly looked scared, as if he'd seen something that might just have been a ghost.

'Something about the timer . . .' Danny muttered.

'*What?*' Jack was leaning forward, and Danny flinched in her arms.

'Jack, you're scaring him!' she said, and her voice was high, accusatory. It suddenly came to her that they were all scared. But of what?

'I don't know, I don't know,' Danny was saying to his father. 'What . . . what did I say, Daddy?'

'Nothing,' Jack muttered. He took his handkerchief from his back pocket and wiped his mouth with it. Wendy had a moment of that sickening time-is-running-backward feeling again. It was a gesture she remembered well from his drinking days.

'Why did you lock the door, Danny?' she asked gently. 'Why did you do that?'

'Tony,' he said. 'Tony told me to.'

They exchanged a glance over the top of his head.

'Did Tony say why, son?' Jack asked quietly.

'I was brushing my teeth and I was thinking about my reading,' Danny said. 'Thinking real hard. And . . . and I saw Tony way down in the mirror. He said he had to show me again.'

'You mean he was behind you?' Wendy asked.

'No, he was *in* the mirror.' Danny was very emphatic on this point. 'Way down deep. And then I went through the mirror. The next thing I remember Daddy was shaking me and I thought I was being bad again.'

Jack winced as if struck.

'No, doc,' he said gently.

'Tony told you to lock the door?' Wendy asked, brushing his hair.

'Yes.'

'And what did he want to show you?'

Danny tensed in her arms; it was as if the muscles in his body had turned into something like piano wire. 'I don't remember,' he said, distraught. 'I don't remember. Don't ask me. I . . . *I don't remember nothing!*'

'Shh,' Wendy said, alarmed. She began to rock him again. 'It's all right if you don't remember, hon. Sure it is.'

At last Danny began to relax again.

'Do you want me to stay a little while? Read you a story?'

'No. Just the night light.' He looked shyly at his father. 'Would you stay, Daddy? For a minute?'

'Sure, doc.'

Wendy sighed. 'I'll be in the living room, Jack.'

'Okay.'

She got up and watched as Danny slid under the covers. He seemed very small.

'Are you sure you're okay, Danny?'

'I'm okay. Just plug in Snoopy, Mom.'

'Sure.'

She plugged in the night light, which showed Snoopy lying fast asleep on top of his doghouse. He had never wanted a night light until they moved into the Overlook, and then he had specifically requested one. She turned off the lamp and the overhead and looked back at them, the small white circle of Danny's face, and Jack's above it. She hesitated a moment

(*and then I went through the mirror*)

and then left them quietly.

'You sleepy?' Jack asked, brushing Danny's hair off his forehead.

'Yeah.'

'Want a drink of water?'

'No . . .'

There was silence for five minutes. Danny was still beneath his hand. Thinking the boy had dropped off, he was about to get up and leave quietly when Danny said from the brink of sleep:

'Roque.'

Jack turned back, all zero at the bone.

'Danny—?'

'You'd never hurt Mommy, would you, Daddy?'

'No.'

'Or me?'

'No.'

Silence again, spinning out.

'Daddy?'

'What?'

'Tony came and told me about roque.'

'Did he, doc? What did he say?'

'I don't remember much. Except he said it was in innings. Like baseball. Isn't that funny?'

'Yes.' Jack's heart was thudding dully in his chest. How could the boy possibly know a thing like that? Roque was played by innings, not like baseball but like cricket.

'Daddy . . . ?' He was almost asleep now.

'What?'

'What's redrum?'

'Red drum? Sounds like something an Indian might take on the warpath.'

Silence.

'Hey, doc?'

But Danny was asleep, breathing in long, slow strokes. Jack sat looking down at him for a moment, and a rush of love pushed through him like tidal water. Why had he yelled at the boy like that? It was perfectly normal for him to stutter a little. He had been coming out of a daze or some weird kind of trance, and stuttering was perfectly normal under those circumstances. Perfectly. And he hadn't said *timer* at all. It had been something else, nonsense, gibberish.

How had he known roque was played in innings? Had someone told him? Ullman? Hallorann?

He looked down at his hands. They were made into tight, clenched fists of tension

(*god how i need a drink*)

and the nails were digging into his palms like tiny brands. Slowly he forced them to open.

'I love you, Danny,' he whispered. 'God knows I do.'

He left the room. He had lost his temper again, only a little, but enough to make him feel sick and afraid. A drink would blunt that feeling, oh yes. It would blunt that.

(Something about the timer)

and everything else. There was no mistake about those words at all. None. Each had come out clear as a bell. He paused in the hallway, looking back, and automatically wiped his lips with his handkerchief.

★★★

Their shapes were only dark silhouettes in the glow of the night light. Wendy, wearing only panties, went to his bed and tucked him in again; he had kicked the covers back. Jack stood in the doorway, watching as she put her inner wrist against his forehead.

'Is he feverish?'

'No.' She kissed his cheek.

'Thank God you made that appointment,' he said as she came back to the doorway. 'You think that guy knows his stuff?'

'The checker said he was very good. That's all I know.'

'If there's something wrong, I'm going to send you and him to your mother's, Wendy.'

'No.'

'I know,' he said, putting an arm around her, 'how you feel.'

'You don't know how I feel at all about her.'

'Wendy, there's no place else I can send you. You know that.'

'If you came—'

'Without this job we're done,' he said simply. 'You know that.'

Her silhouette nodded slowly. She knew it.

'When I had that interview with Ullman, I thought he was just blowing off his bazoo. Now I'm not so sure. Maybe I really shouldn't have tried this with you two along. Forty miles from nowhere.'

'I love you,' she said. 'And Danny loves you even more, if that's possible. He would have been heartbroken, Jack. He will be, if you send us away.'

'Don't make it sound that way.'

'If the doctor says there's something wrong, I'll look for a job in Sidewinder,' she said. 'If I can't get one in Sidewinder, Danny and I will go to Boulder. I can't go to my mother, Jack. Not on those terms. Don't ask me. I . . . I just can't.'

'I guess I know that. Cheer up. Maybe it's nothing.'

'Maybe.'

'The appointment's at two?'

'Yes.'

'Let's leave the bedroom door open, Wendy.'

'I want to. But I think he'll sleep through now.'

But he didn't.

***

Boom . . . boom . . . boom boomBOOMBOOM—

He fled the heavy, crashing, echoing sounds through twisting, mazelike corridors, his bare feet whispering over a deep-pile jungle of blue and black. Each time he heard the roque mallet smash into the wall somewhere behind him he wanted to scream aloud. But he mustn't. He mustn't. A scream would give him away and then

(then *RED RUM*)

(*Come out here and take your medicine, you fucking cry-baby!*)

Oh and he could hear the owner of that voice coming, coming for him, charging up the hall like a tiger in an alien blue-black jungle. A man-eater.

(*Come out here, you little son of a bitch!*)

If he could get to the stairs going down, if he could get off this third floor, he might be all right. Even the elevator. If he could remember what had been forgotten. But it was dark and in his terror he had lost his orientation. He had turned down one corridor and then another, his heart leaping into his mouth like a hot lump of ice, fearing that each turn would bring him face to face with the human tiger in these halls.

The booming was right behind him now, the awful hoarse shouting.

The whistle the head of the mallet made cutting through the air

(*roque . . . stroke . . . roque . . . stroke . . . RED RUM*)

before it crashed into the wall. The soft whisper of feet on the jungle carpet. Panic squirting in his mouth like bitter juice.

(*You will remember what was forgotten . . .* but would he? What was it?)

He fled around another corner and saw with creeping, utter horror that he was in a cul-de-sac. Locked doors frowned down at him from three sides. The west wing. He was in the west wing and outside he could hear the storm whooping and screaming, seeming to choke on its own dark throat filled with snow.

He backed up against the wall, weeping with terror now, his heart racing like the heart of a rabbit caught in a snare. When his back was against the light blue silk wallpaper with the embossed pattern of wavy lines, his legs gave way and he collapsed to the carpet, hands splayed on the jungle of woven vines and creepers, the breath whistling in and out of his throat.

Louder. Louder.

There was a tiger in the hall, and now the tiger was just around the corner, still crying out in that shrill and petulant and lunatic rage, the roque mallet slamming, because this tiger walked on two legs and it was—

He woke with a sudden indrawn gasp, sitting bolt upright in bed, eyes wide and staring into the darkness, hands crossed in front of his face.

Something on one hand. Crawling.

Wasps. Three of them.

They stung him then, seeming to needle all at once, and that was when all the images broke apart and fell on him in a dark flood and he began to shriek into the dark, the wasps clinging to his left hand stinging again and again.

The lights went on and Daddy was standing there in his

shorts, his eyes glaring. Mommy behind him, sleepy and scared.

'*Get them off me!*' Danny screamed.

'Oh my God,' Jack said. He saw.

'Jack, what's wrong with him? *What's wrong?*'

He didn't answer her. He ran to the bed, scooped up Danny's pillow, and slapped Danny's thrashing left hand with it. Again. Again. Wendy saw lumbering, insectile forms rise into the air, droning.

'Get a magazine!' he yelled over his shoulder. 'Kill them!'

'Wasps?' she said, and for a moment she was inside herself, almost detached in her realization. That her mind cross-patched, and knowledge was connected to emotion. 'Wasps, oh Jesus, Jack, you said—'

'*Shut the fuck up and kill them!*' he roared. '*Will you do what I say!*'

One of them had landed on Danny's reading desk. She took a coloring book off his worktable and slammed it down on the wasp. It left a viscous brown smear.

'There's another one on the curtain,' he said, and ran out past her with Danny in his arms.

He took the boy into their bedroom and put him on Wendy's side of the makeshift double. 'Lie right there, Danny. Don't come back until I tell you. Understand?'

His face puffed and streaked with tears, Danny nodded.

'That's my brave boy.'

Jack ran back down the hall to the stairs. Behind him he heard the coloring book slap twice, and then his wife screamed in pain. He didn't slow but went down the stairs two by two into the darkened lobby. He went through Ullman's office into the kitchen, slamming the heavy part of his thigh into the corner of Ullman's oak desk, barely feeling it. He slapped on the kitchen overheads and crossed to the sink. The washed dishes from supper were still heaped up in the drainer, where Wendy had left them to drip-dry. He snatched the big Pyrex bowl off the top. A dish fell to the floor and exploded. Ignoring it, he turned and ran back through the office and up the stairs.

Wendy was standing outside Danny's door, breathing hard. Her face was the color of table linen. Her eyes were shiny and flat; her hair hung damply against her neck. 'I got all of them,' she said dully, 'but one stung me. Jack, you said they were all dead.' She began to cry.

He slipped past her without answering and carried the Pyrex bowl over to the nest by Danny's bed. It was still. Nothing there. On the outside, anyway. He slammed the bowl down over the nest.

'There,' he said. 'Come on.'

They went back into their bedroom.

'Where did it get you?' He asked her.

'My . . . on my wrist.'

'Let's see.'

She showed it to him. Just above the bracelet of lines between wrist and palm, there was a small circular hole. The flesh around it was puffing up.

'Are you allergic to stings?' he asked. 'Think hard! If you are, Danny might be. The fucking little bastards got him five or six times.'

'No,' she said, more calmly. 'I . . . I just hate them, that's all. *Hate* them.'

Danny was sitting on the foot of the bed, holding his left hand and looking at them. His eyes, circled with the white of shock, looked at Jack reproachfully.

'Daddy, you said you killed them all. My hand . . . it really hurts.'

'Let's see it, doc . . . no, I'm not going to touch it. That would make it hurt even more. Just hold it out.'

He did and Wendy moaned. 'Oh Danny . . . oh, your poor hand!'

Later the doctor would count eleven separate stings. Now all they saw was a dotting of small holes, as if his palm and fingers had been sprinkled with grains of red paper. The swelling was bad. His hand had begun to look like one of those cartoon images where Bugs Bunny or Daffy Duck has just slammed himself with a hammer.

'Wendy, go get that spray stuff in the bathroom,' he said.

She went after it, and he sat down next to Danny and slipped an arm around his shoulders.

'After we spray your hand, I want to take some Polaroids of it, doc. Then you sleep the rest of the night with us, 'kay?'

'Sure,' Danny said. 'But why are you going to take pictures?'

'So maybe we can sue the ass out of some people.'

Wendy came back with a spray tube in the shape of a chemical fire extinguisher.

'This won't hurt, honey,' she said, taking off the cap.

Danny held out his hand and she sprayed both sides until it gleamed. He let out a long, shuddery sigh.

'Does it smart?' she asked.

'No. Feels better.'

'Now these. Crunch them up.' She held out five orange-flavored baby aspirin. Danny took them and popped them into his mouth one by one.

'Isn't that a lot of aspirin?' Jack asked.

'It's a lot of stings,' she snapped at him angrily. 'You go and get rid of that nest, John Torrance. Right now.'

'Just a minute.'

He went to the dresser and took his Polaroid Square Shooter out of the top drawer. He rummaged deeper and found some flashcubes.

'Jack, what are you doing?' she asked, a little hysterically.

'He's gonna take some pictures of my hand,' Danny said gravely, 'and then we're gonna sue the ass out of some people. Right, Dad?'

'Right,' Jack said grimly. He had found the flash attachment, and he jabbed it onto the camera. 'Hold it out, son. I figure about five thousand dollars a sting.'

'What are you *talking* about?' Wendy nearly screamed.

'I'll tell you what,' he said. 'I followed the directions on that fucking bug bomb. We're going to sue them. The damn thing was defective. Had to have been. How else can you explain this?'

'Oh,' she said in a small voice.

He took four pictures, pulling out each covered print for Wendy to time on the small locket watch she wore around her neck. Danny, fascinated with the idea that his stung hand might be worth thousands and thousands of dollars, began to lose some of his fright and take an active interest. The hand throbbed dully, and he had a small headache.

When Jack had put the camera away and spread the prints out on top of the dresser to dry, Wendy said: 'Should we take him to the doctor tonight?'

'Not unless he's really in pain,' Jack said. 'If a person has a strong allergy to wasp venom, it hits within thirty seconds.'

'Hits? What do you—'

'A coma. Or convulsions.'

'Oh. Oh my Jesus.' She cupped her hands over her elbows and hugged herself, looking pale and wan.

'How do you feel, son? Think you could sleep?'

Danny blinked at them. The nightmare had faded to a dull, featureless background in his mind, but he was still frightened.

'If I can sleep with you.'

'Of course,' Wendy said. 'Oh honey, I'm so sorry.'

'It's okay, Mommy.'

She began to cry again, and Jack put his hands on her shoulders. 'Wendy, I swear to you that I followed the directions.'

'Will you get rid of it in the morning? Please?'

'Of course I will.'

The three of them got in bed together, and Jack was about to snap off the light over the bed when he paused and pushed the covers back instead. 'Want a picture of the nest, too.'

'Come right back.'

'I will.'

He went to the dresser, got the camera and the last flashcube, and gave Danny a closed thumb-and-forefinger circle. Danny smiled and gave it back with his good hand.

Quite a kid, he thought as he walked down to Danny's room. *All of that and then some.*

The overhead was still on. Jack crossed to the bunk setup, and as he glanced at the table beside it, his skin crawled into goose flesh. The short hairs on his neck prickled and tried to stand erect.

He could hardly see the nest through the clear Pyrex bowl. The inside of the glass was crawling with wasps. It was hard to tell how many. Fifty at least. Maybe a hundred.

His heart thudding slowly in his chest, he took his pictures and then set the camera down to wait for them to develop. He wiped his lips with the palm of his hand. One thought played over and over in his mind, echoing with

(*You lost your temper. You lost your temper. You lost your temper.*)

an almost superstitious dread. They had come back. He had killed the wasps but they had come back.

In his mind he heard himself screaming into his frightened, crying son's face: *Don't stutter!*

He wiped his lips again.

He went to Danny's worktable, rummaged in its drawers, and came up with a big jigsaw puzzle with a fiberboard backing. He took it over to the bedtable and carefully slid the bowl and the nest onto it. The wasps buzzed angrily inside their prison. Then, putting his hand firmly on top of the bowl so it wouldn't slip, he went out into the hall.

'Coming to bed, Jack?' Wendy asked.

'Coming to bed, Daddy?'

'Have to go downstairs for a minute,' he said, making his voice light.

How had it happened? How in God's name?

The bomb sure hadn't been a dud. He had seen the thick white smoke start to puff out of it when he had pulled the ring. And when he had gone up two hours later, he had shaken a drift of small dead bodies out of the hole in the top.

Then how? Spontaneous regeneration?

That was crazy. Seventeenth-century bullshit. Insects didn't regenerate. And even if wasp eggs could mature full-grown insects in twelve hours, this wasn't the season in which the queen laid. That happened in April or May. Fall was their dying time.

A living contradiction, the wasps buzzed furiously under the bowl.

He took them downstairs and through the kitchen. In back there was a door which gave on the outside. A cold night wind blew against his nearly naked body, and his feet went numb almost instantly against the cold concrete of the platform he was standing on, the platform where milk deliveries were made during the hotel's operating season. He put the puzzle and the bowl down carefully, and when he stood up he looked at the thermometer nailed outside the door. FRESH UP WITH 7-UP, the thermometer said, and the mercury stood at an even twenty-five degrees. The cold would kill them by morning. He went in and shut the door firmly. After a moment's thought he locked it, too.

He crossed the kitchen again and shut off the lights. He stood in the darkness for a moment, thinking, wanting a drink. Suddenly the hotel seemed full of a thousand stealthy sounds: creakings and groans and the sly sniff of the wind under the eaves where more wasps' nests might be hanging like deadly fruit.

They had come back.

And suddenly he found that he didn't like the Overlook so well anymore, as if it wasn't wasps that had stung his son, wasps that had miraculously lived through the bug bomb assault, but the hotel itself.

His last thought before going upstairs to his wife and son

(from now on you will hold your temper. No Matter What.)

was firm and hard and sure.

As he went down the hall to them he wiped his lips with the back of his hand.

CHAPTER SEVENTEEN
THE DOCTOR'S OFFICE

Stripped to his underpants, lying on the examination table, Danny Torrance looked very small. He was looking up at Dr ('Just call me Bill') Edmonds, who was wheeling a large black machine up beside him. Danny rolled his eyes to get a better look at it.

'Don't let it scare you, guy,' Bill Edmonds said. 'It's an electroencephalograph, and it doesn't hurt.'

'Electro—'

'We call it EEG for short. I'm going to hook a bunch of wires to your head – no, not stick them in, only tape them – and the pens in this part of the gadget will record your brain waves.'

'Like on "The Six Million Dollar Man"?'

'About the same. Would you like to be like Steve Austin when you grow up?'

'No way,' Danny said as the nurse began to tape the wires to a number of tiny shaved spots on his scalp. 'My daddy says that someday he'll get a short circuit and then he'll be up sh . . . he'll be up the creek.'

'I know that creek well,' Dr Edmonds said amiably. 'I've been up it a few times myself, *sans* paddle. An EEG can tell us lots of things, Danny.'

'Like what?'

'Like for instance if you have epilepsy. That's a little problem where—'

'Yeah, I know what epilepsy is.'

'Really?'

'Sure. There was a kid in my nursery school back in Vermont – I went to nursery school when I was a little kid – and he had it. He wasn't supposed to use the flashboard.'

'What was that, Dan?' He had turned on the machine. Thin lines began to trace their ways across graph paper.

'It had all these lights, all different colors. And when you turned it on, some colors would flash but not all. And you had to count the colors and if you pushed the right button, you could turn it off. Brent couldn't use that.'

'That's because bright flashing lights sometimes cause an epileptic seizure.'

'You mean using the flashboard might've made Brent pitch a fit?'

Edmonds, and the nurse exchanged a brief, amused glance. 'Inelegantly but accurately put, Danny.'

'What?'

'I said you're right, except you should say "seizure" instead of "pitch a fit". That's not nice . . . okay, lie just as still as a mouse now.'

'Okay.'

'Danny, when you have these . . . whatever they ares, do you ever recall seeing bright flashing lights before?'

'No.'

'Funny noises? Ringing? Or chimes like a doorbell?'

'Huh-uh.'

'How about a funny smell, maybe like oranges or sawdust? Or a smell like something rotten?'

'No, sir.'

'Sometimes do you feel like crying before you pass out? Even though you don't feel sad?'

'No way.'

'That's fine, then.'

'Have I got epilepsy, Dr Bill?'

'I don't think so, Danny. Just lie still. Almost done.'

The machine hummed and scratched for another five minutes and then Dr Edmonds shut it off.

'All done, guy,' Edmonds said briskly. 'Let Sally get those electrodes off you and then come into the next room. I want to have a little talk with you. Okay?'

'Sure.'

'Sally, you go ahead and give him a tine test before he comes in.'

'All right.'

Edmonds ripped off the long curl of paper the machine had extruded and went into the next room, looking at it.

'I'm going to prick your arm just a little,' the nurse said after Danny had pulled up his pants. 'It's to make sure you don't have TB.'

'They gave me that at my school just last year,' Danny said without much hope.

'But that was a long time ago and you're a big boy now, right?'

'I guess so,' Danny sighed, and offered his arm up for sacrifice.

When he had his shirt and shoes on, he went through the sliding door and into Dr Edmonds's office. Edmonds was sitting on the edge of his desk, swinging his legs thoughtfully.

'Hi, Danny.'

'Hi.'

'How's that hand now?' He pointed at Danny's left hand, which was lightly bandaged.

'Pretty good.'

'Good. I looked at your EEG and it seems fine. But I'm going to send it to a friend of mine in Denver who makes his living reading those things. I just want to make sure.'

'Yes, sir.'

'Tell me about Tony, Dan.'

Danny shuffled his feet. 'He's just an invisible friend,' he said. 'I made him up. To keep me company.'

Edmonds laughed and put his hands on Danny's shoulders. 'Now that's what your Mom and Dad say. But this is just between us, guy. I'm your doctor. Tell me the truth and I'll promise not to tell them unless you say I can.'

Danny thought about it. He looked at Edmonds and then, with a small effort of concentration, he tried to catch Edmonds's thoughts or at least the color of his mood. And suddenly he got an oddly comforting image in his head: file cabinets, their doors sliding shut one after another, locking with a click. Written on the small tabs in the center of each door was: A–C, SECRET; D–G, SECRET; and so on. This made Danny feel a little easier.

Cautiously he said: 'I don't know who Tony is.'

'Is he your age?'

'No. He's at least eleven. I think he might be even older. I've never seen him right up close. He might be old enough to drive a car.'

'You just see him at a distance, huh?'

'Yes, sir.'

'And he always comes just before you pass out?'

'Well, I don't pass out. It's like I go with him. And he shows me things.'

'What kind of things?'

'Well . . .' Danny debated for a moment and then told Edmonds about Daddy's trunk with all his writing in it, and about how the movers hadn't lost it between Vermont and Colorado after all. It had been right under the stairs all along.

'And your daddy found it where Tony said he would?'

'Oh yes, sir. Only Tony didn't *tell* me. He showed me.'

'I understand. Danny, what did Tony show you last night? When you locked yourself in the bathroom?'

'I don't remember,' Danny said quickly.

'Are you sure?'

'Yes, sir.'

'A moment ago I said *you* locked the bathroom door. But that wasn't right, was it? *Tony* locked the door.'

'No, sir. Tony couldn't lock the door because he isn't real. He wanted me to do it, so I did. I locked it.'

'Does Tony always show you where lost things are?'

'No, sir. Sometimes he shows me things that are going to happen.'

'Really?'

'Sure. Like one time Tony showed me the amusements and wild animal park in Great Barrington. Tony said Daddy was going to take me there for my birthday. He did, too.'

'What else does he show you?'

Danny frowned. 'Signs. He's always showing me stupid old *signs*. And I can't read them, hardly ever.'

'Why do you suppose Tony would do that, Danny?'

'I don't know.' Danny brightened. 'But my daddy and mommy are teaching me to read, and I'm trying real hard.'

'So you can read Tony's signs.'

'Well, I really want to learn. But that too, yeah.'

'Do you like Tony, Danny?'

Danny looked at the tile floor and said nothing.

'Danny?'

'It's hard to tell,' Danny said. 'I used to. I used to hope he'd come every day, because he always showed me good things, especially since Mommy and Daddy don't think about DIVORCE anymore.' Dr Edmonds's gaze sharpened, but Danny didn't notice. He was looking hard at the floor, concentrating on expressing himself. 'But now whenever he comes he shows me bad things. *Awful* things. Like in the bathroom last night. The things he shows me, they sting me like those wasps stung me. Only Tony's things sting me up here.' He cocked a finger gravely at his temple, a small boy unconsciously burlesquing suicide.

'What things, Danny?'

'I can't remember!' Danny cried out, agonized. 'I'd tell you if I could! It's like I can't remember because it's so bad I don't *want* to remember. All I can remember when I wake up is REDRUM.'

'Red *drum* or red *rum*?'

'Rum.'

'What's that, Danny?'

'I don't know.'

'Danny?'

'Yes, sir?'

'Can you make Tony come now?'

'I don't know. He doesn't always come. I don't even know if I want him to come anymore.'

'Try, Danny. I'll be right here.'

Danny looked at Edmonds doubtfully. Edmonds nodded encouragement.

Danny let out a long, sighing breath and nodded. 'But I don't know if it will work. I never did it with anyone looking at me before. And Tony doesn't always come, anyway.'

'If he doesn't, he doesn't,' Edmonds said. 'I just want you to try.'

'Okay.'

He dropped his gaze to Edmonds's slowly swinging loafers and cast his mind outward toward his mommy and daddy. They were here someplace . . . right beyond that wall with the picture on it, as a matter of fact. In the waiting room where they had come in. Sitting side by side but not talking. Leafing through magazines. Worried. About him.

He concentrated harder, his brow furrowing, trying to get into the feeling of his mommy's thoughts. It was always harder when they weren't right there in the room with him. Then he began to get it. Mommy was thinking about a sister. Her sister. The sister was dead. His mommy was thinking that was the main thing that turned her mommy into such a

(*bitch?*)

into such an old biddy. Because her sister had died. As a little girl she was

(*hit by a car oh god I could never stand anything like that again like aileen but what if he's sick really sick cancer spinal meningitis leukemia brain tumor like john gunther's son or muscular dystrophy oh jeez kids his age get leukemia all the time radium treatments chemotherapy we couldn't afford anything like that but of course they just can't turn you out to die on the street can they and anyway he's all right all right all right you really shouldn't let yourself think*)

(*Danny—*)

(*about aileen and*)

(*Dannee—*)

(*that car*)

(*Dannee—*)

But Tony wasn't there. Only his voice. And as it faded, Danny followed it down into darkness, falling and tumbling down some magic hole between Dr Bill's swinging loafers, past a loud knocking sound, further, a bathtub cruised silently by in the darkness with some horrible thing lolling in it, past a sound like sweetly chiming church bells, past a clock under a dome of glass.

Then the dark was pierced feebly by a single light, festooned with cobwebs. The weak glow disclosed a stone floor that looked damp and unpleasant. Somewhere not far distant was a steady mechanical roaring sound, but muted, not frightening. Soporific. It was the thing that would be forgotten, Danny thought with dreamy surprise.

As his eyes adjusted to the gloom he could see Tony just ahead of him, a silhouette. Tony was looking at something and Danny strained his eyes to see what it was.

(*Your daddy. See your daddy?*)

Of course he did. How could he have missed him, even in the basement light's feeble glow? Daddy was kneeling on the floor, casting the beam of a flashlight over old cardboard boxes and wooden crates. The cardboard boxes were mushy and old; some of them had split open and spilled drifts of paper onto the floor. Newspapers, books, printed pieces of paper that looked like bills. His daddy was examining them with great interest. And then Daddy looked up and shone his flashlight in another direction. Its beam of light impaled another book, a large white one bound with gold string. The cover looked like white leather. It was a scrapbook. Danny suddenly needed to cry out to his daddy, to tell him to leave that book alone, that some books should not be opened. But his daddy was climbing toward it.

The mechanical roaring sound, which he now recognized as the boiler at the Overlook which Daddy checked three or four times every day, had developed an ominous, rhythmic hitching. It began to sound like . . . like pounding. And the smell of mildew and wet, rotting paper was changing to something else – the high, junipery smell of the Bad Stuff. It hung around his daddy like a vapor as he reached for the book . . . and grasped it.

Tony was somewhere in the darkness.

(*This inhuman place makes human monsters. This inhuman place*) repeating the same incomprehensible thing over and over.

(*makes human monsters.*)

Falling through darkness again, now accompanied by the heavy, pounding thunder that was no longer the boiler but the sound of a whistling mallet striking silk-papered walls, knocking out whiffs of plaster dust. Crouching helplessly on the blue-black woven jungle rug.

(*Come out*)

(*This inhuman place*)
(*and take your medicine!*)
(*makes human monsters.*)

With a gasp that echoed in his own head he jerked himself out of the darkness. Hands were on him and at first he shrank back, thinking that the dark thing in the Overlook of Tony's world had somehow followed him back into the world of real things – and then Dr Edmonds was saying: 'You're all right, Danny. You're all right. Everything is fine.'

Danny recognized the doctor, then his surroundings in the office. He began to shudder helplessly. Edmonds held him.

When the reaction began to subside, Edmonds asked, 'You said something about monsters, Danny – what was it?'

'This inhuman place,' he said gutturally. 'Tony told me . . . this inhuman place . . . makes . . . makes . . .' He shook his head. 'Can't remember.'

'Try!'

'I can't.'

'Did Tony come?'

'Yes.'

'What did he show you?'

'Dark. Pounding. I don't remember.'

'Where were you?'

'*Leave me alone! I don't remember! Leave me alone!*' He began to sob helplessly in fear and frustration. It was all gone, dissolved into a sticky mess like a wet bundle of paper, the memory unreadable.

Edmonds went to the water cooler and got him a paper cup of water. Danny drank it and Edmonds got him another one.

'Better?'

'Yes.'

'Danny, I don't want to badger you . . . tease you about this, I mean. But can you remember anything about *before* Tony came?'

'My mommy,' Danny said slowly. 'She's worried about me.'

'Mothers always are, guy.'

'No . . . she had a sister that died when she was a little girl. Aileen. She was thinking about how Aileen got hit by a car and that made her worried about me. I don't remember anything else.'

Edmonds was looking at him sharply. 'Just now she was thinking that? Out in the waiting room?'

'Yes, sir.'

'Danny, how would you know that?'

'I don't know,' Danny said wanly. 'The shining, I guess.'

'The what?'

Danny shook his head very slowly. 'I'm awful tired. Can't I go see my mommy and daddy? I don't want to answer any more questions. I'm tired. And my stomach hurts.'

'Are you going to throw up?'

'No, sir. I just want to go see my mommy and daddy.'

'Okay, Dan.' Edmonds stood up. 'You go on out and see them for a minute, then send them in so I can talk to them. Okay?'

'Yes, sir.'

'There are books out there to look at. You like books, don't you?'

'Yes, sir,' Danny said dutifully.

'You're a good boy, Danny.'

Danny gave him a faint smile.

★★★

'I can't find a thing wrong with him,' Dr Edmonds said to the Torrances. 'Not physically. Mentally, he's bright and rather too imaginative. It happens. Children have to grow into their imaginations like a pair of oversized shoes. Danny's is still way too big for him, ever had his IQ tested?'

'I don't believe in them,' Jack said. 'They strait-jacket the expectations of both parents and teachers.'

Dr Edmonds nodded. 'That may be. But if you did test him, I think you'd find he's right off the scale for his age group. His verbal ability, for a boy who is five going on six, is amazing.'

'We don't talk down to him,' Jack said with a trace of pride.

'I doubt if you've ever had to in order to make yourself understood.' Edmonds paused, fiddling with a pen. 'He went into a trance while I was with him. At my request. Exactly as you described him in the bathroom last night. All his muscles went lax, his body slumped, his eyeballs rotated outward. Textbook autohypnosis. I was amazed. I still am.'

The Torrances sat forward. 'What happened?' Wendy asked tensely, and Edmonds carefully related Danny's trance, the muttered phrase from which Edmonds had only been able to pluck the word 'monsters', the 'dark', the 'pounding'. The aftermath of tears, near-hysteria, and nervous stomach.

'Tony again,' Jack said.

'What does it mean?' Wendy asked. 'Have you any idea?'

'A few. You might not like them.'

'Go ahead anyway,' Jack told him.

'From what Danny told me, his "invisible friend" was truly a friend until you folks moved out here from New England. Tony has only become a threatening figure since that move. The pleasant interludes have become nightmarish, even more frightening to your son because he can't remember exactly what the nightmares are about. That's common enough. We all remember our pleasant dreams more clearly than the scary ones. There seems to be a buffer somewhere between the conscious and the subconscious, and one hell of a bluenose lives in there. This censor only lets through a small amount, and often what does come through is only symbolic. That's oversimplified Freud, but it does pretty much describe what we know of the mind's interaction with itself.'

'You think moving has upset Danny that badly?' Wendy asked.

'It may have, if the move took place under traumatic circumstances,' Edmonds said. 'Did it?'

Wendy and Jack exchanged a glance.

'I was teaching at a prep school,' Jack said slowly. 'I lost my job.'

'I see,' Edmonds said. He put the pen he had been playing with firmly back in its holder. 'There's more here, I'm afraid. It may be painful to you. Your son seems to believe you two have seriously contemplated divorce. He spoke of it in an off-hand way, but only because he believes you are no longer considering it.'

Jack's mouth dropped open, and Wendy recoiled as if slapped. The blood drained from her face.

'We never even discussed it!' she said. 'Not in front of him, not even in front of each other! We—'

'I think it's best if you understand everything, Doctor,' Jack said. 'Shortly after Danny was born, I became an alcoholic. I'd had a drinking problem all the way through college, it subsided a little after Wendy and I met, cropped up worse than ever after Danny was born and the writing I consider to be my real work was going badly. When Danny was three and a half, he spilled some beer on a bunch of papers I was working on . . . papers I was shuffling around, anyway . . . and I . . . well . . . oh shit.' His voice broke, but his eyes remained dry and unflinching. 'It sounds so goddamn beastly said out loud. I broke his arm turning him around to spank him. Three months later I gave up drinking. I haven't touched it since.'

'I see,' Edmonds said neutrally. 'I knew the arm had been broken, of course. It was set well.' He pushed back from his desk a little and crossed his legs. 'If I may be frank, it's obvious that he's been in no way abused since then. Other than the stings, there's nothing on him but the normal bruises and scabs that any kid has in abundance.'

'Of course not,' Wendy said hotly. 'Jack didn't mean—'

'No, Wendy,' Jack said. 'I meant to do it. I guess someplace inside I really did mean to do that to him. Or something even worse.' He looked back at Edmonds again. 'You know something, Doctor? This is the first time the word divorce has been mentioned between us. And alcoholism. And child-beating. Three firsts in five minutes.'

'That may be at the root of the problem,' Edmonds said. 'I am not a psychiatrist. If you want Danny to see a child psychiatrist, I can recommend a good one who works out of the Mission Ridge Medical Center in Boulder. But I am fairly confident of my diagnosis. Danny is an intelligent, imaginative, perceptive boy. I don't believe he would have been as upset by your marital problems as you believed. Small children are great accepters. They don't understand shame, or the need to hide things.'

Jack was studying his hands. Wendy took one of them and squeezed it.

'But he sensed the things that were wrong. Chief among them from his point of view was not the broken arm but the broken – or breaking – link between you two. He mentioned divorce to me, but not the broken arm. When my nurse mentioned the set to him, he simply shrugged it off. It was no pressure thing. "It happened a long time ago" is what I think he said.'

'That kid,' Jack muttered. His jaws were clamped together, the muscles in the cheeks standing out. 'We don't deserve him.'

'You have him, all the same,' Edmonds said dryly. 'At any rate, he retires into a fantasy world from time to time. Nothing unusual about that; lots of kids do. As I recall, I had my own invisible friend when I was Danny's age, a talking rooster named Chug-Chug. Of course no one could see Chug-Chug but me. I had two older brothers who often left me behind, and in such a situation Chug-Chug came in mighty handy. And of course you two must understand why Danny's invisible friend is named Tony instead of Mike or Hal or Dutch.'

'Yes,' Wendy said.

'Have you ever pointed it out to him?'

'No,' Jack said. 'Should we?'

'Why bother? Let him realize it in his own time, by his own logic. You see, Danny's fantasies were considerably deeper than those that grow around the ordinary invisible friend syndrome, but he felt he needed Tony that much more. Tony would come and show him pleasant things. Sometimes amazing things. Always good things. Once Tony showed him where Daddy's lost trunk was . . . under the stairs. Another time Tony showed him that Mommy and Daddy were going to take him to an amusement park for his birthday—'

'At Great Barrington!' Wendy cried. 'But how could he *know* those things? It's eerie, the things he comes out with sometimes. Almost as if—'

'He had second sight?' Edmonds asked, smiling.

'He was born with a caul,' Wendy said weakly.

Edmonds's smile became a good, hearty laugh. Jack and

Wendy exchanged a glance and then also smiled, both of them amazed at how easy it was. Danny's occasional 'lucky guesses' about things was something else they had not discussed much.

'Next you'll be telling me he can levitate,' Edmonds said, still smiling. 'No, no, no, I'm afraid not. It's not extrasensory but good old human perception, which in Danny's case is unusually keen. Mr Torrance, he knew your trunk was under the stairs because you had looked everywhere else. Process of elimination, what? It's so simple Ellery Queen would laugh at it. Sooner or later you would have thought of it yourself.

'As for the amusement park at Great Barrington, whose idea was that originally? Yours or his?'

'His, of course,' Wendy said. 'They advertised on all the morning children's programs. He was wild to go. But the thing is, Doctor, we couldn't afford to take him. And we had told him so.'

'Then a men's magazine I'd sold a story to back in 1971 sent a check for fifty dollars,' Jack said. 'They were reprinting the story in an annual, or something. So we decided to spend it on Danny.'

Edmonds shrugged. 'Wish fulfillment plus a lucky co-incidence.'

'Goddammit, I bet that's just right,' Jack said.

Edmonds smiled a little. 'And Danny himself told me that Tony often showed him things that never occurred. Visions based on faulty perception, that's all. Danny is doing subconsciously what these so-called mystics and mind readers do quite consciously and cynically. I admire him for it. If life doesn't cause him to retract his antennae, I think he'll be quite a man.'

Wendy nodded – of course she thought Danny would be quite a man – but the doctor's explanation struck her as glib. It tasted more like margarine than butter. Edmonds had not lived with them. He had not been there when Danny found lost buttons, told that maybe the *TV Guide* was under the bed, that he thought he better wear his rubbers to nursery school even though the sun was out . . . and later that day they had walked home under her umbrella through the pouring rain. Edmonds couldn't know of the curious way Danny had of preguessing them both. She would decide to have an unusual evening cup of tea, go out in the kitchen and find her cup out with a tea bag in it. She would remember that the books were due at the library and find them all neatly piled up on the hall table, her library card on top. Or Jack would take it into his head to wax the Volkswagen and find Danny already out there, listening to tinny top-forty music on his crystal radio as he sat on the curb to watch.

Aloud she said, 'Then why the nightmares now? Why did Tony tell him to lock the bathroom door?'

'I believe it's because Tony has outlived his usefulness,' Edmonds said. 'He was born – Tony, not Danny – at a time when you and your husband were straining to keep your marriage together. Your husband was drinking too much. There was the incident of the broken arm. The ominous quiet between you.'

Ominous quiet, yes, that phrase was the real thing, anyway. The stiff, tense meals where the only conversation had been please pass the butter or Danny, eat the rest of your carrots or may I be excused, please. The nights when Jack was gone and she had lain down, dry-eyed, on the couch while Danny watched TV. The mornings when she and Jack had stalked around each other like two angry cats with a quivering, frightened mouse between them. It all rang true;

(dear God, do old scars ever stop hurting?)

horribly, horribly true.

Edmonds resumed, 'But things have changed. You know, schizoid behavior is a pretty common thing in children. It's accepted, because all we adults have this unspoken agreement that children are lunatics. They have invisible friends. They may go and sit in the closet when they're depressed, withdrawing from the world. They attach talismanic importance to a special blanket, or a teddy bear, or a stuffed tiger. They suck their thumbs. When an adult sees things that aren't there, we consider him ready for the rubber room. When a child says he's seen a troll in his bedroom or a vampire outside the window, we simply smile indulgently. We have a one-sentence explanation that explains the whole range of such phenomena in children —'

'He'll grow out of it,' Jack said.

Edmonds blinked. 'My very words,' he said. 'Yes. Now I would guess that Danny was in a pretty good position to develop a full-fledged psychosis. Unhappy home life, a big imagination, the invisible friend who was so real to him that he nearly became real to you. Instead of "growing out of" his childhood schizophrenia, he might well have grown into it.'

'And become autistic?' Wendy asked. She had read about autism. The word itself frightened her; it sounded like dread and white silence.

'Possible but not necessarily. He might simply have entered Tony's world someday and never come back to what he calls "real things".'

'God,' Jack said.

'But now the basic situation has changed drastically. Mr Torrance no longer drinks. You are in a new place where conditions have forced the three of you into a tighter family unit than ever before – certainly tighter than my own, where my wife and kids may see me for only two or three hours a day. To my mind, he is in the perfect healing situation. And I think the very fact that he is able to differentiate so sharply between Tony's world and "real things" says a lot about the fundamentally healthy state of his mind. He says that you two are no longer considering divorce. Is he as right as I think he is?'

'Yes,' Wendy said, and Jack squeezed her hand tightly, almost painfully. She squeezed back.

Edmonds nodded. 'He really doesn't need Tony anymore. Danny is flushing him out of his system. Tony no longer brings pleasant visions but hostile nightmares that are too frightening for him to remember except fragmentarily. He internalized Tony during a difficult – desperate – life situation, and Tony is not leaving easily. But he *is* leaving. Your son is a little like a junkie kicking the habit.'

He stood up, and the Torrances stood also.

'As I said, I'm not a psychiatrist. If the nightmares are still continuing when your job at the Overlook ends next spring, Mr Torrance, I would strongly urge you to take him to this man in Boulder.'

'I will.'

'Well, let's go out and tell him he can go home,' Edmonds said.

'I want to thank you,' Jack told him painfully. 'I feel better about all this than I have in a very long time.'

'So do I,' Wendy said.

At the door, Edmonds paused and looked at Wendy. 'Do you or did you have a sister, Mrs Torrance? Named Aileen?'

Wendy looked at him, surprised. 'Yes, I did. She was killed outside our home in Somersworth, New Hampshire, when she was six and I was ten. She chased a ball into the street and was struck by a delivery van.'

'Does Danny know that?'

'I don't know. I don't think so.'

'He says you were thinking about her in the waiting room.'

'I was,' Wendy said slowly. 'For the first time in ... oh, I don't know how long.'

'Does the word "redrum" mean anything to either of you?'

Wendy shook her head but Jack said, 'He mentioned that word last night, just before he went to sleep. Red drum.'

'No, *rum*,' Edmonds corrected. 'He was quite emphatic about that. *Rum*. As in the drink. The alcoholic drink.'

'Oh,' Jack said. 'It fits in, doesn't it?' He took his handkerchief out of his back pocket and wiped his lips with it.

'Does the phrase "the shining" mean anything to you?'

This time they both shook their heads.

'Doesn't matter, I guess,' Edmonds said. He opened the door into the waiting room. 'Anybody here named Danny Torrance that would like to go home?'

'Hi, Daddy! Hi, Mommy!' He stood up from the small table where he had been leafing slowly through a copy of *Where the Wild Things Are* and muttering the words he knew aloud.

He ran to Jack, who scooped him up. Wendy ruffled his hair.

Edmonds peered at him. 'If you don't love your mommy and daddy, you can stay with good old Bill.'

'No, sir!' Danny said emphatically. He slung one arm around

Jack's neck, one arm around Wendy's, and looked radiantly happy.

'Okay,' Edmonds said, smiling. He looked at Wendy. 'You call if you have any problems.'

'Yes.'

'I don't think you will,' Edmonds said, smiling.

CHAPTER EIGHTEEN
THE SCRAPBOOK

Jack found the scrapbook on the first of November, while his wife and son were hiking up the rutted old road that ran from behind the roque court to a deserted sawmill two miles further up. The fine weather still held, and all three of them had acquired improbable autumn suntans.

He had gone down in the basement to knock the press down on the boiler and then, on impulse, he had taken the flashlight from the shelf where the plumbing schematics were and decided to look at some of the old papers. He was also looking for good places to set his traps, although he didn't plan to do that for another month – I want them all to be home from vacation, he had told Wendy.

Shining the flashlight ahead of him, he stepped past the elevator shaft (at Wendy's insistence they hadn't used the elevator since they moved in) and through the small stone arch. His nose wrinkled at the smell of rotting paper. Behind him the boiler kicked on with a thundering *whoosh*, making him jump.

He flickered the light around, whistling tunelessly between his teeth. There was a scale-model Andes range down here: dozens of boxes and crates stuffed with papers, most of them white and shapeless with age and damp. Others had broken open and spilled yellowed sheaves of paper onto the stone floor. There were bales of newspaper tied up with hayrope. Some boxes contained what looked like ledgers, and others contained invoices bound with rubber bands. Jack pulled one out and put the flashlight beam on it.

ROCKY MOUNTAIN EXPRESS INC.
To: OVERLOOK HOTEL
From: SIDEY'S WAREHOUSE, 1210 16th Street, Denver, CO.

Via: CANADIAN PACIFIC RR
Contents: 400 CASES DELSEY TOILET TISSUE,
         1 GROSS/CASE

Signed *D E F*
Date *August 24,1954*

Smiling, Jack let the paper drop back into the box.

He flashed the light above it and it speared a hanging light-bulb, almost buried in cobwebs. There was no chain pull.

He stood on tiptoe and tried screwing the bulb in. It lit weakly. He picked up the toilet-paper invoice again and used it to wipe off some cobwebs. The glow didn't brighten much.

Still using the flashlight, he wandered through the boxes and bales of paper, looking for rat spoor. They had been here, but not for quite a long time ... maybe years. He found some droppings that were powdery with age, and several nests of neatly shredded paper that were old and unused.

Jack pulled a newspaper from one of the bundles and glanced down at the headline.

JOHNSON PROMISES ORDERLY TRANSITION
Says Work Begun by JFK Will Go Forward in Coming Year

The paper was the *Rocky Mountain News*, dated December 19, 1963. He dropped it back onto its pile.

He supposed he was fascinated by that commonplace sense of history that anyone can feel glancing through the fresh news of ten or twenty years ago. He found gaps in the piled newspapers and records; nothing from 1937 to 1945, from 1957 to 1960, from 1962 to 1963. Periods when the hotel had been closed, he guessed. When it had been between suckers grabbing for the brass ring.

Ullman's explanations of the Overlook's chequered career still didn't ring quite true to him. It seemed that the Overlook's spectacular location alone should have guaranteed its continuing success. There had always been an American jet-set, even before jets were invented, and it seemed to Jack that the Overlook should have been one of the bases they touched in their migrations. It even sounded right. The Waldorf in May, the

THE SHINING

Bar Harbor House in June and July, the Overlook in August and early September, before moving on to Bermuda, Havana, Rio, wherever. He found a pile of old desk registers and they bore him out. Nelson Rockefeller in 1950. Henry Ford & Fam, in 1927. Jean Harlow in 1930. Clark Gable and Carole Lombard. In 1956 the whole top floor had been taken for a week by 'Darryl F. Zanuck & Party'. The money must have rolled down the corridors and into the cash registers like a twentieth-century Comstock Lode. The management must have been spectacularly bad.

There was history here, all right, and not just in newspaper headlines. It was buried between the entries in these ledgers and account books and room-service chits where you couldn't quite see it. In 1922 Warren G. Harding had ordered a whole salmon at ten o'clock in the evening, and a case of Coors beer. But whom had he been eating and drinking with? Had it been a poker game? A strategy session? What?

Jack glanced at his watch and was surprised to see that forty-five minutes had somehow slipped by since he had come down here. His hands and arms were grimy, and he probably smelled bad. He decided to go up and take a shower before Wendy and Danny got back.

He walked slowly between the mountains of paper, his mind alive and ticking over possibilities in a speedy way that was exhilarating. He hadn't felt this way in years. It suddenly seemed that the book he had semijokingly promised himself might really happen. It might even be right here, buried in these untidy heaps of paper. It could be a work of fiction, or history, or both – a long book exploding out of this central place in a hundred directions.

He stood beneath the cobwebby light, took his handkerchief from his back pocket without thinking, and scrubbed at his lips with it. And that was when he saw the scrapbook.

A pile of five boxes stood on his left like some tottering Pisa. The one on top was stuffed with more invoices and ledgers. Balanced on top of those, keeping its angle of repose for who knew how many years, was a thick scrapbook with white leather covers, its pages bound with two hanks of gold string that had been tied along the binding in gaudy bows.

Curious, he went over and took it down. The top cover was thick with dust. He held it on a plane at lip level, blew the dust off in a cloud, and opened it. As he did so a card fluttered out and he grabbed it in mid-air before it could fall to the stone floor. It was rich and creamy, dominated by a raised engraving of the Overlook with every window alight. The lawn and playground were decorated with glowing Japanese lanterns. It looked almost as though you could step right into it, an Overlook Hotel that had existed thirty years ago.

Horace M. Derwent Requests
The Pleasure of Your Company
At a Masked Ball to Celebrate
The Grand Opening of

THE OVERLOOK HOTEL

Dinner Will Be Served At 8 P.M.
Unmasking And Dancing At Midnight
August 29, 1945   *RSVP*

Dinner at eight! Unmasking at midnight!

He could almost see them in the dining room, the richest men in America and their women. Tuxedos and glimmering starched shirts; evening gowns; the band playing; gleaming high-heeled pumps. The clink of glasses, the jocund pop of champagne corks. The war was over, or almost over. The future lay ahead, clean and shining. America was the colossus of the world and at last she knew it and accepted it.

And later, at midnight, Derwent himself crying: 'Unmask! Unmask!' The masks coming off and . . .

(*The Red Death held sway over all!*)

He frowned. What left field had that come out of? That was Poe, the Great American Hack. And surely the Overlook – this shining, glowing Overlook on the invitation he held in his hands – was the farthest cry from E. A. Poe imaginable.

He put the invitation back and turned to the next page. A paste-up from one of the Denver papers, and scratched beneath it the date: May 15, 1947.

THE SHINING

POSH MOUNTAIN RESORT REOPENS WITH
STELLAR GUEST REGISTER

Derwent Says Overlook Will Be 'Showplace of the World'

By David Felton, Features Editor

The Overlook Hotel has been opened and reopened in its thirty-eight-year history, but rarely with such style and dash as that promised by Horace Derwent, the mysterious California millionaire who is the latest owner of the hostelry.

Derwent, who makes no secret of having sunk more than one million dollars into his newest venture – and some say the figure is closer to three million – says that 'The new Overlook will be one of the world's showplaces, the kind of hotel you will remember overnighting in thirty years later.'

When Derwent, who is rumored to have substantial Las Vegas holdings, was asked if his purchase and refurbishing of the Overlook signaled the opening gun in a battle to legalize casino-style gambling in Colorado, the aircraft, movie, munitions, and shipping magnate denied it . . . with a smile. 'The Overlook would be cheapened by gambling,' he said, 'and don't think I'm knocking Vegas! They've got too many of my markets out there for me to do that! I have no interest in lobbying for legalized gambling in Colorado. It would be spitting into the wind.'

When the Overlook opens officially (there was a gigantic and hugely successful party there some time ago when the actual work was finished), the newly painted, papered and decorated rooms will be occupied by a stellar guest list, ranging from Chic designer Corbat Stani to . . .

Smiling bemusedly, Jack turned the page. Now he was looking at a full-page ad from the New York Sunday *Times* travel section. On the page after that a story on Derwent himself, a balding man with eyes that pierced you even from an old newsprint photo. He was wearing rimless spectacles and a forties-style pencil-line mustache that did nothing at all to make him look like Errol Flynn. His face was that of an accountant. It was the eyes that made him look like someone or something else.

Jack skimmed the article rapidly. He knew most of the information from a *Newsweek* story on Derwent the year before. Born poor in St Paul, never finished high school, joined the Navy instead. Rose rapidly, then left in a bitter wrangle over the patent on a new type of propeller that he had designed. In the tug of war between the Navy and an unknown young man named Horace Derwent, Uncle Sam came off the predictable winner. But Uncle Sam had never gotten another patent, and there had been a lot of them.

In the late twenties and early thirties, Derwent turned to aviation. He bought out a bankrupt cropdusting company, turned it into an airmail service, and prospered. More patents followed: a new monoplane wing design, a bomb carriage used on the Flying Fortresses that had rained fire on Hamburg and Dresden and Berlin, a machine gun that was cooled by alcohol, a prototype of the ejection seat later used in United States jets.

And along the line, the accountant who lived in the same skin as the inventor kept piling up the investments. A piddling string of munitions factories in New York and New Jersey. Five textile mills in New England. Chemical factories in the bankrupt and groaning South. At the end of the Depression his wealth had been nothing but a handful of controlling interests, bought at abysmally low prices, salable only at lower prices still. At one point Derwent boasted that he could liquidate completely and realize the price of a three-year-old Chevrolet.

There had been rumors, Jack recalled, that some of the means employed by Derwent to keep his head above water were less than savory. Involvement with bootlegging. Prostitution in the Midwest. Smuggling in the coastal areas of the South where his fertilizer factories were. Finally an association with the nascent western gambling interests.

Probably Derwent's most famous investment was the purchase of the foundering Top Mark Studios, which had not had a hit since their child star, Little Margery Morris, had died of a heroin overdose in 1934. She was fourteen. Little Margery, who had specialized in sweet seven-year-olds who saved marriages and the lives of dogs unjustly accused of killing chickens, had been given the biggest Hollywood funeral in history by Top

Mark – the official story was that Little Margery had contracted a 'wasting disease' while entertaining at a New York orphanage – and some cynics suggested the studio had laid out all that long green because it knew it was burying itself.

Derwent hired a keen businessman and raging sex maniac named Henry Finkel to run Top Mark, and in the two years before Pearl Harbor the studio ground out sixty movies, fifty-five of which glided right into the face of the Hayes Office and spit on its large blue nose. The other five were government training films. The feature films were huge successes. During one of them an unnamed costume designer had jury-rigged a strapless bra for the heroine to appear in during the Grand Ball scene, where she revealed everything except possibly the birthmark just below the cleft of her buttocks. Derwent received credit for this invention as well, and his reputation – or notoriety – grew.

The war had made him rich and he was still rich. Living in Chicago, seldom seen except for Derwent Enterprises board meetings (which he ran with an iron hand), it was rumored that he owned United Air Lines, Las Vegas (where he was known to have controlling interests in four hotel-casinos and some involvement in at least six others), Los Angeles, and the USA itself. Reputed to be a friend of royalty, presidents, and under-world kingpins, it was supposed by many that he was the richest man in the world.

But he had not been able to make a go of the Overlook, Jack thought. He put the scrapbook down for a moment and took the small notebook and mechanical pencil he always kept with him out of his breast pocket. He jotted 'Look into H. Derwent, Sidwndr lbry?' He put the notebook back and picked up the scrapbook again. His face was preoccupied, his eyes distant. He wiped his mouth constantly with his hand as he turned the pages.

He skimmed the material that followed, making a mental note to read it more closely later. Press releases were pasted into many of the pages. So-and-so was expected at the Overlook next week, thus-and-such would be entertaining in the lounge (in Derwent's time it had been the Red-Eye Lounge). Many of the entertainers were Vegas names, and many of the guests were Top Mark executives and stars.

Then, in a clipping marked February 1, 1952:

MILLIONAIRE EXEC TO SELL COLORADO INVESTMENTS
Deal Made with California Investors on Overlook, Other Investments, Derwent Reveals

By Rodney Conklin, Financial Editor

In a terse communique yesterday from the Chicago offices of the monolithic Derwent Enterprises, it was revealed that millionaire (perhaps billionaire) Horace Derwent has sold out of Colorado in a stunning financial power play that will be completed by October 1, 1954. Derwent's investments include natural gas, coal, hydroelectric power, and a land development company called Colorado Sunshine, Inc., which owns or holds options on better than 500,000 acres of Colorado land.

The most famous Derwent holding in Colorado, the Overlook Hotel, has already been sold, Derwent revealed in a rare interview yesterday. The buyer was a California group of investors headed by Charles Grondin, a former director of the California Land Development Corporation. While Derwent refused to discuss price, informed sources . . .

He had sold out everything, lock, stock, and barrel. It wasn't just the Overlook. But somehow . . . somehow . . .

He wiped his lips with his hand and wished he had a drink. This would go better with a drink. He turned more pages.

The California group had opened the hotel for two seasons, and then sold it to a Colorado group called Mountainview Resorts. Mountainview went bankrupt in 1957 amid charges of corruption, nest-feathering, and cheating the stockholders. The president of the company shot himself two days after being subpoenaed to appear before a grand jury.

The hotel had been closed for the rest of the decade. There was a single story about it, a Sunday feature headlined FORMER GRAND HOTEL SINKING INTO DECAY. The accompanying photos wrenched at Jack's heart: the paint on the front porch peeling, the lawn a bald and scabrous mess, windows broken by storms and stones. This would be a part of the book, if he actually wrote it, too – the phoenix going down into the ashes to be reborn. He promised himself he would take care of the place, very good care. It seemed that before today he had never really understood the breadth of his responsibility to the Overlook. It was almost like having a responsibility to history.

In 1961 four writers, two of them Pulitzer Prize winners, had leased the Overlook and reopened it as a writers' school. That had lasted one year. One of the students had gotten drunk in his third-floor room, crashed out of the window somehow, and fell to his death on the cement terrace below. The paper hinted that it might have been suicide.

Any big hotels have got scandals, Watson had said, *just like every big hotel has got a ghost. Why? Hell, people come and go . . .*

Suddenly it seemed that he could almost feel the weight of the Overlook bearing down on him from above, one hundred and ten guest rooms, the storage rooms, kitchen, pantry, freezer, lounge, ballroom, dining room . . .

(*In the room the women come and go*)

(*. . . and the Red Death held sway over all.*)

He rubbed his lips and turned to the next page in the scrapbook. He was in the last third of it now, and for the first time he wondered consciously whose book this was, left atop the highest pile of records in the cellar.

A new headline, this one dated April 10, 1963.

LAS VEGAS GROUP BUYS FAMED COLORADO HOTEL
Scenic Overlook to Become Key Club

Robert T. Leffing, spokesman for a group of investors going under the name of High Country Investments, announced today in Las Vegas that High Country has negotiated a deal for the famous Overlook Hotel, a resort located high in the Rockies. Leffing declined to mention the names of specific investors, but said the hotel would be turned into an exclusive 'key club'. He said that the group he represents hopes to sell memberships to high-echelon executives in American and foreign companies.

High Country also owns hotels in Montana, Wyoming, and Utah.

The Overlook became world-known in the years 1946 to 1952 when it was owned by elusive mega-millionaire Horace Derwent, who . . .

The item on the next page was a mere squib, dated four months later. The Overlook had opened under its new management. Apparently the paper hadn't been able to find out or wasn't interested in who the key holders were, because no name was mentioned but High Country Investments – the most anonymous-sounding company Jack had ever heard except for a chain of bike and appliance shops in western New England that went under the name of Business, Inc.

He turned the page and blinked down at the clipping pasted there.

MILLIONAIRE DERWENT BACK IN COLORADO VIA BACK DOOR?

High Country Exec Revealed to be Charles Grondin

By Rodney Conklin, Financial Editor

The Overlook Hotel, a scenic pleasure palace in the Colorado high country and once the private plaything of millionaire Horace Derwent, is at the center of a financial tangle which is only now beginning to come to light.

On April 10 of last year the hotel was purchased by a Las Vegas firm, High Country Investments, as a key club for wealthy executives of both foreign and domestic breeds. Now informed sources say that High Country is headed by Charles Grondin, 53, who was the head of California Land Development Corp, until 1959, when he resigned to take the position of executive veep in the Chicago home office of Derwent Enterprises.

This has led to speculation that High Country Investments may be controlled by Derwent, who may have acquired the Overlook for the second time, and under decidedly peculiar circumstances.

Grondin, who was indicted and acquitted on charges of

tax evasion in 1960, could not be reached for comment, and Horace Derwent, who guards his own privacy jealously, had no comment when reached by telephone. State Representative Dick Bows of Golden has called for a complete investigation into . . .

That clipping was dated July 27, 1964. The next was a column from a Sunday paper that September. The byline belonged to Josh Brannigar, a muck-raking investigator of the Jack Anderson breed. Jack vaguely recalled that Brannigar had died in 1968 or '69.

MAFIA FREE-ZONE IN COLORADO

By Josh Brannigar

It now seems possible that the newest r&r spot of Organization overlords in the US is located at an out-of-the-way hotel nestled in the center of the Rockies. The Overlook Hotel, a white elephant that has been run lucklessly by almost a dozen different groups and individuals since it first opened its doors in 1910, is now being operated as a security-jacketed 'key club', ostensibly for unwinding businessmen. The question is, what business are the Overlook's key holders *really* in?

The members present during the week of August 16–23 may give us an idea. The list below was obtained by a former employee of High Country Investments, a company first believed to be a dummy company owned by Derwent Enterprises. It now seems more likely that Derwent's interest in High Country (if any) is outweighed by those of several Las Vegas gambling barons. And these same gaming honchos have been linked in the past to both suspected and convicted underworld kingpins.

Present at the Overlook during that sunny week in August were:

Charles Grondin, President of High Country Investments. When it became known in July of this year that he was running the High Country ship it was announced – considerably after the fact – that he had resigned his position in

Derwent Enterprises previously. The silver-maned Grondin, who refused to talk to me for this column, has been tried once and acquitted on tax evasion charges (1960).

Charles 'Baby Charlie' Battaglia, a 60-year-old Vegas impresario (controlling interests in The Greenback and The Lucky Bones on the Strip). Battaglia is a close personal friend of Grondin. His arrest record stretches back to 1932, when he was tried and acquitted in the gangland-style murder of Jack 'Dutchy' Morgan. Federal authorities suspect his involvement in the drug traffic, prostitution, and murder for hire, but 'Baby Charlie' has only been behind bars once, for income tax evasion in 1955–56.

Richard Scarne, the principal stockholder of Fun Time Automatic Machines. Fun Time makes slot machines for the Nevada crowd, pinball machines, and jukeboxes (Melody-Coin) for the rest of the country. He has done time for assault with a deadly weapon (1940), carrying a concealed weapon (1948), and conspiracy to commit tax fraud (1961).

Peter Zeiss, a Miami-based importer, now nearing 70. For the last five years Zeiss has been fighting deportation as an undesirable person. He has been convicted on charges of receiving and concealing stolen property (1958), and conspiracy to commit tax fraud (1954). Charming, distinguished, and courtly, Pete Zeiss is called 'Poppa' by his intimates and has been tried on charges of murder and accessory to murder. A large stockholder to Scarne's Fun Time company, he also has known interests to four Las Vegas casinos.

Vittorio Gienelli, also known as 'Vito the Chopper', tried twice for gangland-style murders, one of them the ax-murder of Boston vice overlord Frank Scoffy. Gienelli has been indicted twenty-three times, tried fourteen times, and convicted only once, for shoplifting in 1940. It has been said that in recent years Gienelli has become a power in the organization's western operation, which is centered in Las Vegas.

Carl 'Jimmy-Ricks' Prashkin, a San Francisco investor, reputed to be the heir apparent of the power Gienelli now wields. Prashkin owns large blocks of stock in Derwent

Enterprises, High Country Investments, Fun Time Automatic Machines, and three Vegas casinos. Prashkin is clean in America, but was indicted in Mexico on fraud charges that were dropped quickly three weeks after they were brought. It has been suggested that Prashkin may be in charge of laundering money skimmed from Vegas casino operations and funneling the big bucks back into the organization's legitimate western operations. And such operations may now include the Overlook Hotel in Colorado.

Other visitors during the current season include . . .

There was more but Jack only skimmed it, constantly wiping his lips with his hand. A banker with Las Vegas connections. Men from New York who were apparently doing more in the Garment District than making clothes. Men reputed to be involved with drugs, vice, robbery, murder.

God, what a story! And they had all been here, right above him, in those empty rooms. Screwing expensive whores on the third floor, maybe. Drinking magnums of champagne. Making deals that would turn over millions of dollars, maybe in the very suite of rooms where Presidents had stayed. There was a story, all right. One hell of a story. A little frantically, he took out his notebook and jotted down another memo to check all of these people out at the library in Denver when the caretaking job was over. Every hotel has its ghost? The Overlook had a whole coven of them. First suicide, then the Mafia, what next?

The next clipping was an angry denial of Brannigar's charges by Charles Grondin. Jack smirked at it.

The clipping on the next page was so large that it had been folded. Jack unfolded it and gasped harshly. The picture there seemed to leap out at him: the wallpaper had been changed since June of 1966, but he knew that window and the view perfectly well. It was the western exposure of the Presidential Suite. Murder came next. The sitting room wall by the door leading into the bedroom was splashed with blood and what could only be white flecks of brain matter. A blank-faced cop was standing over a corpse hidden by a blanket. Jack stared, fascinated, and then his eyes moved up to the headline.

STEPHEN KING

GANGLAND-STYLE SHOOTING AT COLORADO HOTEL
Reputed Crime Overlord Shot at Mountain Key Club
Two Others Dead

SIDEWINDER, COLO (UPI) – Forty miles from this sleepy
Colorado town, a gangland-style execution has occurred in
the heart of the Rocky Mountains. The Overlook Hotel,
purchased three years ago as an exclusive key club by a Las
Vegas firm, was the site of a triple shotgun slaying. Two of the
men were either the companions or bodyguard of Vittorio
Gienelli, also known as 'The Chopper' for his reputed
involvement in a Boston slaying twenty years ago.

Police were summoned by Robert Norman, manager of
the Overlook, who said he heard shots and that some of the
guests reported two men wearing stockings on their faces
and carrying guns had fled down the fire escape and driven
off in a late-model tan convertible.

State Trooper Benjamin Moorer discovered two dead
men, later identified as Victor T. Boorman and Roger
Macassi, both of Las Vegas, outside the door of the Presidential Suite where two American Presidents have stayed. Inside,
Moorer found the body of Gienelli sprawled on the floor.
Gienelli was apparently fleeing his attackers when he was cut
down. Moorer said Gienelli had been shot with heavy-gauge
shotguns at close range.

Charles Grondin, the representative of the company
which now owns the Overlook, could not be reached for . . .

Below the clipping, in heavy strokes of a ball point pen,
someone had written: *They took his balls along with them.* Jack
stared at that for a long time, feeling cold. Whose book was
this?

He turned the page at last, swallowing a click in his throat.
Another column from Josh Brannigar, this one dated early 1967.
He only read the headline: NOTORIOUS HOTEL SOLD FOLLOW-
ING MURDER OF UNDERWORLD FIGURE.

The sheets following that clipping were blank.

(*They took his balls along with them.*)

He flipped back to the beginning, looking for a name or

180

address. Even a room number. Because he felt quite sure that whoever had kept this little book of memories had stayed at the hotel. But there was nothing.

He was getting ready to go through all the clippings, more closely this time, when a voice called down the stairs: 'Jack? Hon?'

He started, almost guiltily, as if he had been drinking secretly and she would smell the fumes on him. Ridiculous. He scrubbed his lips with his hand and called back, 'Yeah, babe. Lookin for rats.'

She was coming down. He heard her on the stairs, then crossing the boiler room. Quickly, without thinking why he might be doing it, he stuffed the scrapbook under a pile of bills and invoices. He stood up as she came through the arch.

'What in the world have you been doing down here? It's almost three o'clock!'

He smiled. 'Is it that late? I got rooting around through all this stuff. Trying to find out where the bodies are buried, I guess.'

The words clanged back viciously in his mind.

She came closer, looking at him, and he unconsciously retreated a step, unable to stop himself. He knew what she was doing. She was trying to smell liquor on him. Perhaps she wasn't even aware of it herself, but he was, and it made him feel both guilty and angry.

'Your mouth is bleeding,' she said in curiously flat tone.

'Huh?' He put his hand to his lips and winced at the thin stinging. His index finger came away bloody. His guilt increased.

'You've been rubbing your mouth again,' she said.

He looked down and shrugged. 'Yeah, I guess I have.'

'It's been hell for you, hasn't it?'

'No, not so bad.'

'Has it gotten any easier?'

He looked up at her and made his feet start moving. Once they were actually in motion it was easier. He crossed to his wife and slipped an arm around her waist. He brushed aside a sheaf of her blond hair and kissed her neck. 'Yes,' he said. 'Where's Danny?'

'Oh, he's around somewhere. It's started to cloud up outside. Hungry?'

He slipped a hand over her taut, jeans-clad bottom with counterfeit lechery. 'Like ze bear, madame.'

'Watch out, slugger. Don't start something you can't finish.'

'Fig-fig, madame?' he asked, still rubbing. 'Dirty peectures? Unnatural positions?' As they went through the arch, he threw one glance back at the box where the scrapbook

(*whose?*)

was hidden. With the light out it was only a shadow. He was relieved that he had gotten Wendy away. His lust became less acted, more natural, as they approached the stairs.

'Maybe,' she said. 'After we get you a sandwich – *yeek*!' She twisted away from him, giggling. 'That tickles!'

'It teekles nozzing like Jock Torrance would like to teekle you, madame.'

'Lay off, Jack. How about a ham and cheese . . . for the first course?'

They went up the stairs together, and Jack didn't look over his shoulder again. But he thought of Watson's words:

Every big hotel has got a ghost. Why? Hell, people come and go . . .

Then Wendy shut the basement door behind them, closing it into darkness.

CHAPTER NINETEEN
OUTSIDE 217

Danny was remembering the words of someone else who had worked at the Overlook during the season:

Her saying she'd seen something in one of the rooms where . . . a bad thing happened. That was in Room 217 and I want you to promise me you won't go in there, Danny . . . steer right clear . . .

It was a perfectly ordinary door, no different from any other door on the first two floors of the hotel. It was dark gray, halfway down a corridor that ran at right angles to the main second-floor hallway. The numbers on the door looked no different from the house numbers on the Boulder apartment building they had lived in. A 2, a 1, and a 7. Big deal. Just below them was a tiny glass circle, a peephole. Danny had tried several of them. From the inside you got a wide fish-eye view of the corridor. From outside you could screw up your eye seven ways to Sunday and still not see a thing. A dirty gyp.

(*Why are you here?*)

After the walk behind the Overlook, he and Mommy had come back and she had fixed him his favorite lunch, a cheese and bologna sandwich plus Campbell's Bean Soup. They ate in Dick's kitchen and talked. The radio was on, getting thin and crackly music from the Estes Park station. The kitchen was his favorite place in the hotel, and he guessed that Mommy and Daddy must feel the same way, because after trying their meals in the dining room for three days or so, they had begun eating in the kitchen by mutual consent, setting up chairs around Dick Hallorann's butcher block, which was almost as big as their dining room table back in Stovington, anyway. The dining room had been too depressing, even with the lights on and the music playing from the tape cassette system in the office. You were still just one of three people sitting at a table surrounded by dozens of other tables, all empty, all covered with those transparent plastic dustcloths. Mommy said it was like having dinner in the middle of a Horace Walpole novel, and Daddy had laughed and agreed. Danny had no idea who Horace Walpole was, but he did know that Mommy's cooking had begun to taste better as soon as they began to eat it in the kitchen. He kept discovering little flashes of Dick Hallorann's personality lying around, and they reassured him like a warm touch.

Mommy had eaten half a sandwich, no soup. She said Daddy must have gone out for a walk of his own since both the VW and the hotel truck were in the parking lot. She said she was tired and might lie down for an hour or so, if he thought he could amuse himself and not get into trouble. Danny told her around a mouthful of cheese and bologna that he thought he could.

'Why don't you go out into the playground?' she asked him. 'I thought you'd love that place, with a sandbox for your trucks and all.'

He swallowed and the food went down his throat in a lump that was dry and hard. 'Maybe I will,' he said, turning to the radio and fiddling with it.

'And all those neat hedge animals,' she said, taking his empty plate. 'Your father's got to get out and trim them pretty soon.'

'Yeah,' he said.

(*Just nasty things . . . once it had to do with those damn hedges clipped to look like animals . . .*)

'If you see your father before I do, tell him I'm lying down.'
'Sure, Mom.'

She put the dirty dishes in the sink and came back over to him. 'Are you happy here, Danny?'

He looked at her guilelessly, a milk mustache on his lip. 'Uh-huh.'

'No more bad dreams?'

'No.' Tony had come to him once, one night while he was lying in bed, calling his name faintly and from far away. Danny had squeezed his eyes tightly shut until Tony had gone.

'You sure?'
'Yes, Mom.'

She seemed satisfied. 'How's your hand?'

He flexed it for her. 'All better.'

She nodded. Jack had taken the nest under the Pyrex bowl, full of frozen wasps, out to the incinerator in back of the equipment shed and burned it. They had seen no more wasps since. He had written to a lawyer in Boulder, enclosing the snaps of Danny's hand, and the lawyer had called back two days ago – that had put Jack in a foul temper all afternoon. The lawyer doubted if the company that had manufactured the bug bomb could be sued successfully because there was only Jack to testify that he had followed directions printed on the package. Jack had asked the lawyer if they couldn't purchase some others and test them for the same defect. Yes, the lawyer said, but the results were highly doubtful even if all the test bombs malfunctioned. He told Jack of a case that involved an extension ladder company and a man who had broken his back. Wendy had commiserated with Jack, but privately she had just been glad that Danny had gotten off as cheaply as he had. It was best to leave lawsuits to people who understood them, and that did not include the Torrances. And they had seen no more wasps since.

'Go and play, doc. Have fun.'

But he hadn't had fun. He had wandered aimlessly around the hotel, poking into the maid's closets and the janitor's rooms, looking for something interesting, not finding it, a small boy padding along a dark blue carpet woven with twisting black lines. He had tried a room door from time to time, but of course they were all locked. The passkey was hanging down in the office, he knew where, but Daddy had told him he shouldn't touch that. And he didn't want to. Did he?

(*Why are you here?*)

There was nothing aimless about it after all. He had been drawn to room 217 by a morbid kind of curiosity. He remembered a story Daddy had read to him once when he was drunk. That had been a long time ago, but the story was just as vivid now as when Daddy had read it to him. Mommy had scolded Daddy and asked what he was doing, reading a three-year-old baby something so horrible. The name of the story was *Bluebeard*. That was clear in his mind too, because he had thought at first Daddy was saying *Bluebird*, and there were no bluebirds in the story, or birds of any kind for that matter. Actually the story was about *Bluebeard*'s wife, a pretty lady that had corn-colored hair like Mommy. After *Bluebeard* married her, they lived in a big and ominous castle that was not unlike the Overlook. And every day *Bluebeard* went off to work and every day he would tell his pretty little wife not to look in a certain room, although the key to that room was hanging right on a hook, just like the passkey was hanging on the office wall downstairs. *Bluebeard*'s wife had gotten more and more curious about the locked room. She tried to peep through the keyhole the way Danny had tried to look through Room 217's peephole with similar unsatisfying results. There was even a picture of her getting down on her knees and trying to look *under* the door, but the crack wasn't wide enough. The door swung wide and . . .

The old fairy tale book had depicted her discovery in ghastly, loving detail. The image was burned on Danny's mind. The severed heads of *Bluebeard*'s seven previous wives were in the room, each one on its own pedestal, the eyes turned up to whites, the mouths unhinged and gaping in silent screams. They were somehow balanced on necks ragged from the broadsword's decapitating swing, and there was blood running down the pedestals.

Terrified, she had turned to flee from the room and the castle, only to discover *Bluebeard* standing in the doorway, his terrible eyes blazing. 'I told you not to enter this room,' *Bluebeard* said, unsheathing his sword. 'Alas, in your curiosity you are like the other seven, and though I loved you best of all, your ending shall be as was theirs. Prepare to die, wretched woman!'

It seemed vaguely to Danny that the story had had a happy ending, but that had paled to insignificance beside the two dominant images: the taunting, maddening locked door with some great secret behind it, and the grisly secret itself, repeated more than half a dozen times. The locked door and behind it the heads, the severed heads.

His hand reached out and stroked the room's doorknob,

almost furtively. He had no idea how long he had been here, standing hypnotized before the bland gray locked door.

(*And maybe three times I've thought I've seen things . . . nasty things . . .*)

But Mr Hallorann – Dick – had also said he didn't think those things could hurt you. They were like scary pictures in a book, that was all. And maybe he wouldn't see anything. On the other hand . . .

He plunged his left hand into his pocket and it came out holding the passkey. It had been there all along, of course.

He held it by the square metal tab on the end which had OFFICE printed on it in Magic Marker. He twirled the key on its chain, watching it go around and around. After several minutes of this he stopped and slipped the passkey into the lock. It slid in smoothly, with no hitch, as if it had wanted to be there all along.

(*I've thought I've seen things . . . nasty things . . . promise me you won't go in there.*)

(*I promise.*)

And a promise was, of course, very important. Still, his curiosity itched at him as maddeningly as poison ivy in a place you aren't supposed to scratch. But it was a dreadful kind of curiosity, the kind that makes you peek through your fingers during the scariest parts of a scary movie. What was beyond that door would be no movie.

(*I don't think those things can hurt you . . . like scary pictures in a book . . .*)

Suddenly he reached out with his left hand, not sure of what it was going to do until it had removed the passkey and stuffed it back into his pocket. He stared at the door a moment longer, blue-gray eyes wide, then turned quickly and walked back down the corridor toward the main hallway that ran at right angles to the corridor he was in.

Something made him pause there and he wasn't sure what for a moment. Then he remembered that directly around this corner, on the way back to the stairs, there was one of those old-fashioned fire extinguishers curled up against the wall. Curled there like a dozing snake.

They weren't chemical-type extinguishers at all, Daddy said, although there were several of those in the kitchen. These were the forerunner of the modern sprinkler system. The long canvas hoses hooked directly into the Overlook's plumbing system, and by turning a single valve you could become a one-man fire department. Daddy said that the chemical extinguishers, which sprayed foam or CO_2 were much better. The chemicals smothered fires, took away the oxygen they needed to burn, while a high-pressure spray might just spread the flames around. Daddy said that Mr Ullman should replace the old-fashioned hoses right along with the old-fashioned broiler, but Mr Ullman would probably do neither because he was a CHEAP PRICK. Danny knew that this was one of the worst epithets his father could summon. It was applied to certain doctors, dentists, and appliance repairmen, and also to the head of his English Department at Stovington, who had disallowed some of Daddy's book orders because he said the books would put them over budget. 'Over budget, hell,' he had fumed to Wendy – Danny had been listening from his bedroom where he was supposed to be asleep. 'He's just saving the last five hundred bucks for himself, the CHEAP PRICK.'

Danny looked around the corner.

The extinguisher was there, a flat hose folded back a dozen times on itself, the red tank attached to the wall. Above it was an ax in a glass case like a museum exhibit, with white words printed on a red background: IN CASE OF EMERGENCY, BREAK GLASS. Danny could read the word EMERGENCY, which was also the name of one of his favorite TV shows, but was unsure of the rest. But he didn't like the way the word was used in connection with that long flat hose. EMERGENCY was fire explosions, car crashes, hospitals, sometimes death. And he didn't like the way that hose hung there so blandly on the wall. When he was alone, he always skittered past these extinguishers as fast as he could. No particular reason. It just felt better to go faster. It felt safer.

Now, heart thumping loudly in his chest, he came around the corner and looked down the hall past the extinguisher to the stairs. Mommy was down there, sleeping. And if Daddy was back from his walk, he would probably be sitting in the kitchen, eating a sandwich and reading a book. He would just walk right past that old extinguisher and go downstairs.

He started toward it, moving closer to the far wall until his right arm was brushing the expensive silk paper. Twenty steps away. Fifteen. A dozen.

When he was ten steps away, the brass nozzle suddenly rolled off the fat loop it had been lying

(sleeping?)

on and fell to the hall carpet with a dull thump. It lay there, the dark bore of its muzzle pointing at Danny. He stopped immediately, his shoulders twitching forward with the suddenness of his scare. His blood thumped thickly in his ears and temples. His mouth had gone dry and sour, his hands curled into fists. Yet the nozzle of the hose only lay there, its brass casing glowing mellowly, a loop of flat canvas leading back up to the redpainted frame bolted to the wall.

So it had fallen off, so what? It was only a fire extinguisher, nothing else. It was stupid to think that it looked like some poison snake from 'Wide World of Animals' that had heard him and woken up. Even if the stitched canvas did look a little bit like scales. He would just step over it and go down the hall to the stairs, walking a little bit fast, maybe, to make sure it didn't snap out after him and curl around his foot . . .

He wiped his lips with his left hand, in unconscious imitation of his father, and took a step forward. No movement from the hose. Another step. Nothing. There, see how stupid you are? You got all worked up thinking about that dumb room and that dumb *Bluebeard* story and that hose was probably ready to fall off for the last five years. That's all.

Danny stared at the hose on the floor and thought of wasps.

Eight steps away, the nozzle of the hose gleamed peacefully at him from the rug as if to say: *Don't worry. I'm just a hose, that's all. And even if that isn't all, what I do to you won't be much worse than a bee sting. Or a wasp sting. What would I want to do to a nice little boy like you . . . except bite . . . and bite . . . and bite?*

Danny took another step, and another. His breath was dry and harsh in his throat. Panic was close now. He began to wish the hose *would* move, then at last he would know, he would be sure. He took another step and now he was within striking distance. But it's not going to *strike* at you, he thought hysterically. How can it *strike* at you, *bite* at you, when it's just a hose?

Maybe it's full of wasps.

His internal temperature plummeted to ten below zero. He stared at the black bore in the center of the nozzle, nearly hypnotized. Maybe it *was* full of wasps, secret wasps, their brown bodies bloated with poison, so full of autumn poison that it dripped from their stingers in clear drops of fluid.

Suddenly he knew that he was nearly frozen with terror, if he did not make his feet go now, they would become locked to the carpet and he would stay here, staring at the black hole in the center of the brass nozzle like a bird staring at a snake, he would stay here until his daddy found him and then what would happen?

With a high moan, he made himself run. As he reached the hose some trick of the light made the nozzle seem to move, to revolve as if to strike, and he leaped high in the air above it; in his panicky state it seemed that his legs pushed him nearly all the way to the ceiling, that he could feel the stiff back hairs that formed his cowlick brushing the hallway's plaster ceiling, although later he knew that couldn't have been so.

He came down on the other side of the hose and ran, and suddenly he heard it behind him, coming for him, the soft dry whicker of that brass snake's head as it slithered rapidly along the carpet after him like a rattlesnake moving swiftly through a dry field of grass. It was coming for him, and suddenly the stairs seemed very far away; they seemed to retreat a running step into the distance for each running step he took toward them.

Daddy! he tried to scream, but his closed throat would not allow a word to pass. He was on his own. Behind him the sound grew louder, the dry sliding sound of the snake, slipping swiftly over the carpet's dry shackles. At his heels now, perhaps rising up with clear poison dribbling from its brass snout.

Danny reached the stairs and had to pinwheel his arms crazily for balance. For one moment it seemed sure that he would cartwheel over and go head-for-heels to the bottom.

He threw a glance back over his shoulder.

The hose had not moved. It lay as it had lain, one loop off the frame, the brass nozzle pointing disinterestedly away from him. You see, stupid? he berated himself. You made it all up, scaredycat. It was all your imagination, scaredy-cat, scaredy-cat.

He clung to the stairway railing, his legs trembling in reaction.

(*It never chased you*)

his mind told him, and seized on that thought, and played it back.

(*never chased you, never chased you, never did, never did*)

It was nothing to be afraid of. Why, he could go back and put that hose right into its frame, if he wanted to. He could, but he didn't think he would. Because what if it had chased him and had gone back when it saw that it couldn't . . . quite . . . catch him?

The hose lay on the carpet, almost seeming to ask him if he would like to come back and try again.

Panting, Danny ran downstairs.

CHAPTER TWENTY
TALKING TO MR ULLMAN

The Sidewinder Public Library was a small, retiring building one block down from the town's business area. It was a modest, vine-covered building, and the wide concrete walk up to the door was lined with the corpses of last summer's flowers. On the lawn was a large bronze statue of a Civil War general Jack had never heard of, although he had been something of a Civil War buff in his teenage years.

The newspaper files were kept downstairs. They consisted of the Sidewinder *Gazette* that had gone bust in 1963, the Estes Park daily, and the Boulder *Camera*. No Denver papers at all.

Sighing, Jack settled for the *Camera*.

When the files reached 1965, the actual newspapers were replaced by spools of microfilm ('A federal grant,' the librarian told him brightly. 'We hope to do 1958 to '64 when the next check comes through, but they're so slow, aren't they? You will be careful, won't you? I just know you will. Call if you need me.'). The only reading machine had a lens that had somehow gotten warped, and by the time Wendy put her hand on his shoulder some forty-five minutes after he had switched from the actual papers, he had a juicy thumper of a headache.

'Danny's in the park,' she said, 'but I don't want him outside too long. How much longer do you think you'll be?'

'Ten minutes,' he said. Actually he had traced down the last of the Overlook's fascinating history – the years between the gangland shooting and the takeover by Stuart Ullman & Co. But he felt the same reticence about telling Wendy.

'What are you up to, anyway?' she asked. She ruffled his hair as she said it, but her voice was only half-teasing.

'Looking up some old Overlook history,' he said.

'Any particular reason?'

'No.

(and why the hell are you so interested anyway?)

just curiosity.'

'Find anything interesting?'

'Not much,' he said, having to strive to keep his voice pleasant now. She was prying, just the way she had always pried and poked at him when they had been at Stovington and Danny was still a crib-infant. *Where are you going, Jack? When will you be back? How much money do you have with you? Are you going to take the car? Is Al going to be with you? Will one of you stay sober?* On and on. She had, pardon the expression, driven him to drink. Maybe that hadn't been the only reason, but by Christ let's tell the truth here and admit it was one of them. Nag and nag and nag until you wanted to clout her one just to shut her up and stop the

(Where? When? How? Are you? Will you?)

endless flow of questions. It could give you a real

(headache? hangover?)

headache. The reader. The damned reader with its distorted print. That was why he had such a cunt of a headache.

'Jack, are you all right? You look pale—'

He snapped his head away from her fingers. '*I am fine!*'

She recoiled from his hot eyes and tried on a smile that was a size too small. 'Well . . . if you are . . . I'll just go and wait in the park with Danny . . .' She was starting away now, her smile dissolving into a bewildered expression of hurt.

He called to her: 'Wendy?'

She looked back from the foot of the stairs. 'What, Jack?'

He got up and went over to her. 'I'm sorry, babe. I guess I'm really not all right. That machine . . . the lens is distorted. I've got a really bad headache. Got any aspirin?'

'Sure.' She pawed in her purse and came up with a tin of Anacin. 'You keep them.'

He took the tin. 'No Excedrin?' He saw the small recoil on her face and understood. It had been a bitter sort of joke between them at first, before the drinking had gotten too bad for jokes. He had claimed that Excedrin was the only non-prescription drug ever invented that could stop a hangover dead in its tracks.

Absolutely the only one. He had begun to think of his morning-after thumpers as Excedrin Headache Number Vat 69.

'No Excedrin,' she said. 'Sorry.'

'That's okay,' he said, 'these'll do just fine.' But of course they wouldn't, and she should have known it, too. At times she could be the stupidest bitch . . .

'Want some water?' she asked brightly.

(*No I just want you to GET THE FUCK OUT OF HERE!*)

'I'll get some at the drinking fountain when I go up. Thanks.'

'Okay.' She started up the stairs, good legs moving gracefully under a short tan wool skirt. 'We'll be in the park.'

'Right.' He slipped the tin of Anacin absently into his pocket, went back to the reader, and turned it off. When he was sure she was gone, he went upstairs himself. God, but it was a lousy headache. If you were going to have a vise-gripper like this one, you ought to at least be allowed the pleasure of a few drinks to balance it off.

He tried to put the thought from his mind, more ill tempered than ever. He went to the main desk, fingering a matchbook cover with a telephone number on it.

'Ma'am, do you have a pay telephone?'

'No, sir, but you can use mine if it's local.'

'It's long-distance, sorry.'

'Well then, I guess the drugstore would be your best bet. They have a booth.'

'Thanks.'

He went out and down the walk, past the anonymous Civil War general. He began to walk toward the business block, hands stuffed in his pockets, head thudding like a leaden bell. The sky was also leaden; it was November 7, and with the new month the weather had become threatening. There had been a number of snow flurries. There had been snow in October too, but that had melted. The new flurries had stayed, a light frosting over everything – it sparkled in the sunlight like fine crystal. But there had been no sunlight today, and even as he reached the drugstore it began to spit snow again.

The phone booth was at the back of the building, and he was halfway down an aisle of patent medicines, jingling his change in his pocket, when his eyes fell on the white boxes with their green print. He took one of them to the cashier, paid, and went back to the telephone booth. He pulled the door closed, put his change and matchbook cover on the counter, and dialed 0.

'Your call, please?'

'Fort Lauderdale, Florida, operator.' He gave her the number there and the number in the booth. When she told him it would be a dollar ninety for the first three minutes, he dropped eight quarters into the slot, wincing each time the bell bonged in his ear.

Then, left in limbo with only the faraway clickings and gab-blings of connection-making, he took the green bottle of Exced-rin out of its box, pried up the white cap, and dropped the wad of cotton batting to the floor of the booth. Cradling the phone receiver between his ear and shoulder, he shook out three of the white tablets and lined them up on the counter beside his remaining change. He recapped the bottle and put it in his pocket.

At the other end, the phone was picked up on the first ring.

'Surf-Sand Resort, how may we help you?' the perky female voice asked.

'I'd like to speak with the manager, please.'

'Do you mean Mr Trent or—'

'I mean Mr Ullman.'

'I believe Mr Ullman is busy, but if you would like me to check—'

'I would. Tell him it's Jack Torrance calling from Colorado.'

'One moment, please.' She put him on hold.

Jack's dislike for that cheap, self-important little prick Ullman came flooding back. He took one of the Excedrins from the counter, regarded it for a moment, then put it into his mouth and began to chew it slowly and with relish. The taste flooded back like memory, making his saliva squirt in mingled pleasure and unhappiness. A dry, bitter taste, but a compelling one. He swallowed with a grimace. Chewing aspirin had been a habit with him in his drinking days; he hadn't done it at all since then. But when your headache was bad enough, a hangover headache or one like this one, chewing them seemed to make them get to work quicker. He had read somewhere that chewing aspirin could become addictive. Where had he read that, anyway? Frowning, he tried to think. And then Ullman came on the line.

'Torrance? What's the trouble?'

'No trouble,' he said. 'The boiler's okay and I haven't even gotten around to murdering my wife yet. I'm saving that until after the holidays, when things get dull.'

'Very funny. Why are you calling? I'm a busy—'

'Busy man, yes, I understand that. I'm calling about some things that you didn't tell me during your history of the Overlook's great and honorable past. Like how Horace Derwent sold it to a bunch of Las Vegas sharpies who dealt it through so many dummy corporations that not even the IRS knew who really owned it. About how they waited until the time was right and then turned it into a playground for Mafia bigwigs, and about how it had to be shut down in 1966 when one of them got a little bit dead. Along with his bodyguards, who were standing outside the door to the Presidential Suite. Great place, the Overlook's Presidential Suite. Wilson, Harding, Roosevelt, Nixon, and Vito the Chopper, right?'

There was a moment of surprised silence on the other end of the line, and then Ullman said quietly: 'I don't see how that can have any bearing on your job, Mr Torrance. It—'

'The best part happened after Gienelli was shot, though, don't you think? Two more quick shuffles, now you see it and now you don't, and then the Overlook is suddenly owned by a private citizen, a woman named Sylvia Hunter . . . who just happened to be Sylvia Hunter Derwent from 1942 to 1948.'

'Your three minutes are up,' the operator said. 'Signal when through.'

'My dear Mr Torrance, all of this is public knowledge . . . and ancient history.'

'It formed no part of my knowledge,' Jack said. 'I doubt if many other people know it, either. Not all of it. They remember the Gienelli shooting, maybe, but I doubt if anybody has put together all the wondrous and strange shuffles the Overlook has been through since 1945. And it always seems like Derwent or a Derwent associate comes up with the door prize. What was Sylvia Hunter running up there in '67 and '68, Mr Ullman? It was a whorehouse, wasn't it?'

'*Torrance!*' His shock crackled across two thousand miles of telephone cable without losing a thing.

Smiling, Jack popped another Excedrin into his mouth and chewed it.

'She sold out after a rather well known US senator died of a heart attack up there. There were rumors that he was found naked except for black nylon stockings and a garter belt and a pair of high-heeled pumps. Patent-leather pumps, as a matter of fact.'

'That's a vicious, damnable lie!' Ullman cried.

'Is it?' Jack asked. He was beginning to feel better. The headache was draining away. He took the last Excedrin and chewed it up, enjoying the bitter, powdery taste as the tablet shredded in his mouth.

'It was a very unfortunate occurrence,' Ullman said. 'Now what is the point, Torrance? If you're planning to write some ugly smear article . . . if this is some ill-conceived, stupid black-mail idea . . .'

'Nothing of the sort,' Jack said. 'I called because I didn't think you played square with me. And because—'

'Didn't play *square*? Ullman cried. 'My God, did you think I was going to share a large pile of dirty laundry with the hotel's *caretaker*? Who in heaven's name do you think you are? And how could those old stories possibly affect you anyway? Or do you think there are ghosts parading up and down the halls of the west wing wearing bedsheets and crying "Woe!"?

'No, I don't think there are any ghosts. But you raked up a lot of my personal history before you gave me the job. You had me on the carpet, quizzing me about my ability to take care of your hotel like a little boy in front of the teacher's desk for peeing in the coatroom. You embarrassed me.'

'I just do not believe your cheek, your bloody damned imper-tinence,' Ullman said. He sounded as if he might be choking. 'I'd like to sack you. And perhaps I will.'

'I think Al Shockley might object. Strenuously.'

'And I think you may have finally overestimated Mr Shockley's commitment to you, Mr Torrance.'

For a moment Jack's headache came back in all its thudding glory, and he closed his eyes against the pain. As if from a distance away he heard himself ask: 'Who owns the Overlook now? Is it still Derwent Enterprises? Or are you too smallfry to know?'

'I think that will do, Mr Torrance. You are an employee of the hotel, no different from a busboy or a kitchen pot scrubber. I have no intention of—'

'Okay, I'll write Al,' Jack said. 'He'll know; after all, he's on the Board of Directors. And I might just add a little PS to the effect that—'

'Derwent doesn't own it.'

'What? I couldn't quite make that out.'

'I said Derwent doesn't own it. The stockholders are all Easterners. Your friend Mr Shockley owns the largest block of stock himself, better than thirty-five per cent. You would know better than I if he has any ties to Derwent.'

'Who else?'

'I have no intention of divulging the names of the other stockholders to you, Mr Torrance. I intend to bring this whole matter to the attention of—'

'One other question.'

'I am under no obligation to you.'

'Most of the Overlook's history – savory and unsavory alike – I found in a scrapbook that was in the cellar. Big thing with white leather covers. Gold thread for binding. Do you have any idea whose scrapbook that might be?'

'None at all.'

'Is it possible it could have belonged to Grady? The caretaker who killed himself?'

'Mr Torrance,' Ullman said in tones of deepest frost, 'I am by no means sure that Mr Grady could read, let alone dig out the rotten apples you have been wasting my time with.'

'I'm thinking of writing a book about the Overlook Hotel. I thought if I actually got through it, the owner of the scrapbook would like to have an acknowledgment at the front.'

'I think writing a book about the Overlook would be very unwise,' Ullman said. 'Especially a book done from your . . . uh, point of view.'

'Your opinion doesn't surprise me.' His headache was all gone now. There had been that one flash of pain, and that was all. His mind felt sharp and accurate, all the way down to millimeters. It was the way he usually felt only when the writing was going extremely well or when he had a three-drink buzz on. That was another thing he had forgotten about Excedrin; he didn't know if it worked for others, but for him crunching three tablets was like an instant high.

Now he said: 'What you'd like is some sort of commissioned guidebook that you could hand out free to the guests when they checked in. Something with a lot of glossy photos of the mountains at sunrise and sunset and a lemon-meringue text to go with it. Also a section on the colorful people who have stayed there, of course excluding the really colorful ones like Gienelli and his friends.'

'If I felt I could fire you and be a hundred per cent certain of my own job instead of just ninety-five per cent,' Ullman said in clipped, strangled tones, 'I would fire you right this minute, over the telephone. But since I feel that five per cent of uncertainty, I intend to call Mr Shockley the moment you're off the line . . . which will be soon, or so I devoutly hope.'

Jack said. 'There isn't going to be anything in the book that isn't true, you know. There's no need to dress it up.'

(*Why are you baiting him? Do you want to be fired?*)

'I don't care if Chapter Five is about the Pope of Rome screwing the shade of the Virgin Mary,' Ullman said, his voice rising. 'I want you out of my hotel!'

'*It's not your hotel!*' Jack screamed, and slammed the receiver into its cradle.

He sat on the stool breathing hard, a little scared now, (a little? hell, a lot)

wondering why in the name of God he had called Ullman in the first place.

(*You lost your temper again, Jack.*)

Yes. Yes, he had. No sense trying to deny it. And the hell of it was, he had no idea how much influence that cheap little prick had over Al, no more than he knew how much bullshit Al would take from him in the name of auld lang syne. If Ullman was as good as he claimed to be, and if he gave Al a he-goes-or-I-go ultimatum, might not Al be forced to take it? He closed his eyes and tried to imagine telling Wendy. Guess what, babe? I lost another job. This time I had to go through two thousand miles of Bell Telephone cable to find someone to punch out, but I managed it.

He opened his eyes and wiped his mouth with his handkerchief. He wanted a drink. Hell, he *needed* one. There was a café just down the street, surely he had time for a quick beer on his way up to the park, just one to lay the dust . . .

He clenched his hands together helplessly.

The question recurred: Why had he called Ullman in the first place? The number of the Surf-Sand in Lauderdale had been written in a small notebook by the phone and the CB radio in the office – plumbers' numbers, carpenters, glaziers, electricians, others. Jack had copied it onto the matchbook cover shortly after getting out of bed, the idea of calling Ullman fullblown and gleeful in his mind. But to what purpose? Once, during the drinking phase, Wendy had accused him of desiring his own destruction but not possessing the necessary moral fiber to support a fullblown deathwish. So he manufactured ways in which other people could do it, lopping a piece at a time off himself and their family. Could it be true? Was he afraid somewhere inside that the Overlook might be just what he needed to finish his play and generally collect up his shit and get it together? Was he blowing the whistle on himself? Please God no, don't let it be that way. Please.

He closed his eyes and an image immediately arose on the darkened screen of his inner lids: sticking his hand through that hole in the shingles to pull out the rotted flashing, the sudden needling sting, his own agonized, startled cry in the still and unheeding air: *Oh you goddam fucking son of a bitch . . .*

Replaced with an image two years earlier, himself stumbling into the house at three in the morning, drunk, falling over a table and sprawling full-length on the floor, cursing, waking Wendy up on the couch. Wendy turning on the light, seeing his clothes ripped and smeared from some cloudy parking-lot scuffle that had occurred at a vaguely remembered honky-tonk just over the New Hampshire border hours before, crusted blood under his nose, now looking up at his wife, blinking stupidly in the light like a mole in the sunshine, and Wendy saying dully, *You son of a bitch, you woke Danny up. If you don't care about yourself can't you care a little bit about us? Oh, why do I even bother talking to you?*

The telephone rang, making him jump. He snatched it off the cradle, illogically sure it must be either Ullman or Al Shockley. 'What?' he barked.

'Your overtime, sir. Three dollars and fifty cents.'

'I'll have to break some ones,' he said. 'Wait a minute.'

He put the phone on the shelf, deposited his last six quarters, then went out to the cashier to get more. He performed the transaction automatically, his mind running in a single closed circle like a squirrel on an exercise wheel.

Why had he called Ullman?

Because Ullman had embarrassed him? He had been embarrassed before, and by real masters – the Grand Master, of course, being himself. Simply to crow at the man, expose his hypocrisy? Jack didn't think he was that petty. His mind tried to seize on the scrapbook as a valid reason, but that wouldn't hold water either. The chances of Ullman knowing who the owner was were no more than two in a thousand. At the interview, he had treated the cellar as another country – a nasty under-developed one at that. If he had really wanted to know, he would have called Watson, whose winter number was also in the office notebook. Even Watson would not have been a sure thing, but surer than Ullman.

And telling him about the book idea, that had been another stupid thing. Incredibly stupid. Besides jeopardizing his job, he could be closing off wide channels of information once Ullman called around and told people to beware of New Englanders bearing questions about the Overlook Hotel. He could have done his researches quietly, mailing off polite letters, perhaps even arranging some interviews in the spring . . . and then laughed up his sleeve at Ullman's rage when the book came out and he was safely away – The Masked Author Strikes Again. Instead he had made that damned senseless call, lost his temper, antagonized Ullman, and brought out all of the hotel manager's Little Caesar tendencies. Why? If it wasn't an effort to get himself thrown out of the good job Al had snagged for him, then what was it?

He deposited the rest of the money in the slots and hung up the phone. It really was the senseless kind of thing he might have done if he had been drunk. But he had been sober; dead cold sober.

Walking out of the drugstore he crunched another Excedrin into his mouth, grimacing yet relishing the bitter taste.

On the walk outside he met Wendy and Danny.

'Hey, we were just coming after you,' Wendy said. 'Snowing, don't you know.'

Jack blinked up. 'So it is.' It was snowing hard. Sidewinder's main street was already heavily powdered, the center line obscured. Danny had his head tilted up to the white sky, his mouth open and his tongue out to catch some of the fat flakes drifting down.

'Do you think this is it?' Wendy asked.

Jack shrugged. 'I don't know. I was hoping for another week or two of grace. We still might get it.'

Grace, that was it.

(*I'm sorry, Al. Grace, your mercy. For your mercy. One more chance. I am heartily sorry*—)

How many times, over how many years, had he – a grown man – asked for the mercy of another chance? He was suddenly so sick of himself, so revolted, that he could have groaned aloud.

'How's your headache?' she asked, studying him closely.

He put an arm around her and hugged her tight. 'Better. Come on, you two, let's go home while we still can.'

They walked back to where the hotel truck was slant-parked against the curb, Jack in the middle, his left arm around Wendy's shoulders, his right hand holding Danny's hand. He had called it home for the first time, for better or worse.

THE SHINING

As he got behind the truck's wheel it occurred to him that while he was fascinated by the Overlook, he didn't much like it. He wasn't sure it was good for either his wife or his son or himself. Maybe that was why he had called Ullman.

To be fired while there was still time.

He backed the truck out of its parking space and headed them out of town and up into the mountains.

CHAPTER TWENTY-ONE
NIGHT THOUGHTS

It was ten o'clock. Their quarters were filled with counterfeit sleep.

Jack lay on his side facing the wall, eyes open, listening to Wendy's slow and regular breathing. The taste of dissolved aspirin was still on his tongue, making it feel rough and slightly numb. Al Shockley had called at quarter of six, quarter of eight back East. Wendy had been downstairs with Danny, sitting in front of the lobby fireplace and reading.

'Person to person,' the operator said, 'for Mr Jack Torrance.'

'Speaking.' He had switched the phone to his right hand, had dug his handkerchief out of his back pocket with his left, and had wiped his tender lips with it. Then he lit a cigarette.

Al's voice then, strong in his ear: 'Jacky-boy, what in the name of God are you up to?'

'Hi, Al.' He snuffed the cigarette and groped for the Excedrin bottle.

'What's going on, Jack? I got this *weird* phone call from Stuart Ullman this afternoon. And when Stu Ullman calls long-distance out of his own pocket, you know the shit has hit the fan.'

'Ullman has nothing to worry about, Al. Neither do you.'

'What exactly is the nothing we don't have to worry about? Stu made it sound like a cross between blackmail and a *National Enquirer* feature on the Overlook. Talk to me, boy.'

'I wanted to poke him a little,' Jack said. 'When I came up here to be interviewed, he had to drag out all my dirty laundry. Drinking problem. Lost your last job for racking over a student. Wonder if you're the right man for this. Et cetera. The thing that bugged me was that he was bringing all this up because he loved the goddam hotel so much. The beautiful Overlook. The traditional Overlook. The bloody sacred Overlook. Well,

I found a scrapbook in the basement. Somebody had put together all the less savory aspects of Ullman's cathedral, and it looked to me like a little black mass had been going on after hours.'

'I hope that's metaphorical, Jack.' Al's voice sounded frighteningly cold.

'It is. But I did find out—'

'I know the hotel's history.'

Jack ran a hand through his hair. 'So I called him up and poked him with it. I admit it wasn't very bright, and I sure wouldn't do it again. End of story.'

'Stu says you're planning to do a little dirty-laundry-airing yourself.'

'Stu is an asshole!' he barked into the phone. 'I told him I had an idea of writing about the Overlook, yes. I do. I think this place forms an index of the whole post-World War II American character. That sounds like an inflated claim, stated so baldly . . . I know it does . . . but it's all here, Al! My God, it could be a *great* book. But it's far in the future, I can promise you that, I've got more on my plate right now than I can eat, and—'

'Jack, that's not good enough.'

He found himself gaping at the black receiver of the phone, unable to believe what he had surely heard. 'What? Al, did you say—?'

'I said what I said. How long is far in the future, Jack? For you it may be two years, maybe five. For me it's thirty or forty, because I expect to be associated with the Overlook for a long time. The thought of you doing some sort of a scum-job on my hotel and passing it off as a great piece of American writing, that makes me sick.'

Jack was speechless.

'I tried to help you, Jacky-boy. We went through the war together, and I thought I owed you some help. You remember the war?'

'I remember it,' he muttered, but the coals of resentment had begun to glow around his heart. First Ullman, then Wendy, now Al. What was this? National Let's Pick Jack Torrance Apart

STEPHEN KING

Week? He clamped his lips more tightly together, reached for his cigarettes, and knocked them off onto the floor. Had he ever liked this cheap prick talking to him from his mahogany-lined den in Vermont? Had he really?

'Before you hit that Hatfield kid,' Al was saying, 'I had talked the Board out of letting you go and even had them swung around to considering tenure. You blew that one for yourself. I got you this hotel thing, a nice quiet place for you to get yourself together, finish your play, and wait it out until Harry Effinger and I could convince the rest of those guys that they made a big mistake. Now it looks like you want to chew my arm off on your way to a bigger killing. Is that the way you say thanks to your friends, Jack?'

'No,' he whispered.

He didn't dare say more. His head was throbbing with the hot, acid-etched words that wanted to get out. He tried desperately to think of Danny and Wendy, depending on him, Danny and Wendy sitting peacefully downstairs in front of the fire and working on the first of the second-grade reading primers, thinking everything was A-OK. If he lost this job, what then? Off to California in that tired old VW with the disintegrating fuel pump like a family of dustbowl Okies? He told himself he would get down on his knees and beg Al before he let that happen, but still the words struggled to pour out, and the hand holding the hot wires of his rage felt greased.

'What?' Al said sharply.

'No,' he said. 'That is not the way I treat my friends. And you know it.'

'How do I know it? At the worst, you're planning to smear my hotel by digging up bodies that were decently buried years ago. At the best, you call up my temperamental but extremely competent hotel manager and work him into a frenzy as part of some . . . some stupid kid's game.'

'It was more than a game, Al. It's easier for you. You don't have to take some rich friend's charity. You don't need a friend in court because you *are* the court. The fact that you were one step from a brown-bag lush goes pretty much unmentioned, doesn't it?'

'I suppose it does,' Al said. His voice had dropped a notch and he sounded tired of the whole thing. 'But Jack, Jack . . . I can't help that. I can't change that.'

'I know,' Jack said emptily. 'Am I fired? I guess you better tell me if I am.'

'Not if you'll do two things for me.'

'All right.'

'Hadn't you better hear the conditions before you accept them?'

'No. Give me your deal and I'll take it. There's Wendy and Danny to think about. If you want my balls, I'll send them airmail.'

'Are you sure selfpity is a luxury you can afford, Jack?'

He had closed his eyes and slid an Excedrin between his dry lips. 'At this point I feel it's the only one I can afford. Fire away . . . no pun intended.'

Al was silent for a moment. Then he said: 'First, no more calls to Ullman. Not even if the place burns down. If that happens, call the maintenance man, that guy who swears all the time, you know who I mean . . .'

'Watson.'

'Yes.'

'Okay. Done.'

'Second, you promise me, Jack. Word of honor. No book about a famous Colorado mountain hotel with a history.'

For a moment his rage was so great that he literally could not speak. The blood beat loudly in his ears. It was like getting a call from some twentieth-century Medici prince . . . no portraits of my family with their warts showing, please, or back to the rabble you'll go. I subsidize no pictures but pretty pictures. When you paint the daughter of my good friend and business partner, please omit birthmark or back to the rabble you'll go. Of course we're friends . . . we are both civilized men, aren't we? We've shared bed and board and bottle. We'll always be friends, and the dog collar I have on you will always be ignored by mutual consent, and I'll take good and benevolent care of you. All I ask in return is your soul. Small item. We can even ignore the fact that you've handed it over, the way we ignore the dog collar. Remember, my talented friend, there are Michelangelos begging everywhere in the streets of Rome . . .

'Jack? You there?'

He made a strangled noise that was intended to be the word yes.

Al's voice was firm and very sure of itself. 'I really don't think I'm asking so much, Jack. And there will be other books. You just can't expect me to subsidize you while you . . .'

'All right, agreed.'

'I don't want you to think I'm trying to control your artistic life, Jack. You know me better than that. It's just that—'

'Al?'

'What?'

'Is Derwent still involved with the Overlook? Somehow?'

'I don't see how that can possibly be any concern of yours, Jack.'

'No,' he said distantly. 'I suppose it isn't. Listen, Al, I think I hear Wendy calling me for something. I'll get back to you.'

'Sure thing, Jacky-boy. We'll have a good talk. How are things? Dry?'

(YOU'VE GOT YOUR POUND OF FLESH BLOOD AND ALL NOW CAN'T YOU LEAVE ME ALONE?)

'As a bone.'

'Here too. I'm actually beginning to enjoy sobriety. If—'

'I'll get back, Al. Wendy—'

'Sure. Okay.'

And so he had hung up and that was when the cramps had come, hitting him like lightning bolts, making him curl up in front of the telephone like a penitent, hands over his belly, head throbbing like a monstrous bladder.

The moving wasp, having stung, moves on . . .

It had passed a little when Wendy came upstairs and asked him who had been on the phone.

'Al,' he said. 'He called to ask how things were going. I said they were fine.'

'Jack, you look terrible. Are you sick?'

'Headache's back. I'm going to bed early. No sense trying to write.'

'Can I get you some warm milk?'

He smiled wanly. 'That would be nice.'

And now he lay beside her, feeling her warm and sleeping thigh against his own. Thinking of the conversation with Al, how he had groveled, still made him hot and cold by turns. Someday there would be a reckoning. Someday there would be a book, not the soft and thoughtful thing he had first considered, but a gem-hard work of research, photo section and all, and he would pull apart the entire Overlook history, nasty, incestuous ownership deals and all. He would spread it all out for the reader like a dissected crayfish. And if Al Shockley had connections with the Derwent empire, then God help him.

Strung up like piano wire, he lay staring into the dark, knowing it might be hours yet before he could sleep.

***

Wendy Torrance lay on her back, eyes closed, listening to the sound of her husband's slumber – the long inhale, the brief hold, the slightly guttural exhale. Where did he go when he slept, she wondered. To some amusement park, a Great Barrington of dreams where all the rides were free and there was no wife mother along to tell them they'd had enough hotdogs or that they'd better be going if they wanted to get home by dark? Or was it some fathoms-deep bar where the drinking never stopped and the batwings were always propped open and all the old companions were gathered around the electronic hockey game, glasses in hand, Al Shockley prominent among them with his tie loosened and the top button of his shirt undone? A place where both she and Danny were excluded and the boogie went on endlessly?

Wendy was worried about him, the old, helpless worry that she had hoped was behind her forever in Vermont, as if worry could somehow not cross state lines. She didn't like what the Overlook seemed to be doing to Jack and Danny.

The most frightening thing, vaporous and unmentioned, perhaps unmentionable, was that all of Jack's drinking symptoms had come back, one by one . . . all but the drink itself. The constant wiping of the lips with hand or handkerchief, as if to rid them of excess moisture. Long pauses at the typewriter, more balls of paper in the wastebasket. There had been a bottle of Excedrin on the telephone table tonight after Al had called him, but no water glass. He had been chewing them again. He got irritated over little things. He would unconsciously start snapping his fingers in a nervous rhythm when things got too quiet. Increased profanity. She had begun to worry about his temper, too. It would almost come as a relief if he would lose it, blow off steam, in much the same way that he went down to the basement first thing in the morning and last thing at night to dump the press on the boiler. It would almost be good to see him curse and kick a chair across the room or slam a door. But those things, always an integral part of his temperament, had almost wholly ceased. Yet she had the feeling that Jack was more and more often angry with her or Danny, but was refusing to let it out. The boiler had a pressure gauge: old, cracked, clotted with grease, but still workable. Jack had none. She had never been able to read him very well. Danny could, but Danny wasn't talking.

And the call from Al. At about the same time it had come, Danny had lost all interest in the story they had been reading. He left her to sit by the fire and crossed to the main desk where Jack had constructed a roadway for his matchbox cars and trucks. The Violent Violet Volkswagen was there and Danny had begun to push it rapidly back and forth. Pretending to read her own book but actually looking at Danny over the top of it, she had seen an odd amalgam of the ways she and Jack expressed anxiety. The wiping of the lips. Running both hands nervously through his hair, as she had done while waiting for Jack to come home from his round of the bars. She couldn't believe Al had called just to 'ask how things were going.' If you wanted to shoot the bull, you called Al. When Al called you, that was business.

Later, when she had come back downstairs, she had found Danny curled up by the fire again, reading the second-grade-primer adventures of Joe and Rachel at the circus with their daddy in complete, absorbed attention. The fidgety distraction had completely disappeared. Watching him, she had been struck again by the eerie certainty that Danny knew more and understood more than there was room for in Dr ('Just can me Bill') Edmonds's philosophy.

'Hey, time for bed, doc,' she'd said.

'Yeah, okay.' He marked his place in the book and stood up.

'Wash up and brush your teeth.'

'Okay.'

'Don't forget to use the floss.'

'I won't.'

They stood side by side for a moment, watching the wax and wane of the coals of the fire. Most of the lobby was chilly and drafty, but this circle around the fireplace was magically warm, and hard to leave.

'It was Uncle Al on the phone,' she said casually.

'Oh yeah?' Totally unsurprised.

'I wonder if Uncle Al was mad at Daddy,' she said, still casually.

'Yeah, he sure was,' Danny said, still watching the fire. 'He didn't want Daddy to write the book.'

'What book, Danny?'

'About the hotel.'

The question framed on her lips was one she and Jack had asked Danny a thousand times: *How do you know that?* she hadn't asked him. She didn't want to upset him before bed, or make him aware that they were casually discussing his knowledge of things he had no way of knowing at all. And he *did* know, she was convinced of that. Dr Edmonds's patter about inductive reasoning and subconscious logic was just that: patter. Her sister . . . how had Danny known she was thinking about Aileen in the waiting room that day? And

(*I dreamed Daddy had an accident.*)

She shook her head, as if to clear it. 'Go wash up, doc.'

'Okay.' He ran up the stairs toward their quarters. Frowning, she had gone into the kitchen to warm Jack's milk in a saucepan.

And now, lying wakeful in her bed and listening to her husband's breathing and the wind outside (miraculously, they'd had only another flurry that afternoon; still no heavy snow), she let her mind turn fully to her lovely, troubling son, born with a caul over his face, a simple tissue of membrane that doctors saw perhaps once in every seven hundred births, a tissue that the old wives' tales said betokened the second sight.

She decided that it was time to talk to Danny about the Overlook . . . and high time she tried to get Danny to talk to her. Tomorrow. For sure. The two of them would be going down to the Sidewinder Public Library to see if they could get him some second-grade-level books on an extended loan through the winter, and she would talk to him. And frankly. With that thought she felt a little easier, and at last began to drift toward sleep.

★★★

Danny lay awake in his bedroom, eyes open, left arm encircling his aged and slightly worse-for-wear Pooh (Pooh had lost one shoe-button eye and was oozing stuffing from half a dozen sprung seams), listening to his parents sleep in their bedroom. He felt as if he were standing unwilling guard over them. The nights were the worst of all. He hated the nights and the constant howl of the wind around the west side of the hotel.

His glider floated overhead from a string. On his bureau the VW model, brought up from the roadway setup downstairs, glowed a dimly fluorescent purple. His books were in the book-case, his coloring books on the desk. *A place for everything and everything in its place*, Mommy said. *Then you know where it is when you want it.* But now things had been misplaced. Things were missing. Worse still, things had been *added*, things you couldn't quite see, like in one of those pictures that said CAN YOU SEE THE INDIANS? And if you strained and squinted, you could see some of them – the thing you had taken for a cactus at first glance was really a brave with a knife clamped in his teeth, and there were others hiding in the rocks, and you could even see one of their evil, merciless faces peering through the spokes of a covered wagon wheel. But you could never see all of them, and that was what made you uneasy. Because it was the ones you couldn't see that would sneak up behind you, a tomahawk in one hand and a scalping knife in the other . . .

He shifted uneasily in his bed, his eyes searching out the

comforting glow of the night light. Things were worse here. He knew that much for sure. At first they hadn't been so bad, but little by little . . . his daddy thought about drinking a lot more. Sometimes he was angry at Mommy and didn't know why. He went around wiping his lips with his handkerchief and his eyes were far away and cloudy. Mommy was worried about him and Danny, too. He didn't have to shine into her to know that; it had been in the anxious way she had questioned him on the day the fire hose had seemed to turn into a snake. Mr Hallorann said he thought all mothers could shine a little bit, and she had known on that day that something had happened. But not what.

He had almost told her, but a couple of things had held him back. He knew that the doctor in Sidewinder had dismissed Tony and the things that Tony had showed him as perfectly

(well almost)

normal. His mother might not believe him if he told her about the hose. Worse, she might believe him in the wrong way, might think he was LOSING HIS MARBLES. He understood a little about LOSING YOUR MARBLES, not as much as he did about GETTING A BABY, which his mommy had explained to him the year before at some length, but enough.

Once, at nursery school, his friend Scott had pointed out a boy named Robin Stenger, who was moping around the swings with a face almost long enough to step on. Robin's father taught arithmetic at Daddy's school, and Scott's daddy taught history there. Most of the kids at the nursery school were associated either with Stovington Prep or with the small IBM plant just outside of town. The prep kids chummed in one group, the IBM kids in another. There were cross-friendships, of course, but it was natural enough for the kids whose fathers knew each other to more or less stick together. When there was an adult scandal in one group, it almost always filtered down to the children in some wildly mutated form or other, but it rarely jumped to the other group.

He and Scotty were sitting in the play rocketship when Scotty jerked his thumb at Robin and said: 'You know that kid?'

'Yeah,' Danny said.

Scott leaned forward. 'His dad LOST HIS MARBLES last night. They took him away.'

'Yeah? Just for losing some marbles?'

Scotty looked disgusted. 'He went crazy. You know.' Scott crossed his eyes, flopped out his tongue, and twirled his index fingers in large elliptical orbits around his ears. 'They took him to THE BUGHOUSE.'

'Wow,' Danny said. 'When will they let him come back?'

'Never-never-never,' Scotty said darkly.

In the course of that day and the next, Danny heard that

a.) Mr Stenger had tried to kill everybody in his family, including Robin, with his World War II souvenir pistol;

b.) Mr Stenger ripped the house to pieces while he was STINKO;

c.) Mr Stenger had been discovered eating a bowl of dead bugs and grass like they were cereal and milk and crying while he did it;

d.) Mr Stenger had tried to strangle his wife with a stocking when the Red Sox lost a big ball game.

Finally, too troubled to keep it to himself, he had asked Daddy about Mr Stenger. His daddy had taken him on his lap and had explained that Mr Stenger had been under a great deal of strain, some of it about his family and some about his job and some of it about things that nobody but doctors could understand. He had been having crying fits, and three nights ago he had gotten crying and couldn't stop it and had broken a lot of things in the Stenger home. It wasn't LOSING YOUR MARBLES, Daddy said, it was HAVING A BREAKDOWN, and Mr Stenger wasn't in a BUGHOUSE but in a SANNY-TARIUM. But despite Daddy's careful explanations, Danny was scared. There didn't seem to be any difference at all between LOSING YOUR MARBLES and HAVING A BREAKDOWN, and whether you called it a BUGHOUSE or a SANNY-TARIUM, there were still bars on the windows and they wouldn't let you out if you wanted to go. And his father, quite innocently, had confirmed another of Scotty's phrases unchanged, one that filled Danny with a vague and unformed dread. In the place where Mr Stenger now lived, there were THE MEN IN THE WHITE COATS. They came to get you in a truck with no windows, a truck that was gravestone gray. It rolled up to the curb in front of your house and THE MEN IN THE WHITE COATS got out and took you away from your family and made you live in a room with soft walls. And if you wanted to write home, you had to do it with Crayolas.

'When will they let him come back?' Danny asked his father.

'Just as soon as he's better, doc.'

'But when will that be?' Danny had persisted.

'Dan,' Jack said, 'NO ONE KNOWS.'

And that was the worst of all. It was another way of saying never-never-never. A month later, Robin's mother took him out of nursery school and they moved away from Stovington without Mr Stenger.

That had been over a year ago, after Daddy stopped taking the Bad Stuff but before he had lost his job. Danny still thought about it often. Sometimes when he fell down or bumped his head or had a bellyache, he would begin to cry and the memory would flash over him, accompanied by the fear that he would not be able to stop crying, that he would just go on and on, weeping and wailing, until his daddy went to the phone, dialed it, and said: 'Hello? This is Jack Torrance at 149 Mapleline Way. My son here can't stop crying. Please send THE MEN IN THE WHITE COATS to take him to the SANNY-TARIUM. That's right, he's LOST HIS MARBLES. Thank you.' And the gray truck with no windows would come rolling up to *his* door, they would load him in, still weeping hysterically, and take him away. When would he see his mommy and daddy again? NO ONE KNOWS.

It was this fear that had kept him silent. A year older, he was quite sure that his daddy and mommy wouldn't let him be taken away for thinking a fire hose was a snake, his *rational* mind was sure of that, but still, when he thought of telling them, that old memory rose up like a stone filling his mouth and blocking words. It wasn't like Tony; Tony had always seemed perfectly natural (until the bad dreams, of course), and his parents had also seemed to accept Tony as a more or less natural phenomenon. Things like Tony came from being BRIGHT, which they both assumed he was (the same way they assumed they were BRIGHT), but a fire hose that turned into a snake, or seeing blood and brains on the wall of the Presidential Sweet when no one else could, those things would not be natural. They had already taken him to see a regular doctor. Was it not reasonable to assume that THE MEN IN THE WHITE COATS might come next?

Still he might have told them except he was sure, sooner or later, that they would want to take him away from the hotel. And he wanted desperately to get away from the Overlook. But he also knew that this was his daddy's last chance, that he was here at the Overlook to do more than take care of the place. He was here to work on his papers. To get over losing his job. To love Mommy/Wendy. And until very recently, it had seemed that all those things were happening. It was only lately that Daddy had begun to have trouble. Since he found those papers.

(*This inhuman place makes human monsters.*)

What did that mean? He had prayed to God, but God hadn't told him. And what would Daddy do if he stopped working here? He had tried to find out from Daddy's mind, and had become more and more convinced that Daddy didn't know. The strongest proof had come earlier this evening when Uncle Al had called his daddy up on the phone and said mean things and Daddy didn't dare say anything back because Uncle Al could fire him from this job just the way that Mr Crommert, the Stovington headmaster, and the Board of Directors had fired him from his schoolteaching job. And Daddy was scared to death of that, for him and Mommy as well as himself.

So he didn't dare say anything. He could only watch helplessly and hope that there really weren't any Indians at all, or if there were that they would be content to wait for bigger game and let their little three-wagon train pass unmolested.

But he couldn't believe it, no matter how hard he tried.

Things were worse at the Overlook now.

The snow was coming, and when it did, any poor options he had would be abrogated. And after the snow, what? What then, when they were shut in and at the mercy of whatever might have only been toying with them before?

(*Come out here and take your medicine!*)

What then? REDRUM.

He shivered to his bed and turned over again. He could read more now. Tomorrow maybe he would try to call Tony, he would try to make Tony show him exactly what REDRUM was and if there was any way he could prevent it. He would risk the nightmares. He had to *know*.

Danny was still awake long after his parents' false sleep had become the real thing. He rolled in his bed, twisting the sheets, grappling with a problem years too big for him, awake in the night like a single sentinel on picket. And sometime after midnight, he slept too and then only the wind was awake, prying at the hotel and hooting in its gables under the bright gimlet gaze of the stars.

CHAPTER TWENTY-TWO
IN THE TRUCK

I see a bad moon a-rising.
I see trouble on the way.
I see earthquakes and lightnin'.
I see bad times today.
Don't go 'round tonight,
It's bound to take your life,
There's a bad moon on the rise. *

Someone had added a very old Buick car radio under the hotel truck's dashboard, and now, tinny and choked with static, the distinctive sound of John Fogerty's Creedence Clearwater Revival band came out of the speaker. Wendy and Danny were on their way down to Sidewinder. The day was clear and bright. Danny was turning Jack's orange library card over and over in his hands and seemed cheerful enough, but Wendy thought he looked drawn and tired, as if he hadn't been sleeping enough and was going on nervous energy alone.

The song ended and the disc jockey came on. 'Yeah, that's Creedence. And speakin of bad moon, it looks like it may be risin over the KMTX listening area before long, hard as it is to believe with the beautiful, springlike weather we've enjoyed for the last couple-three days. The KMTX Fearless Forecaster says high pressure will give way by one o'clock this afternoon to a widespread low-pressure area which is just gonna grind to a stop in our KMTX area, up where the air is rare. Temperatures will fall rapidly, and precipitation should start around dusk. Elevations under seven thousand feet, including the metro-Denver

---

area, can expect a mixture of sleet and snow, perhaps freezing on some roads, and nothin but snow up here, cuz. We're lookin at one to three inches below seven thousand and possible accumulations of six to ten inches in Central Colorado and on the Slope. The Highway Advisory Board says that if you're plannin to tour the mountains in your car this afternoon or tonight, you should remember that the chain law will be in effect. And don't go nowhere unless you have to. Remember,' the announcer added jocularly, 'that's how the Donners got into trouble. They just weren't as close to the nearest Seven-Eleven as they thought.'

A Clairol commercial came on, and Wendy reached down and snapped the radio off. 'You mind?'

'Huh-uh, that's okay.' He glanced out at the sky, which was bright blue. 'Guess Daddy picked just the right day to trim those hedge animals, didn't he?'

'I guess he did,' Wendy said.

'Sure doesn't look much like snow, though,' Danny added hopefully.

'Getting cold feet?' Wendy asked. She was still thinking about that crack the disc jockey had made about the Donner Party.

'Nah, I guess not.'

Well, she thought, this is the time. If you're going to bring it up, do it now or forever hold your peace.

'Danny,' she said, making her voice as casual as possible, 'would you be happier if we went away from the Overlook? If we didn't stay the winter?'

Danny looked down at his hands. 'I guess so,' he said. 'Yeah. But it's Daddy's job.'

'Sometimes,' she said carefully, 'I get the idea that Daddy might be happier away from the Overlook, too.' They passed a sign which read SIDEWINDER 18 MI. and then she took the truck cautiously around a hairpin and shifted up into second. She took no chances on these downgrades; they scared her silly.

'Do you really think so?' Danny asked. He looked at her with interest for a moment and then shook his head. 'No, I don't think so.'

'Why not?'

'Because he's worried about us,' Danny said, choosing his words carefully. It was hard to explain, he understood so little of it himself. He found himself harking back to an incident he had told Mr Hallorann about, the big kid looking at department store TV sets and wanting to steal one. That had been distressing, but at least it had been clear what was going on, even to Danny, then little more than an infant. But grownups were always in a turmoil, every possible action muddied over by thoughts of the consequences, by self-doubt, by *selfimage*, by feelings of love and responsibility. Every possible choice seemed to have drawbacks, and sometimes he didn't understand why the drawbacks *were* drawbacks. It was very hard.

'He thinks . . .' Danny began again, and then looked at his mother quickly. She was watching the road, not looking at him, and he felt he could go on.

'He thinks maybe we'll be lonely. And then he thinks that he likes it here and it's a good place for us. He loves us and doesn't want us to be lonely . . . or sad . . . but he thinks even if we are, it might be okay in the LONGRUN. Do you know LONGRUN?'

She nodded. 'Yes, dear. I do.'

'He's worried that if we left he couldn't get another job. That we'd have to beg, or something.'

'Is that all?'

'No, but the rest is all mixed up. Because he's different now.'

'Yes,' she said, almost sighing. The grade eased a little and she shifted cautiously back to third gear.

'I'm not making this up, Mommy. Honest to God.'

'I know that,' she said, and smiled. 'Did Tony tell you?'

'No,' he said. 'I just know. That doctor didn't believe in Tony, did he?'

'Never mind that doctor,' she said. 'I believe in Tony. I don't know what he is or who he is, if he's a part of you that's special or if he comes from . . . somewhere outside, but I do believe in him, Danny. And if you . . . he . . . think we should go, we will. The two of us will go and be together with Daddy again in the spring.'

He looked at her with sharp hope. 'Where? A motel?'

'Hon, we couldn't afford a motel. It would have to be at my mother's.'

The hope in Danny's face died out. 'I know—' he said, and stopped.

'What?'

'Nothing,' he muttered.

She shifted back to second as the grade steepened again. 'No, doc, please don't say that. This talk is something we should have had weeks ago, I think. So please. What is it you know? I won't be mad. I can't be mad, because this is too important. Talk straight to me.'

'I know how you feel about her,' Danny said, and sighed.

'How do I feel?'

'Bad,' Danny said, and then rhyming, singsong, frightening her: 'Bad. Sad. Mad. It's like she wasn't your mommy at all. Like she wanted to eat you.' He looked at her, frightened. 'And I don't like it there. She's always thinking about how she would be better for me than you. And how she could get me away from you. Mommy, I don't want to go there. I'd rather be at the Overlook than there.'

Wendy was shaken. Was it that bad between her and her mother? God, what hell for the boy if it was and he could really read their thoughts for each other. She suddenly felt more naked than naked, as if she had been caught in an obscene act.

'All right,' she said. 'All right, Danny.'

'You're mad at me,' he said in a small, near-to-tears voice.

'No, I'm not. Really I'm not. I'm just sort of shook up.' They were passing a SIDEWINDER 15 MI sign, and Wendy relaxed a little. From here on in the road was better.

'I want to ask you one more question, Danny. I want you to answer it as truthfully as you can. Will you do that?'

'Yes, Mommy,' he said, almost whispering.

'Has your daddy been drinking again?'

'No,' he said, and smothered the two words that rose behind his lips after that simple negative: *Not yet*.

Wendy relaxed a little more. She put a hand on Danny's jeans-clad leg and squeezed it. 'Your daddy has tried very hard,' she said softly. 'Because he loves us. And we love him, don't we?'

He nodded gravely.

Speaking almost to herself she went on: 'He's not a perfect man, but he has tried . . . Danny, he's tried so hard! When he . . . stopped . . . he went through a kind of hell. He's still going through it. I think if it hadn't been for us, he would have just let go. I want to do what's right. And I don't know. Should we go? Stay? It's like a choice between the fat and the fire.'

'I know.'

'Would you do something for me, doc?'

'What?'

'Try to make Tony come. Right now. Ask him if we're safe at the Overlook.'

'I already tried,' Danny said slowly. 'This morning.'

'What happened?' Wendy asked. 'What did he say?'

'He didn't come,' Danny said. 'Tony didn't come.' And he suddenly burst into tears.

'Danny,' she said, alarmed. 'Honey, don't do that. Please —' The truck swerved across the double yellow line and she pulled it back, scared.

'Don't take me to Gramma's,' Danny said through his tears. 'Please, Mommy, I don't want to go there, I want to stay with Daddy —'

'All right,' she said softly. 'All right, that's what we'll do.' She took a Kleenex out of the pocket of her Western-style shirt and handed it to him. 'We'll stay. And everything will be fine. Just fine.'

CHAPTER TWENTY-THREE
IN THE PLAYGROUND

Jack came out onto the porch, tugging the tab of his zipper up under his chin, blinking into the bright air. In his left hand he was holding a battery-powered hedge-clipper. He tugged a fresh handkerchief out of his back pocket with his right hand, swiped his lips with it, and tucked it away. Snow, they had said on the radio. It was hard to believe, even though he could see the clouds building up on the far horizon.

He started down the path to the topiary, switching the hedge-clipper over to the other hand. It wouldn't be a long job, he thought; a little touch-up would do it. The cold nights had surely stunted their growth. The rabbit's ears looked a little fuzzy, and two of the dog's legs had grown fuzzy green bonespurs, but the lions and the buffalo looked fine. Just a little haircut would do the trick, and then let the snow come.

The concrete path ended as abruptly as a diving board. He stepped off it and walked past the drained pool to the gravel path which wound through the hedge sculptures and into the playground itself. He walked over to the rabbit and pushed the button on the handle of the clippers. It hummed into quiet life.

'Hi, Br'er Rabbit,' Jack said. 'How are you today? A little off the top and get some of the extra off your ears? Fine. Say, did you hear the one about the traveling salesman and the old lady with a pet poodle?'

His voice sounded unnatural and stupid in his ears, and he stopped. It occurred to him that he didn't care much for these hedge animals. It had always seemed slightly perverted to him to clip and torture a plain old hedge into something that it wasn't. Along one of the highways in Vermont there had been a hedge billboard on a high slope overlooking the road, advertising some kind of ice cream. Making nature peddle ice cream, that was just wrong. It was grotesque.

(*You weren't hired to philosophize, Torrance.*)

Ah, that was true. So true. He clipped along the rabbit's ears, brushing a small litter of sticks and twigs off onto the grass. The hedge-clipper hummed in that low and rather disgustingly metallic way that all battery-powered appliances seem to have. The sun was brilliant but it held no warmth, and now it wasn't so hard to believe that snow was coming.

Working quickly, knowing that to stop and think when you were at this kind of task usually meant making a mistake, Jack touched up the rabbit's 'face' (up this close it didn't look like a face at all, but he knew that at a distance of twenty paces or so light and shadow would seem to suggest one; that, and the viewer's imagination) and then zipped the clippers along its belly.

That done, he shut the clippers off, walked down toward the playground, and then turned back abruptly to get it all at once, the entire rabbit. Yes, it looked all right. Well, he would do the dog next.

'But if it was my hotel,' he said, 'I'd cut the whole damn bunch of you down.' He would, too. Just cut them down and resod the lawn where they'd been and put in half a dozen small metal tables with gaily colored umbrellas. People could have cocktails on the Overlook's lawn in the summer sun. Sloe gin fizzes and margaritas and pink ladies and all those sweet tourist drinks. A rum and tonic, maybe. Jack took his handkerchief out of his back pocket and slowly rubbed his lips with it.

'Come on, come on,' he said softly. That was nothing to be thinking about.

He was going to start back, and then some impulse made him change his mind and he went down to the playground instead. It was funny how you never knew kids, he thought. He and Wendy had expected Danny to love the playground; it had everything a kid could want. But Jack didn't think the boy had been down half a dozen times, if that. He supposed if there had been another kid to play with, it would have been different.

The gate squeaked slightly as he let himself in, and then there was crushed gravel crunching under his feet. He went first to the playhouse, the perfect scale model of the Overlook itself. It came up to his lower thigh, just about Danny's height when he was standing up. Jack hunkered down and looked in the thirdfloor windows.

'The giant has come to eat you all up in your beds,' he said hollowly. 'Kiss your Triple A rating goodbye.' But that wasn't funny, either. You could open the house simply by pulling it apart – it opened on a hidden hinge. The inside was a disappointment. The walls were painted, but the place was mostly hollow. But of course it would have to be, he told himself, or how else could the kids get inside? What play furniture might go with the place in the summer was gone, probably packed away in the equipment shed. He closed it up and heard the small click as the latch closed.

He walked over to the slide, set the hedge-clipper down, and after a glance back at the driveway to make sure Wendy and Danny hadn't returned, he climbed to the top and sat down. This was the big kid's slide, but the fit was still uncomfortably tight for his grownup ass. How long had it been since he had been on a slide? Twenty years? It didn't seem possible it could be that long, it didn't *feel* that long, but it had to be that, or more. He could remember his old man taking him to the park in Berlin when he had been Danny's age, and he had done the whole bit – slide, swings, teeter-totters, everything. He and the old man would have a hotdog lunch and buy peanuts from the man with the cart afterward. They would sit on a bench to eat them and dusky clouds of pigeons would flock around their feet.

'Goddam scavenger birds,' his dad would say, 'don't you feed them, Jacky.' But they would both end up feeding them, and giggling at the way they ran after the nuts, the greedy way they ran after the nuts. Jack didn't think the old man had ever taken his brothers to the park. Jack had been his favorite, and even so Jack had taken his lumps when the old man was drunk, which was a lot of the time. But Jack had loved him for as long as he was able, long after the rest of the family could only hate and fear him.

He pushed off with his hands and went to the bottom, but the trip was unsatisfying. The slide, unused, had too much friction and no really pleasant speed could be built up. And his ass was just too big. His adult feet thumped into the slight dip where thousands of children's feet had landed before him. He stood up, brushed at the seat of his pants, and looked at the hedge-clipper. But instead of going back to it he went to the swings, which were also a disappointment. The chains had built up rust since the close of the season, and they squealed like things in pain. Jack promised himself he would oil them in the spring.

You better stop it, he advised himself. You're not a kid anymore. You don't need this place to prove it.

But he went on the cement rings – they were too small for him and he passed them up – and then to the security fence which marked the edge of the grounds. He curled his fingers through the links and looked through, the sun crosshatching shadow-lines on his face like a man behind bars. He recognized the similarity himself and he shook the chain link fence, put a harried expression on his face and whispered: 'Lemme outta here! Lemme outta here!' But for the third time, not funny. It was time to get back to work.

That was when he heard the sound behind him.

He turned around quickly, frowning, embarrassed, wondering if someone had seen him fooling around down here in kiddie country. His eyes ticked off the slides, the opposing angles of the seesaws, the swings in which only the wind sat. Beyond all that to the gate and the low fence that divided the playground from the lawn and the topiary – the lions gathered protectively around the path, the rabbit bent over as if to crop grass, the buffalo ready to charge, the crouching dog. Beyond them, the putting green and the hotel itself. From here he could even see the raised lip of the roque court on the Overlook's western side.

Everything was just as it had been. So why had the flesh of his face and hands begun to creep, and why had the hair along the back of his neck begun to stand up, as if the flesh back there had suddenly tightened?

THE SHINING

He squinted up at the hotel again, but that was no answer. It simply stood there, its windows dark, a tiny thread of smoke curling from the chimney, coming from the banked fire in the lobby.

(Buster, you better get going or they're going to come back and wonder if you were doing anything all the while.)

Sure, get going. Because the snow was coming and he had to get the damn hedges trimmed. It was part of the agreement. Besides, they wouldn't dare—

(Who wouldn't? What wouldn't? Dare do what?)

He began to walk back toward the hedge-clipper at the foot of the big kid's slide, and the sound of his feet crunching on the crushed stone seemed abnormally loud. Now the flesh on his testicles had begun to creep too, and his buttocks felt hard and heavy, like stone.

(*Jesus, what is this?*)

He stopped by the hedge-clipper, but made no move to pick it up. Yes, there was something different. In the topiary. And it was so simple, so easy to see, that he just wasn't picking it up. Come on, he scolded himself, you just trimmed the fucking rabbit, so what's the

(that's it)

His breath stopped in his throat.

The rabbit was down on all fours, cropping grass. Its belly was against the ground. But not ten minutes ago it had been up on its hind legs, of course it had been, he had trimmed its ears . . . and its belly.

His eyes darted to the dog. When he had come down the path it had been sitting up, as if begging for a sweet. Now it was crouched, head tilted, the clipped wedge of mouth seeming to snarl silently. And the lions—

(oh no, baby, oh no, uh-uh, no way)

the lions were closer to the path. The two on his right had subtly changed positions, had drawn closer together. The tail of the one on the left now almost jutted out over the path. When he had come past them and through the gate, that lion had been on the right and he was quite sure its tail had been curled around it.

227

They were no longer protecting the path; they were blocking it.

Jack put his hand suddenly over his eyes and then took it away. The picture didn't change. A soft sigh, too quiet to be a groan, escaped him. In his drinking days he had always been afraid of something like this happening. But when you were a heavy drinker you called it the DTs – good old Ray Milland in *Lost Weekend*, seeing the bugs coming out of the walls.

What did you call it when you were cold sober?

The question was meant to be rhetorical, but his mind answered it

(you call it insanity)

nevertheless

Staring at the hedge animals, he realized something *had* changed while he had his hand over his eyes. The dog had moved closer. No longer crouching, it seemed to be in a running posture, haunches flexed, one front leg forward, the other back. The hedge mouth yawned wider, the pruned sticks looked sharp and vicious And now he fancied he could see faint eye indentations in the greenery as well. Looking at him.

Why do they have to be trimmed? he thought hysterically. *They're perfect.*

Another soft sound. He involuntarily backed up a step when he looked at the lions. One of the two on the right seemed to have drawn slightly ahead of the other. Its head was lowered. One paw had stolen almost all the way to the low fence. Dear God, what next?

(*next it leaps over and gobbles you up like something in an evil nursery fable*)

It was like that game they had played when they were kids, red light. One person was 'it', and while he turned his back and counted to ten, the other players crept forward. When 'it' got to ten, he whirled around and if he caught anyone moving, they were out of the game. The others remained frozen in statue postures until 'it' turned his back and counted again. They got closer and closer, and at last, somewhere between five and ten, you would feel a hand on your back . . .

Gravel rattled on the path.

THE SHINING

He jerked his head around to look at the dog and it was halfway down the pathway, just behind the lions now, its mouth wide and yawning. Before, it had only been a hedge clipped in the general shape of a dog, something that lost all definition when you got up close to it. But now Jack could see that it had been clipped to look like a German shepherd, and shepherds could be mean. You could train shepherds to kill.

A low rustling sound.

The lion on the left had advanced all the way to the fence now; its muzzle was touching the boards. It seemed to be grinning at him. Jack backed up another two steps. His head was thudding crazily and he could feel the dry rasp of his breath in his throat. Now the buffalo had moved, circling to the right, behind and around the rabbit. The head was lowered, the green hedge horns pointing at him. The thing was, you couldn't watch all of them. Not all at once.

He began to make a whining sound, unaware in his locked concentration that he was making any sound at all. His eyes darted from one hedge creature to the next, trying to *see* them move. The wind gusted, making a hungry rattling sound in the close-matted branches. What kind of sound would there be if they got him? But of course he knew. A snapping, rending, breaking sound. It would be—

(*no no NO NO I WILL NOT BELIEVE THIS NOT AT ALL!*)

He clapped his hands over his eyes, clutching at his hair, his forehead, his throbbing temples. And he stood like that for a long time, dread building until he could stand it no longer and he pulled his hands away with a cry.

By the putting green the dog was sitting up, as if begging for a scrap. The buffalo was gazing with disinterest back toward the roque court, as it had been when Jack had come down with the clippers. The rabbit stood on its hind legs, ears up to catch the faintest sound, freshly clipped belly exposed. The lions, rooted into place, stood beside the path.

He stood frozen for a long time, the harsh breath in his throat finally slowing. He reached for his cigarettes and shook four of them out onto the gravel. He stooped down and picked them up, groped for them, never taking his eyes from the topiary for fear the animals would begin to move again. He picked them up, stuffed three carelessly back into the pack, and lit the fourth. After two deep drags he dropped it and crushed it out. He went to the hedge-clipper and picked it up.

'I'm very tired,' he said, and now it seemed okay to talk out loud. It didn't seem crazy at all. 'I've been under a strain. The wasps . . . the play . . . Al calling me like that. But it's all right.'

He began to trudge back up to the hotel. Part of his mind tugged fretfully at him, tried to make him detour around the hedge animals, but he went directly up the gravel path, through them. A faint breeze rattled through them, that was all. He had imagined the whole thing. He had had a bad scare but it was over now.

In the Overlook's kitchen he paused to take two Excedrin and then went downstairs and looked at papers until he heard the dim sound of the hotel truck rattling into the driveway. He went up to meet them. He felt all right. He saw no need to mention his hallucination. He'd had a bad scare but it was over now.

CHAPTER TWENTY-FOUR
SNOW

It was dusk.

They stood on the porch in the fading light, Jack in the middle, his left arm around Danny's shoulders and his right arm around Wendy's waist. Together they watched as the decision was taken out of their hands.

The sky had been completely clouded over by two-thirty and it had begun to snow an hour later, and this time you didn't need a weatherman to tell you it was serious snow, no flurry that was going to melt or blow away when the evening wind started to whoop. At first it had fallen in perfectly straight lines, building up a snowcover that coated everything evenly, but now, an hour after it had started, the wind had begun to blow from the northwest and the snow had begun to drift against the porch and the sides of the Overlook's driveway. Beyond the grounds the highway had disappeared under an even blanket of white. The hedge animals were also gone, but when Wendy and Danny had gotten home, she had commended him on the good job he had done. Do you think so? he had asked, and said no more. Now the hedges were buried under amorphous white cloaks.

Curiously, all of them were thinking different thoughts but feeling the same emotion: relief. The bridge had been crossed.

'Will it ever be spring?' Wendy murmured.

Jack squeezed her tighter. 'Before you know it. What do you say we go in and have some supper? It's cold out here.'

She smiled. All afternoon Jack had seemed distant and . . . well, odd. Now he sounded more like his normal self. 'Fine by me. How about you, Danny?'

'Sure.'

So they went in together, leaving the wind to build to the

low-pitched scream that would go on all night – a sound they would get to know well. Flakes of snow swirled and danced across the porch. The Overlook faced it as it had for nearly three quarters of a century, its darkened windows now bearded with snow, indifferent to the fact that it was now cut off from the world. Or possibly it was pleased with the prospect. Inside its shell the three of them went about their early evening routine, like microbes trapped in the intestine of a monster.

CHAPTER TWENTY-FIVE
INSIDE 217

A week and a half later two feet of snow lay white and crisp and even on the grounds of the Overlook Hotel. The hedge menagerie was buried up to its haunches; the rabbit, frozen on its hind legs, seemed to be rising from a white pool. Some of the drifts were over five feet deep. The wind was constantly changing them, sculpting them into sinuous, dunelike shapes. Twice Jack had snowshoed clumsily around to the equipment shed for his shovel to clear the porch, the third time he shrugged, simply cleared a path through the towering drift lying against the door, and let Danny amuse himself by sledding to the right and left of the path. The truly heroic drifts lay against the Overlook's west side; some of them towered to a height of twenty feet, and beyond them the ground was scoured bare to the grass by the constant windflow. The first-floor windows were covered, and the view from the dining room which Jack had so admired on closing day was now no more exciting than a view of a blank movie screen. Their phone had been out for the last eight days, and the CB radio in Ullman's office was now their only communications link with the outside world.

It snowed every day now, sometimes only brief flurries that powdered the glittering snow crust, sometimes for real, the low whistle of the wind cranking up to a womanish shriek that made the old hotel rock and groan alarmingly even in its deep cradle of snow. Night temperatures had not gotten above 10°, and although the thermometer by the kitchen service entrance sometimes got as high as 25° in the early afternoons, the steady knife edge of the wind made it uncomfortable to go out without a ski mask. But they all did go out on the days when the sun shone, usually wearing two sets of clothing and mittens on over their gloves. Getting out was almost a compulsive thing; the hotel was circled with the double track of Danny's Flexible Flyer. The permutations were nearly endless: Danny riding while his parents pulled; Danny riding and laughing while Wendy and Danny tried to pull (it was just possible for them to pull him on the icy crust, and flatly impossible when powder covered it); Danny and Mommy riding; Wendy riding by herself while her menfolk pulled and puffed white vapor like drayhorses, pretending she was heavier than she was. They laughed a great deal on these sled excursions around the house, but the whooping and impersonal voice of the wind, so huge and hollowly sincere, made their laughter seem tinny and forced.

They had seen caribou tracks in the snow and once the caribou themselves, a group of five standing motionlessly below the security fence. They had all taken turns with Jack's Zeiss-Ikon binoculars to see them better, and looking at them had given Wendy a weird, unreal feeling: they were standing leg-deep in the snow that covered the highway, and it came to her that between now and the spring thaw, the road belonged more to the caribou than it did to them. Now the things that men had made up here were neutralized. The caribou understood that, she believed. She had put the binoculars down and had said something about starting lunch and in the kitchen she had cried a little, trying to rid herself of the awful pent-up feeling that sometimes fell on her like a large, pressing hand over her heart. She thought of the caribou. She thought of the wasps Jack had put out on the service entrance platform, under the Pyrex bowl, to freeze.

There were plenty of snowshoes hung from nails in the equipment shed, and Jack found a pair to fit each of them, although Danny's pair was quite a bit outsized. Jack did well with them. Although he had not snowshoed since his boyhood in Berlin, New Hampshire, he retaught himself quickly. Wendy didn't care much for it — even fifteen minutes of tramping around on the outsized laced paddles made her legs and ankles ache outrageously — but Danny was intrigued and working hard to pick up the knack. He still fell often, but Jack was pleased with his progress. He said that by February Danny would be skipping circles around both of them.

***

This day was overcast, and by noon the sky had already begun to spit snow. The radio was promising another eight to twelve inches and chanting hosannas to Precipitation, that great god of Colorado skiers. Wendy, sitting in the bedroom and knitting a scarf, thought to herself that she knew exactly what the skiers could do with all that snow. She knew exactly where they could put it.

Jack was in the cellar. He had gone down to check the furnace and boiler – such checks had become a ritual with him since the snow had closed them in – and after satisfying himself that everything was going well he had wandered through the arch, screwed the lightbulb on, and had seated himself in an old and cobwebby camp chair he had found. He was leafing through the old records and papers, constantly wiping his mouth with his handkerchief as he did so. Confinement had leached his skin of its autumn tan, and as he sat hunched over the yellowed, crackling sheets, his reddish-blond hair tumbling untidily over his forehead, he looked slightly lunatic. He had found some odd things tucked in among the invoices, bills of lading, receipts. Disquieting things. A bloody strip of sheeting. A dismembered teddy bear that seemed to have been slashed to pieces. A crumpled sheet of violet ladies' stationery, a ghost of perfume still clinging to it beneath the musk of age, a note begun and left unfinished in faded blue ink: 'Dearest Tommy, I can't think so well up here as I'd hoped, about us I mean, of course, who else? Ha. Ha. Things keep getting in the way. I've had strange dreams about things going bump in the night, can you believe that and' That was all. The note was dated June 27, 1934. He found a hand puppet that seemed to be either a witch or a warlock . . . something with long teeth and a pointy hat, at any rate. It had been improbably tucked between a bundle of natural-gas receipts and a bundle of receipts for Vichy water. And something that seemed to be a poem, scribbled on the back of a menu in dark pencil: 'Medoc/are you here?/I've been sleepwalking again, my dear./The *plants are moving under the rug.*' No date on the menu, and no name on the poem, if it was a poem. Elusive, but fascinating. It seemed to him that these things were like pieces in a jigsaw, things that would eventually fit together if he could find the right linking pieces. And so he kept looking, jumping and wiping his lips every time the furnace roared into life behind him.

★★★

Danny was standing outside room 217 again.

The passkey was in his pocket. He was staring at the door with a kind of drugged avidity, and his upper body seemed to twitch and jiggle beneath his flannel shirt. He was humming softly and tunelessly.

He hadn't wanted to come here, not after the fire hose. He was scared to come here. He was scared that he had taken the pass-key again, disobeying his father.

He *had* wanted to come here. Curiosity

(killed the cat; satisfaction brought him back)

was like a constant fishhook in his brain, a kind of nagging siren song that would not be appeased. And hadn't Mr Hallorann said, 'I don't think there's anything here that can hurt you'?

(You promised.)

(*Promises were made to be broken.*)

He jumped at that. It was as if that thought had come from outside, insectile, buzzing, softly cajoling.

(*Promises were made to be broken my dear redrum, to be broken. splintered. shattered. hammered apart. FORE!*)

His nervous humming broke into low, atonal song: 'Lou, Lou, skip to m' Lou, skip to m'Lou my daaarlin . . .'

Hadn't Mr Hallorann been right? Hadn't that been, in the end, the reason why he had kept silent and allowed the snow to close them in?

Just close your eyes and it will be gone.

What he had seen in the Presidential Sweet had gone away. And the snake had only been a fire hose that had fallen onto the rug. Yes, even the blood in the Presidential Sweet had been harmless, something old, something that had happened long before he was born or even thought of, something that was done with. Like a movie that only he could see. There was nothing, really nothing, in this hotel that could hurt him, and if he had to prove that to himself by going into this room, shouldn't he do so?

'Lou, Lou, skip to m'Lou . . .'

(*Curiosity killed the cat my dear redrum, redrum my dear, satisfaction brought him back safe and sound, from toes to crown; from head to ground he was safe and sound. He knew that those things*)

(*are like scary pictures, they can't hurt you, but oh my god*)

(*what big teeth you have grandma and is that a wolf in a* (*BLUEBEARD suit or a BLUEBEARD in a wolf suit and I'm so*)

(*glad you asked because curiosity killed that cat and it was the HOPE of satisfaction that brought him*)

up the hall, treading softly over the blue and twisting jungle carpet. He had stopped by the fire extinguisher, had put the brass nozzle back in the frame, and then had poked it repeatedly with his finger, heart thumping, whispering: 'Come on and hurt me. Come on and hurt me, you cheap prick. Can't do it, can you? Huh? You're nothing but a cheap fire hose. Can't do nothin but lie there. Come on, come on!' He had felt insane with bravado. And nothing had happened. It was only a hose after all, only canvas and brass, you could hack it to pieces and it would never complain, never twist and jerk and bleed green slime all over the blue carpet, because it was only a hose, not a nose and not a rose, not glass buttons or satin bows, not a snake in a sleepy doze . . . and he had hurried on, had hurried on because he was

('late, I'm late,' said the white rabbit.)

the white rabbit. Yes. Now there was a white rabbit out by the playground, once it had been green but now it was white, as if something had shocked it repeatedly on the snowy, windy nights and turned it old . . .

Danny took the passkey from his pocket and slid it into the lock.

'Lou, Lou . . .'

(*the white rabbit had been on its way to a croquet party to the Red Queen's croquet party storks for mallets hedgehogs for balls*)

He touched the key, let his fingers wander over it. His head felt dry and sick. He turned the key and the tumblers thumped back smoothly.

(*OFF WITH HIS HEAD! OFF WITH HIS HEAD! OFF WITH HIS HEAD!*)

(*this game isn't croquet though the mallets are too short this game is*)

(*WHACK-BOOM! Straight through the wicket.*)

(*OFF WITH HIS HEEEEEAAAAAAAD—*)

Danny pushed the door open. It swung smoothly, without a creak. He was standing just outside a large combination bedsitting room, and although the snow had not reached up this far – the highest drifts were still a foot below the second-floor windows – the room was dark because Daddy had closed all the shutters on the western exposure two weeks ago.

He stood in the doorway, fumbled to his right, and found the switch plate. Two bulbs in an overhead cut-glass fixture came on. Danny stepped further in and looked around. The rug was deep and soft, a quiet rose color. Soothing. A double bed with a white coverlet. A writing desk

(*Pray tell me: Why is a raven like a writing desk?*)

by the large shuttered window. During the season the Constant Writer

(*having a wonderful time, wish you were fear*)

would have a pretty view of the mountains to describe to the folks back home.

He stepped further in. Nothing here, nothing at all. Only an empty room, cold because Daddy was heating the east wing today. A bureau. A closet, its door open to reveal a clutch of hotel hangers, the kind you can't steal. A Gideon Bible on an endtable. To his left was the bathroom door, a full-length mirror on it reflecting his own white-faced image. That door was ajar and—

He watched his double nod slowly.

Yes, that's where it was, whatever it was. In there. In the bathroom. His double walked forward, as if to escape the glass. It put its hand out, pressed it against his own. Then it fell away at an angle as the bathroom door swung open. He looked in.

A long room, old-fashioned, like a Pullman car. Tiny white

hexagonal tiles on the floor. At the far end, a toilet with the lid up. At the right, a washbasin and another mirror above it, the kind that hides a medicine cabinet. To the left, a huge white tub on claw feet, the shower curtain pulled closed. Danny stepped into the bathroom and walked toward the tub dreamily, as if propelled from outside himself, as if this whole thing were one of the dreams Tony had brought him, that he would perhaps see something nice when he pulled the shower curtain back, something Daddy had forgotten or Mommy had lost, something that would make them both happy—

So he pulled the shower curtain back.

The woman in the tub had been dead for a long time. She was bloated and purple, her gas-filled belly rising out of the cold, ice-rimmed water like some fleshy island. Her eyes were fixed on Danny's, glassy and huge, like marbles. She was grinning, her purple lips pulled back in a grimace. Her breasts lolled. Her pubic hair floated. Her hands were frozen on the knurled porcelain sides of the tub like crab claws.

Danny shrieked. But the sound never escaped his lips; turning inward and inward, it fell down in his darkness like a stone in a well. He took a single blundering step backward, hearing his heels clack on the white hexagonal tiles, and at the same moment his urine broke, spilling effortlessly out of him.

The woman was sitting up.

Still grinning, her huge marble eyes fixed on him, she was sitting up. Her dead palms made squittering noises on the porcelain. Her breasts swayed like ancient cracked punching bags. There was the minute sound of breaking ice shards. She was not breathing. She was a corpse, and dead long years.

Danny turned and ran. Bolting through the bathroom door, his eyes starting from their sockets, his hair on end like the hair of a hedgehog about to be turned into a sacrificial

(croquet? or roque?) ball, his mouth open and soundless. He ran full-tilt into the outside door of 217, which was now closed. He began hammering on it, far beyond realizing that it was unlocked, and he had only to turn the knob to let himself out. His mouth pealed forth deafening screams that were beyond human auditory range. He could only hammer on the door and hear the dead woman coming for him, bloated belly, dry hair, outstretched hands – something that had lain slain in that tub for perhaps years, embalmed there in magic.

The door would not open, would not, would not, would not.

And then the voice of Dick Hallorann came to him, so sudden and unexpected, so calm, that his locked vocal cords opened and he began to cry weakly – not with fear but with blessed relief.

(*I don't think they can hurt you . . . they're like pictures in a book . . . close your eyes and they'll be gone.*)

His eyelids snapped down. His hands curled into balls. His shoulders hunched with the effort of his concentration:

(*Nothing there nothing there not there at all NOTHING THERE THERE IS NOTHING!*)

Time passed. And he was just beginning to relax, just beginning to realize that the door must be unlocked and he could go, when the years–damp, bloat, fish-smelling hands closed softly around his throat and he was turned implacably around to stare into that dead and purple face.

PART FOUR
SNOWBOUND

CHAPTER TWENTY-SIX
DREAMLAND

Knitting made her sleepy. Today even Bartók would have made her sleepy, and it wasn't Bartók on the little phonograph, it was Bach. Her hands grew slower and slower, and at the time her son was making the acquaintance of Room 217's long-term resident, Wendy was asleep with her knitting on her lap. The yarn and needles rose in the slow time of her breathing. Her sleep was deep and she did not dream.

★★★

Jack Torrance had fallen asleep too, but his sleep was light and uneasy, populated by dreams that seemed too vivid to be mere dreams – they were certainly more vivid than any dreams he had ever had before.

His eyes had begun to get heavy as he leafed through packets of milk bills, a hundred to a packet, seemingly tens of thousands all together. Yet he gave each one a cursory glance, afraid that by not being thorough he might miss exactly the piece of Overlookiana he needed to make the mystic connection that he was sure must be here somewhere. He felt like a man with a power cord in one hand, groping around a dark and unfamiliar room for a socket. If he could find it he would be rewarded with a view of wonders.

He had come to grips with Al Shockley's phone call and his request; his strange experience in the playground had helped him to do that. That had been too damned close to some kind of breakdown, and he was convinced that it was his mind in revolt against Al's high-goddam-handed request that he chuck his book project. It had maybe been a signal that his own sense of self-respect could only be pushed so far before disintegrating entirely. He would write the book. If it meant the end of his association with Al Shockley, that would have to be. He would write the hotel's biography, write it straight from the shoulder, and the introduction would be his hallucination that the topiary animals had moved. The title would be uninspired but workable: *Strange, The Story of the Overlook Hotel.* Straight from the shoulder, yes, but it would not be written vindictively, in any effort to get back at Al or Stuart Ullman or George Hatfield or his father (miserable, bullying drunk that he had been) or anyone else, for that matter. He would write it because the Overlook had enchanted him − could any other explanation be so simple or so true? He would write it for the reason he felt that all great literature, fiction and nonfiction, was written: truth comes out, in the end it always comes out. He would write it because he felt he had to.

Five hundred gals whole milk. One hundred gals skim milk. Pd. Billed to acc't. Three hundred pts orange juice. Pd.

He slipped down further in his chair, still holding a clutch of the receipts, but his eyes no longer looking at what was printed there. They had come unfocused. His lids were slow and heavy. His mind had slipped from the Overlook to his father, who had been a male nurse at the Berlin Community Hospital. Big man. A fat man who had towered to six feet two inches, he had been taller than Jack even when Jack got his full growth of six feet even - not that the old man had still been around then. 'Runt of the litter,' he would say, and then cuff Jack lovingly and laugh. There had been two other brothers, both taller than their father, and Becky, who at five-ten had only been two inches shorter than Jack and taller than he for most of their childhood.

His relationship with his father had been like the unfurling of some flower of beautiful potential, which, when wholly opened, turned out to be blighted inside. Until he had been seven he had loved the tall, big-bellied man uncritically and strongly in spite of the spankings, the black-and-blues, the occasional black eye.

He could remember velvet summer nights, the house quiet, oldest brother Brett out with his girl, middle brother Mike studying something, Becky and their mother in the living room, watching something on the balky old TV; and he would sit in the hall dressed in a pajama singlet and nothing else, ostensibly playing with his trucks, actually waiting for the moment when the silence would be broken by the door swinging open with a large bang, the bellow of his father's welcome when he saw Jacky was waiting, his own happy squeal in answer as this big man came down the hall, his pink scalp glowing beneath his crewcut in the glow of the hall light. In that light he always looked like some soft and flapping oversized ghost in his hospital whites, the shirt always untucked (and sometimes bloody), the pants cuffs drooping down over the black shoes.

His father would sweep him into his arms and Jacky would be propelled deliriously upward, so fast it seemed he could feel air pressure settling against his skull like a cap made out of lead, up and up, both of them crying 'Elevator! Elevator!'; and there had been nights when his father in his drunkenness had not stopped the upward lift of his slabmuscled arms soon enough and Jacky had gone right over his father's flattopped head like a human projectile to crash-land on the hall floor behind his dad. But on other nights his father would only sweep him into a giggling ecstasy, through the zone of air where beer hung around his father's face like a mist of raindrops, to be twisted and turned and shaken like a laughing rag, and finally to be set down on his feet, hiccupping with reaction.

The receipts slipped from his relaxing hand and seesawed down through the air to land lazily on the floor, his eyelids, which had settled shut with his father's image tattooed on their backs like stereopticon images, opened a little bit and then slipped back down again. He twitched a little. Consciousness, like the receipts, like autumn aspen leaves, seesawed lazily downward.

That had been the first phase of his relationship with his father, and as it was drawing to its end he had become aware that Becky and his brothers, all of them older, hated the father and that their mother, a nondescript woman who rarely spoke above a mutter, only suffered him because her Catholic upbringing said that she must. In those days it had not seemed strange to Jack that the father won all his arguments with his children by use of his fists, and it had not seemed strange that his own love should go hand-in-hand with his fear: fear of the elevator game which might end in a splintering crash on any given night; fear that his father's bearish good humor on his day off might suddenly change to boarish bellowing and the smack of his '*good right hand*'; and sometimes, he remembered, he had even been afraid that his father's shadow might fall over him while he was at play. It was near the end of this phase that he began to notice that Brett never brought his dates home, or Mike and Becky their chums.

Love began to curdle at nine, when his father put his mother into the hospital with his cane. He had begun to carry the cane a year earlier, when a car accident had left him lame. After that he was never without it, long and black and thick and gold-headed. Now, dozing, Jack's body twitched in a remembered cringe at the sound it made in the air, a murderous swish, and its heavy crack against the wall . . . or against flesh. He had beaten their mother for no good reason at all, suddenly and without warning. They had been at the supper table. The cane had been standing by his chair. It was a Sunday night, the end of a three day weekend for Daddy, a weekend which he had boozed away in his usual inimitable style. Roast chicken. Peas. Mashed potatoes. Daddy at the head of the table, his plate heaped high, snoozing or nearly snoozing. His mother passing plates. And suddenly Daddy had been wide awake, his eyes set deeply into their fat eyesockets, glittering with a kind of stupid, evil petulance. They flickered from one member of the family to the next, and the vein in the center of his forehead was standing out prominently, always a bad sign. One of his large freckled hands had dropped to the gold knob of his cane, caressing it. He said something about coffee – to this day Jack was sure it had been 'coffee' that his father said. Momma had opened her mouth to answer and then the cane was whickering through the air, smashing against her face. Blood spurted from her nose. Becky screamed. Momma's spectacles dropped into her gravy. The cane had been drawn back, had come down again, this time on top of her head, splitting the scalp. Momma had dropped to the floor. He had been out of his chair and around to where she lay dazed on the carpet, brandishing the cane, moving with a fat man's grotesque speed and agility, little eyes flashing, jowls quivering as he spoke to her just as he had always spoken to his children during such outbursts. 'Now. Now by Christ. I guess you'll take your medicine now. Goddam puppy. Whelp. Come on and take your medicine.' The cane had gone up and down on her seven more times before Brett and Mike got hold of him, dragged him away, wrestled the cane out of his hand. Jack

(little Jacky now he was little Jacky now dozing and mumbling on a cobwebby camp chair while the furnace roared into hollow life behind him)

knew exactly how many blows it had been because each soft *whump* against his mother's body had been engraved on his memory like the irrational swipe of a chisel on stone. Seven *whumps*. No more, no less. He and Becky crying, unbelieving, looking at their mother's spectacles lying in her mashed potatoes, one cracked lens smeared with gravy. Brett shouting at Daddy from the back hall, telling him he'd kill him if he moved. And Daddy saying over and over: 'Damn little puppy. Damn little whelp. Give me my cane, you damn little pup. Give it to me.' Brett brandishing it hysterically, saying yes, yes, I'll give it to you, just you move a little bit and I'll give you all you want and two extra. I'll give you *plenty*. Momma getting slowly to her feet, dazed, her face already puffed and swelling like an old tire with too much air in it, bleeding in four or five different places, and she had said a terrible thing, perhaps the only thing Momma had ever said which Jacky could recall word for word: 'Who's got the newspaper? Your daddy wants the funnies. Is it raining yet?' And then she sank to her knees again, her hair hanging in her puffed and bleeding face. Mike calling the doctor, babbling into the phone. Could he come right away? It was their mother. No, he couldn't say what the trouble was, not over the phone, not over a party line he couldn't. Just *come*. The doctor came and took Momma away to the hospital where Daddy had worked all of his adult life. Daddy, sobered up some (or perhaps only with the stupid cunning of any hard-pressed animal), told the doctor she had fallen downstairs. There was blood on the tablecloth because he had tried to wipe her dear face with it. Had her glasses flown all the way through the living room and into the dining room to land in her mashed potatoes and gravy? the doctor asked with a kind of horrid, grinning sarcasm. Is that what happened, Mark? I have heard of folks who can get a radio station on their gold fillings and I have seen a man get shot between the eyes and live to tell about it, but that is a new one on me. Daddy had merely shook his head and said he didn't know; they must have fallen off her face when he brought her through into the dining room. The four children had been stunned to silence by the calm stupendousness of the lie. Four days later Brett quit his job in the mill and joined the Army. Jack had always felt it was not just the sudden and irrational beating his father had administered at the dinner table but the fact that, in the hospital, their mother had corroborated their father's story while holding the hand of the parish priest. Revolted, Brett had left them to whatever might come. He had been killed in Dong Ho province in 1965, the year when Jack Torrance, undergraduate, had joined the active college agitation to end the war. He had waved his brother's bloody shirt at rallies that were increasingly well attended, but it was not Brett's face that hung before his eyes when he spoke – it was the face of his mother's, dazed, uncomprehending face, his mother saying: 'Who's got the newspaper?'

Mike escaped three years later when Jack was twelve – he went to UNH on a hefty Merit Scholarship. A year after that their father died of a sudden, massive stroke which occurred while he was prepping a patient for surgery. He had collapsed in his flapping and untucked hospital whites, dead possibly even before he hit the industrial black-and-red hospital tiles, and three days later the man who had dominated Jacky's life, the irrational white ghost-god, was under ground.

The stone read *Mark Anthony Torrance, Loving Father*. To that Jack would have added one line: *He Knew How to Play Elevator*.

There had been a great lot of insurance money. There are people who collect insurance as compulsively as others collect coins and stamps, and Mark Torrance had been that type. The insurance money came in at the same time the monthly policy payments and liquor bills stopped. For five years they had been rich. Nearly rich . . .

In his shallow, uneasy sleep his face rose before him as if in a glass, his face but not his face, the wide eyes and innocent bowed mouth of a boy sitting in the hall with his trucks, waiting for his daddy, waiting for the white ghost-god, waiting for the elevator to rise up with dizzying, exhilarating speed through the salt-and-sawdust mist of exhaled taverns, waiting perhaps for it to go crashing down, spilling old clocksprings out of his ears while his daddy roared with laughter, and it

(transformed into Danny's face, so much like his own had been, his eyes had been light blue while Danny's were cloudy gray, but the lips still made a bow and the complexion was fair; Danny in his study, wearing training pants, all his papers soggy and the fine misty smell of beer rising . . . a dreadful batter all in ferment, rising on the wings of yeast, the breath of taverns . . . snap of bone . . . his own voice, mewling drunkenly *Danny, you okay doc? . . . Oh God oh God your poor sweet arm . . .* and that face transformed into)

(momma's dazed face rising up from below the table, punched and bleeding, and momma was saying)

('—*from your father. I repeat, an enormously important announcement from your father. Please stay tuned or tune immediately to the Happy Jack frequency. Repeat, tune immediately to the Happy Hour frequency. I repeat—*')

A slow dissolve. Disembodied voices echoing up to him as if along an endless, cloudy hallway.

(*Things keep getting in the way, dear Tommy . . .*)

(*Medoc, are you here? I've been sleepwalking again, my dear. It's the inhuman monsters that I fear . . .*)

('*Excuse me, Mr Ullman, but isn't this the . . .*')

. . . office, with its file cabinets, Ullman's big desk, a blank reservations book for next year already in place – never misses a trick, that Ullman – all the keys hanging neatly on their hooks

(except for one, which one, which key, passkey – passkey, passkey, who's got the passkey? if we went upstairs perhaps we'd see)

and the big two-way radio on its shelf.

He snapped it on. CBB transmissions coming in short, crackly bursts. He switched the band and dialed across bursts of music, news, a preacher haranguing a softly moaning congregation, a weather report. And another voice which he dialed back to. It was his father's voice.

'—kill him. You have to kill him, Jacky, and her, too. Because a real artist must suffer. Because each man kills the thing he loves. Because they'll always be conspiring against you, trying to hold you back and drag you down. Right this minute that boy of yours is in where he shouldn't be. Trespassing. That's what he's doing. He's a goddam little pup. Cane him for it, Jacky, cane him within an inch of his life. Have a drink, Jacky my boy, and we'll play the elevator game. Then I'll go with you while you give him his medicine. I know you can do it, of course you can. You must kill him. You have to kill him, Jacky, and her, too. Because a real artist must suffer. Because each man—'

His father's voice, going up higher and higher, becoming something maddening, not human at all, something squealing and petulant and maddening, the voice of the Ghost-God, the Pig-God, coming dead at him out of the radio and

'*No!*' he screamed back. 'You're *dead*, you're in your *grave*, you're not in me at all!' Because he had cut all the father out of him and it was not right that he should come back, creeping through this hotel two thousand miles from the New England town where his father had lived and died.

He raised the radio up and brought it down, and it smashed on the floor spilling old clocksprings and tubes like the result of some crazy elevator game gone awry, making his father's voice gone, leaving only his voice, Jack's voice, Jacky's voice, chanting in the cold reality of the office:

'—*dead, you're dead, you're dead!*'

And the startled sound of Wendy's feet hitting the floor over his head, and Wendy's startled, frightened voice: 'Jack? *Jack!*'

He stood, blinking down at the shattered radio. Now there was only the snowmobile in the equipment shed to link them to the outside world.

He put his hands over his eyes and clutched at his temples. He was getting a headache.

CHAPTER TWENTY-SEVEN
CATATONIC

Wendy ran down the hall in her stocking feet and ran down the main stairs to the lobby two at a time. She didn't look up at the carpeted flight that led to the second floor, but if she had, she would have seen Danny standing at the top of them, still and silent, his unfocused eyes directed out into indifferent space, his thumb in his mouth, the collar and shoulders of his shirt damp. There were puffy bruises on his neck and just below his chin.

Jack's cries had ceased, but that did nothing to ease her fear. Ripped out of her sleep by his voice, raised in that old hectoring pitch she remembered so well, she still felt that she was dreaming – but another part knew she was awake, and that terrified her more. She half-expected to burst into the office and find him standing over Danny's sprawled-out body, drunk and confused.

She pushed through the door and Jack was standing there, rubbing at his temples with his fingers. His face was ghost-white. The two-way CB radio lay at his feet in a sprinkling of broken glass.

'Wendy?' He asked uncertainly. 'Wendy—?'

The bewilderment seemed to grow and for a moment she saw his true face, the one he ordinarily kept so well hidden, and it was a face of desperate unhappiness, the face of an animal caught in a snare beyond its ability to decipher and render harmless. Then the muscles began to work, began to writhe under the skin, the mouth began to tremble infirmly, the Adam's apple began to rise and fall.

Her own bewilderment and surprise were overlaid by shock: he was going to cry. She had seen him cry before, but never since he stopped drinking . . . and never in those days unless he was very drunk and pathetically remorseful. He was a tight man, drum-tight and his loss of control frightened her all over again.

He came toward her, the tears brimming over his lower lids now, his head shaking involuntarily as if in a fruitless effort to ward off this emotional storm, and his chest drew in a convulsive gasp that was expelled in a huge, racking sob. His feet, clad in Hush Puppies, stumbled over the wreck of the radio and he almost fell into her arms, making her stagger back with his weight. His breath blew into her face and there was no smell of liquor on it. Of course not; there was no liquor up here.

'What's wrong?' She held him as best she could. 'Jack, what is it?'

But he could do nothing at first but sob, clinging to her, almost crushing the wind from her, his head turning on her shoulder in that helpless, shaking, warding-off gesture. His sobs were heavy and fierce. He was shuddering all over, his muscles jerking beneath his plaid shirt and jeans.

'Jack? What? Tell me what's wrong!'

At last the sobs began to change themselves into words, most of them incoherent at first, but coming clearer as his tears began to spend themselves.

'. . . dream, I guess it was a dream, but it was so real, I . . . it was my mother saying that Daddy was going to be on the radio and I . . . he was . . . he was telling me to . . . I don't know, he was *yelling* at me . . . and so I broke the radio . . . to shut him up. To shut him up. He's dead. I don't even want to dream about him. He's dead. My God, Wendy, my God. I never had a nightmare like that. I never want to have another one. Christ! It was awful.'

'You just fell asleep in the office?'

'No . . . not here. Downstairs.' He was straightening a little now, his weight coming off her, and the steady back-and-forth motion of his head first slowed and then stopped.

'I was looking through those old papers. Sitting on a chair I set up down there. Milk receipts. Dull stuff. And I guess I just drowsed off. That's when I started to dream. I must have sleepwalked up here.' He essayed a shaky little laugh against her neck. 'Another first.'

'Where is Danny, Jack?'

'I don't know. Isn't he with you?'

'He wasn't . . . downstairs with you?'

'He looked over his shoulder and his face tightened at what he saw on her face.

'Never going to let me forget that, are you, Wendy?'

'Jack—'

'When I'm on my deathbed you'll lean over and say, "It serves you right, remember the time you broke Danny's arm?"'

'Jack!'

'Jack what?' he asked hotly, and jumped to his feet. 'Are you denying that's what you're thinking? That I hurt him? That I hurt him once before and I could hurt him again?'

'I want to know where he is, that's all!'

'Go ahead, yell your fucking head off, that'll make everything okay, won't it?'

She turned and walked out the door.

He watched her go, frozen for a moment, a blotter covered with fragments of broken glass in one hand. Then he dropped it into the wastebasket, went after her, and caught her by the lobby desk. He put his hands on her shoulders and turned her around. Her face was carefully set.

'Wendy, I'm sorry. It was the dream. I'm upset. Forgive?'

'Of course,' she said, her face not changing expression. Her wooden shoulders slipped out of his hands. She walked to the middle of the lobby and called: '*Hey, doc! Where are you?*'

Silence came back. She walked toward the double lobby doors, opened one of them, and stepped out onto the path Jack had shoveled. It was more like a trench; the packed and drifted snow through which the path was cut came to her shoulders. She called him again, her breath coming out in a white plume. When she came back in she had begun to look scared.

Controlling his irritation with her, he said reasonably: 'Are you sure he's not sleeping in his room?'

'I told you, he was playing somewhere when I was knitting. I could hear him downstairs.'

'Did you fall asleep?'

'What's that got to do with it? Yes. *Danny?*'

'Did you look to his room when you came downstairs just now?'

'I—' She stopped.

He nodded. 'I didn't really think so.'

He started up the stairs without waiting for her. She followed him, half-running, but he was taking the risers two at a time. She almost crashed into his back when he came to a dead stop on the first-floor landing. He was rooted there, looking up, his eyes wide.

'What –?' she began, and followed his gaze.

Danny still stood there, his eyes blank, sucking his thumb. The marks on his throat were cruelly visible in the light of the hall's electric flambeaux.

'*Danny!*' she shrieked.

It broke Jack's paralysis and they rushed up the stairs together to where he stood. Wendy fell on her knees beside him and swept the boy into her arms. Danny came pliantly enough, but he did not hug her back. It was like hugging a padded stick, and the sweet taste of horror flooded her mouth. He only sucked his thumb and stared with indifferent blankness out into the stairwell beyond both of them.

'Danny, what happened?' Jack asked. He put out his hand to touch the puffy side of Danny's neck. 'Who did this to y—'

'*Don't you touch him!*' Wendy hissed. She clutched Danny in her arms, lifted him, and had retreated halfway down the stairs before Jack could do more than stand up, confused.

'What? Wendy, what the hell are you t—'

'Don't you touch him! I'll kill you if you lay your hands on him again!'

'Wendy—'

'You bastard!'

She turned and ran down the rest of the stairs to the first floor. Danny's head jounced mildly up and down as she ran. His thumb was lodged securely in his mouth. His eyes were soaped windows. She turned right at the foot of the stairs, and Jack heard her feet retreat to the end of it. Their bedroom door slammed. The bolt was run home. The lock turned. Brief silence. Then the soft, muttered sounds of comforting.

He stood for an unknown length of time, literally paralyzed by all that had happened in such a short space of time. His dream was still with him, painting everything a slightly unreal shade. It was as if he had taken a very mild mescaline hit. Had he maybe hurt Danny as Wendy thought? Tried to strangle his son at his dead father's request? No. He would never hurt Danny.

(*He fell down the stairs, Doctor.*)

He would never hurt Danny *now*.

(*How could I know the bug bomb was defective?*)

Never in his life had he been willfully vicious when he was sober.

(*Except when you almost killed George Hatfield.*)

'No!' he cried into the darkness. He brought both fists crashing down on his legs, again and again and again.

★★★

Wendy sat in the overstuffed chair by the window with Danny on her lap, holding him, crooning the old meaningless words, the ones you never remember afterward no matter how a thing turns out. He had folded onto her lap with neither protest nor gladness, like a paper cutout of himself, and his eyes didn't even shift toward the door when Jack cried out 'No!' somewhere in the hallway.

The confusion had receded a little bit in her mind, but she now discovered something even worse behind it. Panic.

Jack had done this, she had no doubt of it. His denials meant nothing to her. She thought it was perfectly possible that Jack had tried to throttle Danny in his sleep just as he had smashed the CB radio in his sleep. He was having a breakdown of some kind. But what was she going to do about it? She couldn't stay locked in here forever. They would have to eat.

There was really only one question, and it was asked in a mental voice of utter coldness and pragmatism, the voice of her maternity, a cold and passionless voice once it was directed away from the closed circle of mother and child and out toward Jack. It was a voice that spoke of self-preservation only after son-preservation and its question was:

(Exactly how dangerous is he?)

He had denied doing it. He had been horrified at the bruises, at Danny's soft and implacable disconnection. If he had done it, a separate section of himself had been responsible. The fact that he had done it when he was asleep was – in a terrible, twisted way – encouraging. Wasn't it possible that he could be trusted to get them out of here? To get them down and away. And after that . . .

But she could see no further than she and Danny arriving safe at Dr Edmonds's office in Sidewinder. She had no particular need to see further. The present crisis was more than enough to keep her occupied.

She crooned to Danny, rocking him on her breasts. Her fingers, on his shoulder, had noticed that his T-shirt was damp, but they had not bothered reporting the information to her brain in more than a cursory way. If it had been reported, she might have remembered that Jack's hands, as he had hugged her in the office and sobbed against her neck, had been dry. It might have given her pause. But her mind was still on other things. The decision had to be made – to approach Jack or not?

Actually it was not much of a decision. There was nothing she could do alone, not even carry Danny down to the office and call for help on the CB radio. He had suffered a great shock. He ought to be taken out quickly before any permanent damage could be done. She refused to let herself believe that permanent damage might already have been done.

And still she agonized over it, looking for another alternative. She did not want to put Danny back within Jack's reach. She was aware now that she had made one bad decision when she had gone against her feelings (and Danny's) and allowed the snow to close them in . . . for Jack's sake. Another bad decision when she had shelved the idea of divorce. Now she was nearly paralyzed by the idea that she might be making another mistake, one she would regret every minute of every day of the rest of her life.

There was not a gun in the place. There were knives hanging from the magnetized runners in the kitchen, but Jack was between her and them.

THE SHINING

In her striving to make the right decision, to find the alternative, the bitter irony of her thoughts did not occur: an hour ago she had been asleep, firmly convinced that things were all right and soon would be even better. Now she was considering the possibility of using a butcher knife on her husband if he tried to interfere with her and her son.

At last she stood up with Danny in her arms, her legs trembling. There was no other way. She would have to assume that Jack awake was Jack sane, and that he would help her get Danny down to Sidewinder and Dr Edmonds. And if Jack tried to do anything *but* help, God help *him*.

She went to the door and unlocked it. Shifting Danny up to her shoulder, she opened it and went out into the hall.

'Jack?' she called nervously, and got no answer.

With growing trepidation she walked down to the stairwell, but Jack was not there. And as she stood there on the landing, wondering what to do next, the singing came up from below, rich, angry, bitterly satiric:

> *'Roll me over*
> *In the clo-ho-ver,*
> *Roll me over, lay me down and do It again.'*

She was frightened even more by the sound of him than she had been by his silence, but there was still no alternative. She started down the stairs.

CHAPTER TWENTY-EIGHT
'IT WAS HER!'

Jack had stood on the stairs, listening to the crooning, comforting sounds coming muffled through the locked door, and slowly his confusion had given way to anger. Things had never really changed. Not to Wendy. He could be off the juice for twenty years and still when he came home at night and she embraced him at the door, he would see/sense that little flare of her nostrils as she tried to divine scotch or gin fumes riding the outboard train of his exhalation. She was always going to assume the worst; if he and Danny got in a car accident with a drunken blindman who had had a stroke just before the collision, she would silently blame Danny's injuries on him and turn away.

Her face as she had snatched Danny away – it rose up before him and he suddenly wanted to wipe the anger that had been on it out with his fist.

She had no goddam right!

Yes, maybe at first. He had been a lush, he had done terrible things. Breaking Danny's arm had been a terrible thing. But if a man reforms, doesn't he deserve to have his reformation credited sooner or later? And if he doesn't get it, doesn't he deserve the game to go with the name? If a father constantly accuses his virginal daughter of screwing every boy in junior high, must she not at last grow weary (enough) of it to earn her scoldings? And if a wife secretly – and not so secretly – continues to believe that her teetotaling husband is a drunk . . .

He got up, walked slowly down to the first-floor landing, and stood there for a moment. He took his handkerchief from his back pocket, wiped his lips with it, and considered going down and pounding on the bedroom door, demanding to be let in so he could see his son. She had no right to be so goddam highhanded.

Well, sooner or later she'd have to come out, unless she planned a radical sort of diet for the two of them. A rather ugly grin touched his lips at the thought. Let her come to him. She would in time.

He went downstairs to the ground floor, stood aimlessly by the lobby desk for a moment then turned right. He went into the dining room and stood just inside the door. The empty tables, their white linen cloths neatly cleaned and pressed beneath their clear plastic covers glimmered up at him. All was deserted now but

(Dinner Will Be Served At 8 PM)
Unmasking and Dancing At Midnight)

Jack walked among the tables, momentarily forgetting his wife and son upstairs, forgetting the dream, the smashed radio, the bruises. He trailed his fingers over the slick plastic dust covers, trying to imagine how it must have been on that hot August night in 1945, the war won, the future stretching ahead so various and new, like a land of dreams. The bright and particolored Japanese lanterns hung the whole length of the circular drive, the golden-yellow light spilling from these high windows that were now drifted over with snow. Men and women in costume, here a glittering princess, there a high-booted cavalier, flashing jewelry and flashing wit everywhere, dancing, liquor flowing freely, first wine and then cocktails and then perhaps boilermakers, the level of conversation going up and up until the jolly cry rang out from the bandmaster's podium, the cry of 'Unmask! Unmask!'

(And the Red Death held sway . . .)

He found himself standing on the other side of the dining room, just outside the stylized batwing doors of the Colorado Lounge, where, on that night in 1945, all the booze would have been free.

(Belly up to the bar, pardner, the drinks're on the house.)

He stepped through the batwings and into the deep, folded shadows of the bar. And a strange thing occurred. He had been in here before, once to check the inventory sheet Ullman had left, and he knew the place had been stripped clean. The shelves were totally bare. But now, lit only murkily by the light which filtered through from the dining room (which was itself only dimly lit because of the snow blocking the windows), he thought he saw ranks and ranks of bottles twinkling mutedly behind the bar, and syphons, and even beer dripping from the spigots of all three highly polished taps. Yes, he could even *smell* beer, that damp and fermented and yeasty odor, no different from the smell that had hung finely misted around his father's face every night when he came home from work.

Eyes widening, he fumbled for the wall switch, and the low, intimate bar-lighting came on, circles of twenty-watt bulbs emplanted on the tops of the three wagon-wheel chandeliers overhead.

The shelves were all empty. They had not even as yet gathered a good coat of dust. The beer taps were dry, as were the chrome drains beneath them. To his left and right, the velvet-upholstered booths stood like men with high backs, each one designed to give a maximum of privacy to the couple inside. Straight ahead, across the red-carpeted floor, forty barstools stood around the horseshoe-shaped bar. Each stool was upholstered in leather and embossed with cattle brands – Circle H, Bar D Bar (that was fitting), Rocking W, Lazy B.

He approached it, giving his head a little shake in bewilderment as he did so. It was like that day on the playground when . . . but there was no sense in thinking about that. Still he could have sworn he had seen those bottles, vaguely, it was true, the way you see the darkened shapes of furniture in a room where the curtains have been drawn. Mild glints on glass. The only thing that remained was that smell of beer, and Jack knew that was a smell that faded into the woodwork of every bar in the world after a certain period of time, not to be eradicated by any cleaner invented. Yet the smell here seemed sharp . . . almost fresh.

He sat down on one of the stools and propped his elbows on the bar's leather-cushioned edge. At his left hand was a bowl for peanuts – now empty, of course. The first bar he'd been in for nineteen months and the damned thing was dry – just his luck. All the same, a bitterly powerful wave of nostalgia swept over him, and the physical craving for a drink seemed to work itself up from his belly to his throat to his mouth and nose, shriveling and wrinkling the tissues as it went, making them cry out for something wet and long and cold.

He glanced at the shelves again in wild, irrational hope but the shelves were just as empty as before. He grinned in pain and frustration. His fists, clenching slowly, made minute scratchings on the bar's leather-padded edge.

'Hi, Lloyd,' he said. 'A little slow tonight, isn't it?'

Lloyd said it was. Lloyd asked him what it would be.

'Now I'm really glad you asked me that,' Jack said, 'really glad. Because I happen to have two twenties and two tens in my wallet and I was afraid they'd be sitting right there until sometime next April. There isn't a Seven-Eleven around here, would you believe it? And I thought they had Seven-Elevens on the fucking *moon*.'

Lloyd sympathized.

'So here's what,' Jack said. 'You set me up an even twenty martinis. An even twenty, just like that, kazang. One for every month I've been on the wagon and one to grow on. You can do that, can't you? You aren't too busy?'

Lloyd said he wasn't busy at all.

'Good man. You line those martians up right along the bar and I'm going to take them down, one by one. White man's burden, Lloyd my man.'

Lloyd turned to do the job. Jack reached into his pocket for his money clip and came out with an Excedrin bottle instead. His money clip was on the bedroom bureau, and of course his skinny-shanks wife had locked him out of the bedroom. Nice going, Wendy. You bleeding bitch.

'I seem to be momentarily light,' Jack said. 'How's my credit in this joint, anyhow?'

Lloyd said his credit was fine.

'That's super. I like you, Lloyd. You were always the best of them. Best damned barkeep between Barre and Portland, Maine. Portland, *Oregon*, for that matter.'

Lloyd thanked him for saying so.

Jack thumped the cap from his Excedrin bottle, shook two

tablets out, and flipped them into his mouth. The familiar acid-compelling taste flooded in.

He had a sudden sensation that people were watching him, curiously and with some contempt. The booths behind him were full – there were graying, distinguished men and beautiful young girls, all of them in costume, watching this sad exercise in the dramatic arts with cold amusement.

Jack whirled on his stool.

The booths were all empty, stretching away from the lounge door to the left and right, the line on his left cornering to flank the bar's horseshoe curve down the short length of the room. Padded leather seats and backs. Gleaming dark Formica tables, an ashtray on each one, a book of matches in each ashtray, the words *Colorado Lounge* stamped on each in gold leaf above the batwing-door logo.

He turned back, swallowing the rest of the dissolving Excedrin with a grimace.

'Lloyd, you're a wonder,' he said. 'Set up already. Your speed is only exceeded by the soulful beauty of your Neapolitan eyes. *Salud.*'

Jack contemplated the twenty imaginary drinks, the martini glasses blushing droplets of condensation, each with a swizzle poked through a plump green olive. He could almost smell gin on the air.

'The wagon,' he said. 'Have you ever been acquainted with a gentleman who has hopped up on the wagon?'

Lloyd allowed as how he had met such men from time to time.

'Have you ever renewed acquaintances with such a man after he hopped back off?'

Lloyd could not, in all honesty, recall.

'You never did, then,' Jack said. He curled his hand around the first drink, carried his fist to his mouth, which was open, and turned his fist up. He swallowed and then tossed the imaginary glass over his shoulder. The people were back again, fresh from their costume ball, studying him, laughing behind their hands. He could feel them. If the backbar had featured a mirror instead of those damn stupid empty shelves, he could have seen them. Let them stare. Fuck them. Let anybody stare who wanted to stare.

'No, you never did,' he told Lloyd. 'Few men ever return from the fabled Wagon, but those who do come with a fearful tale to tell. When you jump on it, it seems like the brightest, cleanest Wagon you ever saw, with ten-foot wheels to keep the bed of it high out of the gutter where all the drunks are laying around with their brown bags and their Thunderbird and their Granddad Flash's Popskull Bourbon. You're away from all the people who throw you nasty looks and tell you to clean up your act or go put it on in another town. From the gutter, that's finest-lookin Wagon you ever saw, Lloyd my boy. All hung with bunting and a brass band in front and three majorettes to each side, twirling their batons and flashing their panties at you. Man, you got to get on that Wagon and away from the juicers that are straining canned heat and smelling their own puke to get high again and poking along the gutter for butts with half an inch left below the filter.'

He drained two more imaginary drinks and tossed the glasses back over his shoulder. He could almost hear them smashing on the floor. And goddam if he wasn't starting to feel high. It was the Excedrin.

'So you climb up,' he told Lloyd, 'and ain't you glad to be there. My God yes, that's affirmative. That Wagon is the biggest and best float in the whole parade, and everybody is lining the streets and clapping and cheering and waving, all for you. Except for the winos passed out in the gutter. Those guys used to be your friends, but that's all behind you now.'

He carried his empty fist to his mouth and sluiced down another – four down, sixteen to go. Making excellent progress. He swayed a little on the stool. Let em stare, if that was how they got off. Take a picture, folks, it'll last longer.

Then you start to see things, Lloydy-my-boy. Things you missed from the gutter. Like how the floor of the Wagon is nothing but straight pine boards, so fresh they're still bleeding sap, and if you took your shoes off you'd be sure to get a splinter. Like how the only furniture in the Wagon is these long benches with high backs and no cushions to sit on, and in fact they are nothing but pews with a songbook every five feet or so. Like how all the people sitting in the pews on the Wagon are those flat-chested el birdos in long dresses with a little lace around the collar and their hair pulled back into buns until it's so tight you can almost hear it screaming. And every face is flat and pale and shiny, and they're all singing "Shall we gather at the riiiiver, the beautiful, the beautiful, the *riiiiver*," and up front there's this reekin bitch with blond hair playing the organ and tellin em to sing louder, sing louder. And somebody slams a songbook into your hands and says, "Sing it out, brother. If you expect to stay on this Wagon, you got to sing morning, noon, and night. Especially at night." And that's when you realize what the Wagon really is, Lloyd. It's a church with bars on the windows, a church for women and a prison for you.'

He stopped. Lloyd was gone. Worse still, he had never been there. The drinks had never been there. Only the people in the booths, the people from the costume party, and he could almost hear their muffled laughter as they held their hands to their mouths and pointed, their eyes sparkling with cruel pinpoints of light.

He whirled around again. 'Leave me —'

(alone?)

All the booths were empty. The sound of laughter had died like a stir of autumn leaves. Jack stared at the empty lounge for a tick of time, his eyes wide and dark. A pulse beat noticeably in the center of his forehead. In the very center of him a cold certainty was forming and the certainty was that he was losing his mind. He felt an urge to pick up the bar stool next to him, reverse it, and go through the place like an avenging whirlwind. Instead he whirled back around to the bar and began to bellow:

> *'Roll me over*
> *In the Clo-ho-ver,*
> *Roll me over, lay me down and do it again.'*

Danny's face rose before him, not Danny's normal face, lively and alert, the eyes sparkling and open, but the catatonic, zombielike face of a stranger, the eyes dull and opaque, the mouth pursed babyishly around his thumb. What was he doing, sitting here and talking to himself like a sulky teen-ager when his son was upstairs someplace, acting like something that belonged in a padded room, acting the way Wally Hollis said Vic Stenger had been before the men in the white coats had to come and take him away?

(*But I never put a hand on him! Goddammit, I didn't!*)

'Jack?' The voice was timid, hesitant.

He was so startled he almost fell off the stool whirling it around. Wendy was standing just inside the batwing doors, Danny cradled in her arms like some waxen horror show dummy. The three of them made a tableau that Jack felt very strongly: it was just before the curtain of Act II in some old time temperance play, one so poorly mounted that the prop man had forgotten to stock the shelves of the Den of Iniquity.

'I never touched him,' Jack said thickly. 'I never have since the night I broke his arm. Not even to spank him.'

'Jack, that doesn't matter now. What matters is—'

'*This matters!*' he shouted. He brought one fist crashing down on the bar, hard enough to make the empty peanut dishes jump. '*It matters, goddammit, it matters!*'

'Jack, we have to get him off the mountain. He's—'

Danny began to stir in her arms. The slack, empty expression on his face had begun to break up like a thick matte of ice over some buried surface. His lips twisted, as if at some weird taste. His eyes widened. His hands came up as if to cover them and then dropped back.

Abruptly he stiffened in her arms. His back arched into a bow, making Wendy stagger. And he suddenly began to shriek, mad sounds that escaped his straining throat in bolt after crazy, echoing bolt. The sound seemed to fill the empty downstairs and come back at them like banshees. There might have been a hundred Dannys, all screaming at once.

'*Jack!*' she cried in terror. '*Oh God Jack what's wrong with him?*'

He came off the stool, numb from the waist down, more frightened than he had ever been in his life. What hole had his son poked through and into? What dark nest? And what had been in there to sting him?

'Danny!' he roared. '*Danny!*'

Danny saw him. He broke his mother's grip with a sudden, fierce strength that gave her no chance to hold him. She stumbled back against one of the booths and nearly fell into it.

'*Daddy!*' he screamed, running to Jack, his eyes huge and affrighted. '*Oh Daddy Daddy, it was her! Her! Her! Oh Daaaaahdeee—*'

He slammed into Jack's arms like a blunt arrow, making Jack rock on his feet. Danny clutched at him furiously, at first seeming to pummel him like a fighter, then clutching his belt and sobbing against his shirt. Jack could feel his son's face, hot and working, against his belly.

Daddy, it was her.

Jack looked slowly up into Wendy's face. His eyes were like small silver coins.

'Wendy?' Voice soft, nearly purring. 'Wendy, what did you do to him?'

Wendy stared back at him in stunned disbelief, her face pallid. She shook her head.

'Oh Jack, you must know—'

Outside it had begun to snow again.

CHAPTER TWENTY-NINE
KITCHEN TALK

Jack carried Danny into the kitchen. The boy was still sobbing wildly, refusing to look up from Jack's chest. In the kitchen he gave Danny back to Wendy, who still seemed stunned and disbelieving.

'Jack, I don't know what he's talking about. Please, you must believe that.'

'I do believe it,' he said, although he had to admit to himself that it gave him a certain amount of pleasure to see the shoe switched to the other foot with such dazzling, unexpected speed. But his anger at Wendy had been only a passing gut twitch. In his heart he knew Wendy would pour a can of gasoline over herself and strike a match before harming Danny.

The large tea kettle was on the back burner, poking along on low heat. Jack dropped a teabag into his own large ceramic cup and poured hot water halfway.

'Got cooking sherry, don't you?' he asked Wendy.

'What? . . . oh, sure. Two or three bottles of it.'

'Which cupboard?'

She pointed, and Jack took one of the bottles down. He poured a hefty dollop into the teacup, put the sherry back, and filled the last quarter of the cup with milk. Then he added three tablespoons of sugar and stirred. He brought it to Danny, whose sobs had tapered off to snifflings and hitchings. But he was trembling all over, and his eyes were wide and starey.

'Want you to drink this, doc,' Jack said. 'It's going to taste frigging awful, but it'll make you feel better. Can you drink it for your daddy?'

Danny nodded that he could and took the cup. He drank a little, grimaced, and looked questioningly at Jack. Jack nodded, Danny drank again. Wendy felt the familiar twist of jealousy somewhere in her middle, knowing the boy would not have drunk it for her.

On the heels of that came an uncomfortable, even startling thought: Had she *wanted* to think Jack was to blame? Was she that jealous? It was the way her mother would have thought, that was the really terrible thing. She could remember a Sunday when her Dad had taken her to the park and she had toppled from the second tier of the jungle gym, cutting both knees. When her father brought her home, her mother had shrieked at him: *What did you do? Why weren't you watching her? What kind of a father are you?*

(She hounded him to his grave; by the time he divorced her it was too late.)

She had never even given Jack the benefit of the doubt. Not the smallest. Wendy felt her face burn yet knew with a kind of helpless finality that if the whole thing were to be played over again, she would do and think the same way. She carried part of her mother with her always, for good or bad.

'Jack—' she began, not sure if she meant to apologize or justify. Either, she knew, would be useless.

'Not now,' he said.

It took Danny fifteen minutes to drink half of the big cup's contents, and by that time he had calmed visibly. The shakes were almost gone.

Jack put his hands solemnly on his son's shoulders. 'Danny, do you think you can tell us exactly what happened to you? It's very important.'

Danny looked from Jack to Wendy, then back again. In the silent pause, their setting and situation made themselves known: the whoop of the wind outside, driving fresh snow down from the northwest; the creaking and groaning of the old hotel as it settled into another storm. The fact of their disconnect came to Wendy with unexpected force as it sometimes did, like a blow under the heart.

'I want . . . to tell you everything,' Danny said. 'I wish I had before.' He picked up the cup and held it, as if comforted by the warmth.

'Why didn't you, son?' Jack brushed Danny's sweaty, tumbled hair back gently from his brow.

'Because Uncle Al got you the job. And I couldn't figure out how it was good for you here and bad for you here at the same time. It was . . .' He looked at them for help. He did not have the necessary word.

'A dilemma?' Wendy asked gently. 'When neither choice seems any good?'

'Yes, that.' He nodded, relieved.

Wendy said: 'The day that you trimmed the hedges, Danny and I had a talk in the truck. The day the first real snow came. Remember?'

Jack nodded. The day he had trimmed the hedges was very clear in his mind.

Wendy sighed. 'I guess we didn't talk enough. Did we, doc?'

Danny, the picture of woe, shook his head.

'Exactly what did you talk about?' Jack asked. 'I'm not sure how much I like my wife and son—'

'—discussing how much they love you?'

'Whatever it was, I don't understand it. I feel like I came into a movie just after the intermission.'

'We were discussing you,' Wendy said quietly. 'And maybe we didn't say it all in words, but we both knew. Me because I'm your wife and Danny because he . . . just understands things.'

Jack was silent.

'Danny said it just right. The place seemed good for you. You were away from all the pressures that made you so unhappy at Stovington. You were your own boss, working with your hands so you could save your brain – all of your brain – for your evenings writing. Then . . . I don't know just when . . . the place began to seem bad for you. Spending all that time down in the cellar, sifting through those old papers, all that old history. Talking in your sleep—'

'In my sleep?' Jack asked. His face wore a cautious, startled expression. 'I talk in my sleep?'

'Most of it is slurry. Once I got up to use the bathroom and you were saying, "To hell with it, bring in the slots at least, no one will know, no one will ever know." Another time you woke me right up, practically yelling, "Unmask, unmask, unmask."'

'Jesus Christ,' he said, and rubbed a hand over his face. He looked ill.

'All your old drinking habits, too. Chewing Excedrin. Wiping your mouth all the time. Cranky in the morning. And you haven't been able to finish the play yet, have you?'

'No. Not yet, but it's only a matter of time. I've been thinking about something else . . . a new project—'

'This hotel. The project Al Shockley called you about. The one he wanted you to drop.'

'How do you know about that?' Jack barked. 'Were you listening in? You—'

'No,' she said. 'I couldn't have listened in if I'd wanted to, and you'd know that if you were thinking straight. Danny and I were downstairs that night. The switchboard is shut down. Our phone upstairs was the only one in the hotel that was working, because it's patched directly into the outside line. You told me so yourself.'

'Then how could you know what Al told me?'

'Danny told me. Danny knew. The same way he sometimes knows when things are misplaced, or when people are thinking about divorce.'

'The doctor said—'

She shook her head impatiently. 'The doctor was full of shit and we both know it. We've known it all the time. Remember when Danny said he wanted to see the firetrucks? That was no hunch. *He was just a baby*. He *knows* things. And now I'm afraid . . .' She looked at the bruises on Danny's neck.

'Did you really know Uncle Al had called me, Danny?'

Danny nodded. 'He was really mad, Daddy. Because you called Mr Ullman and Mr Ullman called him. Uncle Al didn't want you to write anything about the hotel.'

'Jesus,' Jack said again. 'The bruises, Danny. Who tried to strangle you?'

Danny's face went dark. '*Her*,' he said. 'The woman in that room. In 217. The dead lady.' His lips began to tremble again, and he seized the teacup and drank.

Jack and Wendy exchanged a scared look over his bowed head.

'Do you know anything about this?' he asked her.

She shook her head. 'Not about this, no.'

'Danny?' He raised the boy's frightened face. 'Try, son. We're right here.'

'I knew it was bad here,' Danny said in a low voice. 'Ever since we were in Boulder. Because Tony gave me dreams about it.'

'What dreams?'

'I can't remember everything. He showed me the Overlook at night, with a skull and crossbones on the front. And there was pounding. Something . . . I don't remember what . . . chasing after me. A monster. Tony showed me about redrum.'

'What's that, doc?' Wendy asked.

He shook his head. 'I don't know.'

'Rum, like yo-ho-ho and a bottle of rum?' Jack asked.

Danny shook his head again. 'I don't know. Then we got here, and Mr Hallorann talked to me in his car. Because he has the shine, too.'

'Shine?'

'It's . . .' Danny made a sweeping, all-encompassing gesture with his hands. 'It's being able to understand things. To know things. Sometimes you see things. Like me knowing Uncle Al called. And Mr Hallorann knowing you call me doc. Mr Hallorann, he was peeling potatoes in the Army when he knew his brother got killed in a train crash. And when he called home it was true.'

'Holy God,' Jack whispered. 'You're not making this up, are you, Dan?'

Danny shook his head violently. 'No, I swear to God.' Then, with a touch of pride he added: 'Mr Hallorann said I had the best shine of anyone he ever met. We could talk back and forth to each other without hardly opening our mouths.'

His parents looked at each other again, frankly stunned.

'Mr Hallorann got me alone because he was worried,' Danny went on. 'He said this was a bad place for people who shine. He said he'd seen things. I saw something, too. Right after I talked to him. When Mr Ullman was taking us around.'

'What was it?' Jack asked.

'In the Presidential Sweet. On the wall by the door going into the bedroom. A whole lot of blood and some other stuff. Gushy stuff. I think . . . that the gushy stuff must have been brains.'

'Oh my God,' Jack said.

Wendy was now very pale, her lips nearly gray.

'This place,' Jack said. 'Some pretty bad types owned it awhile back. Organization people from Las Vegas.'

'Crooks?' Danny said.

'Yeah, crooks.' He looked at Wendy. 'In 1966 a big-time hood named Vito Gienelli got killed up there, along with his two bodyguards. There was a picture in the newspaper. Danny just described the picture.'

'Mr Hallorann said he saw some other stuff,' Danny told them. 'Once about the playground. And once it was something bad in that room. 217. A maid saw it and lost her job because she talked about it. So Mr Hallorann went up and he saw it too. But he didn't talk about it because he didn't want to lose his job. Except he told me never to go in there. But I did. Because I believed him when he said the things you saw here couldn't hurt you.' This last was nearly whispered in a low, husky voice, and Danny touched the puffed circle of bruises on his neck.

'What about the playground?' Jack asked in a strange, casual voice.

'I don't know. The playground, he said. And the hedge animals.'

Jack jumped a little, and Wendy looked at him curiously.

'Have you seen anything down there, Jack?'

'No,' he said. 'Nothing.'

Danny was looking at him.

'Nothing,' he said again, more calmly. And that was true. He had been the victim of an hallucination. And that was *all*.

'Danny, we have to hear about the woman,' Wendy said gently.

So Danny told them, but his words came in cyclic bursts,

sometimes almost verging on incomprehensible garble in his hurry to spit it out and be free of it. He pushed tighter and tighter against his mother's breasts as he talked.

'I went in,' he said. 'I stole the passkey and went in. It was like I couldn't help myself. I had to know. And she ... the lady ... was in the tub. She was dead. All swelled up. She was nuh-nuh ... didn't have no clothes on.' He looked miserably at his mother. 'And she started to get up and she wanted me. I know she did because I could feel it. She wasn't even thinking, not the way you and Daddy think. It was black ... it was hurt-think ... like ... like the wasps that night in my room! Only wanting to hurt. Like the wasps.'

He swallowed and there was silence for a moment, all quiet while the image of the wasps sank into them.

'So I ran,' Danny said. 'I ran but the door was closed. I left it open but it was closed. I didn't think about just opening it again and running out. I was scared. So I just ... I leaned against the door and closed my eyes and thought of how Mr Hallorann said the things here were just like pictures in a book and if I ... kept saying to myself ... *you're not there, go away, you're not there* ... she would go away. But it didn't work.'

His voice began to rise hysterically.

'She grabbed me ... turned me around ... I could see her eyes ... how her eyes were ... and she started to choke me ... I could smell her ... *I could smell how dead she was* ...'

'Stop now, shhh,' Wendy said, alarmed. 'Stop, Danny. It's all right. It—'

She was getting ready to go into her croon again. The Wendy Torrance All-purpose Croon. Pat. Pending.

'Let him finish,' Jack said curtly.

'There isn't any more,' Danny said. 'I passed out. Either because she was choking me or just because I was scared. When I came to, I was dreaming you and Mommy were fighting over me and you wanted to do the Bad Thing again, Daddy. Then I knew it wasn't a dream at all ... and I was awake ... and ... I wet my pants. I wet my pants like a baby.' His head fell back against Wendy's sweater and he began to cry with horrible weakness, his hands lying limp and spent in his lap.

Jack got up. 'Take care of him.'

'What are you going to do?' Her face was full of dread.

'I'm going up to that room, what did you think I was going to do? Have coffee?'

'No! Don't, Jack, please *don't!*'

'Wendy, if there's someone else in the hotel, we have to know.'

'*Don't you dare leave us alone!*' she shrieked at him. Spittle flew from her lips with the force of her cry.

Jack said: 'Wendy, that's a remarkable imitation of your mom.'

She burst into tears then, unable to cover her face because Danny was on her lap.

'I'm sorry,' Jack said. 'But I have to, you know. I'm the goddam caretaker. It's what I'm paid for.'

She only cried harder and he left her that way, going out of the kitchen, rubbing his mouth with his handkerchief as the door swung shut behind him.

'Don't worry, mommy,' Danny said. 'He'll be all right. He doesn't shine. Nothing here can hurt him.'

Through her tears she said, 'No, I don't believe that.'

CHAPTER THIRTY
217 REVISITED

He took the elevator up and it was strange, because none of them had used the elevator since they moved in. He threw the brass handle over and it wheezed vibratoriously up the shaft, the brass grate rattling madly. Wendy had a true claustrophobe's horror of the elevator, he knew. She envisioned the three of them trapped in it between floors while the winter storms raged outside, she could see them growing thinner and weaker, starving to death. Or perhaps dining on each other, the way those Rugby players had. He remembered a bumper sticker he had seen in Boulder, RUGBY PLAYERS EAT THEIR OWN DEAD. He could think of others. YOU ARE WHAT YOU EAT. Or menu items. Welcome to the Overlook Dining Room, Pride of the Rockies. Eat in Splendor at the Roof of the World. Human Haunch Broiled Over Matches *La Spécialité de la Maison*. The contemptuous smile flicked over his features again. As the number 2 rose on the shaft wall, he threw the brass handle back to the home position and the elevator car creaked to a stop. He took his Excedrin from his pocket, shook three of them into his hand, and opened the elevator door. Nothing in the Overlook frightened him. He felt that he and it were *simpático*.

He walked up the hall flipping his Excedrin into his mouth and chewing them one by one. He rounded the corner into the short corridor off the main hall. The door to Room 217 was ajar, and the passkey hung from the lock on its white paddle.

He frowned, feeling a wave of irritation and even real anger. Whatever had come of it, the boy had been trespassing. He had been told, and told bluntly, that certain areas of the hotel were off limits: the equipment shed, the basement, and all of the guest rooms. He would talk to Danny about that just as soon as the boy was over his fright. He would talk to him reasonably but sternly. There were plenty of fathers who would have done more than just talk. They would have administered a good shaking, and perhaps that was what Danny needed. If the boy had gotten a scare, wasn't that at least his just deserts?

He walked down to the door, removed the passkey, dropped it into his pocket, and stepped inside. The overhead light was on. He glanced at the bed, saw it was not rumpled, and then walked directly across to the bathroom door. A curious certainty had grown in him. Although Watson had mentioned no names or room numbers, Jack felt sure that this was the room the lawyer's wife and her stud had shared, that this was the bathroom where she had been found dead, full of barbiturates and Colorado Lounge booze.

He pushed the mirror-backed bathroom door open and stepped through. The light in here was off. He turned it on and observed the long, Pullman-car room, furnished in the distinctive early nineteen-hundreds-remodeled-in-the-twenties style that seemed common to all Overlook bathrooms, except for the ones on the third floor – those were properly Byzantine, as befitted the royalty, politicians, movie stars, and capos who had stayed there over the years.

The shower curtain, a pallid pastel pink, was drawn protectively around the long claw-footed tub.

(nevertheless they *did* move)

And for the first time he felt his new sense of sureness (almost cockiness) that had come over him when Danny ran to him shouting *It was her! It was her!* deserting him. A chilled finger pressed gently against the base of his spine, cooling him off ten degrees. It was joined by others and they suddenly rippled all the way up his back to his medulla oblongata, playing his spine like a jungle instrument.

His anger at Danny evaporated, and as he stepped forward and pushed the shower curtain back his mouth was dry and he felt only sympathy for his son and terror for himself.

The tub was dry and empty.

Relief and irritation vented in a sudden 'Pah!' sound that escaped his compressed lips like a very small explosive. The tub had been scrubbed clean at the end of the season; except for the rust stain under the twin faucets, it sparkled. There was a faint but definable smell of cleanser, the kind that can irritate your nose with the smell of its own righteousness for weeks, even months, after it has been used.

He bent down and ran his fingertips along the bottom of the tub. Dry as a bone. Not even a hint of moisture. The boy had been either hallucinating or outright lying. He felt angry again. That was when the bathmat on the floor caught his attention. He frowned down at it. What was a bathmat doing in here? It should be down in the linen cupboard at the end of the wing with the rest of the sheets and towels and pillow slips. All the linen was supposed to be there. Not even the beds were really made up in these guest rooms; the mattresses had been zipped into clear plastic and then covered with bedspreads. He supposed Danny might have gone down and gotten it – the passkey would open the linen cupboard – but why? He brushed the tips of his fingers back and forth across it. The bathmat was bone dry.

He went back to the bathroom door and stood in it. Everything was all right. The boy had been dreaming. There was not a thing out of place. It was a little puzzling about the bathmat, granted, but the logical explanation was that some chambermaid, hurrying like mad on the last day of the season, had just forgotten to pick it up. Other than that, everything was—

His nostrils flared a little. Disinfectant, that self-righteous smell, cleaner-than-thou. And—

Soap?

Surely not. But once the smell had been identified, it was too clear to dismiss. Soap. And not one of those postcard-size bars of Ivory they provide you with in hotels and motels, either. This scent was light and perfumed, a lady's soap. It had a pink sort of smell, Camay or Lowila, the brand that Wendy had always used in Stovington.

(It's nothing. It's your imagination.)
(yes like the hedges nevertheless they did move)
(They did not move!)

He crossed jerkily to the door which gave on the hall, feeling the irregular thump of a headache beginning at his temples. Too much had happened today, too much by far. He wouldn't spank the boy or shake him, just talk to him, but by God, he wasn't going to add Room 217 to his problems. Not on the basis of a dry bathmath and a faint smell of Lowila soap. He—

There was a sudden rattling, metallic sound behind him. It came just as his hand closed around the doorknob, and an observer might have thought the brushed steel of the knob carried an electric charge. He jerked convulsively, eyes widening, other facial features drawing in, grimacing.

Then he had control of himself, a little, anyway, and he let go of the doorknob and turned carefully around. His joints creaked. He began to walk back to the bathroom door, step by leaden step.

The shower curtain which he had pushed back to look into the tub, was now drawn. The metallic rattle, which had sounded to him like a stir of bones in a crypt, had been the curtain rings on the overhead bar. Jack stared at the curtain. His face felt as if it had been heavily waxed, all dead skin on the outside, live, hot rivulets of fear on the inside. The way he had felt on the playground.

There was something behind the pink plastic shower curtain. There was something in the tub.

He could see it, ill defined and obscure through the plastic, a nearly amorphous shape. It could have been anything. A trick of the light. The shadow of the shower attachment. A woman long dead and reclining in her bath, a bar of Lowila in one stiffening hand as she waited patiently for whatever lover might come.

Jack told himself to step forward boldly and rake the shower curtain back. To expose whatever might be there. Instead he turned with jerky, marionette strides, his heart whamming frightfully in his chest, and went back into the bed/sitting room.

The door to the hall was shut.

He stared at it for a long, immobile second. He could taste his terror now. It was in the back of his throat like a taste of gone-over cherries.

He walked to the door with that same jerky stride and forced his fingers to curl around the knob.

THE SHINING

(It won't open.)

But it did.

He turned off the light with a fumbling gesture, stepped out into the hall, and pulled the door shut without looking back. From inside, he seemed to hear an odd wet thumping sound, far off, dim, as if something had just scrambled belatedly out of the tub, as if to greet a caller, as if it had realized the caller was leaving before the social amenities had been completed and so it was now rushing to the door, all purple and grinning, to invite the caller back inside. Perhaps forever.

Footsteps approaching the door or only the heartbeat in his ears?

He fumbled at the passkey. It seemed sludgy, unwilling to turn in the lock. He attacked the passkey. The tumblers suddenly fell and he stepped back against the corridor's far wall, a little groan of relief escaping him. He closed his eyes and all the old phrases began to parade through his mind, it seemed there must be hundreds of them.

(cracking up not playing with a full deck lostya marbles guy just went loony tunes he went up and over the high side went bananas lost his football crackers nuts half a seabag)

all meaning the same thing: *losing your mind.*

'No,' he whimpered, hardly aware that he had been reduced to this, whimpering with his eyes shut like a child. 'Oh no, God. Please, God, no.'

But below the tumble of his chaotic thoughts, below the triphammer beat of his heart, he could hear the soft and futile sound of the doorknob being turned to and fro as something locked in tried helplessly to get out, something that wanted to meet him, something that would like to be introduced to his family as the storm shrieked around them and white daylight became black night. If he opened his eyes and saw that doorknob moving he would go mad. So he kept them shut, and after an unknowable time, there was stillness.

Jack forced himself to open his eyes, half-convinced that when he did, she would be standing before him. But the hall was empty.

He felt watched just the same.

He looked at the peephole in the center of the door and wondered what would happened if he approached it, stared into it. What would he be eyeball to eyeball with?

His feet were moving.

(feets don't fail me now)

before he realized it. He turned them away from the door and walked down to the main hall, his feet whispering on the blue–black jungle carpet. He stopped halfway to the stairs and looked at the fire extinguisher. He thought that the folds of canvas were arranged in a slightly different manner. And he was quite sure that the brass nozzle had been pointing toward the elevator when he came up the hall. Now it was pointing the other way.

'I didn't see that at all,' Jack Torrance said quite clearly. His face was white and haggard and his mouth kept trying to grin.

But he didn't take the elevator back down. It was too much like an open mouth. Too much by half. He took the stairs.

CHAPTER THIRTY-ONE
THE VERDICT

He stepped into the kitchen and looked at them, bouncing the passkey a few inches up off his left hand, making the chain on the white metal tongue jingle, then catching it again. Danny was pallid and worn out. Wendy had been crying, he saw; her eyes were red and darkly circled. He felt a sudden burst of gladness at this. He wasn't suffering alone, that was sure.

They looked at him without speaking.

'Nothing there,' he said, astounded, by the heartiness of his voice. 'Not a thing.'

He bounced the passkey up and down, up and down, smiling reassuringly at them, watching the relief spread over their faces, and thought he had never in his life wanted a drink so badly as he did right now.

CHAPTER THIRTY-TWO
THE BEDROOM

Late that afternoon Jack got a cot from the first-floor storage room and put it in the corner of their bedroom. Wendy had expected that the boy would be half the night getting to sleep, but Danny was nodding before 'The Waltons' was half over, and fifteen minutes after they had tucked him in he was far down in sleep, moveless, one hand tucked under his cheek. Wendy sat watching him, holding her place in a fat paperback copy of *Cashelmara* with one finger. Jack sat at his desk, looking at his play.

'Oh shit,' Jack said.

Wendy looked up from her contemplation of Danny. 'What?'

'Nothing.'

He looked down at the play with smoldering ill-temper. How could he have thought it was good? It was puerile. It had been done a thousand times. Worse, he had no idea how to finish it. Once it had seemed simple enough. Denker, in a fit of rage, seizes the poker from beside the fireplace and beats saintly Gary to death. Then, standing spread-legged over the body, the bloody poker in one hand, he screams at the audience: 'It's here somewhere and I *will* find it!' Then, as the lights dim and the curtain is slowly drawn, the audience sees Gary's body face down on the forestage as Denker strides to the upstage bookcase and feverishly begins pulling books from the shelves, looking at them, throwing them aside. He had thought it was something old enough to be new, a play whose novelty alone might be enough to see it through a successful Broadway run: a tragedy in five acts.

But, in addition to his sudden diversion of interest to the Overlook's history, something else had happened. He had developed opposing feelings about his characters. This was something quite new. Ordinarily he liked all of his characters, the good and the bad. He was glad he did. It allowed him to try to see all of their sides and understand their motivations more clearly. His favorite story, sold to a small southern Maine magazine called *Contraband for copies*, had been a piece called 'The Monkey Is Here, Paul DeLong'. It had been about a child molester about to commit suicide in his furnished room. The child molester's name had been Paul DeLong, Monkey to his friends. Jack had liked Monkey very much. He sympathized with Monkey's bizarre needs, knowing that Monkey was not the only one to blame for the three rape-murders in his past. There had been bad parents, the father a beater as his own father had been, the mother a limp and silent dishrag as his mother had been. A homosexual experience in grammar school. Public humiliation. Worse experiences in high school and college. He had been arrested and sent to an institution after exposing himself to a pair of little girls getting off a school bus. Worst of all, he had been dismissed from the institution, let back out onto the streets, because the man in charge had decided he was all right. This man's name had been Grimmer. Grimmer had known that Monkey DeLong was exhibiting deviant symptoms, but he had written the good, hopeful report and had let him go anyway. Jack liked and sympathized with Grimmer, too. Grimmer had to run an understaffed and underfunded institution and try to keep the whole thing together with spit, baling wire, and nickle-and-dime appropriations from a state legislature who had to go back and face the voters. Grimmer knew that Monkey could interact with other people, that he did not soil his pants or try to stab his fellow inmates with the scissors. He did not think he was Napoleon. The staff psychiatrist in charge of Monkey's case thought there was a better-than-even chance that Monkey could make it on the street, and they both knew that the longer a man is in an institution the more he comes to need that closed environment, like a junkie with his smack. And meanwhile, people were knocking down the doors. Paranoids, schizoids, cycloids, semicatatonics, men who claimed to have gone to heaven in flying saucers, women who had burned their children's sex organs off with Bic lighters, alcoholics, pyromaniacs, kleptomaniacs, manic-depressives, suicidals. Tough old world, baby. If you're not bolted together tightly, you're gonna shake, rattle, and roll before you turn thirty. Jack could sympathize with Grimmer's problem. He could sympathize with the parents of the murder victims. With the murdered children themselves, of course. And with Monkey DeLong. Let the reader lay blame. In those days he hadn't wanted to judge. The cloak of the moralist sat badly on his shoulders.

He had started *The Little School* in the same optimistic vein. But lately he had begun to choose up sides, and worse still, he had come to loathe his hero, Gary Benson. Originally conceived as a bright boy more cursed with money than blessed with it, a boy who wanted more than anything to compile a good record so he could go to a good university because he had earned admission and not because his father had pulled strings, he had become to Jack a kind of simpering Goody Two-shoes, a postulant before the altar of knowledge rather than a sincere acolyte, an outward paragon of Boy Scout virtues, inwardly cynical, filled not with real brilliance (as he had first been conceived) but only with sly animal cunning. All through the play he unfailingly addressed Denker as 'sir', just as Jack had taught his own son to address those older and those in authority as 'sir'. He thought that Danny used the word quite sincerely, and Gary Benson as originally conceived had too, but as he had begun Act V, it had come more and more strongly to him that Gary was using the word satirically, outwardly straight-faced while the Gary Benson inside was mugging and leering at Denker. Denker, who had never had any of the things Gary had. Denker, who had had to work all his life just to become head of a single little school. Who was now faced with ruin over this handsome, innocent-seeming rich boy who had cheated on his Final Composition and had then cunningly covered his tracks. Jack had seen Denker the teacher as not much different from the strutting South American little Caesars in their banana kingdoms, standing dissidents up against the wall of the handiest squash or handball court, a super-zealot in a comparatively small puddle, a man whose every whim becomes a crusade. In the beginning he had wanted to use his play as a microcosm to say something about the abuse of power. Now he tended more and more to see Denker as a Mr Chips figure, and the tragedy was not the intellectual racking of Gary Benson but rather the destruction of a kindly old teacher and headmaster unable to see through the cynical wiles of this monster masquerading as a boy.

He hadn't been able to finish the play.

Now he sat looking down at it, scowling, wondering if there was any way he could salvage the situation. He didn't really think there was. He had begun with one play and it had somehow turned into another, presto-chango. Well, what the hell. Either way it had been done before. Either way it was a load of shit. And why was he driving himself crazy about it tonight anyway? After the day just gone by it was no wonder he couldn't think straight.

'— get him down?'

He looked up, trying to blink the cobwebs away. 'Huh?'

'I said, how are we going to get him down? We've got to get him out of here, Jack.'

For a moment his wits were so scattered that he wasn't even sure what she was talking about. Then he realized and uttered a short, barking laugh.

'You say that as if it were so easy.'

'I didn't mean —'

'No problem, Wendy. I'll just change clothes in that telephone booth down in the lobby and fly him to Denver on my back. Superman Jack Torrance, they called me in my salad days.'

Her face registered slow hurt.

'I understand the problem, Jack. The radio is broken. The snow . . . but you have to understand Danny's problem. My God, don't you? He was nearly catatonic, Jack! What if he hadn't come out of that?'

'But he did,' Jack said, a trifle shortly. He had been frightened at Danny's blank-eyed, slack-faced state too, of course he had. At first. But the more he thought about it, the more he wondered if it hadn't been a piece of play-acting put on to escape his punishment. He had, after all, been trespassing.

'All the same,' she said. She came to him and sat on the end of the bed by his desk. Her face was both surprised and worried.

'Jack, the bruises on his neck! Something got at him! And I want him away from it!'

'Don't shout,' he said. 'My head aches, Wendy. I'm as worried about this as you are, so please . . . don't . . . shout.'

'All right,' she said, lowering her voice. 'I won't shout. But I don't understand you, Jack. Someone is in here with us. And not a very nice someone, either. We have to get down to Sidewinder, not just Danny but all of us. Quickly. And you . . . you're sitting there reading your *play*!'

' "We have to get down, we have to get down," you keep saying that. You must think I really am Superman.'

'I think you're my husband,' she said softly, and looked down at her hands.

His temper flared. He slammed the playscript down, knocking the edges of the pile out of true again and crumpling the sheets on the bottom.

'It's time you got some of the home truths into you, Wendy. You don't seem to have internalized them, as the sociologists say. They're knocking around up in your head like a bunch of loose cueballs. You need to shoot them into the pockets. You need to understand that *we are snowed in*.'

Danny had suddenly become active in his bed. Still sleeping, he had begun to twist and turn. The way he always did when we fought, Wendy thought dismally. And we're doing it again.

'Don't wake him up, Jack. Please.

He glanced over at Danny and some of the flush went out of his cheeks. 'Okay. I'm sorry. I'm sorry I sounded mad, Wendy. It's not really for you. But I broke the radio. If it's anybody's fault it's mine. That was our big link to the outside. Olly-olly-in-for-free. Please come get us, Mister Ranger. We can't stay out this late.'

'Don't,' she said, and put a hand on his shoulder. He leaned his head against it. She brushed his hair with her other hand. 'I guess you've got a right, after what I accused you of. Sometimes I am like my mother. I can be a bitch. But you have to understand that some things . . . are hard to get over. You have to understand that.'

'Do you mean his arm?' His lips had thinned.

'Yes,' Wendy said, and then she rushed on: 'But it's not just you. I worry when he goes out to play. I worry about him wanting a two-wheeler next year, even one with training wheels. I worry about his teeth and his eyesight and about this thing, what he calls his shine. I worry. Because he's little and he seems very fragile and because . . . because something in this hotel seems to want him. And it will go through us to get him if it has to. That's why we must get him out, Jack. I know that! I feel that! *We must get him out!*'

Her hand tightened painfully on his shoulder in her agitation, but he didn't move away. One hand found the firm weight of her left breast and he began to stroke it through her shirt.

'Wendy,' he said, and stopped. She waited for him to rearrange whatever he had to say. His strong hand on her breast felt good, soothing. 'I could snowshoe him down. He could walk part of the way himself, but I would mostly have to carry him. It would mean camping out one, two, maybe three nights. That would mean building a travois to carry supplies and bedrolls on. We have the AM/FM radio, so we could pick a day when the weather forecast called for a three-day spell of good weather. But if the forecast was wrong,' he finished, his voice soft and measured, 'I think we might die.'

Her face had paled. It looked shiny, almost ghostly. He continued to stroke her breast, rubbing the ball of his thumb gently over the nipple.

She made a soft sound – from his words or in reaction to his gentle pressure on her breast, he couldn't tell. He raised his hand slightly and undid the top button of her shirt. Wendy shifted her legs slightly. All at once her jeans seemed too tight, slightly irritating in a pleasant sort of way.

'It would mean leaving you alone because you can't snowshoe worth beans. It would be maybe three days of not knowing. Would you want that?' His hand dropped to the second button, slipped it, and the beginning of her cleavage was exposed.

'No,' she said in a voice that was slightly thick. She glanced over at Danny. He had stopped twisting and turning. His thumb had crept back into his mouth. So that was all right. But Jack was leaving something out of the picture. It was too bleak. There was something else . . . what?

'If we stay put,' Jack said, unbuttoning the third and fourth buttons with that same deliberate slowness, 'a ranger from the park or a game warden is going to poke in here just to find out how we're doing. At that point we simply tell him we want down. He'll see to it.' He slipped her naked breasts into the wide V of the open shirt, bent, and molded his lips around the stem of a nipple. It hard and erect. He slipped his tongue slowly back and forth across it in a way he knew she liked. Wendy moaned a little and arched her back.

(*?Something I've forgotten?*)

'Honey?' she asked. On their own her hands sought the back of his head so that when he answered his voice was muffled against her flesh.

'How would the ranger take us out?'

He raised his head slightly to answer and then settled his mouth against the other nipple.

'If the helicopter was spoken for I guess it would have to be by snowmobile.'

(*!!!*)

'But we have one of those! Ullman said so!'

His mouth froze against her breast for a moment, and then he sat up. Her own face was slightly flushed, her eyes overbright. Jack's, on the other hand, was calm, as if he had been reading a rather dull book instead of engaging in foreplay with his wife.

'If there's a snowmobile there's no problem,' she said excitedly. 'We can all three go down together.'

'Wendy, I've never driven a snowmobile in my life.'

'It can't be that hard to learn. Back in Vermont you see ten-year-olds driving them in the fields . . . although what their parents can be thinking of I don't know. And you had a motor-cycle when we met.' He had, a Honda 350cc. He had traded it in on a Saab shortly after he and Wendy took up residence together.

'I suppose I could,' he said slowly. 'But I wonder how well it's been maintained. Ullman and Watson . . . they run this place from May to October. They have summertime minds. I know it won't have gas in it. There may not be plugs or a battery, either. I don't want you to get your hopes up over your head, Wendy.'

She was totally excited now, leaning over him, her breasts tumbling out of her shirt. He had a sudden impulse to seize one and twist it until she shrieked. Maybe that would teach her to shut up.

'The gas is no problem,' she said. 'The VW and the hotel truck are both full. There's gas for the emergency generator downstairs, too. And there must be a gascan out in that shed so you could carry extra.'

'Yes,' he said. 'There is.' Actually there were three of them, two five-gallons and a two-gallon.

'I'll bet the sparkplugs and the battery are out there too. Nobody would store their snowmobiles in one place and the plugs and battery someplace else, would they?'

'Doesn't seem likely, does it?' He got up and walked over to where Danny lay sleeping. A spill of hair had fallen across his forehead and Jack brushed it away gently. Danny didn't stir.

'And if you can get it running you'll take us out?' she asked from behind him. 'On the first day the radio says good weather?'

For a moment he didn't answer. He stood looking down at his son, and his mixed feelings dissolved in a wave of love. He was the way she had said, vulnerable, fragile. The marks on his neck were very prominent

'Yes,' he said. 'I'll get it running and we'll get out as quick as we can.'

'Thank God!'

He turned around. She had taken off her shirt and lay on the bed, her belly flat, her breasts aimed perkily at the ceiling. She was playing with them lazily, flicking at the nipples. 'Hurry up, gentlemen,' she said softly, 'time.'

★★★

After, with no light burning in the room but the night light that Danny had brought with him from his room, she lay in the crook of his arm, feeling deliciously at peace. She found it hard to believe they could be sharing the Overlook with a murderous stowaway.

'Jack?'

'Hmmmm?'

'What got at him?'

He didn't answer her directly. 'He does have something. Some talent the rest of us are missing. The most of us, beg pardon. And maybe the Overlook has something, too.'

'Ghosts?'

'I don't know. Not in the Algernon Blackwood sense, that's for sure. More like the residues of the feelings of the people who have stayed here. Good things and bad things. In that sense, I suppose that every big hotel has got its ghosts. Especially the old ones.'

'But a dead woman in the tub . . . Jack, he's not losing his mind, is he?'

He gave her a brief squeeze. 'We know he goes into . . . well, trances, for want of a better word . . . from time to time. We know that when he's in them he sometimes . . . sees? . . . things he doesn't understand. If precognitive trances are possible, they're probably functions of the subconscious mind. Freud said that the subconscious never speaks to us in literal language. Only in symbols. If you dream about being in a bakery where no one speaks English, you may be worried about your ability to support your family. Or maybe just that no one understands you. I've read that the falling dream is a standard outlet for feelings of insecurity. Games, little games. Conscious on one side of the net, subconscious on the other, serving some cocka-mamie image back and forth. Same with mental illness, with hunches, all of that. Why should precognition be any different? Maybe Danny really did see blood all over the walls of the Presidential Suite. To a kid his age, the image of blood and the concept of death are nearly interchangeable. To kids, the image is always more accessible than the concept, anyway. William Carlos Williams knew that, he was a pediatrician. When we grow up, concepts gradually get easier and we leave the images to the poets . . . and I'm just rambling on.'

'I like to hear you ramble.'

'She said it, folks. She said it. You all heard it.'

'The marks on his neck, Jack. Those are real.'

'Yes.'

There was nothing else for a long time. She had begun to think he must have gone to sleep and she was slipping into a drowse herself when he said:

'I can think of two explanations for those. And neither of them involves a fourth party in the hotel.'

'What?' She came up on one elbow.

'Stigmata, maybe,' he said.

'Stigmata? Isn't that when people bleed on Good Friday or something?'

'Yes. Sometimes people who believe deeply in Christ's divinity exhibit bleeding marks on their hands and feet during the Holy Week. It was more common in the Middle Ages than now. In those days such people were considered blessed by God. I don't think the Catholic Church proclaimed any of it as out-and-out miracles, which was pretty smart of them. Stigmata isn't much different from some of the things the yogis can do. It's better understood now, that's all. The people who understand the interaction between the mind and the body – study it, I mean, no one understands it – believe we have a lot more control over our involuntary functions than they used to think. You can slow your heartbeat if you think about it enough. Speed up your own metabolism. Make yourself sweat more. Or make yourself bleed.'

'You think Danny *thought* those bruises onto his neck? Jack, I just can't believe that.'

'I can believe it's possible, although it seems unlikely to me, too. What's more likely is that he did it to himself.'

'*To himself?*'

'He's gone into these "trances" and hurt himself in the past. Do you remember the time at the supper table? About two years ago, I think. We were super-pissed at each other. Nobody talking very much. Then, all at once, his eyes rolled up in his head and he went face-first into his dinner. Then onto the floor. Remember?'

'Yes,' she said. 'I sure do. I thought he was having a convulsion.'

'Another time we were in the park,' he said. 'Just Danny and I. Saturday afternoon. He was sitting on a swing, coasting back and forth. He collapsed onto the ground. It was like he'd been shot. I ran over and picked him up and all of a sudden he just came around. He sort of blinked at me and said, "I hurt my tummy. Tell Mommy to close the bedroom windows if it rains." And that night it rained like hell.'

'Yes, but—'

'And he's always coming in with cuts and scraped elbows. His shins look like a battlefield in distress. And when you ask him how he got this one or that one, he says "Oh, I was playing," and that's the end of it.'

'Jack, all kids get bumped and bruised up. With little boys it's almost constant from the time they learn to walk until they're twelve or thirteen.'

'And I'm sure Danny gets his share,' Jack responded. 'He's an active kid. But I remember that day in the park and that night at the supper table. And I wonder if some of our kid's bumps and bruises come from just keeling over. That Dr Edmonds said Danny did it right in his office, for Christ's sake!'

'All right. But those bruises were *fingers*. I'd swear to it. He didn't get them falling down.'

'He goes into a trance,' Jack said. 'Maybe he sees something that happened in that room. An argument. Maybe a suicide. Violent emotions. It isn't like watching a movie; he's in a highly suggestible state. He's right in the damn thing. His subconscious is maybe visualizing whatever happened in a symbolic way . . . as a dead woman who's alive again, zombie, undead, ghoul, you pick your term.'

'You're giving me goose-bumps,' she said thickly.

'I'm giving myself a few. I'm no psychiatrist, but it seems to fit so well. The walking dead woman as a symbol for dead emotions, dead lives, that just won't give up and go away . . . but because she's a subconscious figure, she's also *him*. In the trance state, the conscious Danny is submerged. The subconscious figure is pulling the strings. So Danny put his hands around his own neck and—'

'Stop,' she said. 'I get the picture. I think that's more frightening than having a stranger creeping around the halls, Jack. You can move away from a stranger. You can't move away from yourself. You're talking about schizophrenia.'

'Of a very limited type,' he said, but a trifle uneasily. 'And of a very special nature. Because he does seem able to read thoughts, and he really does seem to have precognitive flashes from time to time. I can't think of that as mental illness no matter how hard I try. We all have schizo deposits in us anyway. I think as Danny gets older, he'll get this under control.'

'If you're right, then it's imperative that we get him out. Whatever he has, this hotel is making it worse.'

'I wouldn't say that,' he objected. 'If he'd done as he was told, he never would have gone up to that room in the first place. It never would have happened.'

'My God, Jack! Are you implying that being half-strangled was a . . . a fitting punishment for being off limits?'

'No . . . no. Of course not. But—'

'No buts,' she said, shaking her head violently. 'The truth is, we're guessing. We don't have any idea when he might turn a corner and run into one of those . . . air pockets, one-reel horror movies, whatever they are. We have to get him *away*.' She laughed a little in the darkness. 'Next thing we'll be seeing things.'

'Don't talk nonsense,' he said, and in the darkness of the room he saw the hedge lions bunching around the path, no longer flanking it but guarding it, hungry November lions. Cold sweat sprang out on his brow.

'You didn't really see anything, did you?' she was asking. 'I mean, when you went up to that room. You didn't see anything?'

The lions were gone. Now he saw a pink pastel shower curtain with a dark shape lounging behind it. The closed doors. That muffled, hurried thump, and sounds after it that might have been running footsteps. The horrible, lurching beat of his own heart as he struggled with the passkey.

'Nothing,' he said, and that was true. He had been strung up, not sure of what was happening. He hadn't had a chance to sift through his thoughts for a reasonable explanation concerning the bruises on his son's neck. He had been pretty damn suggestible himself. Hallucinations could sometimes be catching.

'And you haven't changed your mind? About the snow-mobile, I mean?'

His hands clamped into sudden tight fists

(*Stop nagging me!*)

by his sides. 'I said I would, didn't I? I will. Now go to sleep. It's been a long hard day.'

'And how,' she said. There was a rustle of bedclothes as she turned toward him and kissed his shoulder. 'I love you, Jack.'

'I love you too,' he said, but he was only mouthing the words. His hands were still clenched into fists. They felt like rocks on the ends of his arms. The pulse beat prominently in his forehead. She hadn't said a word about what was going to happen to them *after* they got down, when the party was over. Not one word. It had been Danny this and Danny that and Jack I'm so scared. Oh yes, she was scared of a lot of closet boogeymen and jumping shadows, plenty scared. But there was no lack of real ones, either. When they got down to Sidewinder they would arrive with sixty dollars and the clothes they stood up in. Not even a car. Even if Sidewinder had a pawnshop, which it didn't, they had nothing to hock but Wendy's ninety-dollar diamond engagement ring and the Sony AM/FM radio. A pawnbroker might give them twenty bucks. A *kind* pawnbroker. There would be no job, not even part-time or seasonal, except maybe shoveling out driveways for three dollars a shot. The picture of John Torrance, thirty years old, who had once published in *Esquire* and who had harbored dreams – not at all unreasonable dreams, he felt – of becoming a major American writer during the next decade, with a shovel from the Side-winder Western Auto on his shoulder, ringing doorbells . . . that picture suddenly came to him much more clearly than the hedge lions and he clenched his fists tighter still, feeling the fingernails sink into his palms and draw blood in mystic quarter-moon shapes. John Torrance, standing in line to change his sixty dollars into food stamps, standing in line again at the Sidewinder Methodist Church to get donated commodities and dirty looks from the locals. John Torrance explaining to Al that they just had to leave, had to shut down the boiler, had to leave the Overlook and all it contained open to vandals or thieves on snow machines because, you see, Al, *attendez-vous*, Al, there are ghosts up there and they have it in for my boy. Good-by, Al. Thoughts of Chapter Four, Spring Comes for John Torrance. What then? Whatever then? They might be able to get to the West Coast in the VW, he supposed. A new fuel pump would do it. Fifty miles west of here and it was all downhill, you could damn near put the bug in neutral and coast to Utah. On to sunny California, land of oranges and opportunity. A man with his sterling record of alcoholism, student-beating, and ghost-chasing would undoubtedly be able to write his own ticket. Anything you like. Custodial engineer – swamping out Greyhound buses. The automotive business – washing cars in a rubber suit. The culinary arts, perhaps, washing dishes in a diner. Or possibly a more responsible position, such as pumping gas. A job like that even held the intellectual stimulation of making change and writing out credit slips. *I can give you twenty-five hours a week at the minimum wage.* That was heavy tunes in a year when Wonder bread went for sixty cents a loaf.

Blood had begun to trickle down from his palms. Like stigmata, oh yes. He squeezed tighter, savaging himself with pain. His wife was asleep beside him, why not? There were no problems. He had agreed to take her and Danny away from the big bad boogeyman and there were no problems. *So you see, Al, I thought the best thing to do would be to—*

(kill her.)

The thought rose up from nowhere, naked and unadorned. The urge to tumble her out of bed, naked, bewildered, just beginning to wake up; to pounce on her, seize her neck like the green limb of a young aspen and to throttle her, thumbs on windpipe, fingers pressing against the top of her spine, jerking her head up and ramming it back down against the floorboards, again and again, whamming, whacking, smashing, crashing.

Jitter and jive, baby. Shake, rattle, and roll. He would make her take her medicine. Every drop. Every last bitter drop.

He was dimly aware of a muffled noise somewhere, just outside his hot and racing inner world. He looked across the room and Danny was thrashing again, twisting in his bed and rumpling the blankets. The boy was moaning deep in his throat, a small, caged sound. What nightmare? A purple woman, long dead, shambling after him down twisting hotel corridors? Somehow he didn't think so. Something else chased Danny in his dreams. Something worse.

The bitter shock of his emotions was broken. He got out of bed, and went across to the boy, feeling sick and ashamed of himself. It was Danny he had to think of, not Wendy, not himself. Only Danny. And no matter what shape he wrestled the facts into, he knew in his heart that Danny must be taken out. He straightened the boy's blankets and added the quilt from the foot of the bed. Danny had quieted again now. Jack touched the sleeping forehead

(what monsters capering just behind that ridge of bone?)

and found it warm, but not overly so. And he was sleeping peacefully again. Queer.

He got back into bed and tried to sleep. It eluded him.

It was so unfair that things should turn out this way – bad luck seemed to stalk them. They hadn't been able to shake it by coming up here after all. By the time they arrived in Sidewinder tomorrow afternoon, the golden opportunity would have evaporated – gone the way of the blue suede shoe, as an old roommate of his had been wont to say. Consider the difference if they didn't go down, if they could somehow stick it out. The play would get finished. One way or the other, he would tack an ending onto it. His own uncertainty about his characters might add an appealing touch of ambiguity to his original ending. Perhaps it would even make him some money, it wasn't impossible. Even lacking that, Al might well convince the Stovington Board to rehire him. He would be on pro of course, maybe for as long as three years, but if he could stay sober and keep writing, he might not have to stay at Stovington for three years. Of course he hadn't cared much for Stovington before, he had felt stifled, buried alive, but that had been an immature reaction. Furthermore, how much could a man enjoy teaching when he went through his first three classes with a skull-busting hangover every second or third day? It wouldn't be that way again. He would be able to handle his responsibilities much better. He was sure of it.

Somewhere in the midst of that thought, things began to break up and he drifted down into sleep. His last thought followed him down like a sounding bell:

It seemed that he might be able to find peace here. At last. If they would only let him.

★★★

When he woke up he was standing in the bathroom of 217.

(been walking in my sleep again – why? – no radios to break up here)

The bathroom light was on, the room behind him in darkness. The shower curtain was drawn around the long claw-footed tub. The bathmat beside it was wrinkled and wet.

He began to feel afraid, but the very dreamlike quality of his fear told him this was not real. Yet that could not contain the fear. So many things at the Overlook seemed like dreams.

He moved across the floor to the tub, not wanting to but helpless to turn his feet back.

He flung the curtain open.

Lying in the tub, naked, lolling almost weightless in the water, was George Hatfield, a knife stuck in his chest. The water around him was stained a bright pink. George's eyes were closed. His penis floated limply, like kelp.

'George —' he heard himself say.

At the word, George's eyes snapped open. They were silver, not human eyes at all. George's hands, fish-white, found the sides of the tub and he pulled himself up to a sitting position. The knife stuck straight out from his chest, equidistantly placed between nipples. The wound was lipless.

'You set the timer ahead,' silver-eyed George told him.

'No, George, I didn't. I—'

'I don't stutter.'

George was standing now, still fixing him with that inhuman silver glare, but his mouth had drawn back in a dead and grimacing smile. He threw one leg over the porcelained side of the tub. One white and wrinkled foot placed itself on the bathmat.

'First you tried to run me over on my bike and then you set the timer ahead and then you tried to stab me to death but *I still don't stutter*.' George was coming for him, his hands out, the fingers slightly curled. He smelled moldy and wet, like leaves that had been rained on.

'It was for your own good,' Jack said, backing up. 'I set it ahead for your own good. Furthermore, I happen to know you cheated on your Final Composition.'

'I don't cheat . . . and I don't stutter.'

George's hands touched his neck.

Jack turned and ran, ran with the floating, weightless slowness that is so common to dreams.

'You did! You did cheat!' he screamed in fear and anger as he crossed the darkened bed/sitting room. 'I'll prove it!'

George's hands were on his neck again. Jack's heart swelled with fear until he was sure it would burst. And then, at last, his hand curled around the doorknob and it turned under his hand and he yanked the door open. He plunged out, not into the second-floor hallway, but into the basement room beyond the arch. The cobwebby light was on. His campchair, stark and geometrical, stood beneath it. And all around it was a miniature mountain range of boxes and crates and banded bundles of records and invoices and God knew what. Relief surged through him.

'I'll find it!' he heard himself screaming. He seized a damp and moldering cardboard box; it split apart in his hands, spilling out a waterfall of yellow flimsies. 'It's here somewhere! *I will find it!*' He plunged his hands deep into the pile of papers and came up with a dry, papery wasps' nest in one hand and a timer in the other. The timer was ticking. Attached to its back was a length of electrical cord and attached to the other end of the cord was a bundle of dynamite. '*Here!*' he screamed. '*Here, take it!*'

His relief became absolute triumph. He had done more than

escape George; he had conquered. With these talismanic objects in his hands, George would never touch him again. George would flee in terror.

He began to turn so he could confront George, and that was when George's hands settled around his neck, squeezing, stopping his breath, damming up his respiration entirely after one final dragging gasp.

'*I don't stutter,*' whispered George from behind him.

He dropped the wasps' nest and wasps boiled out of it in a furious brown and yellow wave. His lungs were on fire. His wavering sight fell on the timer and the sense of triumph returned, along with a cresting wave of righteous wrath. Instead of connecting the timer to dynamite, the cord ran to the gold knob of a stout black cane, like the one his father had carried after the accident with the milk truck.

He grasped it and the cord parted. The cane felt heavy and right in his hands. He swung it back over his shoulder. On the way up it glanced against the wire from which the light bulb depended and the light began to swing back and forth, making the room's hooded shadows rock monstrously against the floor and walls. On the way down the cane struck something much harder. George screamed. The grip on Jack's throat loosened.

He tore free of George's grip and whirled. George was on his knees, his head drooping, his hands laced together on top of it. Blood welled through his fingers.

'Please,' George whispered humbly. 'Give me a break, Mr Torrance.'

'Now you'll take your medicine,' Jack grunted. 'Now by God, won't you. Young pup. Young worthless cur. Now by God, right now. Every drop. Every single drop!'

As the light swayed above him and the shadows danced and flapped, he began to swing the cane, bringing it down again and again, his arm rising and falling like a machine. George's bloody protecting fingers fell away from his head and Jack brought the cane down again and again, and on his neck and shoulders and back and arms. Except that the cane was no longer precisely a cane; it seemed to be a mallet with some kind of brightly striped handle. A mallet with a hard side and soft side.

The business end was clotted with blood and hair. And the flat, whacking sound of the mallet against flesh had been replaced with a hollow booming sound, echoing and reverberating. His own voice had taken on this same quality, bellowing, disembodied. And yet, paradoxically, it sounded weaker, slurred, petulant . . . as if he were drunk.

The figure on its knees slowly raised its head, as if in supplication. There was not a face, precisely, but only a mask of blood through which eyes peered. He brought the mallet back for a final whistling downstroke and it was fully launched before he saw that the supplicating face below him was not George's but Danny's. It was the face of his son.

'*Daddy*—'

And then the mallet crashed home, striking Danny right between the eyes, closing them forever. And something somewhere seemed to be laughing—

(*! No !*)

***

He came out of it standing naked over Danny's bed, his hands empty, his body sheened with sweat. His final scream had only been in his mind. He voiced it again, this time in a whisper.

'No. No, Danny. Never.'

He went back to bed on legs that had turned to rubber. Wendy was sleeping deeply. The clock on the nightstand said it was quarter to five. He lay sleepless until seven, when Danny began to stir awake. Then he put his legs over the edge of the bed and began to dress. It was time to go downstairs and check the boiler.

CHAPTER THIRTY-THREE
THE SNOWMOBILE

Sometime after midnight, while they all slept uneasily, the snow had stopped after dumping a fresh eight inches on the old crust. The clouds had broken, a fresh wind had swept them away, and now Jack stood in a dusty ingot of sunlight, which slanted through the dirty window set into the eastern side of the equipment shed.

The place was about as long as a freight car, and about as high. It smelled of grease and oil and gasoline and – faint, nostalgic smell – sweet grass. Four power lawnmowers were ranked like soldiers on review against the south wall, two of them the riding type that look like small tractors. To their left were posthole diggers, round-bladed shovels made for doing surgery on the putting green, a chain saw, the electric hedge-clippers, and a long thin steel pole with a red flag at the top. Caddy, fetch my ball in under ten seconds and there's a quarter in it for you. Yes, *sir*.

Against the eastern wall, where the morning sun slanted in most strongly, three Ping-Pong tables leaned one against the other like a drunken house of cards. Their nets had been removed and flopped down from the shelf above. In the corner was a stack of shuffleboard weights and a roque set – the wickets banded together with twists of wire, the brightly painted balls in an egg-carton sort of thing (strange hens you have up here, Watson . . . yes, and you should see the animals down on the front lawn, ha-ha), and the mallets, two sets of them, standing in their racks.

He walked over to them, stepping over an old eight-cell battery (which had once sat beneath the hood of the hotel truck, no doubt) and a battery charger and a pair of J. C. Penny jumper cables coiled between them. He slipped one of the short-handled mallets out of the front rack and held it up in front of his face, like a knight bound for battle saluting his king.

Fragments of his dream (it was all jumbled now, fading) recurred, something about George Hatfield and his father's cane, just enough to make him uneasy and, absurdly enough, a trifle guilty about holding a plain old garden-variety roque mallet. Not that roque was such a common garden-variety game anymore; its more modern cousin, croquet, was much more popular now . . . and a child's version of the game at that. Roque, however . . . that must have been quite a game. Jack had found a mildewed rule book down in the basement, from one of the years in the early twenties when a North American Roque Tournament had been held at the Overlook. Quite a game.

(*schizo*)

He frowned a little, then smiled. Yes, it was a schizo sort of game at that. The mallet expressed that perfectly. A soft end and a hard end. A game of finesse and aim, and a game of raw, bludgeoning power.

He swung the mallet through the air . . . *whhhooop*. He smiled a little at the powerful, whistling sound it made. Then he replaced it in the rack and turned to his left. What he saw there made him frown again.

The snowmobile sat almost in the middle of the equipment shed, a fairly new one, and Jack didn't care for its looks at all. *Bombardier Skidoo* was written on the side of the engine cowling facing him in black letters which had been raked backward, presumably to connote speed. The protruding skis were also black. There was black piping to the right and left of the cowling, what they would call racing stripes on a sports car. But the actual paintjob was a bright, sneering yellow, and that was what he didn't like about it. Sitting there in its shaft of morning sun, yellow body and black piping, black skis and black upholstered open cockpit, it looked like a monstrous mechanized wasp. When it was running it would sound like that too. Whining and buzzing and ready to sting. But then, what else should it look like? It wasn't flying under false colors, at least. Because after it had done its job, they were going to be hurting plenty. All of them. By spring the Torrance family would be hurting so badly that what those wasps had done to Danny's hand would look like a mother's kisses.

He pulled his handkerchief from his back pocket, wiped his mouth with it, and walked over to the Skidoo. He stood looking down at it, the frown very deep now, and stuffed his handkerchief back into his pocket. Outside a sudden gust of wind slammed against the equipment shed, making it rock and creak. He looked out the window and saw the gust carrying a sheet of sparkling snow crystals toward the drifted-in rear of the hotel, whirling them high into the hard blue sky.

The wind dropped and he went back to looking at the machine. It was a disgusting thing, really. You almost expected to see a long, limber stinger protruding from the rear of it. He had always disliked the goddam snowmobiles. They shivered the cathedral silence of winter into a million rattling fragments. They startled the wildlife. They sent out huge and pollutive clouds of blue and billowing oilsmoke behind them – cough, cough, gag, gag, let me breathe. They were perhaps the final grotesque toy of the unwinding fossil fuel age, given to ten-year-olds for Christmas.

He remembered a newspaper article he had read in Stivington, a story datelined someplace in Maine. A kid on a snowmobile, barrel-assing up a road he'd never traveled before at better than thirty miles an hour. Night. His headlight off. There had been a heavy chain strung between two posts with a NO TRESPASSING sign hung from the middle. They said that in all probability the kid never saw it. The moon might have gone behind a cloud. The chain had decapitated him. Reading the story Jack had been almost glad, and now, looking down at this machine, the feeling recurred.

(If it wasn't for Danny, I would take great pleasure in grabbing one of those mallets, opening the cowling, and just pounding until)

He let his pent-up breath escape him in a long slow sigh. Wendy was right. Come hell, high water, or the welfare line, Wendy was right. Pounding this machine to death would be the height of folly, no matter how pleasant an aspect that folly made. It would almost be tantamount to pounding his own son to death.

'Fucking Luddite,' he said aloud.

He went to the back of the machine and unscrewed the gascap. He found a dipstick on one of the shelves that ran at chest-height around the walls and slipped it in. The last eighth of an inch came out wet. Not very much, but enough to see if the damn thing would run. Later he could siphon more from the Volks and the hotel truck.

He screwed the cap back on and opened the cowling. No sparkplugs, no battery. He went to the shelf again and began to poke along it, pushing aside screwdrivers and adjustable wrenches, a one-lung carburetor that had been taken out of an old lawn mower, plastic boxes of screws and nails and bolts of varying sizes. The shelf was thick and dark with old grease, and the years' accumulation of dust had stuck to it like fur. He didn't like touching it.

He found a small, oil-stained box with the abbreviation *Skid*. laconically marked on it in pencil. He shook it and something rattled inside. Plugs. He held one of them up to the light, trying to estimate the gap without hunting around for the gapping tool. Fuck it, he thought resentfully, and dropped the plug back into the box. If the gap's wrong, that's just too damn bad. Tough fucking titty.

There was a stool behind the door. He dragged it over, sat down, and installed the four sparkplugs, then fitted the small rubber caps over each. That done, he let his fingers play briefly over the magneto. They laughed when I sat down at the piano.

Back to the shelves. This time he couldn't find what he wanted, a small battery. A three- or four-cell. There were socket wrenches, a case filled with drills and drillbits, bags of lawn fertilizer and Vigoro for the flower beds, but no snowmobile battery. It didn't bother him in the slightest. In fact, it made him feel glad. He was relieved. I did my best, Captain, but I could not get through. That's fine, son. I'm going to put you in for the Silver Star and the Purple Snowmobile. You're a credit to your regiment. Thank you, sir. I did try.

He began to whistle 'Red River Valley' uptempo as he poked along the last two or three feet of shelf. The notes came out in little puffs of white smoke. He had made a complete circuit of the shed and the thing wasn't there. Maybe somebody had lifted it. Maybe Watson had. He laughed aloud. The old office bootleg trick. A few paperclips, a couple of reams of paper, nobody will miss this tablecloth or this Golden Regal place setting . . . and what about this fine snowmobile battery? Yes, that might come in handy. Toss it in the sack. White-collar crime, Baby. Everybody has sticky fingers. Under-the-jacket discount, we used to call it when we were kids.

He walked back to the snowmobile and gave the side of it a good healthy kick as he went by. Well, that was the end of it. He would just have to tell Wendy sorry, baby, but—

There was a box sitting in the corner by the door. The stool had been right over it. Written on the top, in pencil, was the abreviation *Skid*.

He looked at it, the smile drying up on his lips. Look, sir, it's the cavalry. Looks like your smoke signals must have worked after all.

It wasn't fair.

Goddammit, it just wasn't fair.

Something – luck, fate, providence – had been trying to save him. Some other luck, white luck. And at the last moment bad old Jack Torrance luck had stepped back in. The lousy run of cards wasn't over yet.

Resentment, a gray, sullen wave of it, pushed up his throat. His hands had clenched into fists again.

(*Not fair, goddammit, not fair!*)

Why couldn't he have looked someplace else? Anyplace! Why hadn't he had a crick in his neck or an itch in his nose or the need to blink? Just one of those little things. He never would have seen it.

Well, he hadn't. That was all. It was an hallucination, no different from what had happened yesterday outside that room on the second floor or the goddam hedge menagerie. A momentary strain, that was all. Fancy, I thought I saw a snowmobile, battery in that corner. Nothing there now. Combat fatigue. I guess, sir. Sorry. Keep your pecker up, son. It happens to all of us sooner or later.

He yanked the door open almost hard enough to snap the

hinges and pulled his snowshoes inside. They were clotted with snow and he slapped them down hard enough on the floor to raise a cloud of it. He put his left foot on the left shoe . . . and paused.

Danny was out there, by the milk platform. Trying to make a snowman, by the looks. Not much luck; the snow was too cold to stick together. Still, he was giving it the old college try, out there in the flashing morning, a speck of a bundled-up boy above the brilliant snow and below the brilliant sky. Wearing his hat turned around backward like Carlton Fiske.

(*What in the name of God were you thinking of?*)

The answer came back with no pause.

(*Me. I was thinking of me.*)

He suddenly remembered lying in bed the night before, lying there and suddenly he had been contemplating the murder of his wife.

In that instant, kneeling there, everything came clear to him. It was not just Danny the Overlook was working on. It was working on him, too. It wasn't Danny who was the weak link, it was him. He was the vulnerable one, the one who could be bent and twisted until something snapped.

(until i let go and sleep . . . and when i do that if i do that)

He looked up at the banks of windows and the sun threw back an almost blinding glare from their many-paned surfaces but he looked anyway. For the first time he noticed how much they seemed like eyes. They reflected away the sun and held their own darkness within. It was not Danny they were looking at. It was him.

In those few seconds he understood everything. There was a certain black-and-white picture he remembered seeing as a child, in catechism class. The nun had presented it to them on an easel and called it a miracle of God. The class had looked at it blankly, seeing nothing but a jumble of whites and blacks, senseless and patternless. Then one of the children in the third row had gasped, 'It's Jesus!' and that child had gone home with a brand-new Testament and also a calendar because he had been first. The others stared even harder, Jacky Torrance among them. One by one the other kids had given a similar gasp, one little girl transported in near-ecstasy, crying out shrilly: 'I *see* Him! I *see* Him!' She had also been rewarded with a Testament. At last everyone had seen the face of Jesus in the jumble of blacks and whites except Jacky. He strained harder and harder, scared now, part of him cynically thinking that everyone else was simply putting on to please Sister Beatrice, part of him secretly convinced that he wasn't seeing it because God had decided he was the worst sinner in the class. 'Don't you see it, Jacky?' Sister Beatrice had asked him in her sad, sweet manner. I see your *tits*, he had thought in vicious desperation. He began to shake his head, then faked excitement and said: 'Yes, I do! Wow! It *is* Jesus!' And everyone in class had laughed and applauded him, making him feel triumphant, ashamed, and scared. Later, when everyone else had tumbled their way up from the church basement and out onto the street he had lingered behind, looking at the meaningless black-and-white jumble that Sister Beatrice had left on the easel. He hated it. They had all made it up the way he had, even Sister herself. It was a big fake. 'Shitfire-hellfire-shitfire,' he had whispered under his breath, and as he turned to go he had seen the face of Jesus from the corner of his eye, sad and wise. He turned back, his heart in his throat. Everything had suddenly clicked into place and he had stared at the picture with fearful wonder, unable to believe he had missed it. The eyes, the zigzag of shadow across the care-worn brow, the fine nose, the compassionate lips. Looking at Jacky Torrance. What had only been a meaningless sprawl had suddenly been transformed into a stark black-and-white etching of the face of Christ-Our-Lord. Fearful wonder became terror. He had cussed in front of a picture of Jesus. He would be damned. He would be in hell with the sinners. The face of Christ had been in the picture all along. All along.

Now, kneeling in the sun and watching his son playing in the shadow of the hotel, he knew that it was all true. The hotel wanted Danny, maybe all of them but Danny for sure. The hedges had really walked. There was a dead woman in 217, a woman that was perhaps only a spirit and harmless under most circumstances, but a woman who was now an active danger. Like some malevolent clockwork toy she had been wound up and set in motion by Danny's own odd mind . . . and his own. Had it been Watson who had told him a man had dropped dead of a stroke one day on the roque court? Or had it been Ullman? It didn't matter. There had been an assassination on the third floor. How many old quarrels, suicides, strokes? How many murders? Was Grady lurking somewhere in the west wing with his ax, just waiting for Danny to start him up so he could come back out of the woodwork?

The puffed circle of bruises around Danny's neck.

The twinkling, half-seen bottles in the deserted lounge.

The radio.

The dreams.

The scrapbook he had found in the cellar.

(*Medoc, are you here? I've been sleepwalking again, my dear . . .*)

He got up suddenly, thrusting the snowshoes back out the door. He was shaking all over. He slammed the door and picked up the box with the battery in it. It slipped through his shaking fingers

(*oh christ what if i cracked it*)

and thumped over on its side. He pulled the flaps of the carton open and yanked the battery out, heedless of the acid that might be leaking through the battery's casing if it had cracked. But it hadn't. It was whole. A little sigh escaped his lips.

Cradling it, he took it over to the Skidoo and put it on its platform near the front of the engine. He found a small adjustable wrench on one of the shelves and attached the battery cables quickly and with no trouble. The battery was live; no need to use the charger on it. There had been a crackle of electricity and a small odor of ozone when he slipped the positive cable onto its terminal. The job done, he stood away, wiping his hands nervously on his faded denim jacket. There. It should work. No reason why not. No reason at all except that it was part of the Overlook and the Overlook really didn't want them out of here. Not at all. The Overlook was having one hell of a good time. There was a little boy to terrorize, a man and his woman to set one against the other, and if it played its cards right they could end up flitting through the Overlook's halls like insubstantial shades in a Shirley Jackson novel, whatever walked in Hill House walked alone, but you wouldn't be alone in the Overlook, oh no, there would be plenty of company here. But there was really no reason why the snowmobile shouldn't start. Except of course

(*Except he still didn't really want to go.*)

yes, except for that.

He stood looking at the Skidoo, his breath puffing out in frozen little plumes. He wanted it to be the way it had been. When he had come in here he'd had no doubts. Going down would be the wrong decision, he had known that then. Wendy was only scared of the boogeyman summoned up by a single hysterical little boy. Now, suddenly, he could see her side. It was like his play, his damnable play. He no longer knew which side he was on, or how things should come out. Once you saw the face of a god in those jumbled blacks and whites, it was everybody out of the pool – you could never unsee it. Others might laugh and say it's nothing, just a lot of splotches with no meaning, give me a good old Craftmaster paint-by-the-numbers any day, but *you* would always see the face of Christ-Our-Lord looking out at you. You had seen it in one gestalt leap, the conscious and unconscious melding in that one shocking moment of understanding. You would always see it. You were damned to always see it.

(*I've been sleepwalking again, my dear . . .*)

It had been all right until he had seen Danny playing in the snow. It was Danny's fault. Everything had been Danny's fault. He was the one with the shining, or whatever it was. It wasn't a shining, it was a curse. If he and Wendy had been here alone, they could have passed the winter quite nicely. No pain, no strain on the brain.

(*Don't want to leave. ?Can't?*)

The Overlook didn't want them to go and he didn't want them to go either. Not even Danny. Maybe he was a part of it, now. Perhaps the Overlook, large and rambling Samuel Johnson that it was, had picked him to be its Boswell. You say the new caretaker writes? Very good, sign him on. Time we told our side. Let's get rid of the woman and his snotnosed kid first, however. We don't want him to be distracted. We don't—

He was standing by the snowmobile's cockpit, his head starting to ache again. What did it come down to? Go or stay. Very simple. Keep it simple. Shall we go or shall we stay?

If we go, how long will it be before you find the local hole in Sidewinder? a voice inside him asked. The dark place with the lousy color TV that unshaven and unemployed men spend the day watching game shows on? Where the piss in the men's room smells two thousand years old and there's always a sodden Camel butt unraveling in the toilet bowl? Where the beer is thirty cents a glass and you cut it with salt and the jukebox is loaded with seventy country oldies?

How long? Oh Christ, he was so afraid it wouldn't be long at all.

'I can't win,' he said, very softly. That was it. It was like trying to play solitaire with one of the aces missing from the deck.

Abruptly he leaned over the Skidoo's motor compartment and yanked off the magneto. It came off with sickening ease. He looked at it for a moment, then went to the equipment shed's back door and opened it.

From here the view of the mountains was unobstructed, picture-postcard beautiful in the twinkling brightness of morning. An unbroken field of snow rose to the first pines about a mile distant. He flung the magneto as far out into the snow as he could. It went much further than it should have. There was a light puff of snow when it fell. The light breeze carried the snow granules away to fresh resting places. Disperse there, I say. There's nothing to see. It's all over. Disperse.

He felt at peace.

He stood in the doorway for a long time, breathing the good mountain air, and then he closed it firmly and went back out the other door to tell Wendy they would be staying. On the way, he stopped and had a snowball fight with Danny.

CHAPTER THIRTY-FOUR
THE HEDGES

It was November 29, three days after Thanksgiving. The last week had been a good one, the Thanksgiving dinner the best they'd ever had as a family. Wendy had cooked Dick Hallorann's turkey to a turn and they had all eaten to bursting without even coming close to demolishing the jolly bird. Jack had groaned that they would be eating turkey for the rest of the winter – creamed turkey, turkey sandwiches, turkey and noodles, turkey surprise.

No, Wendy told him with a little smile. Only until Christmas. Then we have the capon.

Jack and Danny groaned together.

The bruises on Danny's neck had faded, and their fears seemed to have faded with them. On Thanksgiving afternoon Wendy had been pulling Danny around on his sled while Jack worked on the play, which was now almost done.

'Are you still afraid, doc?' she had asked, not knowing how to put the question less baldly.

'Yes,' he answered simply. 'But now I stay in the safe places.'

'Your daddy says that sooner or later the forest rangers will wonder why we're not checking in on the CB radio. They'll come to see if anything is wrong. We might go down then. You and I. And let your daddy finish the winter. He has good reasons for wanting to. In a way, doc . . . I know this is hard for you to understand . . . our backs are against the wall.'

'Yes,' he had answered noncommittally.

On this sparkling afternoon the two of them were upstairs, and Danny knew that they had been making love. They were dozing now. They were happy, he knew. His mother was still a little bit afraid, but his father's attitude was strange. It was a feeling that he had done something that was very hard and had done it right. But Danny could not seem to see exactly what the something was. His father was guarding that carefully, even in his own mind. Was it possible, Danny wondered, to be glad you had done something and still be so ashamed of that something that you tried not to think of it? The question was a disturbing one. He didn't think such a thing was possible . . . in a normal mind. His hardest probings at his father had only brought him a dim picture of something like an octopus, whirling up into the hard blue sky. And on both occasions that he had concentrated hard enough to get this, Daddy had suddenly been staring at him in a sharp and frightening way, as if he knew what Danny was doing.

Now he was in the lobby, getting ready to go out. He went out a lot taking his sled or wearing his snowshoes. He liked to get out of the hotel. When he was out in the sunshine, it seemed like a weight had slipped from his shoulders.

He pulled a chair over, stood on it, and got his parka and snow pants out of the ballroom closet, and then sat down on the chair to put them on. His boots were in the boot box and he pulled them on, his tongue creeping out into the corner of his mouth in concentration as he laced them and tied the rawhide into careful granny knots. He pulled on his mittens and his ski mask and was ready.

He tramped out through the kitchen to the back door, then paused. He was tired of playing out back, and at this time of day the hotel's shadow would be cast over his play area. He didn't even like being in the Overlook's shadow. He decided he would put on his snowshoes and go down to the playground instead. Dick Hallorann had told him to stay away from the topiary, but the thought of the hedge animals did not bother him much. They were buried under snowdrifts now, nothing showing but a vague hump that was the rabbit's head and the lions' tails. Sticking out of the snow the way they were, the tails looked more absurd than frightening.

Danny opened the back door and got his snowshoes from the milk platform. Five minutes later he was strapping them to his feet on the front porch. His daddy had told him that he (Danny) had the hang of using the snowshoes – the lazy, shuffling stride, the twist of ankle that shook the powdery snow from the lacings just before the boot came back down – and all that remained was for him to build up the necessary muscles in his thighs and calves and ankles. Danny found that his ankles got tired the fastest. Snowshoeing was almost as hard on your ankles as skating, because you had to keep clearing the lacings. Every five minutes or so he had to stop with his legs spread and the snowshoes flat on the snow to rest them.

But he didn't have to rest on his way down to the playground because it was all downhill. Less than ten minutes after he struggled up and over the monstrous snow-dune that had drifted in on the Overlook's front porch he was standing with his mittened hand on the playground slide. He wasn't even breathing hard.

The playground seemed much nicer in the deep snow than it ever had during the autumn. It looked like a fairyland sculpture. The swing chains had been frozen in strange positions, the seats of the big kids' swings resting flush against the snow. The jungle gym was an ice-cave guarded by dripping icicle teeth. Only the chimneys of the play-Overlook stuck up over the snow

(wish the other one was buried that way only not with us in it)

and the tops of the cement rings protruded in two places like Eskimo igloos. Danny tramped over there, squatted, and began to dig. Before long he had uncovered the dark mouth of one of them and he slipped into the cold tunnel. In his mind he was Patrick McGoohan, the Secret Agent Man (they had shown the reruns of that program twice on the Burlington TV channel and his daddy never missed them; he would skip a party to stay home and watch 'Secret Agent' or 'The Avengers', and Danny had always watched with him), on the run from the KGB agents in the mountains of Switzerland. There had been avalanches in the area and the notorious KGB agent Slobbo had killed his girlfriend with a poison dart, but somewhere near was the Russian antigravity machine. Perhaps at the end of this very tunnel. He drew his automatic and went along the concrete tunnel, his eyes wide and alert, his breath pluming out.

The far end of the concrete ring was solidly blocked with snow. He tried digging through it and was amazed (and a little uneasy) to see how solid it was, almost like ice from the cold and the constant weight of more snow on top of it.

His make-believe game collapsed around him and he was suddenly aware that he felt closed in and extremely nervous in this tight ring of cement. He could hear his breathing; it sounded dank and quick and hollow. He was under the snow, and hardly any light filtered down the hole he had dug to get in here. Suddenly he wanted to be out in the sunlight more than anything, suddenly he remembered his daddy and mommy were sleeping and didn't know where he was, that if the hole he dug caved in he would be trapped, and the Overlook didn't like him.

Danny got turned around with some difficulty and crawled back along the length of the concrete ring, his snowshoes clacking woodenly together behind him, his palms crackling in last fall's dead aspen leaves beneath him. He had just reached the end and the cold spill of light coming down from above when the snow *did* give in, a minor fall, but enough to powder his face and clog the opening he had wriggled down through and leave him in darkness.

For a moment his brain froze in utter panic and he could not think. Then, as if from far off, he heard his daddy telling him that he must never play at the Stovington dump, because sometimes stupid people hauled old refrigerators off to the dump without removing the doors and if you got in one and the door happened to shut on you, there was no way to get out. You would die in the darkness.

(You wouldn't want a thing like that to happen to you, would you, doc?)

(No, Daddy.)

But it *had* happened, his frenzied mind told him, it *had* happened, he was in the dark, he was closed in, and it was as cold as a refrigerator. And—

(*something is in here with me.*)

His breath stopped in a gasp. An almost drowsy terror stole through his veins. Yes. Yes. There was something in here with him, some awful thing the Overlook had saved for just such a chance as this. Maybe a huge spider that had burrowed down under the dead leaves, or a rat . . . or maybe the corpse of some little kid that had died here on the playground. Had that ever happened? Yes, he thought maybe it had. He thought of the woman in the tub. The blood and brains on the wall of the Presidential Sweet. Of some little kid, its head split open from a fall from the monkey bars or a swing, crawling after him in the dark, grinning, looking for one final playmate in its endless playground. Forever. In a moment he would hear it coming.

At the far end of the concrete ring, Danny heard the stealthy crackle of dead leaves as something came for him on its hands and knees. At any moment he would feel its cold hand close over his ankle—

That thought broke his paralysis. He was digging at the loose fall of snow that choked the end of the concrete ring, throwing it back between his legs in powdery bursts like a dog digging for a bone. Blue light filtered down from above and Danny thrust himself up at it like a diver coming out of deep water. He scraped his back on the lip of the concrete ring. One of his snow-shoes twisted behind the other. Snow spilled down inside his ski mask and into the collar of his parka. He dug at the snow, clawed at it. It seemed to be trying to hold him, to suck him back down, back into the concrete ring where that unseen, leaf-crackling *thing* was, and keep him there. Forever.

Then he was out, his face was turned up to the sun, and he was crawling through the snow, crawling away from the half-buried cement ring, gasping harshly, his face almost comically white with powdered snow – a living fright-mask. He hobbled over to the jungle gym and sat down to readjust his snowshoes and get his breath. As he set them to rights and tightened the straps again, he never took his eyes from the hole at the end of the concrete ring. He waited to see if something would come out. Nothing did, and after three or four minutes, Danny's breathing began to slow down. Whatever it was, it couldn't stand the sunlight. It was cooped up down there, maybe only able to come out when it was dark . . . or when both ends of its circular prison were plugged with snow.

(but i'm safe now i'm safe i'll just go back because now i'm)

Something thumped softly behind him.

He turned around, toward the hotel, and looked. But even before he looked

(Can you see the Indians in this picture?)

he knew what he would see, because he knew what that soft thumping sound had been. It was the sound of a large clump of snow falling, the way it sounded when it slid off the roof of the hotel and fell to the ground.

(Can you see—?)

Yes. He could. The snow had fallen off the hedge dog. When he came down it had only been a harmless lump of snow outside the playground. Now it stood revealed, an incongruous splash of green in all the eye-watering whiteness. It was sitting up, as if to beg a sweet or a scrap.

But this time he wouldn't go crazy, he wouldn't blow his cool. Because at least he wasn't trapped in some dark old hole. He was in the sunlight. And it was just a dog. It's pretty warm out today, he thought hopefully. Maybe the sun just melted enough snow off that old dog so the rest fell off in a bunch. Maybe that's all it is.

(Don't go near that place . . . steer right clear.)

His snowshoe bindings were as tight as they were ever going to be. He stood up and stared back at the concrete ring, almost completely submerged in the snow, and what he saw at the end he had exited from froze his heart. There was a circular patch of darkness at the end of it, a fold of shadow that marked the hole he'd dug to get down inside. Now, in spite of the snow-dazzle, he thought he could see something there. Something moving. A hand. The waving hand of some desperately unhappy child, waving hand, pleading hand, drowning hand.

(Save me O please save me If you can't save me at least come play with me . . . Forever. And Forever. And Forever.)

'No,' Danny whispered huskily. The word fell dry and bare from his mouth, which was stripped of moisture. He could feel his mind wavering now, trying to go away the way it had when the woman in the room had . . . no, better not think of that.

He grasped at the strings of reality and held them tightly. He had to get out of here. Concentrate on that. Be cool. Be like the Secret Agent Man. Would Patrick McGoohan be crying and peeing in his pants like a little baby?

Would his daddy?'

That calmed him somewhat.

From behind him, that soft *flump* sound of falling snow came again. He turned around and the head of one of the hedge lions was sticking out of the snow now, snarling at him. It was closer than it should have been, almost up to the gate of the playground.

Terror tried to rise up and he quelled it. He was the Secret Agent Man, and he *would* escape.

He began to walk out of the playground, taking the same roundabout course his father had taken on the day that the snow flew. He concentrated on operating the snowshoes. Slow, flat strides. Don't lift your foot too high or you'll lose your balance. Twist your ankle and spill the snow off the crisscrossed lacings. It seemed so *slow*. He reached the corner of the playground. The snow was drifted high here and he was able to step over the fence. He got halfway over and then almost fell flat when the snowshoe on his behind foot caught on one of the fence posts. He leaned on the outside edge of gravity, pinwheeling his arms, remembering how hard it was to get up once you fell down.

From his right; that soft sound again, falling clumps of snow. He looked over and saw the other two lions, clear of snow now down to their forepaws, side by side, about sixty paces away. The green indentations that were their eyes were fixed on him. The dog had turned its head.

(*It only happens when you're not looking.*)

'Oh! Hey—'

His snowshoes had crossed and he plunged forward into the snow, arms waving uselessly. More snow got inside his hood and down his neck and into the tops of his boots. He struggled out of the snow and tried to get the snowshoes under him, heart hammering crazily now

(*Secret Agent Man remember you're the Secret Agent*)

and overbalanced backward. For a moment he lay there looking at the sky, thinking it would be simpler to just give up.

Then he thought of the thing in the concrete tunnel and knew he could not. He gained his feet and stared over at the topiary. All three lions were bunched together now, not forty feet away. The dog had ranged off to their left, as if to block Danny's retreat. They were bare of snow now except for powdery ruffs around their necks and muzzles. They were all staring at him.

His breath was racing now, and the panic was like a rat behind his forehead, twisting and gnawing. He fought the panic and he fought the snowshoes.

(*Daddy's voice: No, don't fight them, doc. Walk on them like they were your own feet. Walk with them.*)

(*Yes, Daddy.*)

He began to walk again, trying to regain the easy rhythm he had practiced with his daddy. Little by little it began to come, but with the rhythm came an awareness of just how tired he was, how much his fear had exhausted him. The tendons of his thighs and calves and ankles were hot and trembly. Ahead he could see the Overlook, mockingly distant, seeming to stare at him with its many windows, as if this were some sort of contest in which it was mildly interested.

Danny looked back over his shoulder and his hurried breathing caught for a moment and then hurried on even faster. The nearest lion was now only twenty feet behind, breasting through the snow like a dog paddling in a pond. The two others were to its right and left, pacing it. They were like an army platoon on patrol, the dog, still off to their left, the scout. The closest lion had its head down. The shoulders bunched powerfully above its neck. The tail was up, as if in the instant before he had turned to look it had been swishing back and forth, back and forth. He thought it looked like a great big housecat that was having a good time playing with a mouse before killing it.

(—*falling*—)

No, if he fell he was dead. They would never let him get up. They would pounce. He pinwheeled his arms madly and lunged ahead, his center of gravity dancing just beyond his nose.

He caught it and hurried on, snapping glances back over his shoulder. The air whistled in and out of his dry throat like hot glass.

The world closed down to the dazzling snow, the green hedges, and the whispery sound of his snowshoes. And something else. A soft, muffled padding sound. He tried to hurry faster and couldn't. He was walking over the buried driveway now, a small boy with his face almost buried in the shadow of his parka hood. The afternoon was still and bright.

When he looked back again, the point lion was only five feet behind. It was grinning. Its mouth was open, its haunches tensed down like a clockspring. Behind it and the others he could see the rabbit, its head now sticking out of the snow, bright green, as if it had turned its horrid blank face to watch the end of the stalk.

Now, on the Overlook's front lawn between the circular drive and the porch, he let the panic loose and began to run clumsily in the snowshoes, not daring to look back now, tilting further and further forward, his arms out ahead of him like a blind man feeling for obstacles. His hood fell back, revealing his complexion, paste white giving way to hectic red blotches on his cheeks, his eyes bulging with terror. The porch was very close now.

Behind him he heard the sudden hard crunch of snow as something leaped.

He fell on the porch steps, screaming without sound, and scrambled up them on his hands and knees, snowshoes clattering and askew behind him.

There was a slashing sound in the air and sudden pain in his leg. The ripping sound of cloth. Something else that might have – *must* have – been in his mind.

Bellowing, angry roar.

Smell of blood and evergreen.

He fell full-length on the porch, sobbing hoarsely, the rich, metallic taste of copper in his mouth. His heart was thundering in his chest. There was a small trickle of blood coming from his nose.

He had no idea how long he lay there before the lobby doors

flew open and Jack ran out, wearing just his jeans and a pair of slippers. Wendy was behind him.

'*Danny!*' she screamed.

'Doc! Danny, for Christ's sake! What's wrong? What happened?'

Daddy was helping him up. Below the knee his snowpants were ripped open. Inside, his woollen ski sock had been ripped open and his calf had been shallowly scratched . . . as if he had tried to push his way through a closely grown evergreen hedge and the branches had clawed him.

He looked over his shoulder. Far down the lawn, past the putting green, were a number of vague, snow-cowled humps. The hedge animals. Between them and the playground. Between them and the road.

His legs gave way. Jack caught him. He began to cry.

CHAPTER THIRTY-FIVE
THE LOBBY

He had told them everything except what had happened to him when the snow had blocked the end of the concrete ring. He couldn't bring himself to repeat that. And he didn't know the right words to express the creeping, lassitudinous sense of terror he had felt when he heard the dead aspen leaves begin to crackle furtively down there in the cold darkness. But he told them about the soft sound of snow falling in clumps. About the lion with its head and its bunched shoulders working its way up and out of the snow to chase him. He even told them about how the rabbit had turned its head to watch near the end.

The three of them were in the lobby. Jack had built a roaring blaze in the fireplace. Danny was bundled up in a blanket on the small sofa where once, a million years ago, three nuns had sat laughing like girls while they waited for the line at the desk to thin out. He was sipping hot noodle soup from a mug. Wendy sat beside him, stroking his hair. Jack had sat on the floor, his face seeming to grow more and more still, more and more set as Danny told his story. Twice he pulled his handkerchief out of his back pocket and rubbed his sore-looking lips with it.

'Then they chased me,' he finished. Jack got up and went over to the window, his back to them. He looked at his mommy. 'They chased me all the way up to the porch.' He was struggling to keep his voice calm, because if he stayed calm maybe they would believe him. Mr Stenger hadn't stayed calm. He had started to cry and hadn't been able to stop so THE MEN IN THE WHITE COATS had come to take him away because if you couldn't stop crying it meant you had LOST YOUR MARBLES and when would you be back? NO ONE KNOWS. His parka and snowpants and the clotted snowshoes lay on the rug just inside the big double doors.

(*I won't cry I won't let myself cry*)

And he thought he could do that, but he couldn't stop shaking. He looked into the fire and waited for Daddy to say something. High yellow flames danced on the dark stone hearth. A pine-knot exploded with a bang and sparks rushed up the flue.

'Danny, come over here.' Jack turned around. His face still had that pinched, deathly look. Danny didn't like to look at it.

'Jack —'

'I just want the boy over here for a minute.'

Danny slipped off the sofa and came over beside his daddy.

'Good boy. Now what do you see?'

Danny had known what he would see even before he got to the window. Below the clutter of boot tracks, sled tracks, and snowshoe tracks that marked their usual exercise area, the snowfield that covered the Overlook's lawns sloped down to the topiary and the playground beyond. It was marred by two sets of tracks, one of them in a straight line from the porch to the playground, the other a long, looping line coming back up.

'Only my tracks, Daddy. But —'

'What about the hedges, Danny?'

Danny's lips began to tremble. He was going to cry. What if he couldn't stop?

(*i won't cry I Won't Cry Won't Won't WON'T*)

'All covered with snow,' he whispered. 'But, Daddy —'

'What? I couldn't hear you!'

'Jack, you're cross-examining him! Can't you see he's upset, he's —'

'Shut up! Well, Danny?'

'They scratched me, Daddy. My leg —'

'You must have cut your leg on the crust of the snow.'

Then Wendy was between them, her face pale and angry. 'What are you trying to make him do?' she asked him. 'Confess to murder? *What's wrong with you?*'

The strangeness in his eyes seemed to break then. 'I'm trying to help him find the difference between something real and something that was only an hallucination, that's all.' He squatted by Danny so they were on an eye-to-eye level, and then hugged him tight. 'Danny, it didn't really happen. Okay? It was like one of those trances you have sometimes. That's all.'

'Daddy?'

'What, Dan?'

'I didn't cut my leg on the crust. There isn't any crust. It's all powdery snow. It won't even stick together to make snowballs. Remember we tried to have a snowball fight and couldn't?'

He felt his father stiffen against him. 'The porch step, then.'

Danny pulled away. Suddenly he had it. It flashed into his mind all at once, the way things sometimes did, the way it had about the woman wanting to be in that gray man's pants. He stared at his father with widening eyes.

'You know I'm telling the truth,' he whispered, shocked.

'Danny—' Jack's face, tightening.

'You know because you saw—'

The sound of Jack's open palm striking Danny's face was flat, not dramatic at all. The boy's head rocked back, the palmprint reddening on his cheek like a brand.

Wendy made a moaning noise.

For a moment they were still, the three of them, and then Jack grabbed for his son and said, 'Danny, I'm sorry, you okay, doc?'

'You hit him, you bastard!' Wendy cried. 'You dirty bastard!'

She grabbed his other arm and for a moment Danny was pulled between them.

'*Oh please stop pulling me!*' he screamed at them, and there was such agony in his voice that they both let go of him, and then the tears had to come and he collapsed, weeping, between the sofa and the window, his parents staring at him helplessly, the way children might stare at a toy broken in a furious tussle over to whom it belonged. In the fireplace another pine knot exploded like a hand grenade, making them all jump.

★★★

Wendy gave him baby aspirin and Jack slipped him, unprotesting, between the sheets of his cot. He was asleep in no time with his thumb in his mouth.

'I don't like that,' she said. 'It's a regression.'

Jack didn't reply.

She looked at him softly, without anger, without a smile, either. 'You want me to apologize for calling you a bastard? All right, I apologize. I'm sorry. You still shouldn't have hit him.'

'I know,' he muttered. 'I know that. I don't know what the hell came over me.'

'You promised you'd never hit him again.'

He looked at her furiously, and then the fury collapsed. Suddenly, with pity and horror, she saw what Jack would be like as an old man. She had never seen him look that way before.

(?what way?)

Defeated, she answered herself. *He looks beaten.*

He said: 'I always thought I could keep my promises.'

She went to him and put her hands on his arm. 'All right, it's over. And when the ranger comes to check us, we'll tell him we all want to go down. All right?'

'All right,' Jack said, and at the moment, at least, he meant it. The same way he had always meant it on those mornings after, looking at his pale and haggard face in the bathroom mirror. *I'm going to stop, going to cut it off flat.* But morning gave way to afternoon, and in the afternoons he felt a little better. And afternoon gave way to night. As some great twentieth-century thinker had said, night must fall.

He found himself wishing that Wendy would ask him about the hedges, would ask him what Danny meant when he said *You know because you saw—* If she did, he would tell her everything. Everything. The hedges, the woman in the room, even about the fire hose that seemed to have switched positions. But where did confession stop? Could he tell her he'd thrown the magneto away, that they could all be down in Sidewinder right now if he hadn't done that?

What she said was, 'Do you want tea?'

'Yes. A cup of tea would be good.'

She went to the door and paused there, rubbing her forearms through her sweater. 'It's my fault as much as yours,' she said. 'What were we doing while he was going through that . . . dream, or whatever it was?'

'Wendy—'

'We were sleeping,' she said. 'Sleeping like a couple of teen-age kids with their itch nicely scratched.'

'Stop it,' he said. 'It's over.'

'No,' Wendy answered, and gave him a strange, restless smile. 'It's not over.'

She went out to make tea, leaving him to keep watch over their son.

CHAPTER THIRTY-SIX
THE ELEVATOR

Jack awoke from a thin and uneasy sleep where huge and ill-defined shapes chased him through endless snowfields to what he first thought was another dream: darkness, and in it, a sudden mechanical jumble of noises – clicks and clanks, hummings, rattlings, snaps and whooshes.

Then Wendy sat up beside him and he knew it was no dream.

'What's that?' Her hand, cold marble, gripped his wrist. He restrained an urge to shake it off – how in the hell was he supposed to know what it was? The illuminated clock on his nightstand said it was five minutes to twelve.

The humming sound again. Loud and steady, varying the slightest bit. Followed by a clank as the humming ceased. A rattling bang. A thump. Then the humming resumed.

It was the elevator.

Danny was sitting up. 'Daddy? *Daddy?*' His voice was sleepy and scared.

'Right here, doc,' Jack said. 'Come on over and jump in. Your mom's awake, too.'

The bedclothes rustled as Danny got on the bed between them. 'It's the elevator,' he whispered.

'That's right,' Jack said. 'Just the elevator.'

'What do you mean, *just?*' Wendy demanded. There was an ice-skim of hysteria on her voice. 'It's the middle of the night. *Who's running it?*'

Hummmmmmm. Click/clank. Above them now. The rattle of the gate accordioning back, the bump of the doors opening and closing. Then the hum of the motor and the cables again.

Danny began to whimper.

Jack swung his feet out of bed and onto the floor. 'It's probably a short. I'll check.'

'Don't you dare go out of this room!'

'Don't be stupid,' he said, pulling on his robe. 'It's my job.'

She was out of bed herself a moment later, pulling Danny with her.

'We'll go, too.'

'Wendy—'

'What's wrong?' Danny asked somberly. 'What's wrong, Daddy?'

Instead of answering he turned away, his face angry and set. He belted his robe around him at the door, opened it, and stepped out into the dark hall.

Wendy hesitated for a moment, and it was actually Danny who began to move first. She caught up quickly, and they went out together.

Jack hadn't bothered with the lights. She fumbled for the switch that lit the four spaced overheads in the hallway that led to the main corridor. Up ahead, Jack was already turning the corner. This time Danny found the switchplate and flicked all three switches up. The hallway leading down to the stairs and the elevator shaft came alight.

Jack was standing at the elevator station, which was flanked by benches and cigarette urns. He was standing motionless in front of the closed elevator door. In his faded tartan bathrobe and brown leather slippers with the rundown heels, his hair all in sleep corkscrews and Alfalfa cowlicks, he looked to her like an absurd twentieth-century Hamlet, an indecisive figure so mesmerized by onrushing tragedy that he was helpless to divert its course or alter it in any way.

(*jesus stop thinking so crazy—*)

Danny's hand had tightened painfully on her own. He was looking up at her intently, his face strained and anxious. He had been catching the drift of her thoughts, she realized. Just how much or how little of them he was getting was impossible to say, but she flushed, feeling much the same as if he had caught her in a masturbatory act.

'Come on,' she said, and they went down the hall to Jack.

The hummings and clankings and thumpings were louder here, terrifying in a disconnected, benumbed way. Jack was staring at the closed door with feverish intensity. Through the diamond-shaped window in the center of the elevator door she thought she could make out the cables, thrumming slightly. The elevator clanked to a stop below them, at lobby level. They heard the doors thump open. And . . .

(party)

Why had she thought party? The word had simply jumped into her head for no reason at all. The silence in the Overlook was complete and intense except for the weird noises coming up the elevator shaft.

(must have been quite a party)

(???WHAT PARTY???)

For just a moment her mind had filled with an image so real that it seemed to be a memory . . . not just any memory but one of those you treasure, one of those you keep for very special occasions and rarely mention aloud. Lights . . . hundreds, maybe thousands of them. Lights and colors, the pop of champagne corks, a forty-piece orchestra playing Glenn Miller's 'In the Mood'. But Glenn Miller had gone down in his bomber before she was born, how could she have a memory of Glenn Miller?

She looked down at Danny and saw his head had cocked to one side, as if he was hearing something she couldn't hear. His face was very pale.

Thump.

The door had slid shut down there. A humming whine as the elevator began to rise. She saw the engine housing on top of the car first through the diamond-shaped window, then the interior of the car, seen through the further diamond shapes made by the brass gate. Warm yellow light from the car's overhead. It was empty. The car was empty. It was empty but

(on the night of the party they must have crowded in by the dozens, crowded the car way beyond its safety limit but of course it had been new then and all of them wearing masks)

(????WHAT MASKS????)

The car stopped above them, on the third floor. She looked at Danny. His face was all eyes. His mouth was pressed into a frightened, bloodless slit. Above them, the brass gate rattled back.

The elevator door thumped open, it thumped open because it was time, the time had come, it was time to say

(Goodnight . . . goodnight . . . yes, it was lovely . . . no, I really can't stay for the unmasking . . . early to bed, early to rise . . . oh, was that Sheila? . . . the monk? . . . isn't that witty, Sheila coming as a monk? . . . yes, goodnight . . . good)

Thump.

Gears clashed. The motor engaged. The car began to whine back down.

'Jack,' she whispered. 'What is it? What's wrong with it?'

'A short circuit,' he said. His face was like wood. 'I told you, it was a short circuit.'

'I keep hearing voices in my head!' she cried. 'What is it? What's wrong? I feel like I'm going crazy!'

'What voices?' He looked at her with deadly blandness.

She turned to Danny. 'Did you—?'

Danny nodded slowly. 'Yes. And music. Like from a long time ago. In my head.'

The elevator car stopped again. The hotel was silent, creaking, deserted. Outside, the wind whined around the eaves in the darkness.

'Maybe you are both crazy,' Jack said conversationally. 'I don't hear a goddamned thing except that elevator having a case of the electrical hiccups. If you two want to have duet hysterics, fine. But count me out.'

The elevator was coming down again.

Jack stepped to the right, where a glass-fronted box was mounted on the wall at chest height. He smashed his bare fist against it. Glass tinkled inward. Blood dripped from two of his knuckles. He reached in and took out a key with a long, smooth barrel.

'Jack, no. Don't.'

'I am going to do my job. Now leave me alone, Wendy!'

She tried to grab his arm. He pushed her backward. Her feet tangled in the hem of her robe and she fell to the carpet with an ungainly thump. Danny cried out shrilly and fell on his knees beside her. Jack turned back to the elevator and thrust the key into the socket.

The elevator cables disappeared and the bottom of the car came into view in the small window. A second later Jack turned the key hard. There was a grating, screeching sound as the elevator car came to an instant standstill. For a moment the declutched motor in the basement whined even louder, and then its circuit breaker cut in and the Overlook went unearthly still. The night wind outside seemed very loud by comparison. Jack looked stupidly at the gray metal elevator door. There were three splotches of blood below the keyhole from his lacerated knuckles.

He turned back to Wendy and Danny for a moment. She was sitting up, and Danny had his arm around her. They were both staring at him carefully, as if he was a stranger they had never seen before, possibly a dangerous one. He opened his mouth, not sure what was going to come out.

'It . . . Wendy, it's my job.'

She said clearly: 'Fuck your job.'

He turned back to the elevator, worked his fingers into the crack that ran down the right side of the door, and got it open a little way. Then he was able to get his whole weight on it and threw the door open.

The car had stopped halfway, its floor at Jack's chest level. Warm light still spilled out on it, contrasting with the oily darkness of the shaft below.

He looked in for what seemed a long time.

'It's empty,' he said then. 'A short circuit, like I said.' He hooked his fingers into the slot behind the door and began to pull it closed . . . then her hand was on his shoulder, surprisingly strong, yanking him away.

'Wendy!' he shouted. But she had already caught the car's bottom edge and pulled herself up enough so she could look in. Then, with a convulsive heave of her shoulder and belly muscles, she tried to boost herself all the way up. For a moment the issue was in doubt. Her feet tottered over the blackness of the shaft and one pink slipper fell from her foot and slipped out of sight.

'*Mommy!*' Danny screamed.

Then she was up, her cheeks flushed, her forehead as pale

and shining as a spirit lamp. 'What about this, Jack? Is this a short circuit?' She threw something and suddenly the hall was full of drifting confetti, red and white and blue and yellow. 'Is *this*?' A green party streamer, faded to a pale pastel color with age.

'And *this*?'

She tossed it out and it came to rest on the blue-black jungle carpet, a black silk cat's-eye mask, dusted with sequins at the temples.

'*Does that look like a short circuit to you, Jack?*' she screamed at him.

Jack stepped slowly away from it, shaking his head mechanically back and forth. The cat's-eye mask stared up blankly at the ceiling from the confetti-strewn hallway carpet.

CHAPTER THIRTY-SEVEN
THE BALLROOM

It was the first of December.

Danny was in the east-wing ballroom, standing on an over-stuffed, high-backed wing chair, looking at the clock under glass. It stood in the center of the ballroom's high, ornamental mantelpiece, flanked by two large ivory elephants. He almost expected the elephants would begin to move and try to gore him with their tusks as he stood there, but they were moveless. They were 'safe'. Since the night of the elevator he had come to divide all things at the Overlook into two categories. The elevator, the basement, the playground, Room 217, and the Presidential Suite (it was Suite, not Sweet; he had seen the correct spelling in an account book Daddy had been reading at supper last night and had memorized it carefully) – those places were 'unsafe'. Their quarters, the lobby, and the porch were 'safe'. Apparently the ballroom was, too.

(The elephants are, anyway.)

He was not sure about other places and so avoided them on general principle.

He looked at the clock inside the glass dome. It was under glass because all its wheels and cogs and springs were showing. A chrome or steel track ran around the outside of these works, and directly below the clockface there was a small axis bar with a pair of meshing cogs at either end. The hands of the clock stood at quarter past XI, and although he didn't know Roman numerals he could guess by the configuration of the hands at what time the clock had stopped. The clock stood on a velvet base. In front of it, slightly distorted by the curve of the dome, was a carefully carved silver key.

He supposed that the clock was one of the things he wasn't supposed to touch, like the decorative fire-tools in their brass-bound cabinet by the lobby fireplace or the tall china highboy at the back of the dining room.

A sense of injustice and a feeling of angry rebellion suddenly rose in him and

(*never mind what i'm not supposed to touch, just never mind. touched me, hasn't it? played with me, hasn't it?*)

It had. And it hadn't been particularly careful not to break him, either.

Danny put his hands out, grasped the glass dome, and lifted it aside. He let one finger play over the works for a moment, the pad of his index finger denting the cogs, running smoothly over the wheels. He picked up the silver key. For an adult it would have been uncomfortably small, but it fitted his own fingers perfectly. He placed it in the keyhole at the center of the clockface. It went firmly home with a tiny click, more felt than heard. It wound to the right, of course: clockwise.

Danny turned the key until it would turn no more and then removed it. The clock began to tick. Cogs turned. A large balance wheel rocked back and forth in semicircles. The hands were moving. If you kept your head perfectly motionless and your eyes wide open, you could see the minute hand inching along toward its meeting some forty-five minutes from now with the hour hand. At XII.

(*And the Red Death held sway over all.*)

He frowned, and then shook the thought away. It was a thought with no meaning or reference for him.

He reached his index finger out again and pushed the minute hand up to the hour, curious about what might happen. It obviously wasn't a cuckoo clock, but that steel rail had to have some purpose.

There was a small, ratcheting series of clicks, and then the clock began to tinkle Strauss's 'Blue Danube Waltz'. A punched roll of cloth no more than two inches in width began to unwind. A small series of brass strikers rose and fell. From behind the clockface two figures glided into view along the steel track, ballet dancers, on the left a girl in a fluffy skirt and white stockings, on the right a boy in a black leotard and ballet slippers.

Their hands were held in arches over their heads. They came together in the middle, in front of VI.

Danny espied tiny grooves in their sides, just below their armpits. The axis bar slipped into these grooves and he heard another small click. The cogs at either end of the bar began to turn. 'The Blue Danube' tinkled. The dancers' arms came down around each other. The boy flipped the girl up over his head and then whirled over the bar. They were now lying prone, the boy's head buried beneath the girl's short ballet skirt, the girl's face pressed against the center of the boy's leotard. They writhed in a mechanical frenzy.

Danny's nose wrinkled. They were kissing peepees. That made him feel sick.

A moment later and things began to run backward. The boy whirled back over the axis bar. He flipped the girl into an upright position. They seemed to nod knowingly to each other as their hands arched back over their heads. They retreated the way they had come, disappearing just as 'The Blue Danube' finished. The clock began to strike a count of five chimes.

(Midnight! Stroke of midnight!)
(Hooray for masks!)

Danny whirled on the chair, almost falling down. The ballroom was empty. Beyond the double cathedral window he could see fresh snow begining to sift down. The huge ballroom rug (rolled up for dancing, of course), a rich tangle of red and gold embroidery, lay undisturbed on the floor. Spaced around it were small, intimate tables for two, the spidery chairs that went with each upended with legs pointing at the ceiling.

The whole place was empty.

But it wasn't really empty. Because here in the Overlook things just went on and on. Here in the Overlook all times were one. There was an endless night in August of 1945, with laughter and drinks and a chosen shining few going up and coming down in the elevator, drinking champagne and popping party favors in each other's faces. It was a not-yet-light morning in June some twenty years later and the organization hitters endlessly pumped shotgun shells into the torn and bleeding bodies of three men who went through their agony endlessly.

In a room on the second floor a woman lolled in her tub and waited for visitors.

In the Overlook all things had a sort of life. It was as if the whole place had been wound up with a silver key. The clock was running. The clock was running.

He was that key, Danny thought sadly. Tony had warned him and he had just let things go on.

(I'm just five!)

he cried to some half-felt presence in the room.

(Doesn't it make any difference that I'm just five?)

There was no answer.

He turned reluctantly back to the clock.

He had been putting it off, hoping that something would happen to help him avoid trying to call Tony again, that a ranger would come, or a helicopter, or the rescue team; they always came in time on his TV programs, the people were saved. On TV the rangers and the SWAT squad and the paramedics were a friendly white force counterbalancing the confused evil that he perceived in the world; when people got in trouble they were helped out of it, they were fixed up. They did not have to help themselves out of trouble.

(Please?)

There was no answer.

No answer, and if Tony came would it be the same nightmare? The blooming, the hoarse and petulant voice, the blue-black rug like snakes? *Redrum?*

But what else?

(Please oh please)

No answer.

With a trembling sigh, he looked at the clockface. Cogs turned and meshed with other cogs. The balance wheel rocked hypnotically back and forth. And if you held your head perfectly still, you could see the minute hand creeping inexorably down from XII to V. If you held your head perfectly still you could see that—

The clockface was gone. In its place was a round black hole. It led down into forever. It began to swell. The clock was gone. The room behind it. Danny tottered and then fell into the darkness that had been hiding behind the clockface all along.

The small boy in the chair suddenly collapsed and lay in it at a crooked unnatural angle, his head thrown back, his eyes staring sightlessly at the high ballroom ceiling.

Down and down and down and down to—

—the hallway, crouched in the hallway, and he had made a wrong turn, trying to get back to the stairs he had made a wrong turn and now AND NOW—

—he saw he was in the short dead-end corridor that led only to the Presidential Suite and the booming sound was coming closer, the roque mallet whistling savagely through the air, the head of it embedding itself into the wall, cutting the silk paper, letting out small puffs of plaster dust.

(Goddammit, come out here! Take your)

But there was another figure in the hallway, slouched non-chalantly against the wall just behind him. Like a ghost.

No, not a ghost, but all dressed in white. Dressed in whites.

(I'll find you, you goddam little whoremastering RUNT!)

Danny cringed back from the sound. Coming up the main third-floor hall now. Soon the owner of that voice would round the corner.

(Come here! Come here, you little shit!)

The figure dressed in white straightened up a little, removed a cigarette from the corner of his mouth, and plucked a shred of tobacco from his full lower lip. It was Halloran, Danny saw. Dressed in his cook's whites instead of the blue suit he had been wearing on closing day.

'If there *is* trouble,' Halloran said, 'you give a call. A big loud holler like the one that knocked me back a few minutes ago. I might hear you even way down in Florida. And if I do, I'll come on the run. I'll come on the run. I'll come on the—'

(Come on, then! Come now, come NOW! Oh Dick I need you we all need)

'—run. Sorry, but I got to run. Sorry, Danny ole kid ole doc, but I got to run. It's sure been fun, you son of a gun, but I got to hurry, I got to run.'

(No!)

But as he watched, Dick Halloran turned, put his cigarette

back into the corner of his mouth, and stepped nonchalantly through the wall.

Leaving him alone.

And that was when the shadow-figure turned the corner, huge in the hallway's gloom, only the reflected red of its eyes clear.

(*There you are! Now I've got you, you fuck! Now I'll teach you!*)

It lurched toward him in a horrible, shambling run, the roque mallet swinging up and up and up. Danny scrambled backward, screaming, and suddenly he was through the wall and falling, tumbling over and over, down the hole, down the rabbit hole and into a land full of sick wonders.

Tony was far below him, also falling.

(*I can't come anymore, Danny . . . he won't let me near you . . . none of them will let me near you . . . get Dick . . . get Dick . . .*)

'Tony!' he screamed.

But Tony was gone and suddenly he was in a dark room. But not entirely dark. Muted light spilling from somewhere. It was Mommy and Daddy's bedroom. He could see Daddy's desk. But the room was a dreadful shambles. He had been in this room before. Mommy's record player overturned on the floor. Her records scattered on the rug. The mattress half off the bed. Pictures ripped from the walls. His cot lying on its side like a dead dog, the Violent Violet Volkswagen crushed to purple shards of plastic.

The light was coming from the bathroom door, half-open. Just beyond it a hand gangled limply, blood dripping from the tips of the fingers. And in the medicine mirror, the word REDRUM flashing off and on.

Suddenly a huge clock in a glass bowl materialized in front of it. There were no hands or numbers on the clockface, only a date written in red: *DECEMBER* 2. And then, eyes widening in horror, he saw the word REDRUM reflecting dimly from the glass dome, now reflected twice. And he saw that it spelled MURDER.

Danny Torrance screamed in wretched terror. The date was gone from the clockface. The clockface itself was gone, replaced by a circular black hole that swelled and swelled like a dilating iris. It blotted out everything and he fell forward, beginning to fall, falling, he was—

★★★

—falling off the chair.

For a moment he lay on the ballroom floor, breathing hard.

REDRUM.

MURDER.

REDRUM.

MURDER.

(*The Red Death held sway over all!*)

(*Unmask! Unmask!*)

And behind each glittering, lovely mask, the as-yet unseen face of the shape that chased him down these dark alleyways, its red eyes widening, blank and homicidal.

Oh, he was afraid of what face might come to light when the time for unmasking came around at last.

(*DICK!*)

he screamed with all his might. His head seemed to shiver with the force of it.

(*!!! OH DICK OH PLEASE PLEASE PLEASE COME !!!*)

Above him the clock he had wound with the silver key continued to mark off the seconds and minutes and hours.

PART FIVE

MATTERS OF LIFE AND DEATH

CHAPTER THIRTY-EIGHT
FLORIDA

Mrs Hallorann's third son, Dick, dressed in his cook's whites, a Lucky Strike parked in the corner of his mouth, backed his reclaimed Cadillac limo out of its space behind the One-A Wholesale Vegetable Mart and drove slowly around the building. Masterton, part owner now but still walking with the patented shuffle he had adopted back before World War II, was pushing a bin of lettuces into the high, dark building.

Hallorann pushed the button that lowered the passenger side window and hollered: 'Those avocadoes is too damn high, you cheapskate!'

Masterton looked back over his shoulder, grinned widely enough to expose all three gold teeth, and yelled back, 'And I know exactly where you can put em, my good buddy.'

'Remarks like that I keep track of, *bro.*'

Masterton gave him the finger. Hallorann returned the compliment.

'Get your cukes, did you?' Masterton asked.

'I did.'

'You come back early tomorrow, I gonna give you some of the nicest new potatoes you ever seen.'

'I send the boy,' Hallorann said. 'You comin up tonight?'

'You supplyin the juice, *bro*?'

'That's a big ten-four.'

'I be there. You keep that thing off the top end goin home, you hear me? Every cop between here an St Pete knows your name.'

'You know all about it, huh?' Hallorann asked, grinning.

'I know more than you'll ever learn, my man.'

'Listen to this sassy nigger. Would you listen?'

'Go on, get outta here fore I start throwin these lettuces.'

'Go on an throw em. I'll take anything for free.'

Masterton made as if to throw one. Hallorann ducked, rolled up the window, and drove on. He was feeling fine. For the last half hour or so he had been smelling oranges, but he didn't find that queer. For the last half hour he had been in a fruit and vegetable market.

It was 4:30 p.m., EST, the first day of December, Old Man Winter settling his frostbitten rump firmly onto most of the country, but down here the men wore open-throated short-sleeve shirts and the women were in light summer dresses and shorts. On top of the First Bank of Florida building, a digital thermometer bordered with huge grapefruits was flashing 79° over and over. Thank God for Florida, Hallorann thought, mosquitoes and all.

In the back of the limo were two dozen avocadoes, a crate of cucumbers, ditto oranges, ditto grapefruit. Three shopping sacks filled with Bermuda onions, the sweetest vegetable a loving God ever created, some pretty good sweet peas, which would be served with the entree and come back uneaten nine times out of ten, and a single blue Hubbard squash that was strictly for personal consumption.

Hallorann stopped in the turn lane at the Vermont Street light, and when the green arrow showed he pulled out onto state highway 219, pushing up to forty and holding it there until the town began to trickle away into an exurban sprawl of gas stations, Burger Kings and McDonalds. It was a small order today, he could have sent Baedecker after it, but Baedecker had been chafing for his chance to buy the meat, and besides, Hallorann never missed a change to bang it back and forth with Frank Masterton if he could help it. Masterton might show up tonight to watch some TV and drink Hallorann's Bushmill's, or he might not. Either way was all right. But seeing him mattered. Every time it mattered now, because they weren't young anymore. In the last few days it seemed he was thinking of that very fact a great deal. Not so young anymore, when you got up near sixty years old (or – tell the truth and save a lie – past it) you had to start thinking about stepping out. You could go anytime. And that had been on his mind this week, not in a heavy way but as a fact. Dying was a part of living. You had to keep tuning in to that if you expected to be a whole person. And if the fact of your own death was hard to understand, at least it wasn't impossible to accept.

Why this should have been on his mind he could not have said, but his other reason for getting this small order himself was so he could step upstairs to the small office over Frank's Bar and Grill. There was a lawyer up there now (the dentist who had been there last year had apparently gone broke), a young black fellow named McIver. Hallorann had stepped in and told this McIver that he wanted to make a will, and could McIver help him out? Well, McIver asked, how soon do you want the document? Yesterday, said Hallorann, and threw back his head and laughed. Have you got anything complicated in mind? was McIver's next question. Hallorann did not. He had his Cadillac, his bank account – some nine thousand dollars – a piddling checking account, and a closet of clothes. He wanted it all to go to his sister. And if your sister predeceases you? McIver asked. Never mind, Hallorann said. If that happens, I'll make a new will. The document had been completed and signed in less than three hours – fast work for a shyster – and now resided in Hallorann's breast pocket, folded into a stiff blue envelope with the word WILL on the outside in Old English letters.

He could not have said why he had chosen this warm sunny day when he felt so well to do something he had been putting off for years, but the impulse had come on him and he hadn't said no. He was used to following his hunches.

He was pretty well out of town now. He cranked the limo up to an illegal sixty and let it ride there in the left-hand lane, sucking up most of the Petersburg-bound traffic. He knew from experience that the limo would still ride as solid as iron at ninety, and even at a hundred and twenty it didn't seem to lighten up much. But his screamin days were long gone. The thought of putting the limo up to a hundred and twenty on a straight stretch only scared him. He was getting old.

(*Jesus, those oranges smell strong. Wonder if they gone over?*)

Bugs splattered against the window. He dialed the radio

to a Miami soul station and got the soft, wailing voice of Al Green.

> *'What a beautiful time we had together,*
> *Now it's getting late and we must leave each other . . .'*

He unrolled the window, pitched his cigarette butt out, then rolled it further down to clear out the smell of the oranges. He tapped his fingers against the wheel and hummed along under his breath. Hooked over the rearview mirror, his St Christopher's medal swung gently back and forth.

And suddenly the smell of oranges intensified and he knew it was coming, something was coming at him. He saw his own eyes in the rearview, widening, surprised. And then it came all at once, came in a huge blast that drove out everything else: the music, the road ahead, his own absent awareness of himself as a unique human creature. It was as if someone had put a psychic gun to his head and shot him with a .45 caliber scream.

(!!! OH DICK OH PLEASE PLEASE PLEASE
COME !!!)

The limo had just drawn even with a Pinto station wagon driven by a man in workman's clothes. The workman saw the limo drifting into his lane and laid on the horn. When the Cadillac continued to drift he snapped a look at the driver and saw a big black man bolt upright behind the wheel, his eyes looking vaguely upward. Later the workman told his wife that he knew it was just one of those niggery hairdos they were all wearing these days, but at the time it had looked just as if every hair on that coon's head was standing on end. He thought the black man was having a heart attack.

The workman braked hard, dropping back into a luckily-empty space behind him. The rear end of the Cadillac pulled ahead of him, still cutting in, and the workman stared with bemused horror as the long, rocket-shaped rear taillights cut into his lane no more than a quarter of an inch in front of his bumper.

The workman cut to the left, still laying on his horn, and roared around the drunkenly weaving limousine. He invited the driver of the limo to perform an illegal sex act on himself.

To engage in oral congress with various rodents and birds. He articulated his own proposal that all persons of Negro blood return to their native continent. He expressed his sincere belief in the position the limo-driver's soul would occupy in the afterlife. He finished by saying that he believed he had met the limo-driver's mother in a New Orleans house of prostitution.

Then he was ahead and out of danger and suddenly aware that he had wet his pants.

In Hallorann's mind the thought kept repeating

(COME DICK PLEASE COME DICK PLEASE)

but it began to fade off the way a radio station will as you approach the limits of its broadcasting area. He became fuzzily aware that his car was tooling along the soft shoulder at better than fifty miles an hour. He guided it back onto the road, feeling the rear end fishtail for a moment before regaining the composition surface.

There was an A/W Rootbeer stand just ahead. Hallorann signaled and turned in, his heart thudding painfully in his chest, his face a sickly gray color. He pulled into a parking slot, took his handkerchief out of his pocket, and mopped his forehead with it.

(Lord God!)

'May I help you?'

The voice startled him again, even though it wasn't the voice of God but that of a cute little carhop, standing by his open window with an order pad.

'Yeah, baby, a rootbeer float. Two scoops of vanilla, okay?'

'Yes, sir.' She walked away, hips rolling nicely beneath her red nylon uniform.

Hallorann leaned back against the leather seat and closed his eyes. There was nothing left to pick up. The last of it had faded out between pulling in here and giving the waitress his order. All that was left was a sick, thudding headache, as if his brain had been twisted and wrung out and hung up to dry. Like the headache he'd gotten from letting that boy Danny shine at him up there at Ullman's Folly.

But this had been much louder. Then the boy had only been

playing a game with him. This had been pure panic, each word screamed aloud in his head.

He looked down at his arms. Hot sunshine lay on them but they had still goose-bumped. He had told the boy to call him if he needed help, he remembered that. And now the boy was calling.

He suddenly wondered how he could have left that boy up there at all, shining the way he did. There was bound to be trouble, maybe bad trouble.

He suddenly keyed the limo, put it in reverse, and pulled back onto the highway, peeling rubber. The waitress with the rolling hips stood in the A/W stand's archway, a tray with a rootbeer float on it in her hands.

'What is it with you, a fire?' she shouted, but Hallorann was gone.

★★★

The manager was a man named Queems, and when Hallorann came in Queems was conversing with his bookie. He wanted the four-horse at Rockaway. No, no parlay, no quinella, no exacta, no goddam futura. Just the little old four, six hundred dollars on the nose. And the Jets on Sunday. What did he mean, the Jets were playing the Bills? Didn't he know who the Jets were? Five hundred, seven-point spread. When Queems hung up, looking put-out, Hallorann understood how a man could make fifty grand a year running this little spa and still wear suits with shiny seats. He regarded Hallorann with an eye that was still bloodshot from too many glances into last night's Bourbon bottle.

'Problems, Dick?'

'Yes, sir, Mr Queems, I guess so. I need three days off.'

There was a package of Kents in the breast pocket of Queems's sheer yellow shirt. He reached one out of the pocket without removing the pack, tweezing it out, and bit down morosely on the patented Micronite filter. He lit it with his desktop Cricket.

'So do I,' he said. 'But what's on your mind?'

'I need three days,' Hallorann repeated. 'It's my boy.'

Queems's eyes dropped to Hallorann's left hand, which was ringless.

'I been divorced since 1964,' Hallorann said patiently.

'Dick, you know what the weekend situation is. We're full. To the gunnels. Even the cheap seats. We're even filled up in the Florida Room on Sunday night. So take my watch, my wallet, my pension fund. Hell, you can even take my wife if you can stand the sharp edges. But please don't ask me for time off. What is he, sick?'

'Yes, sir,' Hallorann said, still trying to visualize himself twisting a cheap cloth hat and rolling his eyeballs. 'He shot.'

'Shot!' Queems said. He put his Kent down in an ashtray which bore the emblem of Ole Miss, of which he was a business admin graduate.

'Yes, sir,' Hallorann said somberly.

'Hunting accident?'

'No, sir,' Hallorann said, and let his voice drop to a lower, huskier note. 'Jana, she's been livin with this truck driver. A white man. He shot my boy. He's in a hospital in Denver, Colorado. Critical condition.'

'How in hell did you find out? I thought you were buying vegetables.'

'Yes, sir, I was.' He had stopped at the Western Union office just before coming here to reserve an Avis car at Stapleton Airport. Before leaving he had swiped a Western Union flimsy. Now he took the folded and crumpled blank form from his pocket and flashed it before Queems's bloodshot eyes. He put it back in his pocket and, allowing his voice to drop another notch, said: 'Jana sent it. It was waitin in my letterbox when I got back just now.'

'Jesus. Jesus Christ,' Queems said. There was a peculiar tight expression of concern on his face, one Hallorann was familiar with. It was as close to an expression of sympathy as a white man who thought of himself as 'good with the coloreds' could get when the object was a black man or his mythical black son.

'Yeah, okay, you get going,' Queems said. 'Baedecker can take over for three days, I guess. The potboy can help out.'

Hallorann nodded, letting his face get longer still, but the thought of the potboy helping out Baedecker made him grin inside. Even on a good day Hallorann doubted if the potboy could hit the urinal on the first squirt.

'I want to rebate back this week's pay,' Hallorann said. 'The whole thing. I know what a bind this puttin you in, Mr Queems, sir.'

Queems's expression got tighter still; it looked as if he might have a fishbone caught in his throat. 'We can talk about that later. You go on and pack. I'll talk to Baedecker. Want me to make you a plane reservation?'

'No, sir, I'll do it.'

'All right.' Queems stood up, leaned sincerely forward, and inhaled a raft of ascending smoke from his Kent. He coughed heartily, his thin white face turning red. Hallorann struggled hard to keep his somber expression. 'I hope everything turns out, Dick. Call when you get word.'

'I'll do that.'

They shook hands over the desk.

Hallorann made himself get down to the ground floor and across to the hired help's compound before bursting into rich, head-shaking laughter. He was still grinning and mopping his streaming eyes with his handkerchief when the smell of oranges came, thick and gagging, and the bolt followed it, striking him in the head, sending him back against the pink stucco wall in a drunken stagger.

(!!! PLEASE COME DICK PLEASE COME COME QUICK !!!)

He recovered a little at a time and at last felt capable of climbing the outside stairs to his apartment. He kept the latchkey under the rush-plaited doormat, and when he reached down to get it, something fell out of his inner pocket and fell to the second-floor decking with a flat thump. His mind was still so much on the voice that had shivered through his head that for a moment he could only look at the blue envelope blankly, not knowing what it was.

Then he turned it over and the word WILL stared up at him in the black spidery letters.

(Oh my God is it like that?)

He didn't know. But it could be. All week long the thought of his own ending had been on his mind like a . . . well, like a

(Go on, say it)

like a premonition.

Death? For a moment his whole life seemed to flash before him, not in a historical sense, no topography of the ups and downs that Mrs Hallorann's third son, Dick, had lived through, but his life as it was now. Martin Luther King had told them not long before the bullet took him down to his martyr's grave that he had been to the mountain. Dick could not claim that. No mountain, but he had reached a sunny plateau after years of struggle. He had good friends. He had all the references he would ever need to get a job anywhere. When he wanted fuck, why, he could find a friendly one with no questions asked and no big shitty struggle about what it all meant. He had come to terms with his blackness – happy terms. He was up past sixty and thank God, he was cruising.

Was he going to chance the end of that – the end of *him* – for three white people he didn't even know?

But that was a lie, wasn't it?

He knew the boy. They had shared each other the way good friends can't even after forty years of it. He knew the boy and the boy knew him, because they each had a kind of searchlight in their heads, something they hadn't asked for, something that had just been given.

(Naw, you got a flashlight, he the one with the searchlight.)

And sometimes that light, that shine, seemed like a pretty nice thing. You could pick the horses, or like the boy had said, you could tell your daddy where his trunk was when it turned up missing. But that was only dressing, the sauce on the salad, and down below there was as much bitter vetch in that salad as there was cool cucumber. You could taste pain and death and tears. And now the boy was stuck in that place, and he would go. For the boy. Because, speaking to the boy, they had only been different colors when they used their mouths. So he would go. He would do what he could, because if he didn't, the boy was going to die right inside his head.

But because he was human he could not help a bitter wish that the cup had never been passed his way.

★★★

(She had started to get out and come after him.)

He had been dumping a change of clothes into an overnight bag when the thought came to him, freezing him with the power of the memory as it always did when he thought of it. He tried to think of it as seldom as possible.

The maid, Delores Vickery her name was, had been hysterical. Had said some things to the other chambermaids, and worse still, to some of the guests. When the word got back to Ullman, as the silly quiff should have known it would do, he had fired her out of hand. She had come to Hallorann in tears, not about being fired, but about the thing she had seen in that second-floor room. She had gone into 217 to change the towels, she said, and there had been that Mrs Massey, lying dead in the tub. That, of course, was impossible. Mrs Massey had been discreetly taken away the day before and was even then winging her way back to New York – in the shipping hold instead of the first class she'd been accustomed to.

Hallorann hadn't liked Delores much, but he had gone up to look that evening. The maid was an olive-complected girl of twenty-three who waited table near the end of the season when things slowed down. She had a small shining, Hallorann judged, really not more than a twinkle; a mousy-looking man and his escort, wearing a faded cloth coat, would come in for dinner and Delores would trade one of her tables for theirs. The mousy little man would leave a picture of Alexander Hamilton under his plate, bad enough for the girl who had made the trade, but worse, Delores would crow over it. She was lazy, a goof-off in an operation run by a man who allowed no goof-offs. She would sit in a linen closet, reading a confession magazine and smoking, but whenever Ullman went on one of his unscheduled prowls (and woe to the girl he caught resting her feet) he found her working industriously, her magazine hidden under the sheets on a high shelf, her ashtray tucked safely into her uniform pocket. Yeah, Hallorann thought, she'd been a goof-off and a sloven and the other girls had resented her, but Delores had had that little twinkle. It had always greased the skids for her. But what she had seen in 217 had scared her badly enough so she was more than glad to pick up the walking papers Ullman had issued her and go.

Why had she come to him? A shine knows a shine, Hallorann thought, grinning at the pun.

So he had gone up that night and had let himself into the room, which was to be reoccupied the next day. He had used the office passkey to get in, and if Ullman had caught him with that key, he would have joined Delores Vickery on the unemployment line.

The shower curtain around the tub had been drawn. He had pushed it back, but even before he did he'd had a premonition of what he was going to see. Mrs Massey, swollen and purple, lay soggily in the tub, which was half-full of water. He had stood looking down at her, a pulse beating thickly in his throat. There had been other things at the Overlook: a bad dream that recurred at irregular intervals – some sort of costume party and he was catering it in the Overlook's ballroom and at the shout to unmask, everybody exposed faces that were those of rotting insects – and there had been the hedge animals. Twice, maybe three times, he had (or thought he had) seen them move, ever so slightly. That dog would seem to change from his sitting-up posture to a slightly crouched one, and the lions seemed to move forward, as if menacing the little tykes on the playground. Last year in May Ullman had sent him up to the attic to look for the ornate set of firetools that now stood beside the lobby fireplace. While he had been up there the three lightbulbs strung overhead had gone out and he had lost his way back to the trapdoor. He had stumbled around for an unknown length of time, closer and closer to panic, barking his shins on boxes and bumping into things, with a stronger and stronger feeling that something was stalking him in the dark. Some great and frightening creature that had just oozed out of the woodwork when the lights went out. And when he had literally stumbled over the trapdoor's ringbolt he had hurried down as fast as he could, leaving the trap open, sooty and disheveled, with a feeling of disaster barely averted. Later Ullman had come down to the kitchen personally, to inform him he had left the attic trap door open and the lights burning up there. Did Hallorann think the guests wanted to go up there and play treasure hunt? Did he think electricity was free?

And he suspected – no, was nearly positive – that several of the guests had seen or heard things too. In the three years he had been there, the Presidential Suite had been booked nineteen times. Six of the guests who had put up there had left the hotel early, some of them looking markedly ill. Other guests had left other rooms with the same abruptness. One night in August of 1974, near dusk, a man who had won the Bronze and Silver Stars in Korea (that man now sat on the boards of three major corporations and was said to have personally pink-slipped a famous TV news anchorman) unaccountably went into a fit of screaming hysterics on the putting green. And there had been dozens of children during Hallorann's association with the Overlook who simply refused to go into the playground. One child had had a convulsion while playing in the concrete rings, but Hallorann didn't know if that could be attributed to the Overlook's deadly siren song or not – word had gone around among the help that the child, the only daughter of a handsome movie actor, was a medically controlled epileptic who had simply forgotten her medicine that day.

And so, staring down at the corpse of Mrs Massey, he had been frightened but not completely terrified. It was not completely unexpected. Terror came when she opened her eyes to disclose blank silver pupils and began to grin at him. Horror came when

(*she had started to get out and come after him.*)

He had fled, heart racing, and had not felt safe even with the door shut and locked behind him. In fact, he admitted to himself now as he zipped the flightbag shut, he had never felt safe anywhere in the Overlook again.

And now the boy – calling, screaming for help.

He looked at his watch. It was 5:30 p.m. He went to the apartment's door, remembered it would be heavy winter now in Colorado, especially up in the mountains, and went back to his closet. He pulled his long, sheepskin-lined overcoat out of its polyurethane dry-cleaning bag and put it over his arm. It was the only winter garment he owned. He turned off all the lights and looked around. Had he forgotten anything? Yes. One thing. He took the will out of his breast pocket and slipped it into the margin of the dressing table mirror. With luck he would be back to get it.

Sure, with luck.

He left the apartment, locked the door behind him, put the key under the rush mat, and ran down the outside steps to his converted Cadillac.

★★★

Halfway to Miami International, comfortably away from the switchboard where Queems or Queems's toadies were known to listen in, Halloran stopped at a shopping center Laundromat and called United Air Lines. Flights to Denver?

There was one due out at 6:30 p.m. Could the gentleman make that?

Halloran looked at his watch, which showed 6:02, and said he could. What about vacancies on the flight?

Just let me check.

A clunking sound in his ear followed by saccharine Montavani, which was supposed to make being on hold more pleasant. It didn't. Halloran danced from one foot to the other, alternating glances between his watch and a young girl with a sleeping baby in a hammock on her back unloading a coin-op Maytag. She was afraid she was going to get home later than she planned and the roast would burn and her husband – Mark? Mike? Matt? – would be mad.

A minute passed. Two. He had just about made up his mind to drive ahead and take his chances when the canned-sounding voice of the flight reservations clerk came back on. There was an empty seat, a cancellation. It was in first class. Did that make any difference?

No. He wanted it.

Would that be cash or credit card?

Cash, baby, cash. I've got to fly.

And the name was—?

Hallorann, two *l*'s, two *n*'s. Catch you later.

He hung up and hurried toward the door. The girl's simple thought, worry for the roast, broadcast at him over and over until he thought he would go mad. Sometimes it was like that, for no reason at all you would catch a thought, completely isolated, completely pure and clear . . . and usually completely useless.

★★★

He almost made it.

He had the limo cranked up to eighty and the airport was actually in sight when one of Florida's Finest pulled him over.

Hallorann unrolled the electric window and opened his mouth at the cop, who was flipping up pages in his citation book.

'I *know*,' the cop said comfortingly. 'It's a funeral in Cleveland. Your father. It's a wedding in Seattle. Your sister. A fire in San Jose wiped out your gramp's candy store. Some really fine Cambodian Red just waiting in a terminal locker in New York City. I love this piece of road just outside the airport. Even as a kid, story hour was my favorite part of school.'

'Listen, officer, my son is—'

'The only part of the story I can never figure out until the end,' the officer said, finding the right page in his citation book, 'is the driver's-license number of the offending motorist/ storyteller and his registration information. So be a nice guy. Let me peek.'

Hallorann looked into the cop's calm blue eyes, debated telling his my-son-is-in-critical-condition story anyway, and decided that would make things worse. This Smokey was no Queems. He dug out his wallet.

'Wonderful,' the cop said. 'Would you take them out for me, please? I just have to see how it's all going to come out in the end.'

Silently, Hallorann took out his driver's license and his Florida registration and gave them to the traffic cop.

'That's very good. That's so good you win a present.'

'What?' Hallorann asked hopefully.

'When I finish writing down these numbers, I'm going to let you blow up a little balloon for me.'

'Oh, *Jeeeesus!*' Hallorann moaned. 'Officer, my flight—'

'Shhhh,' the traffic cop said. 'Don't be naughty.'

Hallorann closed his eyes.

★★★

He got to the United desk at 6:49, hoping against hope that the flight had been delayed. He didn't even have to ask. The departure monitor over the incoming passengers desk told the story. Flight 901 for Denver, due out at 6:36 EST, had left at 6:40. Nine minutes before.

'Oh shit,' Dick Hallorann said.

And suddenly the smell of oranges, heavy and cloying, he had just time to reach the men's room before it came, deafening, terrified:

(!!! COME PLEASE COME DICK PLEASE PLEASE COME !!!)

CHAPTER THIRTY-NINE
ON THE STAIRS

One of the things they had sold to swell their liquid assets a little before moving from Vermont to Colorado was Jack's collection of two hundred old rock 'n' roll and r & b albums; they had gone at the yard sale for a dollar apiece. One of these albums, Danny's personal favorite, had been an Eddie Cochran double-record set with four pages of bound-in liner notes by Lenny Kaye. Wendy had often been struck by Danny's fascination for this one particular album by a man-boy who had lived fast and died young . . . had died, in fact, when she herself had only been ten years old.

Now, at quarter past seven (mountain time), as Dick Hallorann was telling Queems about his ex-wife's white boyfriend, she came upon Danny sitting halfway up the stairs between the lobby and the first floor, tossing a red rubber ball from hand to hand and singing one of the songs from that album. His voice was low and tuneless.

'So I climb one-two flight three flight four,' Danny sang, 'five flight six flight seven flight more . . . when I get to the top, I'm too tired to rock . . .'

She came around him, sat down on one of the stair risers, and saw that his lower lip had swelled to twice its size and that there was dried blood on his chin. Her heart took a frightened leap in her chest, but she managed to speak neutrally.

'What happened, doc?' she asked, although she was sure she knew. Jack had hit him. Well, of course. That came next, didn't it? The wheels of progress; sooner or later they took you back to where you started from.

'I called Tony,' Danny said. 'In the ballroom. I guess I fell off the chair. It doesn't hurt anymore. Just feels . . . like my lip's too big.'

'Is that what really happened?' she asked, looking at him, troubled.

'Daddy didn't do it,' he answered. 'Not today.'

She gazed at him, feeling eerie. The ball traveled from one hand to the other. He had read her mind. Her son had read her mind.

'What . . . what did Tony tell you, Danny?'

'It doesn't matter.' His face was calm, his voice chillingly indifferent.

'*Danny*—' She gripped his shoulder, harder than she had intended. But he didn't wince, or even try to shake her off.

(*Oh we are wrecking this boy. It's not just Jack, it's me too, and maybe it's not even just us, Jack's father, my mother, are they here too? Sure, why not? The place is lousy with ghosts anyway, why not a couple more? Oh Lord in heaven he's like one of those suitcases they show on TV, run over, dropped from planes, going through factory crushers. Or a Timex watch. Takes a licking and keeps on ticking. Oh Danny I'm so sorry*)

'It doesn't matter,' he said again. The ball went from hand to hand. 'Tony can't come anymore. They won't let him. He's licked.'

'Who won't?'

'The people in the hotel,' he said. He looked at her then, and his eyes weren't indifferent at all. They were deep and scared. 'And the . . . the *things* in the hotel. There's all kinds of them. The hotel is *stuffed* with them.'

'You can see—'

'I don't want to see,' he said low, and then looked back at the rubber ball, arcing from hand to hand. 'But I can hear them sometimes, late at night. They're like the wind, all sighing together. In the attic. The basement. The rooms. All over. I thought it was my fault, because of the way I am. The key. The little silver key.'

'Danny, don't . . . don't upset yourself in this way.'

'But it's *him* too,' Danny said. 'It's Daddy. And it's you. It wants all of us. It's tricking Daddy, it's fooling him, trying to make him think it wants him the most. It wants me the most, but it will take all of us.'

'If only that snowmobile —'

'They wouldn't let him,' Danny said in that same low voice. 'They made him throw part of it away into the snow. Far away. I dreamed it. And he knows that woman really is in 217.' He looked at her with his dark, frightened eyes. 'It doesn't matter whether you believe me or not.'

She slipped an arm around him.

'I believe you. Danny, tell me the truth. Is Jack . . . is he going to try to hurt us?'

'They'll try to make him,' Danny said. 'I've been calling for Mr Hallorann. He said if I ever needed him to just call. And I have been. But it's awful hard. It makes me tired. And the worst part is I don't know if he's hearing me or not. I don't think he can call back because it's too far for him. And I don't know if it's too far for me or not. Tomorrow —'

'What about tomorrow?'

He shook his head. 'Nothing.'

'Where is he now?' she asked. 'Your daddy?'

'He's in the basement. I don't think he'll be up tonight.'

She stood up suddenly. 'Wait right here for me. Five minutes.'

***

The kitchen was cold and deserted under the overhead fluorescent bars. She went to the rack where the carving knives hung from their magnetized strips. She took the longest and sharpest, wrapped it in a dish towel, and left the kitchen, turning off the lights as she went.

***

Danny sat on the stairs, his eyes following the course of his red rubber ball from hand to hand. He sang: 'She lives on the twentieth floor uptown, the elevator is broken down. So I walk one-two flight three flight four . . .'

(—*Lou, Lou, skip to m' Lou*—)

His singing broke off. He listened.

(—*Skip to m' Lou my daarlin'*—)

The voice was in his head, so much a part of him, so frighteningly close that it might have been a part of his own thoughts. It was soft and infinitely sly. Mocking him. Seeming to say:

(*Oh yes, you'll like it here. Try it, you'll like it. Try it, you'll liiiiiike it—*)

Now his ears were open and he could hear them again, the gathering, ghosts or spirits or maybe the hotel itself, a dreadful funhouse where all the sideshows ended in death, where all the specially painted boogies were really alive, where hedges walked, where a small silver key could start the obscenity. Soft and sighing, rustling like the endless winter wind that played under the eaves at night, the deadly lulling wind the summer tourists never heard. It was like the somnolent hum of summer wasps in a ground nest, sleepy, deadly, beginning to wake up. They were ten thousand feet high.

(*Why is a raven like a writing desk? The higher the fewer, of course! Have another cup of tea!*)

It was a living sound, but not voices, not breath. A man of a philosophical bent might have called it the sound of souls. Dick Hallorann's Nana, who had grown up on southern roads in the years before the turn of the century, would have called it ha'ants. A psychic investigator might have had a long name for it – psychic echo, psychokinesis, a telesmic sport. But to Danny it was only the sound of the hotel, the old monster, creaking steadily and ever more closely around them: halls that now stretched back through time as well as distance, hungry shadows, unquiet guests who did not rest easy.

In the darkened ballroom the clock under glass struck seven thirty with a single musical note.

A hoarse voice, made brutal with drink, shouted: '*Unmask and let's fuck!*'

Wendy, halfway across the lobby, jerked to a standstill.

She looked at Danny on the stairs, still tossing the ball from hand to hand. 'Did you hear something?'

Danny only looked at her and continued to toss the ball from hand to hand.

There would be little sleep for them that night, although they slept together behind a locked door.

And in the dark, his eyes open, Danny thought:

(*He wants to be one of them and live forever. That's what he wants.*)

Wendy thought:

(*If I have to, I'll take him further up. If we're going to die I'd rather do it in the mountains.*)

She had left the butcher knife, still wrapped in the towel, under the bed. She kept her hand close to it. They dozed off and on. The hotel creaked around them. Outside snow had begun to spit down from a sky like lead.

CHAPTER FORTY
IN THE BASEMENT

(!!! The boiler the goddam boiler !!!)

The thought came into Jack Torrance's mind full-blown, edged in bright, warning red. On its heels, the voice of Watson:

(If you forget it'll just creep an creep and like as not you an your fambly will end up on the fuckin moon . . . she's rated for two-fifty but she'd blow long before that now . . . I'd be scared to come down and stand next to her at a hundred and eighty.)

He'd been down here all night, poring over the boxes of old records, possessed by a frantic feeling that time was getting short and he would have to hurry. Still the vital clues, the connections that would make everything clear, eluded him. His fingers were yellow and grimy with crumbling old paper. And he'd become so absorbed he hadn't checked the boiler once. He'd dumped it the previous evening around six o'clock, when he first came down. It was now . . .

He looked at his watch and jumped up, kicking over a stack of old invoices.

Christ, it was quarter of five in the morning.

Behind him, the furnace kicked on. The boiler was making a groaning, whistling sound.

He ran to it. His face, which had become thinner in the last month or so, was now heavily shadowed with beardstubble and he had a hollow concentration-camp look.

The boiler pressure gauge stood at two hundred and ten pounds per square inch. He fancied he could almost see the sides of the old patched and welded boiler heaving out with the lethal strain.

(She creeps . . . I'd be scared to come down and stand next to her at a hundred and eighty . . .)

Suddenly a cold and tempting inner voice spoke to him.

(*Let it go. Go get Wendy and Danny and get the fuck out of here. Let it blow sky-high.*)

He could visualize the explosion. A double thunderclap that would first rip the heart from this place, then the soul. The boiler would go with an orange-violet flash that would rain hot and burning shrapnel all over the cellar. In his mind he could see the redhot trinkets of metal careening from floor to walls to ceiling like strange billiard balls, whistling jagged death through the air. Some of them, surely, would whizz right through that stone arch, light on the old papers on the other side, and they would burn merry hell. Destroy the secrets, burn the clues, it's a mystery no living hand will ever solve. Then the gas explosion, a great rumbling crackle of flame, a giant pilot light that would turn the whole center of the hotel into a broiler. Stairs and hallways and ceilings and rooms aflame like the castle in the last reel of a Frankenstein movie. The flames spreading into the wings, hurrying up the black-and-blue-twined carpets like eager guests. The silk wallpaper charring and curling. There were no sprinklers, only those outmoded hoses and no one to use them. And there wasn't a fire engine in the world that could get here before late March. Burn, baby, burn. In twelve hours there would be nothing left but the bare bones.

The needle on the gauge had moved up to two-twelve. The boiler was creaking and groaning like an old woman trying to get out of bed. Hissing jets of steam had begun to play around the edges of old patches; beads of solder had begun to sizzle.

He didn't see, he didn't hear. Frozen with his hand on the valve that would dump off the pressure and damp the fire, Jack's eyes glittered from their sockets like sapphires.

(*It's my last chance.*)

The only thing not cashed in now was the life insurance policy he had taken out jointly with Wendy in the summer between his first and second years at Stovington. Forty-thousand-dollar death benefit, double indemnity if he or she died in a train crash, a plane crash, or a fire. Seven-come-eleven, die the secret death and win a hundred dollars.

(*A fire . . . eighty thousand dollars.*)

They would have time to get out. Even if they were sleeping, they would have time to get out. He believed that. And he didn't think the hedges or anything else would try to hold them back if the Overlook was going up in flames.

(*Flames.*)

The needle inside the greasy, almost opaque dial had danced up to two hundred and fifteen pounds per square inch.

Another memory occurred to him, a childhood memory. There had been a wasps' nest in the lower branches of their apple tree behind the house. One of his older brothers – he couldn't remember which one now – had been stung while swinging in the old tire Daddy had hung from one of the tree's lower branches. It had been late summer, when wasps tend to be at their ugliest.

Their father, just home from work, dressed in his whites, the smell of beer hanging around his face in a fine mist, had gathered all three boys, Brett, Mike, and little Jacky, and told them he was going to get rid of the wasps.

'Now watch,' he had said, smiling and staggering a little (he hadn't been using the cane then, the collision with the milk truck was years in the future). 'Maybe you'll learn something. My father showed me this.'

He had raked a big pile of rain-dampened leaves under the branch where the wasps' nest rested, a deadlier fruit than the shrunken but tasty apples their tree usually produced in late September, which was then still half a month away. He lit the leaves. The day was clear and windless. The leaves smoldered but didn't really burn, and they made a smell – a fragrance – that had echoed back to him each fall when men in Saturday pants and light Windbreakers raked leaves together and burned them. A sweet smell with a bitter undertone, rich and evocative. The smoldering leaves produced great rafts of smoke that drifted up to obscure the nest.

Their father had let the leaves smolder all that afternoon, drinking beer on the porch and dropping the empty Black Label cans into his wife's plastic floorbucket while his two older sons flanked him and little Jacky sat on the steps at his feet, playing with his Bolo Bouncer and singing monotonously over and over: 'Your cheating heart . . . will make you weep . . . your cheating heart . . . is gonna tell on you.'

At quarter of six, just before supper, Daddy had gone out to the apple tree with his sons grouped carefully behind him. In one hand he had a garden hoe. He knocked the leaves apart, leaving little clots spread around to smolder and die. Then he reached the hoe handle up, weaving and blinking, and after two or three tries he knocked the nest to the ground.

The boys fled for the safety of the porch, but Daddy only stood over the nest, swaying and blinking down at it. Jacky crept back to see. A few wasps were crawling sluggishly over the paper terrain of their property, but they were not trying to fly. From the inside of the nest, the black and alien place, came a never-to-be-forgotten sound: a low, somnolent buzz, like the sound of high-tension wires.

'Why don't they try to sting you, Daddy?' he had asked.

'The smoke makes em drunk, Jacky. Go get my gascan.'

He ran to fetch it. Daddy doused the nest with amber gasoline.

'Now step away, Jacky, unless you want to lose your eyebrows.'

He had stepped away. From somewhere in the voluminous folds of his white overblouse, Daddy had produced a wooden kitchen match. He lit it with his thumbnail and flung it onto the nest. There had been a white-orange explosion, almost soundless in its ferocity. Daddy had stepped away, cackling wildly. The wasps' nest had gone up in no time.

'Fire,' Daddy had said, turning to Jacky with a smile. 'Fire will kill anything.'

After supper the boys had come out in the day's waning light to stand solemnly around the charred and blackened nest. From the hot interior had come the sound of wasp bodies popping like corn.

The pressure gauge stood at two-twenty. A low iron wailing sound was building up in the guts of the thing. Jets of steam stood out erect in a hundred places like porcupine quills.

(*Fire will kill anything.*)

Jack suddenly started. He had been dozing off . . . and he

had almost dozed himself right into kingdom come. What in God's name had he been thinking of? Protecting the hotel was his job. He was the caretaker.

A sweat of terror sprang to his hands so quickly that at first he missed his grip on the large valve. Then he curled his fingers around its spokes. He whirled it one turn, two, three. There was a giant hiss of steam, dragon's breath. A warm tropical mist rose from beneath the boiler and veiled him. For a moment he could no longer see the dial but thought he must have waited too long; the groaning, clanking sound inside the boiler increased, followed by a series of heavy rattling sounds and the wrenching screech of metal.

When some of the steam blew away he saw that the pressure gauge had dropped back to two hundred and was still sinking. The jets of steam escaping around the soldered patches began to lose their force. The wrenching, grinding sounds began to diminish.

One-ninety . . . one-eighty . . . one seventy-five . . .

(*He was going downhill, going ninety miles an hour, when the whistle broke into a scream—*)

But he didn't think it would blow now. The press was down to one-sixty.

(*—they found him in the wreck with his hand on the throttle, he was scalded to death by the steam.*)

He stepped away from the boiler, breathing hard, trembling. He looked at his hands and saw that blisters were already rising on his palms. Hell with the blisters, he thought, and laughed shakily. He had almost died with his hand on the throttle, like Casey the engineer in 'The Wreck of the Old 97'. Worse still, he would have killed the Overlook. The final crashing failure. He had failed as a teacher, a writer, a husband, and a father. He had even failed as a drunk. But you couldn't do much better in the old failure category than to blow up the building you were supposed to be taking care of. And this was no ordinary building.

By no means.

Christ, but he needed a drink.

The press had dropped down to eighty psi. Cautiously,

wincing a little at the pain in his hands, he closed the dump valve again. But from now on the boiler would have to be watched more closely than ever. It might have been seriously weakened. He wouldn't trust it at more than one hundred psi for the rest of the winter. And if they were a little chilly, they would just have to grin and bear it.

He had broken two of the blisters. His hands throbbed like rotten teeth.

A drink. A drink would fix him up, and there wasn't a thing in the goddamn house besides cooking sherry. At this point a drink would be medicinal. That was just it, by God. An anesthetic. He had done his duty and now he could use a little anesthetic – something stronger than Excedrin. But there was nothing.

He remembered bottles glittering in the shadows.

He had saved the hotel. The hotel would want to reward him. He felt sure of it. He took his handkerchief out of his back pocket and went to the stairs. He rubbed at his mouth. Just a little drink. Just one. To ease the pain.

He had served the Overlook, and now the Overlook would serve him. He was sure of it. His feet on the stair risers were quick and eager, the hurrying steps of a man who has come home from a long and bitter war. It was 5:20 a.m., MST.

CHAPTER FORTY-ONE
DAYLIGHT

Danny awoke with a muffled gasp from a terrible dream. There had been an explosion. A fire. The Overlook was burning up. He and his mommy were watching it from the front lawn.

Mommy had said: 'Look, Danny, look at the hedges.'

He looked at them and they were all dead. Their leaves had turned a suffocant brown. The tightly packed branches showed through like the skeletons of half-dismembered corpses. And then his daddy had burst out of the Overlook's big double doors, and he was burning like a torch. His clothes were in flames, his skin had acquired a dark and sinister tan that was growing darker by the moment, his hair was a burning bush.

That was when he woke up, his throat tight with fear, his hands clutching at the sheet and blankets. Had he screamed? He looked over at his mother. Wendy lay on her side, the blankets up to her chin, a sheaf of straw-colored hair lying against her cheek. She looked like a child herself. No, he hadn't screamed.

Lying in bed, looking upward, the nightmare began to drain away. He had a curious feeling that some great tragedy

(fire? explosion?)

had been averted by inches. He let his mind drift out, searching for his daddy, and found him standing somewhere below. In the lobby. Danny pushed a little harder, trying to get inside his father. It was not good. Because Daddy was thinking about the Bad Thing. He was thinking how

(*good just one or two would be i don't care sun's over the yardarm somewhere in the world remember how we used to say that al? gin and tonic bourbon with just a dash of bitters scotch and soda rum and coke tweedledum and tweedledee a drink for me and a drink for thee the martians have landed somewhere in the world princeton or houston or stokely on carmichael some fucking place after all tis the season and none of us are)*

(*GET OUT OF HIS MIND, YOU LITTLE SHIT!*)

He recoiled in terror from that mental voice, his eyes widening, his hands tightening into claws on the counterpane. It hadn't been the voice of his father but a clever mimic. A voice he knew. Hoarse, brutal, yet underpointed with a vacuous sort of humor.

Was it so near, then?

He threw the covers back and swung his feet out onto the floor. He kicked his slippers out from under the bed and put them on. He went to the door and pulled it open and hurried up to the main corridor, his slippered feet whispering on the nap of the carpet runner. He turned the corner.

There was a man on all fours halfway down the corridor, between him and the stairs.

Danny froze.

The man looked up at him. His eyes were tiny and red. He was dressed in some sort of silvery, spangled costume. A dog costume, Danny realized. Protruding from the rump of this strange creature was a long and floppy tail with a puff on the end. A zipper ran up the back of the costume to the neck. To the left of him was a dog's or wolf's head, blank eyesockets above the muzzle, the mouth open in a meaningless snarl that showed the rug's black and blue pattern between fangs that appeared to be papier-mâché.

The man's mouth and chin and cheeks were smeared with blood.

He began to growl at Danny. He was grinning, but the growl was real. It was deep in his throat, a chilling primitive sound. Then he began to bark. His teeth were also stained red. He began to crawl toward Danny, dragging his boneless tail behind him. The costume dog's head lay unheeded on the carpet, glaring vacantly over Danny's shoulder.

'Let me by,' Danny said.

'I'm going to eat you, little boy,' the dogman answered, and suddenly a fusillade of barks came from his grinning mouth. They were human imitations, but the savagery in them was real.

THE SHINING

The man's hair was dark, greased with sweat from his confining costume. There was a mixture of scotch and champagne on his breath.

Danny flinched back but didn't run. 'Let me by.'

'Not by the hair of my chinny-chin-chin,' the dogman replied. His small red eyes were fixed attentively on Danny's face. He continued to grin. 'I'm going to eat you up, little boy. And I think I'll start with your plump little *cock*.'

He began to prance skittishly forward, making little leaps and snarling.

Danny's nerve broke. He fled back into the short hallway that led to their quarters, looking back over his shoulder. There was a series of mixed howls and barks and growls, broken by slurred mutterings and giggles.

Danny stood in the hallway, trembling.

'Get it up!' the drunken dogman cried out from around the corner. His voice was both violent and despairing. 'Get it up, Harry you bitch-bastard! I don't care how many casinos and airlines and movie companies you own! I know what you like in the privacy of your own h-home! Get it up! I'll *huff* . . . and I'll *puff* . . . until Harry Derwent's *all blooowwwwn down*!' He ended with a long, chilling howl that seemed to turn into a scream of rage and pain just before it dwindled off.

Danny turned apprehensively to the closed bedroom door at the end of the hallway and walked quietly down to it. He opened it and poked his head through. His mommy was sleeping in exactly the same position. No one was hearing this but him.

He closed the door softly and went back up to the intersection of their corridor and the main hall, hoping the dogman would be gone, the way the blood on the walls of the Presidential Suite had been gone. He peeked around the corner carefully.

The man in the dog costume was still there. He had put his head back on and was now prancing on all fours by the stairwell, chasing his tail. He occasionally leaped off the rug and came down making dog grunts in his throat.

'Woof! Woof! Bowwowwow! *Grrrrr!*'

These sounds came hollowly out of the mask's stylized snarling mouth, and among them were sounds that might have been sobs or laughter.

Danny went back to the bedroom and sat down on his cot, covering his eyes with his hands. The hotel was running things now. Maybe at first the things that had happened had only been accidents. Maybe at first the things he had seen really *were* like scary pictures that couldn't hurt him. But now the hotel was controlling those things and they *could* hurt. The Overlook hadn't wanted him to go to his father. That might spoil all the fun. So it had put the dogman in his way, just as it had put the hedge animals between them and the road.

But his daddy could come here. And sooner or later his daddy would.

He began to cry, the tears rolling silently down his cheeks. It was too late. They were going to die, all three of them, and when the Overlook opened next late spring, they would be right here to greet the guests along with the rest of the spooks. The woman in the tub. The dogman. The horrible dark thing that had been in the cement tunnel. They would be—

(*Stop! Stop that now!*)

He knuckled the tears furiously from his eyes. He would try as hard as he could to keep that from happening. Not to himself, not to his daddy and mommy. He would try as hard as he could.

He closed his eyes and sent his mind out in a high, hard crystal bolt.

(*!!! DICK PLEASE COME QUICK WE'RE IN BAD TROUBLE DICK WE NEED*)

And suddenly, in the darkness behind his eyes the thing that chased him down the Overlook's dark halls in his dreams was *there*, right *there*, a huge creature dressed in white, its prehistoric club raised over its head:

'*I'll make you stop it! You goddam puppy! I'll make you stop it because I am your FATHER!*'

'*No!*' He jerked back to the reality of the bedroom, his eyes wide and staring, the screams tumbling helplessly from his mouth as his mother bolted awake, clutching the sheet to her breasts.

'*No Daddy no no no—*'

And they both heard the vicious, descending swing of the

invisible club, cutting the air somewhere very close, then fading away to silence as he ran to his mother and hugged her, trembling like a rabbit in a snare.

The Overlook was not going to let him call Dick. That might spoil the fun, too.

They were alone.

Outside the snow came harder, curtaining them off from the world.

CHAPTER FORTY-TWO
MID-AIR

Dick Halloriann's flight was called at 6:45 a.m., EST, and the boarding clerk held him by Gate 31, shifting his flight bag nervously from hand to hand, until the last call at 6:55. They were both looking for a man named Carlton Vecker, the only passenger on TWA's Flight 196 from Miami to Denver who hadn't checked in.

'Okay,' the clerk said, and issued Hallorann a blue first-class boarding pass. 'You lucked out. You can board, sir.'

Hallorann hurried up the enclosed boarding ramp and let the mechanically grinning stewardess tear his pass off and give him the stub.

'We're serving breakfast on the flight,' the stew said. 'If you'd like —'

'Just coffee, babe,' he said, and went down the aisle to a seat in the smoking section. He kept expecting the no-show Vecker to pop through the door like a jack-in-the-box at the last second. The woman in the seat by the window was reading *You Can Be Your Own Best Friend* with a sour, unbelieving expression on her face. Hallorann buckled his seat belt and then wrapped his large black hands around the seat's armrests and promised the absent Carlton Vecker that it would take him and five strong TWA flight attendants to drag him out of his seat. He kept his eye on his watch. It dragged off the minutes to the 7:00 takeoff time with maddening slowness.

At 7:05 the stewardess informed them that there would be a slight delay while the ground crew rechecked one of the latches on the cargo door.

'Shit for brains,' Dick Hallorann muttered.

The sharp-faced woman turned her sour, unbelieving expression on him and then went back to her book.

He had spent the night at the airport, going from counter to counter – United, American, TWA, Continental, Braniff – haunting the ticket clerks. Sometime after midnight, drinking his eighth or ninth cup of coffee in the canteen, he had decided he was being an asshole to have taken this whole thing on his own shoulders. There were authorities. He had gone down to the nearest bank of telephones, and after talking to three different operators, he had gotten the emergency number of the Rocky Mountain National Park Authority.

The man who answered the telephone sounded utterly worn out. Hallorann had given a false name and said there was trouble at the Overlook Hotel, west of Sidewinder. Bad trouble.

He was put on hold.

The ranger (Hallorann assumed he was a ranger) came back on in about five minutes.

'They've got a CB,' the ranger said.

'Sure they've got a CB,' Hallorann said.

'We haven't had a Mayday call from them.'

'Man, that don't *matter*. They—'

'Exactly what kind of trouble are they in, Mr Hall?'

'Well, there's a family. The caretaker and his family. I think maybe he's gone a little nuts, you know. I think maybe he might hurt his wife and his little boy.'

'May I ask how you've come by this information, sir?'

Hallorann closed his eyes. 'What's your name, fellow?'

'Tom Staunton, sir.'

'Well, Tom, I *know*. Now I'll be just as straight with you as I can be. There's bad trouble up there. Maybe killin bad, do you dig what I'm saying?'

'Mr Hall, I really have to know how you—'

'Look,' Hallorann had said. 'I'm telling you I *know*. A few years back there was a fellow up there name of Grady. He killed his wife and his two daughters and then pulled the string on himself. I'm telling you it's going to happen again if you guys don't haul your asses out there and stop it!'

'Mr Hall, you're not calling from Colorado.'

'No. But what difference—'

'If you're not in Colorado, you're not in CB range of the

Overlook Hotel. If you're not in CB range you can't possibly have been in contact with the, uh . . .' Faint rattle of papers. 'The Torrance family. While I had you on hold I tried to telephone. It's out, which is nothing unusual. There are still twenty-five miles of aboveground telephone lines between the hotel and the Sidewinder switching station. My conclusion is that you must be some sort of crank.'

'Oh man, you stupid . . .' But this despair was too great to find a noun to go with the adjective. Suddenly, illumination. 'Call them!' he cried.

'Sir?'

'You got the CB, they got the CB. So call them! Call them and ask them what's up!'

There was a brief silence, and the humming of long-distance wires.

'You tried that too, didn't you?' Hallorann asked. That's why you had me on hold so long. You tried the phone and then you tried the CB and you didn't get *nothing* but you don't think nothing's wrong . . . what are you guys doing up there? Sitting on your asses and playing gin rummy?'

'No, we are not,' Staunton said angrily. Hallorann was relieved at the sound of anger in the voice. For the first time he felt he was speaking to a man and not to a recording: 'I'm the only man here, sir. Every other ranger in the park, *plus* game wardens, *plus* volunteers, are up in Hasty Notch, risking their lives because three stupid assholes with six months' experience decided to try the north face of King's Ram. They're stuck halfway up there and maybe they'll get down and maybe they won't. There are two choppers up there and the men who are flying them are risking their lives because it's night here and it's starting to snow. So if you're still having trouble putting it all together, I'll give you a hand with it. Number one, I don't have anybody to send to the Overlook. Number two, the Overlook isn't a priority here – what happens in the park is a priority. Number three, by daybreak neither one of those choppers will be able to fly because it's going to snow like crazy, according to the National Weather Service. Do you understand the situation?'

'Yeah,' Hallorann had said softly. 'I understand.'

'Now my guess as to why I couldn't raise them on the CB is very simple. I don't know what time it is where you are, but out here it's nine-thirty. I think they may have turned it off and gone to bed. Now if you—'

'Good luck with your climbers, man,' Hallorann said. 'But I want you to know that they are not the only ones who are stuck up high because they didn't know what they were getting into.'

He had hung up the phone.

★★★

At 7:20 a.m. the TWA 747 backed lumberingly out of its stall, turned, and rolled out toward the runway. Hallorann let out a long, soundless exhale. Carlton Vecker, wherever you are, eat your heart out.

Flight 196 parted company with the ground at 7:28, and at 7:31, as it gained altitude, the thought-pistol went off in Dick Hallorann's head again. His shoulders hunched uselessly against the smell of oranges and then jerked spasmodically. His forehead wrinkled, his mouth drew down in a grimace of pain.

(*!!! DICK PLEASE COME QUICK WE'RE IN BAD TROUBLE DICK WE NEED*)

And that was all. It was suddenly gone. No fading out this time. The communication had been chopped off cleanly, as if with a knife. It scared him. His hands, still clutching the seat rests, had gone almost white. His mouth was dry. Something had happened to the boy. He was sure of it. If anyone had hurt that little child—

'Do you always react so violently to takeoffs?'

He looked around. It was the woman in the horn-rimmed glasses.

'It wasn't that,' Hallorann said.'I've got a steel plate in my head. From Korea. Every now and then it gives me a twinge. Vibrates, don't you know. Scrambles the signal.'

'Is that so?'

'Yes, ma'am.'

'It is the line soldier who ultimately pays for any foreign intervention,' the sharp-faced woman said grimly.

'Is that so?'

'It is. This country must swear off its dirty little wars. The CIA has been at the root of every dirty little war America has fought in this century. The CIA and dollar diplomacy.'

She opened her book and began to read. The NO SMOKING sign went off. Hallorann watched the receding land and wondered if the boy was all right. He had developed an affectionate feeling for that boy, although his folks hadn't seemed all that much.

He hoped to God they were watching out for Danny.

CHAPTER FORTY-THREE
DRINKS ON THE HOUSE

Jack stood in the dining room just outside the batwing doors leading into the Colorado Lounge, his head cocked, listening. He was smiling faintly.

Around him, he could hear the Overlook Hotel coming to life.

It was hard to say just how he knew, but he guessed it wasn't greatly different from the perceptions Danny had from time to time . . . like father, like son. Wasn't that how it was popularly expressed?

It wasn't a perception of sight or sound, although it was very near to those things, separated from those senses by the filmiest of perceptual curtains. It was as if another Overlook now lay scant inches beyond this one, separated from the real world (if there is such a thing as a 'real world', Jack thought) but gradually coming into balance with it. He was reminded of the 3–D movies he'd seen as a kid. If you looked at the screen without the special glasses, you saw a double image – the sort of thing he was feeling now. But when you put the glasses on, it made sense.

All the hotel's eras were together now, all but this current one, the Torrance Era. And this would be together with the rest very soon now. That was good. That was very good.

He could almost hear the self-important *ding! ding!* of the silver-plated bell on the registration desk, summoning bellboys to the front as men in the fashionable flannels of the 1920s checked in and men in fashionable 1940s double-breasted pin-stripes checked out. There would be three nuns sitting in front of the fireplace as they waited for the check-out line to thin, and standing behind them, nattily dressed with diamond stickpins holding their blue-and-white-figured ties, Charles Grondin and

Vito Gienelli discussed profit and loss, life and death. There was a dozen trucks in the loading bays out back, some laid one over the other like bad time exposures. In the east-wing ballroom, a dozen different business conventions were going on at the same time within temporal centimeters of each other. There was a costume ball going on. There were soirees, wedding receptions, birthday and anniversary parties. Men talking about Neville Chamberlain and the Archduke of Austria. Music. Laughter. Drunkenness. Hysteria. Little love, not here, but a steady undercurrent of sensuousness. And he could almost hear all of them together, drifting through the hotel and making a graceful cacophony. In the dining room where he stood, breakfast, lunch, and dinner for seventy years were all being served simultaneously just behind him. He could almost . . . no, strike the *almost*. He *could* hear them, faintly as yet, but clearly – the way one can hear thunder miles off on a hot summer's day. He could hear all of them, the beautiful strangers. He was becoming aware of them as they must have been aware of him from the very start.

All the rooms of the Overlook were occupied this morning.

A full house.

And beyond the batwings, a low murmur of conversation drifted and swirled like lazy cigarette smoke. More sophisticated, more private. Low, throaty female laughter, the kind that seems to vibrate in a fairy ring around the viscera and the genitals. The sound of a cash register, its window softly lighted in the warm halfdark, ringing up the price of a gin rickey, a Manhattan, a depression bomber, a sloe gin fizz, a zombie. The jukebox, pouring out its drinkers' melodies, each one overlapping the other in time.

He pushed the batwings open and stepped through.

'Hello, boys,' Jack Torrance said softly. 'I've been away but now I'm back.'

'Good evening, Mr Torrance,' Lloyd said, genuinely pleased. 'It's good to see you.'

'It's good to be back, Lloyd,' he said gravely, and hooked his leg over a stool between a man in a sharp blue suit and a bleary-eyed woman in a black dress who was peering into the depths of a singapore sling.

'What will it be, Mr Torrance?'

'Martini,' he said with great pleasure. He looked at the back-bar with its rows of dimly gleaming bottles, capped with their silver siphons. Jim Beam. Wild Turkey, Gilby's, Sharrod's Private Label. Toro. Seagram's. And home again.

'One large martian, if you please,' he said. 'They've landed somewhere in the world, Lloyd.' He took his wallet out and laid a twenty carefully on the bar.

As Lloyd made his drink, Jack looked over his shoulder. Every booth was occupied. Some of the occupants were dressed in costumes . . . a woman in gauzy harem pants and a rhinestone-sparkled brassiere, a man with a foxhead rising slyly out of his evening dress, a man in a silvery dog outfit who was tickling the nose of a woman in a sarong with the puff on the end of his long tail, to the general amusement of all.

'No charge to you, Mr Torrance,' Lloyd said, putting the drink down on Jack's twenty. 'Your money is no good here. Orders from the manager.'

'Manager?'

A faint unease came over him; nevertheless he picked up the martini glass and swirled it, watching the olive at the bottom bob slightly in the drink's chilly depths.

'Of course. The manager.' Lloyd's smile broadened, but his eyes were socketed in shadow and his skin was horribly white, like the skin of a corpse. 'Later he expects to see to your son's wellbeing himself. He is very interested in your son. Danny is a talented boy.'

The juniper fumes of the gin were pleasantly maddening, but they also seemed to be blurring his reason. Danny? What was all of this about Danny? And what was he doing in a bar with a drink in his hand?

He had TAKEN THE PLEDGE. He had GONE ON THE WAGON. He had SWORN OFF.

What could they want with his son? What could they want with Danny? Wendy and Danny weren't in it. He tried to see into Lloyd's shadowed eyes, but it was too dark, too dark, it was like trying to read emotion into the empty orbs of a skull.

(*It's me they must want . . . isn't it? I am the one. Not Danny, not Wendy. I'm the one who loves it here. They wanted to leave. I'm the one who took care of the snowmobile . . . went through the old records . . . dumped the press on the boiler . . . lied . . . practically sold my soul . . . what can they want with him?*)

'Where is the manager?' He tried to ask it casually but his words seemed to come out between lips already numbed by the first drink, like words from a nightmare rather than those in a sweet dream.

Lloyd only smiled.

'What do you want with my son? Danny's not in this . . . is he?' He heard the naked plea in his own voice.

Lloyd's face seemed to be running, changing, becoming something pestilent. The white skin becoming a hepatitic yellow, cracking. Red sores erupting on the skin, bleeding foul-smelling liquid. Droplets of blood sprang out on Lloyd's forehead like sweat and somewhere a silver chime was striking the quarter-hour.

(*Unmask, unmask!*)

'Drink your drink, Mr Torrance,' Lloyd said softly. 'It isn't a matter that concerns you. Not at this point.'

He picked his drink up again, raised it to his lips, and hesitated. He heard the hard, horrible snap as Danny's arm broke. He saw the bicycle flying brokenly up over the hood of Al's car, starring the windshield. He saw a single wheel lying in the road, twisted spokes pointing into the sky like jags of piano wire.

He became aware that all conversation had stopped.

He looked back over his shoulder. They were all looking at him expectantly, silently. The man beside the woman in the sarong had removed his foxhead and Jack saw that it was Horace Derwent, his pallid blond hair spilling across his forehead. Everyone at the bar was watching, too. The woman beside him was looking at him closely, as if trying to focus. Her dress had slipped off one shoulder and looking down he could see a loosely puckered nipple capping one sagging breast. Looking back at her face he began to think that this might be the woman from 217, the one who had tried to strangle Danny. On his other hand, the man in the sharp blue suit had removed a small pearl-handled .32 from his jacket pocket and was idly spinning it on the bar, like a man with Russian roulette on his mind.

(*I want*—)

He realized the words were not passing through his frozen vocal cords and tried again.

'I want to see the manager. I . . . I don't think he understands. My son is not a part of this. He . . .'

'Mr Torrance,' Lloyd said, his voice coming with hideous gentleness from inside his plague-raddled face, 'you will meet the manager in due time. He has, in fact, decided to make you his agent in this matter. Now drink your drink.'

'Drink your drink,' they all echoed.

He picked it up with a badly trembling hand. It was raw gin. He looked into it, and looking was like drowning.

The woman beside him began to sing in a flat, dead voice: 'Roll . . . out . . . the barrel . . . and we'll have . . . a barrel . . . of fun . . .'

Lloyd picked it up. Then the man in the blue suit. The dogman joined in, thumping one paw against the table

'*Now's the time to roll the barrel*—'

Derwent added his voice to the rest. A cigarette was cocked in one corner of his mouth at a jaunty angle. His right arm was around the shoulders of the woman in the sarong, and his right hand was gently and absently stroking her right breast. He was looking at the dog-man with amused contempt as he sang.

'*—because the gang's . . . all . . . here!*'

Jack brought the drink to his mouth and downed it in three long gulps, the gin highballing down his throat like a moving van in a tunnel, exploding in his stomach, rebounding up to his brain in one leap where it seized hold of him with a final convulsing fit of the shakes.

When that passed off, he felt fine.

'Do it again, please,' he said, and pushed the empty glass toward Lloyd.

'Yes, sir,' Lloyd said, taking the glass. Lloyd looked perfectly normal again. The olive-skinned man had put his .32 away. The woman on his right was staring into her singapore sling again. One breast was wholly exposed now, leaning on the bar's leather buffer. A vacuous crooning noise came from her slack mouth. The loom of conversation had begun again, weaving and weaving.

His new drink appeared in front of him.

'*Muchas gracias*, Lloyd,' he said, picking it up.

'Always a pleasure to serve you, Mr Torrance.' Lloyd smiled.

'You were always the best of them, Lloyd.'

'Why, thank you, sir.'

He drank slowly this time, letting it trickle down his throat, tossing a few peanuts down the chute for good luck.

The drink was gone in no time, and he ordered another. Mr President, I have met the martians and am pleased to report they are friendly. While Lloyd fixed another, he began searching his pockets for a quarter to put in the jukebox. He thought of Danny again, but Danny's face was pleasantly fuzzed and nondescript now. He had hurt Danny once, but that had been before he had learned how to handle his liquor. Those days were behind him now. He would never hurt Danny again. Not for the world.

CHAPTER FORTY-FOUR
CONVERSATIONS AT THE PARTY

He was dancing with a beautiful woman

He had no idea what time it was, how long he had spent in the Colorado Lounge or how long he had been here in the ballroom. Time had ceased to matter.

He had vague memories: listening to a man who had once been a successful radio comic and then a variety star in TV's infant days telling a very long and very hilarious joke about incest between Siamese twins; seeing the woman in the harem pants and the sequined bra do a slow and sinuous striptease to some bumping-and-grinding music from the jukebox (it seemed it had been David Rose's theme music from *The Stripper*); crossing the lobby as one of three, the other two men in evening dress that predated the twenties, all of them singing about the stiff patch on Rosie O'Grady's knickers. He seemed to remember looking out the big double doors and seeing Japanese lanterns strung in graceful, curving arcs that followed the sweep of the driveway – they gleamed in soft pastel colors like dusky jewels. The big glass globe on the porch ceiling was on, and night-insects bumped and flittered against it, and a part of him, perhaps the last tiny spark of sobriety, tried to tell him that it was 6 a.m. on a morning in December. But time had been canceled.

(*The arguments against insanity fall through with a soft shrurring sound/layer on layer . . .*)

Who was that? Some poet he had read as an undergraduate? Some undergraduate poet who was now selling washers in Wausau or insurance in Indianapolis? Perhaps an original thought? Didn't matter.

(*The night is dark/the stars are high/a disembodied custard pie/is floating in the sky . . .*)

He giggled helplessly.

'What's funny, honey?'

And here he was again, in the ballroom. The chandelier was lit and couples were circling all around them, some in costume and some not, to the smooth sounds of some postwar band – but which war? Can you be certain?

No, of course not. He was certain of only one thing: he was dancing with a beautiful woman.

She was tall and auburn-haired, dressed in clinging white satin, and she was dancing close to him, her breasts pressed softly and sweetly against his chest. Her white hand was entwined in his. She was wearing a small and sparkly cat's-eye mask and her hair had been brushed over to one side in a soft and gleaming fall that seemed to pool in the valley between their touching shoulders. Her dress was full-skirted but he could feel her thighs against his legs from time to time and had become more and more sure that she was smooth-and-powdered naked under her dress,

(*the better to feel your erection with, my dear*)

and he was sporting a regular railspike. If it offended her she concealed it well; she snuggled even closer to him.

'Nothing funny, honey,' he said, and giggled again.

'I like you,' she whispered, and he thought that her scent was like lilies, secret and hidden in cracks furred with green moss-places where sunshine is short and shadows long.

'I like you, too.'

'We could go upstairs, if you want. I'm supposed to be with Harry, but he'll never notice. He's too busy teasing poor Roger.'

The number ended. There was a spatter of applause and then the band swung into 'Mood Indigo' with scarcely a pause.

Jack looked over her bare shoulder and saw Derwent standing by the refreshment table. The girl in the sarong was with him. There were bottles of champagne in ice buckets ranged along the white lawn covering the table, and Derwent held a foaming bottle in his hand. A knot of people had gathered, laughing. In front of Derwent and the girl in the sarong. Roger capered grotesquely on all fours, his tail dragging limply behind him. He was barking.

'Speak, boy, speak!' Harry Derwent cried.

'Rowf! Rowf!' Roger responded. Everyone clapped; a few of the men whistled.

'Now sit up. Sit up, doggy!'

Roger clambered up on his haunches. The muzzle of his mask was frozen in its eternal snarl. Inside the eyeholes, Roger's eyes rolled with frantic, sweaty hilarity. He held his arms out, dangling the paws.

'Rowf! Rowf!'

Derwent upended the bottle of champagne and it fell in a foamy Niagara onto the upturned mask. Roger made frantic slurping sounds, and everyone applauded again. Some of the women screamed with laughter.

'Isn't Harry a card?' his partner asked him, pressing close again. 'Everyone says so. He's AC/DC, you know. Poor Roger's only DC. He spent a weekend with Harry in Cuba once . . . oh, *months* ago. Now he follows Harry everywhere, wagging his little tail behind him.'

She giggled. The shy scent of lilies drifted up.

'But of course Harry never goes back for seconds . . . not on his *DC* side, anyway . . . and Roger is just *wild*. Harry told him if he came to the masked ball as a doggy, a *cute* little doggy, he might reconsider, and Roger is *such* a silly that he . . .'

The number ended. There was more applause. The band members were filing down for a break.

'Excuse me, sweetness,' she said. 'There's someone I just *must* . . . Darla! Darla, you *dear girl*, where have you *been*?'

She wove her way into the eating, drinking throng and he gazed after her stupidly, wondering how they had happened to be dancing together in the first place. He didn't remember. Incidents seemed to have occurred with no connections. First here, then there, then everywhere. His head was spinning. He smelled lilies and juniper berries. Up by the refreshment table Derwent was now holding a tiny triangular sandwich over Roger's head and urging him, to the general merriment of the onlookers, to do a somersault. The dogmask was turned upward. The silver sides of the dog costume bellowsed in and out. Roger suddenly leaped, tucking his head under, and tried to roll in mid-air. His leap was too low and too exhausted; he landed awkwardly on his back, rapping his head smartly on the tiles. A hollow groan drifted out of the dogmask.

Derwent led the applause. 'Try again, doggy! Try again!'

The onlookers took up the chant – *try again, try again* – and Jack staggered off the other way, feeling vaguely ill.

He almost fell over the drinks cart that was being wheeled along by a low-browed man in a white mess jacket. His foot rapped the lower chromed shelf of the cart; the bottles and siphons on top chattered together musically.

'Sorry,' Jack said thickly. He suddenly felt closed in and claustrophobic; he wanted to get out. He wanted the Overlook back the way it had been . . . free of these unwanted guests. His place was not honored, as the true opener of the way; he was only another of the ten thousand cheering extras, a doggy rolling over and sitting up on command.

'Quite all right,' the man in the white mess jacket said. The polite, clipped English coming from that thug's face was surreal.

'A drink?'

'Martini.'

From behind him, another comber of laughter broke; Roger was howling to the tune of 'Home on the Range'. Someone was picking out accompaniment on the Steinway baby grand.

'Here you are.'

The frosty cold glass was pressed into his hand. Jack drank gratefully, feeling the gin hit and crumble away the first inroads of sobriety.

'Is it all right, sir?'

'Fine.'

'Thank you, sir.' The cart began to roll again.

Jack suddenly reached out and touched the man's shoulder. 'Yes, sir?'

'Pardon me, but . . . what's your name?'

The other showed no surprise. 'Grady, sir, Delbert Grady.'

'But you . . . I mean that . . .'

The bartender was looking at him politely. Jack tried again, although his mouth was mushed by gin and unreality; each word felt as large as an ice cube.

'Weren't you once the caretaker here? When you . . . when . . .' But he couldn't finish. He couldn't say it.

'Why no, sir. I don't believe so.'

'But your wife . . . your daughters . . .'

'My wife is helping in the kitchen, sir. The girls are asleep, of course. It's much too late for them.'

'You were the caretaker. You—' *Oh say it!* 'You killed them.'

Grady's face remained blankly polite. 'I don't have any recollection of that at all, sir.' His glass was empty. Grady plucked it from Jack's unresisting fingers and set about making another drink for him. There was a small white plastic bucket on his cart that was filled with olives. For some reason they reminded Jack of tiny severed heads. Grady speared one deftly, dropped it into the glass, and handed it to him.

'But you—'

'*You're* the caretaker, sir,' Grady said mildly. 'You've *always* been the caretaker. I should know, sir. I've always been here. The same manager hired us both, at the same time. Is it all right, sir?'

Jack gulped at his drink. His head was swirling. 'Mr Ullman—'

'I know no one by that name, sir.'

'But he—'

'The manager,' Grady said. 'The *hotel*, sir. Surely you realize who hired you, sir.'

'No,' he said thickly. 'No, I—'

'I believe you must take it up further with your son, Mr Torrance, sir. He understands everything, although he hasn't enlightened you. Rather naughty of him, if I may be so bold, sir. In fact, he's crossed you at almost every turn, hasn't he? And him not yet six.'

'Yes,' Jack said. 'He has.' There was another wave of laughter from behind them.

'He needs to be corrected, if you don't mind me saying so. He needs a good talking-to, and perhaps a bit more. My own girls, sir, didn't care for the Overlook at first. One of them actually stole a pack of my matches and tried to burn it down.

I corrected them. I corrected them most harshly. And when my wife tried to stop me from doing my duty, I corrected her.' He offered Jack a bland, meaningless smile. 'I find it a sad but true fact that women rarely understand a father's responsibility to his children. Husbands and fathers do have certain responsibilities, don't they, sir?'

'Yes,' Jack said.

'They didn't love the Overlook as I did,' Grady said, beginning to make him another drink. Silver bubbles rose in the upended gin bottle. 'Just as your son and wife don't love it . . . not at present, anyway. But they will come to love it. You must show them the error of their ways, Mr Torrance. Do you agree?'

'Yes. I do.'

He did see. He had been too easy with them. Husbands and fathers did have certain responsibilities. Father Knows Best. They did not understand. That in itself was no crime, but they were *willfully* not understanding. He was not ordinarily a harsh man. But he did believe in punishment. And if his son and his wife had willfully set themselves against his wishes *against the things he knew were best for them*, then didn't he have a certain duty—?

'A thankless child is sharper than a serpent's tooth,' Grady said, handing him his drink. 'I do believe that the manager could bring your son into line. And your wife would shortly follow. Do you agree, sir?'

He was suddenly uncertain. 'I . . . but . . . if they could just leave . . . I mean, after all, it's me the manager wants, isn't it? It must be. Because—' Because why? He should know but suddenly he didn't. Oh, his poor brain was swimming.

'Bad dog!' Derwent was saying, loudly, to a counterpoint of laughter. 'Bad dog to piddle on the floor.'

'Of course you know,' Grady said, leaning confidentially over the cart, 'your son is attempting to bring an outside party into it. Your son has a very great talent, one that the manager could use to even further improve the Overlook, to further . . . enrich it, shall we say? But your son is attempting to use that very talent against us. He is willful, Mr Torrance, sir. Willful.'

'Outside party?' Jack asked stupidly.

Grady nodded.

'Who?'

'A nigger,' Grady said. 'A nigger cook.'

'Hallorann?'

'I believe that is his name, sir, yes.'

Another burst of laughter from behind them was followed by Roger saying something in a whining, protesting voice.

'Yes! Yes! Yes!' Derwent began to chant. The others around him took it up, but before Jack could hear what they wanted Roger to do now, the band began to play again – the tune was 'Tuxedo Junction', with a lot of mellow sax in it but not much soul.

(*Soul? Soul hasn't even been invented yet. Or has it?*)

(*A nigger . . . a nigger cook.*)

He opened his mouth to speak, not knowing what might come out. What did was:

'I was told you hadn't finished high school. But you don't talk like an uneducated man.'

'It's true that I left organized education very early, sir. But the manager takes care of his help. He finds that it pays. Education always pays, don't you agree, sir?'

'Yes,' Jack said dazedly.

'For instance, you show a great interest in learning more about the Overlook Hotel. Very wise of you, sir. Very noble. A certain scrapbook was left in the basement for you to find—'

'By whom?' Jack asked eagerly.

'By the manager, of course. Certain other materials could be put at your disposal, if you wished them . . .'

'I do. Very much.' He tried to control the eagerness in his voice and failed miserably.

'You're a true scholar,' Grady said. 'Pursue the topic to the end. Exhaust all sources.' He dipped his low-browed head, pulled out the lapel of his white mess jacket, and buffed his knuckles at a spot of dirt that was invisible to Jack.

'And the manager puts no strings on his largess,' Grady went on. 'Not at all. Look at me, a tenth-grade dropout. Think how much further you yourself could go in the Overlook's organizational structure. Perhaps . . . in time . . . to the very top.'

'Really?' Jack whispered.

'But that's really up to your son to decide, isn't it?' Grady asked, raising his eyebrows. The delicate gesture went oddly with the brows themselves, which were bushy and somehow savage.

'Up to Danny?' Jack frowned at Grady. 'No, of course not. I wouldn't allow my son to make decisions concerning my career. Not at all. What do you take me for?'

'A dedicated man,' Grady said warmly. 'Perhaps I put it badly, sir. Let us say that your future here is contingent upon how you decide to deal with your son's waywardness.'

'I make my own decisions,' Jack whispered.

'But you must deal with him.'

'I will.'

'Firmly.'

'I will.'

'A man who cannot control his own family holds very little interest for our manager. A man who cannot guide the courses of his own wife and son can hardly be expected to guide himself, let alone assume a position of responsibility in an operation of this magnitude. He—'

'*I said I'll handle him!*' Jack shouted suddenly, enraged.

'Tuxedo Junction' had just concluded and a new tune hadn't begun. His shout fell perfectly into the gap, and conversation suddenly ceased behind him. His skin suddenly felt hot all over. He became fixedly positive that everyone was staring at him. They had finished with Roger and would now commence with him. Roll over. Sit up. Play dead. If you play the game with us, we'll play the game with you. Position of responsibility. They wanted him to sacrifice his son.

(—*Now he follows Harry everywhere, wagging his little tail behind him*—)

(*Roll over. Play dead. Chastise your son.*)

'Right this way, sir,' Grady was saying. 'Something that might interest you.'

The conversation had begun again, lifting and dropping in its own rhythm, weaving in and out of the band music, now doing a swing version of Lennon and McCartney's 'Ticket to Ride'.

(*I've heard better over supermarket loudspeakers.*)

He giggled foolishly. He looked down at his left hand and saw there was another drink in it, half-full. He emptied it at a gulp.

Now he was standing in front of the mantelpiece, the heat from the crackling fire that had been laid in the hearth warming his legs.

(*a fire? . . . in August? . . . yes . . . and no . . . all times are one*)

There was a clock under a glass dome, flanked by two carved ivory elephants. Its hands stood at a minute to midnight. He gazed at it blearily. Had this been what Grady wanted him to see? He turned around to ask, but Grady had left him.

Halfway through 'Ticket to Ride', the band wound up in a brassy flourish.

'The hour is at hand!' Horace Derwent proclaimed. 'Midnight! Unmask! Unmask!'

He tried to turn again, to see what famous faces were hidden beneath the glitter and paint and masks, but he was frozen now, unable to look away from the clock – its hands had come together and pointed straight up.

'*Unmask! Unmask!*' the chant went up.

The clock began to chime delicately. Along the steel runner below the clockface, from the left and right, two figures advanced. Jack watched, fascinated, the unmasking forgotten. Clockwork whirred. Cogs turned and meshed, brass warmly glowing. The balance wheel rocked back and forth precisely.

One of the figures was a man standing on tiptoe, with what looked like a tiny club clasped in his hands. The other was a small boy wearing a dunce cap. The clockwork figures glittered, fantastically precise. Across the front of the boy's dunce cap he could read the engraved word FOOLE.

The two figures slipped onto the opposing ends of a steel axis bar. Somewhere, tinkling on and on, were the strains of a Strauss waltz. An insane commercial jingle began to run through his mind to the tune: *Buy dog food, rowf-rowf, rowf-rowf, buy dog food* . . .

The steel mallet in the clockwork daddy's hands came down on the boy's head. The clockwork son crumbled forward. The mallet rose and fell, rose and fell. The boy's upstretched, protesting hands began to falter. The boy sagged from his crouch to a prone position. And still the hammer rose and fell to the light, tinkling air of the Strauss melody, and it seemed that he could see the man's face, working and knotting and constricting, could see the clockwork daddy's mouth opening and closing as he berated the unconscious, bludgeoned figure of the son.

A spot of red flew up against the inside of the glass dome.

Another followed. Two more splattered beside it.

Now the red liquid was spraying up like an obscene rain shower, striking the glass sides of the dome and running, obscuring what was going on inside, and flecked through the scarlet were tiny gray ribbons of tissue, fragments of bone and brain. And still he could see the hammer rising and falling as the clockwork continued to turn and the cogs continued to mesh the gears and teeth of this cunningly made machine.

'*Unmask! Unmask!*' Derwent was shrieking behind him, and somewhere a dog was howling in human tones.

(*But clockwork can't bleed clockwork can't bleed*)

The entire dome was splashed with blood, he could see clotted bits of hair but nothing else thank God he could see nothing else, and still he thought he would be sick because he could hear the hammerblows still falling, could hear them through the glass just as he could hear the phrases of 'The Blue Danube'. But the sounds were no longer the mechanical *tink-tink-tink* noises of a mechanical hammer striking a mechanical head, but the soft and squashy thudding sounds of a real hammer slicing down and whacking into a spongy, muddy ruin. A ruin that once had been—

'*UNMASK!*'

(—*the Red Death held sway over all!*)

With a miserable, rising scream, he turned away from the clock, his hands outstretched, his feet stumbling against one another like wooden blocks as he begged them to stop, to take him, Danny, Wendy, to take the whole world if they wanted it, but only to stop and leave him a little sanity, a little light.

THE SHINING

The ballroom was empty.

The chairs with their spindly legs were upended on tables covered with plastic dust drops. The red rug with its golden tracings was back on the dance floor, protecting the polished hardwood surface. The bandstand was deserted except for a disassembled microphone stand and a dusty guitar leaning stringless against the wall. Cold morning light, winterlight, fell languidly through the high windows.

His head was still reeling, he still felt drunk, but when he turned back to the mantelpiece, his drink was gone. There were only the ivory elephants . . . and the clock.

He stumbled back across the cold, shadowy lobby and through the dining room. His foot hooked around a table leg and he fell full-length, upsetting the table in a clatter. He struck his nose hard on the floor and it began to bleed. He got up, snuffling back blood and wiping his nose with the back of his hand. He crossed to the Colorado Lounge and shoved through the batwing doors, making them fly back and bang into the walls.

The place was empty . . . but the bar was fully stocked. God be praised! Glass and silver edging on labels glowed warmly in the dark.

Once, he remembered, a very long time ago, he had been angry that there was no backbar mirror. Now he was glad. Looking into it he would have seen just another drunk fresh off the wagon: bloody nose, untucked shirt, hair rumpled, cheeks stubbly.

(*This is what it's like to stick your whole hand into the nest.*)

Loneliness surged over him suddenly and completely. He cried out with sudden wretchedness and honestly wished he were dead. His wife and son were upstairs with the door locked against him. The others had all left. The party was over.

He lurched forward again, reaching the bar.

'Lloyd, where the fuck are you?' he screamed.

There was no answer. In this well-padded

(*cell*)

room, his words did not even echo back to give the illusion of company.

'*Grady!*'

No answer. Only the bottles, standing stiffly at attention.

(*Roll over. Play dead. Fetch. Play dead. Sit up. Play dead.*)

'Never mind, I'll do it myself, goddammit.'

Halfway over the bar he lost his balance and pitched forward, hitting his head a muffled blow on the floor. He got up on his hands and knees, his eyeballs moving disjointed from side to side, fuzzy muttering sounds coming from his mouth. Then he collapsed, his face turned to one side, breathing in harsh tones.

Outside, the wind whooped louder, driving the thickening snow before it. It was 8:30 a.m.

CHAPTER FORTY-FIVE
STAPLETON AIRPORT, DENVER

At 8:31 a.m., MST, a woman on TWA's Flight 196 burst into tears and began to bugle her own opinion, which was perhaps not unshared among some of the other passengers (or even the crew, for that matter), that the plane was going to crash.

The sharp-faced woman next to Hallorann looked up from her book and offered a brief character analysis: 'Ninny,' and went back to her book. She had downed two screwdrivers during the flight, but they seemed not to have thawed her at all.

'It's going to crash!' the woman was crying out shrilly. 'Oh, I just know it is!'

A stewardess hurried to her seat and squatted beside her. Hallorann thought to himself that only stewardesses and very young housewives seemed able to squat with any degree of grace; it was a rare and wonderful talent. He thought about this while the stewardess talked softly and soothingly to the woman, quieting her bit by bit.

Hallorann didn't know about anyone else on 196, but he personally was almost scared enough to shit peachpits. Outside the window there was nothing to be seen but a buffeting curtain of white. The plane rocked sickeningly from side to side with gusts that seemed to come from everywhere. The engines were cranked up to provide partial compensation and as a result the floor was vibrating under their feet. There were several people moaning in Tourist behind them, one stew had gone back with a handful of fresh airsick bags, and a man three rows in front of Hallorann had whoopsed into his *National Observer* and had grinned apologetically at the stewardess who came to help him clean up. 'That's all right,' she comforted him, 'that's how I feel about the *Reader's Digest*.'

Hallorann had flown enough to be able to surmise what had happened. They had been flying against bad headwinds most of the way, the weather over Denver had worsened suddenly and unexpectedly, and now it was just a little late to divert for someplace where the weather was better. *Feets don't fail me now.*

(*Buddy-boy, this is some fucked-up cavalry charge.*)

The stewardess seemed to have succeeded in curbing the worst of the woman's hysterics. She was snuffling and honking into a lace handkerchief, but had ceased broadcasting her opinions about the flight's possible conclusion to the cabin at large. The stew gave her a final pat on the shoulder and stood up just as the 747 gave its worst lurch yet. The stewardess stumbled backward and landed in the lap of the man who had whoopsed into his paper, exposing a lovely length of nyloned thigh. The man blinked and then patted her kindly on the shoulder. She smiled back, but Hallorann thought the strain was showing. It had been one hell of a hard flight this morning.

There was a little ping as the NO SMOKING light reappeared.

'This is the captain speaking,' a soft, slightly southern voice informed them. 'We're ready to begin our descent to Stapleton International Airport. It's been a rough flight, for which I apologize. The landing may be a bit rough also, but we anticipate no real difficulty. Please observe the FASTEN SEAT BELTS and NO SMOKING signs, and we hope you enjoy your stay in the Denver metro area. And we also hope —'

Another hard bump rocked the plane and then dropped her with a sickening elevator plunge. Hallorann's stomach did a queasy hornpipe. Several people – not all women by any means – screamed.

'— that we'll see you again on another TWA flight real soon.'

'Not bloody likely,' someone behind Hallorann said.

'So silly,' the sharp-faced woman next to Hallorann remarked, putting a matchbook cover into her book and shutting it as the plane began to descend. 'When one has seen the horrors of a dirty little war . . . as you have . . . or sensed the degrading immorality of CIA dollar-diplomacy intervention . . .

as I have . . . a rough landing *pales into insignificance*. Am I right, Mr Hallorann?'

'As rain, ma'am,' he said, and looked bleakly out into the wildly blowing snow.

'How is your steel plate reacting to all of this, if I might inquire?'

'Oh, my head's fine,' Hallorann said. 'It's just my stomach that's a mite queasy.'

'A shame.' She reopened her book.

As they descended through the impenetrable clouds of snow, Hallorann thought of a crash that had occurred at Boston's Logan Airport a few years ago. The conditions had been similar, only fog instead of snow had reduced visibility to zero. The plane had caught its undercarriage on a retaining wall near the end of the landing strip. What had been left of the eighty-nine people aboard hadn't looked much different from a Hamburger Helper casserole.

He wouldn't mind so much if it was just himself. He was pretty much alone in the world now, and attendance at his funeral would be mostly held down to the people he had worked with and that old renegade Masterton, who would at least drink to him. But the boy . . . the boy was depending on him. He was maybe all the help that child could expect, and he didn't like the way the boy's last call had been snapped off. He kept thinking of the way those hedge animals had seemed to move . . .

A thin white hand appeared over his.

The woman with the sharp face had taken off her glasses. Without them her features seemed much softer.

'It will be all right,' she said.

Hallorann made a smile and nodded.

As advertised the plane came down hard, reunited with the earth forcefully enough to knock most of the magazines out of the rack at the front and to send plastic trays cascading out of the galley like oversized playing cards. No one screamed, but Hallorann heard several sets of teeth clicking violently together like gypsy castanets.

Then the turbine engines rose to a howl, braking the plane,

and as they dropped in volume the pilot's soft southern voice, perhaps not completely steady, came over the intercom system. 'Ladies and gentlemen, we have landed at Stapleton Airport. Please remain in your seats until the plane has come to a complete stop at the terminal. Thank you.'

The woman beside Hallorann closed her book and uttered a long sigh. 'We live to fight another day, Mr Hallorann.'

'Ma'am, we aren't done with this one, yet.'

'True. Very true. Would you care to have a drink in the lounge with me?'

'I would, but I have an appointment to keep.'

'Pressing?'

'Very pressing,' Hallorann said gravely.

'Something that will improve the general situation in some small way, I hope.'

'I hope so too,' Hallorann said, and smiled. She smiled back at him, ten years dropping silently from her face as she did so.

★★★

Because he had only the flight bag he'd carried for luggage, Hallorann beat the crowd to the Hertz desk on the lower level. Outside the smoked glass windows he could see the snow still falling steadily. The gusting wind drove white clouds of it back and forth, and the people walking across to the parking area were struggling against it. One man lost his hat and Hallorann could commiserate with him as it whirled high, wide, and handsome. The man stared after it and Hallorann thought:

(*Aw, just forget it, man. That homburg ain't comin down until it gets to Arizona.*)

On the heels of that thought:

(*If it's this bad in Denver, what's it going to be like west of Boulder?*)

Best not to think about that, maybe.

'Can I help you, sir?' a girl in Hertz yellow asked him.

'If you got a car, you can help me,' he said with a big grin.

For a heavier-than-average charge he was able to get a heavier-than-average car, a silver and black Buick Electra. He was thinking of the winding mountain roads rather than style;

he would still have to stop somewhere along the way and get chains put on. He wouldn't get far without them.

'How bad is it?' he asked as she handed him the rental agreement to sign.

'They say it's the worst storm since 1969,' she answered brightly. 'Do you have far to drive, sir?'

'Farther than I'd like.'

'If you'd like, sir, I can phone ahead to the Texaco station at the Route 270 junction. They'll put chains on for you.'

'That would be a great blessing, dear.'

She picked up the phone and made the call. 'They'll be expecting you.'

'Thank you very much.'

Leaving the desk, he saw the sharp-faced woman standing on one of the queues that had formed in front of the luggage carousel. She was still reading her book. Halorann winked at her as he went by. She looked up, smiled at him, and gave him a peace sign.

(*shine*)

He turned up his overcoat collar, smiling, and shifted his flight bag to the other hand. Only a little one, but it made him feel better. He was sorry he'd told her that fish story about having a steel plate in his head. He mentally wished her well and as he went out into the howling wind and snow, he thought she wished him the same in return.

★★★

The charge for putting on the chains at the service station was a modest one, but Halorann slipped the man at work in the garage bay an extra ten to get moved up a little way on the waiting list. It was still quarter of ten before he was actually on the road, the windshield wipers clicking and the chains clinking with tuneless monotony on the Buick's big wheels.

The turnpike was a mess. Even with the chains on he could go no faster than thirty. Cars had gone off the road at crazy angles, and on several of the grades traffic was barely struggling along, summer tires spinning helplessly in the drifting powder.

It was the first big storm of the winter down here in the lowlands (if you could call a mile above sealevel 'low'), and it was a mother. Many of them were unprepared, common enough, but Hallorann still found himself cursing them as he inched around them, peering into his snow-clogged outside mirror to be sure nothing was

(*Dashing through the snow . . .*)

coming up in the left-hand lane to cream his black ass.

There was more bad luck waiting for him at the Route 36 entrance ramp. Route 36, the Denver-Boulder turnpike, also goes west to Estes Park, where it connects with Route 7. That road, also known as the Upland Highway, goes through Sidewinder, passes the Overlook Hotel, and finally winds down the Western Slope and into Utah.

The entrance ramp had been blocked by an overturned semi. Bright-burning flares had been scattered around it like birthday candles on some idiot child's cake.

He came to a stop and rolled his window down. A cop with a fur Cossack hat jammed down over his ears gestured with one gloved hand toward the flow of the traffic moving north on I-25.

'You can't get up here!' he bawled to Hallorann over the wind. 'Go down two exits, get on 91, and connect with 36 at Broomfield!'

'I think I could get around him on the left!' Hallorann shouted back. 'That's twenty miles out of my way, what you're rappin!'

'I'll rap your friggin *head*!' the cop shouted back. 'This ramp's closed!'

Hallorann backed up, waited for a break in traffic, and continued on his way up Route 25. The signs informed him it was only a hundred miles to Cheyenne, Wyoming. If he didn't look out for his ramp, he'd wind up there.

He inched his speed up to thirty-five but dared no more; already snow was threatening to clog his wiper blades and the traffic patterns were decidedly crazy. Twenty-mile detour. He cursed, and the feeling that time was growing shorter for the boy welled up in him again, nearly suffocating with its urgency.

And at the same time he felt a fatalistic certainty that he would not be coming back from this trip.

He turned on the radio, dialed past Christmas ads, and found a weather forecast.

'— six inches already, and another foot is expected in the Denver metro area by nightfall. Local and state police urge you not to take your car out of the garage unless it's absolutely necessary, and warn that most mountain passes have already been closed. So stay home and wax up your boards and keep tuned to—'

'Thanks, mother,' Hallorann said, and turned the radio off savagely.

CHAPTER FORTY-SIX
WENDY

Around noon, after Danny had gone into the bathroom to use the toilet, Wendy took the towel-wrapped knife from under her pillow, put it in the pocket of her bathrobe, and went over to the bathroom door.

'Danny?'

'What?'

'I'm going down to make us some lunch. 'Kay?'

'Okay. Do you want me to come down?'

'No, I'll bring it up. How about a cheese omelet and some soup?'

'Sure.'

She hesitated outside the closed door a moment longer. 'Danny, are you sure it's okay?'

'Yeah,' he said. 'Just be careful.'

'Where's your father? Do you know?'

His voice came back, curiously flat: 'No. But it's okay.'

She stifled an urge to keep asking, to keep picking around the edges of the thing. The thing was there, they knew what it was, picking at it was only going to frighten Danny more . . . and herself.

Jack had lost his mind. They had sat together on Danny's cot as the storm began to pick up clout and meanness around eight o'clock this morning and had listened to him downstairs, bellowing and stumbling from one place to another. Most of it had seemed to come from the ballroom. Jack singing tuneless bits of song, Jack holding up one side of an argument, Jack screaming loudly at one point, freezing both of their faces as they stared into one another's eyes. Finally they had heard him stumbling back across the lobby, and Wendy thought she had heard a loud banging noise, as if he had fallen down or pushed a door violently open. Since eight-thirty or so – three and a half hours now – there had been only silence.

She went down the short hall, turned into the main first-floor corridor, and went to the stairs. She stood on the first-floor landing looking down into the lobby. It appeared deserted, but the gray and snowy day had left much of the long room in shadow. Danny could be wrong. Jack could be behind a chair or couch . . . maybe behind the registration desk . . . waiting for her to come down . . .

She wet her lips. 'Jack?'

No answer.

Her hand found the handle of the knife and she began to go down. She had seen the end of her marriage many times, in divorce, in Jack's death at the scene of a drunken car accident (a regular vision in the dark two o'clock of Stovington mornings), and occasionally in daydreams of being discovered by another man, a soap opera Galahad who would sweep Danny and her onto the saddle of his snow-white charger and take them away. But she had never envisioned herself prowling halls and staircases like a nervous felon, with a knife clasped in one hand to use against Jack.

A wave of despair struck through her at the thought and she had to stop halfway down the stairs and holding the railing, afraid her knees would buckle.

(*Admit it. It isn't just Jack, he's just the one solid thing in all of this you can hang the other things on, the things you can't believe and yet are being forced to believe, that thing about the hedges, the party favor in the elevator, the mask*)

She tried to stop the thought but it was too late.

(*and the voices.*)

Because from time to time it had not seemed that there was a solitary crazy man below them, shouting at and holding conversations with the phantoms in his own crumbling mind. From time to time, like a radio signal fading in and out, she had heard – or thought she had – other voices, and music, and laughter. At one moment she would hear Jack holding a conversation with someone named Grady (the name was vaguely familiar to her but she made no actual connection), making statements and asking questions into silence, yet speaking loudly, as if to make himself heard over a steady background racket. And then, eerily, other sounds would be there, seeming to slip into place – a dance band, people clapping, a man with an amused yet authoritative voice who seemed to be trying to persuade somebody to make a speech. For a period of thirty seconds to a minute she would hear this, long enough to grow faint with terror, and then it would be gone again and she would only hear Jack, talking in that commanding yet slightly slurred way she remembered as his drunk-speak voice. But there was nothing in the hotel to drink except cooking sherry. Wasn't that right? Yes, but if she could imagine that the hotel was full of voices and music, couldn't Jack imagine that he was drunk?

She didn't like that thought. Not at all.

Wendy reached the lobby and looked around. The velvet rope that had cordoned off the ballroom had been taken down; the steel post it had been clipped to had been knocked over, as if someone had carelessly bumped it going by. Mellow white light fell through the open door onto the lobby rug from the ballroom's high, narrow windows. Heart thumping, she went to the open ballroom doors and looked in. It was empty and silent, the only sound that curious subaural echo that seems to linger in all large rooms, from the largest cathedral to the smallest hometown bingo parlor.

She went back to the registration desk and stood undecided for a moment, listening to the wind howl outside. It was the worst storm so far, and it was still building up force. Somewhere on the west side a shutter latch had broken and the shutter banged back and forth with a steady flat cracking sound, like a shooting gallery with only one customer.

(*Jack, you really should take care of that. Before something gets in.*)

What would she do if he came at her right now, she wondered. If he should pop up from behind the dark, varnished registration desk with its pile of triplicate forms and its little silver-plated bell, like some murderous jack-in-the-box, pun intended, a grinning jack-in-the-box with a cleaver in one hand

and no sense at all left behind his eyes. Would she stand frozen with terror, or was there enough of the primal mother in her to fight him for her son until one of them was dead? She didn't know. The very thought made her sick – made her feel that her whole life had been a long and easy dream to lull her helplessly into this waking nightmare. She was soft. When trouble came, she slept. Her past was unremarkable. She had never been tried in fire. Now the trial was upon her, not fire but ice, and she would not be allowed to sleep through this. Her son was waiting for her upstairs.

Clutching the haft of the knife tighter, she peered over the desk.

Nothing there.

Her relieved breath escaped her in a long, hitching sigh.

She put the gate up and went through, pausing to glance into the inner office before going in herself. She fumbled through the next door for the bank of kitchen light switches, coldly expecting a hand to close over hers at any second. Then the fluorescents were coming on with minuscule ticking and humming sounds and she could see Mr Hallorann's kitchen – her kitchen now, for better or worse – pale green tiles, gleaming Formica, spotless porcelain, glowing chrome edgings. She had promised him she would keep his kitchen clean, and she had. She felt as if it was one of Danny's safe places. Dick Hallorann's presence seemed to enfold and comfort her. Danny had called for Mr Hallorann, and upstairs, sitting next to Danny in fear as her husband ranted and raved below, that had seemed like the faintest of all hopes. But standing here, in Mr Hallorann's place, it seemed almost possible. Perhaps he was on his way now, intent on getting to them regardless of the storm. Perhaps it was so.

She went across to the pantry, shot the bolt back, and stepped inside. She got a can of tomato soup and closed the pantry door again, and bolted it. The door was tight against the floor. If you kept it bolted, you didn't have to worry about rat or mouse droppings in the rice or flour or sugar.

She opened the can and dropped the slightly jellied contents into a saucepan – *plop*. She went to the refrigerator and got milk and eggs for the omelet. Then to the walk-in freezer for cheese. All of these actions, so common and so much a part of her life before the Overlook had been a part of her life, helped to calm her.

She melted butter in the frying pan, diluted the soup with milk, and then poured the beaten eggs into the pan.

A sudden feeling that someone was standing behind her, reaching for her throat.

She wheeled around, clutching the knife. No one there.

(*! Get ahold of yourself, girl !*)

She grated a bowl of cheese from the block, added it to the omelet, flipped it, and turned the gas ring down to a bare blue flame. The soup was hot. She put the pot on a large tray with silverware, two bowls, two plates, the salt and pepper shakers. When the omelet had puffed slightly, Wendy slid it off onto one of the plates and covered it.

(*Now back the way you came. Turn off the kitchen lights. Go through the inner office. Through the desk gate, collect two hundred dollars.*)

She stopped on the lobby side of the registration desk and set the tray down beside the silver bell. Unreality would stretch only so far; this was like some surreal game of hide-and-seek.

She stood in the shadowy lobby, frowning in thought.

(*Don't push the facts away this time, girl. There are certain realities, as lunatic as this situation may seem. One of them is that you may be the only responsible person left in this grotesque pile. You have a five-going-on-six son to look out for. And your husband, whatever has happened to him and no matter how dangerous he may be . . . maybe he's part of your responsibility, too. And even if he isn't, consider this: Today is December second. You could be stuck up here another four months if a ranger doesn't happen by. Even if they do start to wonder why they haven't heard from us on the CB, no one is going to come today . . . or tomorrow . . . maybe not for weeks. Are you going to spend a month sneaking down to get meals with a knife in your pocket and jumping at every shadow? Do you really think you can avoid Jack for a month? Do you think you can keep Jack out of the upstairs quarters if he wants to get in? He has the passkey and one hard kick would snap the bolt.*)

Leaving the tray on the desk, she walked slowly down to the dining room and looked in. It was deserted. There was one table with the chairs set up around it, the table they had tried eating at until the dining room's emptiness began to freak them out.

'Jack?' she called hesitantly.

At that moment the wind rose in a gust, driving snow against the shutters, but it seemed to her that there had been something. A muffled sort of groan.

'*Jack?*'

No returning sound this time, but her eyes fell on something beneath the batwing doors of the Colorado Lounge, something that gleamed faintly in the subdued light. Jack's cigarette lighter.

Plucking up her courage, she crossed to the batwings and pushed them open. The smell of gin was so strong that her breath snagged in her throat. It wasn't even right to call it a smell; it was a positive reek. But the shelves were empty. Where in God's name had he found it? A bottle hidden at the back of one of the cupboards? *Where?*

There was another groan, low and fuzzy, but perfectly audible this time. Wendy walked slowly to the bar.

'Jack?'

No answer.

She looked over the bar and there he was, sprawled out on the floor in a stupor. Drunk as a lord, by the smell. He must have tried to go right over the top and lost his balance. A wonder he hadn't broken his neck. An old proverb recurred to her: God looks after drunks and little children. Amen.

Yet she was not angry with him; looking down at him she thought he looked like a horribly overtired little boy who had tried to do too much and had fallen asleep in the middle of the living room floor. He had stopped drinking and it was not Jack who had made the decision to start again; there had been no liquor for him to start with . . . so where had it come from?

Resting at every five or six feet along the horseshoe-shaped bar there were wine bottles wrapped in straw, their mouths plugged with candles. Supposed to look bohemian, she supposed. She picked one up and shook it, half-expecting to hear the slosh of gin inside it.

(*new wine in old bottles*)

but there was nothing. She set it back down.

Jack was stirring. She went around the bar, found the gate, and walked back on the inside to where Jack lay, pausing only to look at the gleaming chromium taps. They were dry, but when she passed close to them she could smell beer, wet and new, like a fine mist.

As she reached Jack he rolled over, opened his eyes, and looked up at her. For a moment his gaze was utterly blank, and then it cleared.

'Wendy?' he asked. 'That you?'

'Yes,' she said. 'Do you think you can make it upstairs? If you put your arms around me? Jack, where did you —'

His hand closed brutally around her ankle.

'Jack! What are you —'

'Gotcha!' he said, and began to grin. There was a stale odor of gin and olives about him that seemed to set off an old terror in her, a worse terror than any hotel could provide by itself. A distant part of her thought that the worst thing was that it had all come back to this, she and her drunken husband.

'Jack, I want to help.'

'Oh yeah. You and Danny only want to *help*.' The grip on her ankle was crushing now. Still holding onto her, Jack was getting shakily to his knees. 'You wanted to help us all right out of here. But now . . . I . . . *gotcha!*'

'Jack, you're hurting my ankle —'

'I'll hurt more than your ankle, you *bitch*.'

The word stunned her so completely that she made no effort to move when he let go of her ankle and stumbled from his knees to his feet, where he stood swaying in front of her.

'You never loved me,' he said. 'You want us to leave because you know that'll be the end of me. Did you ever think about my re . . . res . . . respons'bilities? No, I guess to fuck you didn't.

All you ever think about is ways to drag me down. You're just like my mother, you milksop *bitch!*'

'Stop it,' she said, crying. 'You don't know what you're saying. You're drunk. I don't know how, but you're drunk.'

'Oh, I know. I know now. You and him. That little pup upstairs. The two of you, planning together. Isn't that right?'

'No, no! We never planned anything! What are you—'

'*You liar!*' he screamed. 'Oh, I know how you do it! I guess I know that! When I say, "We're going to stay here and I'm going to do my job," you say, "Yes, dear," and he says, "Yes, Daddy," and then you lay your plans. You planned to use the snow-mobile. You planned that. But I knew. I figured it out. *Did you think I wouldn't figure it out? Did you think I was stupid?*'

She stared at him, unable to speak now. He was going to kill her, and then he was going to kill Danny. Then maybe the hotel would be satisfied and allow him to kill himself. Just like that other caretaker. Just like

(*Grady.*)

With almost swooning horror, she realized at last who it was that Jack had been conversing with in the ballroom.

'You turned my son against me. That was the worst.' His face sagged into lines of selfpity. 'My little boy. Now he hates me, too. You saw to that. That was your plan all along, wasn't it? You've always been jealous, haven't you? Just like your mother. You couldn't be satisfied unless you had all the cake, could you? *Could you?*'

She couldn't talk.

'Well, I'll fix you,' he said, and tried to put his hands around her throat.

She took a step backward, then another, and he stumbled against her. She remembered the knife in the pocket of her robe and groped for it, but now his left arm had swept around her, pinning her arm against her side. She could smell sharp gin and the sour odor of his sweat.

'Have to be punished,' he was grunting. 'Chastised. Chastised . . . harshly.'

His right hand found her throat.

As her breath stopped, pure panic took over. His left hand joined his right and now the knife was free to her own hand, but she forgot about it. Both of her hands came up and began to yank helplessly at his larger, stronger ones.

'*Mommy!*' Danny shrieked from somewhere. '*Daddy, stop! You're hurting Mommy!*' He screamed piercingly, a high and crystal sound that she heard from far off.

Red flashes of light leaped in front of her eyes like ballet dancers. The room grew darker. She saw her son clamber up on the bar and throw himself at Jack's shoulders. Suddenly one of the hands that had been crushing her throat was gone as Jack cuffed Danny away with a snarl. The boy fell back against the empty shelves and dropped to the floor, dazed. The hand was on her throat again. The red flashes began to turn black.

Danny was crying weakly. Her chest was burning. Jack was shouting into her face: 'I'll fix you! Goddam you, I'll show you who is boss around here! I'll show you—'

But all sounds were fading down a long dark corridor. Her struggles began to weaken. One of her hands fell away from his and dropped slowly until the arm was stretched out at right angles to her body, the hand dangling limply from the wrist like the hand of a drowning woman.

It touched a bottle – one of the straw-wrapped wine bottles that served as decorative candleholders.

Sightlessly, with the last of her strength, she groped for the bottle's neck and found it, feeling the greasy beads of wax against her hand.

(*and O God if it slips*)

She brought it up and then down, praying for aim, knowing that if it only struck his shoulder or upper arm she was dead.

But the bottle came down squarely on Jack Torrance's head, the glass shattering violently inside the straw. The base of it was thick and heavy, and it made a sound against his skull like a medicine ball dropped on a hardwood floor. He rocked back on his heels, his eyes rolling up in their sockets. The pressure on her throat loosened, then gave way entirely. He put his hands out, as if to steady himself, and then crashed over on his back.

Wendy drew a long, sobbing breath. She almost fell herself, clutched the edge of the bar, and managed to hold herself up. Consciousness wavered in and out. She could hear Danny crying, but she had no idea where he was. It sounded like crying in an echo chamber. Dimly she saw dime-sized drops of blood falling to the dark surface of the bar – from her nose, she thought. She cleared her throat and spat on the floor. It sent a wave of agony up the column of her throat, but the agony subsided to a steady dull press of pain . . . just bearable.

Little by little, she managed to get control of herself.

She let go of the bar, turned around, and saw Jack lying full-length, the shattered bottle beside him. He looked like a felled giant. Danny was crouched below the lounge's cash register, both hands in his mouth, staring at his unconscious father.

Wendy went to him unsteadily and touched his shoulder. Danny cringed away from her.

'Danny, listen to me —'

'No, no,' he muttered in a husky old man's voice. 'Daddy hurt you . . . you hurt Daddy . . . Daddy hurt you . . . I want to go to sleep. Danny wants to go to sleep.'

'Danny —'

'Sleep, sleep. Nighty-night.'

'*No!*'

Pain ripping up her throat again. She winced against it. But he opened his eyes. They looked at her warily from bluish, shadowed sockets.

She made herself speak calmly, her eyes never leaving his. Her voice was low and husky, almost a whisper. It hurt to talk. 'Listen to me, Danny. It wasn't your daddy trying to hurt me. And I didn't want to hurt him. The hotel has gotten into him, Danny. *The Overlook has gotten into your daddy.* Do you understand me?'

Some kind of knowledge came slowly back into Danny's eyes.

'The Bad Stuff,' he whispered. 'There was none of it here before, was there?'

'No. The hotel put it here. The . . .' She broke off in a fit of coughing and spat out more blood. Her throat already felt puffed to twice its size. 'The hotel made him drink it. Did you hear those people he was talking to this morning?'

'Yes . . . the hotel people . . .'

'I heard them too. And that means the hotel is getting stronger. It wants to hurt all of us. But I think . . . I hope . . . that it can only do that through your daddy. He was the only one it could catch. Are you understanding me, Danny? It's desperately important that you understand.'

'The hotel caught Daddy.' He looked at Jack and groaned helplessly.

'I know you love your daddy. I do too. We have to remember that the hotel is trying to hurt him as much as it is us.' And she was convinced that was true. More, she thought that Danny might be the one the hotel really wanted, the reason it was going so far . . . maybe the reason it was *able* to go so far. It might even be that in some unknown fashion it was Danny's shine that was powering it, the way a battery powers the electrical equipment in a car . . . the way a battery gets a car to start. If they got out of here, the Overlook might subside to its old semi-sentient state, able to do no more than present penny-dreadful horror slides to the more psychically aware guests who entered it. Without Danny it was not much more than an amusement park haunted house, where a guest or two might hear rappings or the phantom sounds of a masquerade party, or see an occasional disturbing thing. But if it absorbed Danny . . . Danny's shine or life-force or spirit . . . whatever you wanted to call it . . . into itself – what would it be then?

The thought made her cold all over.

'I wish Daddy was all better,' Danny said, and the tears began to flow again.

'Me too,' she said, and hugged Danny tightly. 'And honey, that's why you've got to help me put your daddy somewhere. Somewhere that the hotel can't make him hurt us and where he can't hurt himself. Then . . . if your friend Dick comes, or a park ranger, we can take him away. And I think he might be all right again. All of us might be all right. I think there's still a chance for that, if we're strong and brave, like you were when you jumped on his back. Do you understand?' She looked at him pleadingly and thought how strange it was; she had never seen him when he looked so much like Jack.

'Yes,' he said, and nodded. 'I think . . . if we can get away from here . . . everything will be like it was. Where could we put him?'

'The pantry. There's food in there, and a good strong bolt on the outside. It's warm. And we can eat up the things from the refrigerator and the freezer. There will be plenty for all three of us until help comes.'

'Do we do it now?'

'Yes, right now. Before he wakes up.'

Danny put the bargate up while she folded Jack's hands on his chest and listened to his breathing for a moment. It was slow but regular. From the smell of him she thought he must have drunk a great deal . . . and he was out of the habit. She thought it might be liquor as much as the crack on the head with the bottle that had put him out.

She picked up his legs and began to drag him along the floor. She had been married to him for nearly seven years, he had lain on top of her countless times – in the thousands – but she had never realized how heavy he was. Her breath whistled painfully in and out of her hurt throat. Nevertheless, she felt better than she had in days. She was alive. Having just brushed so close to death, that was precious. And Jack was alive, too. By blind luck rather than plan, they had perhaps found the only way that would bring them all safely out.

Panting harshly, she paused a moment, holding Jack's feet against her hips. The surroundings reminded her of the old seafaring captain's cry in *Treasure Island* after old blind Pew had passed him the Black Spot: *We'll do em yet!*

And then she remembered, uncomfortably, that the old sea-dog had dropped dead mere seconds later.

'Are you all right, Mommy? Is he . . . is he too heavy?'

'I'll manage.' She began to drag him again. Danny was beside

Jack. One of his hands had fallen off his chest, and Danny replaced it gently, with love.

'Are you sure, Mommy?'

'Yes. It's the best thing, Danny.'

'It's like putting him in jail.'

'Only for awhile.'

'Okay, then. Are you sure you can do it?'

'Yes.'

But it was a near thing, at that. Danny had been cradling his father's head when they went over the doorsills, but his hands slipped in Jack's greasy hair as they went into the kitchen. The back of his head struck the tiles, and Jack began to moan and stir.

'You got to use smoke,' Jack muttered quickly. 'Now run and get me that gascan.'

Wendy and Danny exchanged tight, fearful glances.

'Help me,' she said in a low voice.

For a moment Danny stood as if paralyzed by his father's face, and then he moved jerkily to her side and helped her hold the left leg. They dragged him across the kitchen floor in a nightmare kind of slow motion, the only sounds the faint, insectile buzz of the fluorescent lights and their own labored breathing.

When they reached the pantry, Wendy put Jack's feet down and turned to fumble with the bolt. Danny looked down at Jack, who was lying limp and relaxed again. The shirttail had pulled out of the back of his pants as they dragged him and Danny wondered if Daddy was too drunk to be cold. It seemed wrong to lock him in the pantry like a wild animal, but he had seen what he tried to do to Mommy. Even upstairs he had known Daddy was going to do that. He had heard them arguing in his head.

(*If only we could all be out of here. Or if it was a dream I was having, back in Stovington. If only.*)

The bolt was stuck.

Wendy pulled at it as hard as she could, but it wouldn't move. She couldn't retract the goddam bolt. It was stupid and unfair . . . she had opened it with no trouble at all when she had gone in to get the can of soup. Now it wouldn't move, and what was she going to do? They couldn't put him in the walk-in refrigerator; he would freeze or smother to death. But if they left him out and he woke up . . .

Jack stirred again on the floor.

'I'll take care of it,' he muttered. 'I understand.'

'He's waking up, Mommy!' Danny warned.

Sobbing now, she yanked at the bolt with both hands.

'Danny?' There was something softly menacing, if still blurry, in Jack's voice. 'That you, ole doc?'

'Just go to sleep, Daddy,' Danny said nervously. 'It's bedtime, you know.'

He looked up at his mother, still struggling with the bolt, and saw what was wrong immediately. She had forgotten to rotate the bolt before trying to withdraw it. The little catch was stuck in its notch.

'Here,' he said low, and brushed her trembling hands aside; his own were shaking almost as badly. He knocked the catch loose with the heel of his hand and the bolt drew back easily.

'Quick,' he said. He looked down. Jack's eyes had fluttered open again and this time Daddy was looking directly at him, his gaze strangely flat and speculative.

'You copied it,' Daddy told him. 'I know you did. But it's here somewhere. And I'll find it. That I promise you. I'll find it . . .' His words slurred off again.

Wendy pushed the pantry door open with her knee, hardly noticing the pungent odor of dried fruit that wafted out. She picked up Jack's feet again and dragged him in. She was gasping harshly now, at the limit of her strength. As she yanked the chain pull that turned on the light, Jack's eyes fluttered open again.

'What are you doing? Wendy? What are you doing?'

She stepped over him.

He was quick; amazingly quick. One hand lashed out and she had to sidestep and nearly fall out the door to avoid his grasp. Still, he had caught a handful of her bathrobe and there was a heavy purring noise as it ripped. He was up on his hands and knees now, his hair hanging in his eyes, like some heavy animal. A large dog . . . or a lion.

'Damn you both. I know what you want. But you're not going to get it. This hotel . . . it's mine. It's me they want. Me! Me!'

'The door, Danny!' she screamed. '*Shut the door!*'

He pushed the heavy wooden door shut with a slam, just as Jack leaped. The door latched and Jack thudded uselessly against it.

Danny's small hands groped at the bolt. Wendy was too far away to help; the issue of whether he would be locked in or free was going to be decided in two seconds. Danny missed his grip, found it again, and shot the bolt across just as the latch began to jiggle madly up and down below it. Then it stayed up and there was a series of thuds as Jack slammed his shoulder against the door. The bolt, a quarter inch of steel in diameter, showed no signs of loosening. Wendy let her breath out slowly.

'Let me out of here!' Jack raged. 'Let me out! Danny, doggone it, this is your father and I want to get out! *Now do what I tell you!*'

Danny's hand moved automatically toward the bolt. Wendy caught it and pressed it between her breasts.

'You mind your daddy, Danny! You do what I say! You do it or I'll give you a hiding you'll never forget. *Open this door or I'll bash your fucking brains in!*'

Danny looked at her, pale as window glass.

They could hear his breath tearing in and out behind the half inch of solid oak.

'Wendy, you let me out! Let me out right now! You cheap nickle-plated cold-cunt bitch! You let me out! I mean it! Let me out of here and I'll let it go! If you don't, I'll mess you up! I mean it! I'll mess you up so bad your own mother would pass you on the street! *Now open this door!*'

Danny moaned. Wendy looked at him and saw he was going to faint in a moment.

'Come on, doc,' she said, surprised at the calmness of her own voice. 'It's not your daddy talking, remember. It's the hotel.'

THE SHINING

'Come back here and let me out right NOW!' Jack screamed. There was a scraping, breaking sound as he attacked the inside of the door with his fingernails.

'It's the hotel,' Danny said. 'It's the hotel. I remember.' But he looked back over his shoulder and his face was crumpled and terrified.

CHAPTER FORTY-SEVEN
DANNY

It was three in the afternoon of a long, long day.

They were sitting on the big bed in their quarters. Danny was turning the purple VW model with the monster sticking out of the sun roof over and over in his hands, compulsively.

They had heard Daddy's batterings at the door all the way across the lobby, the batterings and his voice, hoarse and petulantly angry in a weak-king sort of a way, vomiting promises of punishment, vomiting profanity, promising both of them that they would live to regret betraying him after he had slaved his guts out for them over the years.

Danny thought they would no longer be able to hear it upstairs, but the sounds of his rage carried perfectly up the dumb-waiter shaft. Mommy's face was pale, and there were horrible brownish bruises on her neck where Daddy had tried to . . .

He turned the model over and over in his hands. Daddy's prize for having learned his reading lessons.

(. . . *where Daddy had tried to hug her too tight.*)

Mommy put some of her music on the little record player, scratchy and full of horns and flutes. She smiled at him tiredly. He tried to smile back and failed. Even with the volume turned up loud he thought he could still hear Daddy screaming at them and battering the pantry door like an animal in a zoo cage. What if Daddy had to go to the bathroom? What would he do then?

Danny began to cry.

Wendy turned the volume down on the record player at once, held him, rocked him on her lap.

'Danny, love, it will be all right. It will. If Mr Hallorann didn't get your message, someone else will. As soon as the storm is over. No one could get up here until then anyway. Mr Hallorann or anyone else. But when the storm is over, everything will be fine again. We'll leave here. And do you know what we'll do next spring? The three of us?'

Danny shook his head against her breasts. He didn't know. It seemed there could never be spring again.

'We'll go fishing. We'll rent a boat and go fishing, just like we did last year on Chatterton Lake. You and me and your daddy. And maybe you'll catch a bass for our supper. And maybe we won't catch anything, but we're sure to have a good time.'

'I love you, Mommy,' he said, and hugged her.

'Oh, Danny, I love you, too.'

Outside, the wind whooped and screamed.

★★★

Around four-thirty, just as the daylight began to fail, the screams ceased.

They had both been dozing uneasily, Wendy still holding Danny in her arms, and she didn't wake. But Danny did. Somehow the silence was worse, more ominous than the screams and the blows against the strong pantry door. Was Daddy asleep again? Or dead? Or what?

(*Did he get out?*)

Fifteen minutes later the silence was broken by a hard, grating, metallic rattle. There was a heavy grinding, then a mechanical humming. Wendy came awake with a cry.

The elevator was running again.

They listened to it, wide-eyed, hugging each other. It went from floor to floor, the grate rattling back, the brass door slamming open. There was laughter, drunken shouts, occasional screams, and the sounds of breakage.

The Overlook was coming to life around them.

CHAPTER FORTY-EIGHT
JACK

He sat on the floor of the pantry with his legs out in front of him, a box of Triscuit crackers between them, looking at the door. He was eating the crackers one by one, not tasting them, only eating them because he had to eat something. When he got out of here, he was going to need his strength. All of it.

At this precise instant, he thought he had never felt quite so miserable in his entire life. His mind and body together made up a large-writ scripture of pain. His head ached terribly, the sick throb of a hangover. The attendant symptoms were there, too: his mouth tasted like a manure rake had taken a swing through it, his ears rung, his heart had an extra-heavy, thudding beat, like a tom-tom. In addition, both shoulders ached fiercely from throwing himself against the door and his throat felt raw and peeled from useless shouting. He had cut his right hand on the doorlatch.

And when he got out of here, he was going to kick some ass.

He munched the Triscuits one by one, refusing to give in to his wretched stomach, which wanted to vomit up everything. He thought of the Excedrins in his pocket and decided to wait until his stomach had quieted a bit. No sense swallowing a painkiller if you were going to throw it right back up. Have to use your brain. The celebrated Jack Torrance brain. Aren't you the fellow who once was going to live by his wits? Jack Torrance, best-selling author. Jack Torrance, acclaimed playwright and winner of the New York Critics Circle Award. John Torrance, man of letters, esteemed thinker, winner of the Pulitzer Prize at seventy for his trenchant book of memoirs, *My Life in the Twentieth Century*. All any of that shit boiled down to was living by your wits.

Living by your wits is always knowing where the wasps are.

He put another Triscuit into his mouth and crunched it up.

What it really came down to, he supposed, was their lack of trust in him. Their failure to believe that he knew what was best for them and how to get it. His wife had tried to usurp him, first by fair

(sort of)

means, then by foul. When her little hints and whining objections had been overturned by his own well-reasoned arguments, she had turned his boy against him, tried to kill him with a bottle, and then had locked him, of all places, in the goddamned fucking *pantry*.

Still, a small interior voice nagged him.

(*Yes but where did the liquor come from? Isn't that really the central point? You know what happens when you drink, you know it from bitter experience. When you drink, you lose your wits.*)

He hurled the box of Triscuits across the small room. They struck a shelf of canned goods and fell to the floor. He looked at the box, wiped his lips with his hand, and then looked at his watch. It was almost six-thirty. He had been in here for hours. His wife had locked him in here and he'd been here for fucking *hours*.

He could begin to sympathize with his father.

The thing he'd never asked himself, Jack realized now, was exactly what had driven his daddy to drink in the first place. And really ... when you came right down to what his old students had been pleased to call the nitty-gritty ... hadn't it been the woman he was married to? A milksop sponge of a woman, always dragging silently around the house with an expression of doomed martyrdom on her face? A ball and chain around Daddy's ankle? No, not ball and chain. She had never actively tried to make Daddy a prisoner, the way Wendy had done to him. For Jack's father it must have been more like the fate of McTeague the dentist at the end of Frank Norris's great novel: handcuffed to a dead man in the wasteland. Yes, that was better. Mentally and spiritually dead, his mother had been handcuffed to his father by matrimony. Still, Daddy had tried to do right as he dragged her rotting corpse through life. He had tried to bring the four children up to know right from wrong, to understand discipline, and above all, to respect their father.

Well, they had been ingrates, all of them, himself included. And now he was paying the price; his own son had turned out to be an ingrate, too. But there was hope. He would get out of here somehow. He would chastise them both, and harshly. He would set Danny an example, so that the day might come when Danny was grown, a day when Danny would know what to do better than he himself had known.

He remembered the Sunday dinner when his father had caned his mother at the table . . . how horrified he and the others had been. Now he could see how necessary that had been, how his father had only been feigning drunkenness, how his wits had been sharp and alive underneath all along, watching for the slightest sign of disrespect.

Jack crawled after the Triscuits and began to eat them again, sitting by the door she had so treacherously bolted. He wondered exactly what his father had seen, and how he had caught her out by his playacting. Had she been sneering at him behind her hand? Sticking her tongue out? Making obscene finger gestures? Or only looking at him insolently and arrogantly, convinced that he was too stupidly drunk to see? Whatever it had been, he had caught her at it, and he had chastised her sharply. And now, twenty years later, he could finally appreciate Daddy's wisdom.

Of course you could say Daddy had been foolish to marry such a woman, to have handcuffed himself to that corpse in the first place . . . and a disrespectful corpse at that. But when the young marry in haste they must repent in leisure, and perhaps Daddy's daddy had married the same type of woman, so that unconsciously Jack's daddy had also married one, as Jack himself had. Except that *his* wife, instead of being satisfied with the passive role of having wrecked one career and crippled another, had opted for the poisonously active task of trying to destroy his last and best chance: to become a member of the Overlook's staff, and possibly to rise . . . all the way to the position of manager, in time. She was trying to deny him Danny, and

Danny was his ticket of admission. That was foolish, of course – why would they want the son when they could have the father? – but employers often had foolish ideas and that was the condition that had been made.

He wasn't going to be able to reason with her, he could see that now. He had tried to reason with her in the Colorado Lounge, and she had refused to listen, had hit him over the head with a bottle for his pains. But there would be another time, and soon. He would get out of here.

He suddenly held his breath and cocked his head. Somewhere a piano was playing boogie-woogie and people were laughing and clapping along. The sound was muffled through the heavy wooden door, but audible. The song was 'There'll Be a Hot Time in the Old Town Tonight'.

His hands curled helplessly into fists; he had to restrain himself from battering at the door with them. The party had begun again. The liquor would be flowing freely. Somewhere, dancing with someone else, would be the girl who had felt so maddeningly nude under her white silk gown.

'You'll pay for this!' he howled. 'Goddam you two, you'll pay! You'll take your goddam medicine for this, I promise you! You—'

'Here, here, now,' a mild voice said just outside the door. 'No need to shout, old fellow. I can hear you perfectly well.'

Jack lurched to his feet.

'Grady? Is that you?'

'Yes, sir. Indeed it is. You appear to have been locked in.'

'Let me out, Grady. Quickly.'

'I see you can hardly have taken care of the business we discussed, sir. The correction of your wife and son.'

'They're the ones who locked me in. Pull the bolt, for God's sake!'

'You let them lock you in?' Grady's voice registered well-bred surprise. 'Oh, dear. A woman half your size and a little boy? Hardly sets you off as being top managerial timber, does it?'

A pulse began to beat in the clockspring of veins at Jack's right temple. 'Let me out, Grady. I'll take care of them.'

'Will you indeed, sir? I wonder.' Well-bred surprise was replaced by well-bred regret. 'I'm pained to say that I doubt it. I – and others – have really come to believe that your heart is not in this, sir. That you haven't the . . . the belly for it.'

'*I do!*' Jack shouted. '*I do, I swear it!*'

'You would bring us your son?'

'Yes! Yes!'

'Your wife would object to that very strongly, Mr Torrance. And she appears to be . . . somewhat stronger than we had imagined. Somewhat more resourceful. She certainly seems to have gotten the better of *you*.'

Grady tittered.

'Perhaps, Mr Torrance, we should have been dealing with her all along.'

'I'll bring him, I swear it,' Jack said. His face was against the door now. He was sweating. 'She won't object. I swear she won't. She won't be able to.'

'You would have to kill her, I fear,' Grady said coldly.

'I'll do what I have to do. Just *let me out*.'

'You'll give your word on it, sir?' Grady persisted.

'My word, my promise, my sacred vow, whatever in hell you want. If you—'

There was a flat snap as the bolt was drawn back. The door shivered open a quarter of an inch. Jack's words and breath halted. For a moment he felt that death itself was outside the door.

The feeling passed.

He whispered: 'Thank you, Grady. I swear you won't regret it. I swear you won't.'

There was no answer. He became aware that all sounds had stopped except for the cold swooping of the wind outside.

He pushed the pantry door open; the hinges squealed faintly.

The kitchen was empty. Grady was gone. Everything was still and frozen beneath the cold white glare of the fluorescent bars. His eyes caught on the large chopping block where the three of them had eaten their meals.

Standing on top of it was a martini glass, a fifth of gin, and a plastic dish filled with olives.

Leaning against it was one of the roque mallets from the equipment shed.

He looked at it for a long time.

Then a voice, much deeper and much more powerful than Grady's, spoke from somewhere, everywhere ... from inside him.

(Keep your promise, Mr Torrance.)

'I will,' he said. He heard the fawning servility in his own voice but was unable to control it. 'I will.'

He walked to the chopping block and put his hand on the handle of the mallet.

He hefted it.

Swung it.

It hissed viciously through the air.

Jack Torrance began to smile.

CHAPTER FORTY-NINE
HALLORANN, GOING UP
THE COUNTRY

It was quarter of two in the afternoon and according to the snow-clotted signs and the Hertz Buick's odometer, he was less than three miles from Estes Park when he finally went off the road.

In the hills, the snow was falling faster and more furiously than Hallorann had ever seen (which was, perhaps, not to say a great deal, since Hallorann had seen as little snow as he could manage in his lifetime), and the wind was blowing a capricious gale – now from the west, now backing around to the north, sending clouds of powdery snow across his field of vision, making him coldly aware again and again that if he missed a turn he might well plunge two hundred feet off the road, the Electra cartwheeling ass over teapot as it went down. Making it worse was his own amateur status as a winter driver. It scared him to have the yellow center line buried under swirling, drifting snow, and it scared him when the heavy gusts of wind came unimpeded through the notches in the hills and actually made the heavy Buick slew around. It scared him that the road information signs were mostly masked with snow and you could flip a coin as to whether the road was going to break right or left up ahead in the white drive-in movie screen he seemed to be driving through. He was scared, all right. He had driven in a cold sweat since climbing into the hills west of Boulder and Lyons, handling the accelerator and brake as if they were Ming vases. Between rock 'n' roll tunes on the radio, the disc jockey constantly adjured motorists to stay off the main highways and under no conditions to go into the mountains, because many roads were impassable and all of them were dangerous. Scores of minor accidents had been reported, and two serious ones: a party of skiers in a VW microbus and a family that had been bound for Albuquerque through the Sangre de Cristo Mountains. The combined score on both was four dead and five wounded. 'So stay off those roads and get into the good music here at KTLK,' the jock concluded cheerily, and then compounded Hallorann's misery by playing 'Seasons in the Sun'. 'We had joy, we had fun, we had—' Terry Jacks gibbered happily, and Hallorann snapped the radio off viciously, knowing he would have it back on in five minutes. No matter how bad it was, it was better than riding alone through this white madness.

(Admit it. Dis heah black boy has got at least one long stripe of yaller . . . and it runs raht up his ebberlubbin back!)

It wasn't even funny. He would have backed off before he even cleared Boulder if it hadn't been for his compulsion that the boy was in terrible trouble. Even now a small voice in the back of his skull – more the voice of reason than of cowardice, he thought – was telling him to hole up in an Estes Park motel for the night and wait for the plows to at least expose the center stripe again. That voice kept reminding him of the jet's shaky landing at Stapleton, of that sinking feeling that it was going to come in nose-first, delivering its passengers to the gates of hell rather than at Gate 39, Concourse B. But reason would not stand against the compulsion. It had to be today. The snowstorm was his own bad luck. He would have to cope with it. He was afraid that if he didn't, he might have something much worse to cope with in his dreams.

The wind gusted again, this time from the northeast, a little English on the ball if you please, and he was again cut off from the vague shapes of the hills and even from the embankments on either side of the road. He was driving through white null.

And then the high sodium lights of the snowplow loomed out of the soup, bearing down, and to his horror he saw that instead of being to one side, the Buick's nose was pointed directly between those headlamps. The plow was being none too choosy about keeping its own side of the road, and Hallorann had allowed the Buick to drift.

The grinding roar of the plow's diesel engine intruded over

the bellow of the wind, and then the sound of its airhorn, hard, long, almost deafening.

Halloran's testicles turned into two small wrinkled sacs filled with shaved ice. His guts seemed to have been transformed into a large mass of Silly Putty.

Color was materializing out of the white now, snow-clotted orange. He could see the high cab, even the gesticulating figure of the driver behind the single long wiper blade. He could see the V shape of the plow's wing blades, spewing more snow up onto the road's left-hand embankment like pallid, smoking exhaust.

WHAAAAAAAAA! the airhorn bellowed indignantly.

He squeezed the accelerator like the breast of a much-loved woman and the Buick scooted forward and toward the right. There was no embankment over here; the plows headed up instead of down had only to push the snow directly over the drop.

(*The drop, ah yes, the drop*—)

The wingblades on Hallorann's left, fully four feet higher than the Electra's roof, flirted by with no more than an inch or two to spare. Until the plow had actually cleared him, Hallorann had thought a crash inevitable. A prayer which was half an inarticulate apology to the boy flitted through his mind like a torn rag.

Then the plow was past, its revolving blue lights glinting and flashing in Hallorann's rearview mirror.

He jockeyed the Buick's steering wheel back to the left, but nothing doing. The scoot had turned into a skid, and the Buick was floating dreamily toward the lip of the drop, spuming snow from under its mudguards.

He flicked the wheel back the other way, in the skid's direction, and the car's front and rear began to swap places. Panicked now, he pumped the brake hard, and then felt a hard bump. In front of him the road was gone . . . he was looking into a bottomless chasm of swirling snow and vague greenish-gray pines far away and far below.

(*I'm going holy mother of Jesus I'm going off*)

And that was where the car stopped, canting forward at a

thirty-degree angle, the left fender jammed against a guardrail, the rear wheels nearly off the ground. When Hallorann tried reverse, the wheels only spun helplessly. His heart was doing a Gene Krupa drumroll.

He got out – very carefully he got out – and went around to the Buick's back deck.

He was standing there, looking at the back wheels helplessly, when a cheerful voice behind him said: 'Hello there, fella. You must be shit right out of your mind.'

He turned around and saw the plow forty yards further down the road, obscured in the blowing snow except for the raftered dark brown streak of its exhaust and the revolving blue lights on top. The driver was standing just behind him, dressed in a long sheepskin coat and a slicker over it. A blue-and-white pinstriped engineer's cap was perched on his head, and Hallorann could hardly believe it was staying on in the teeth of the wind.

(*Glue. It sure-God must be glue.*)

'Hi,' he said. 'Can you pull me back onto the road?'

'Oh, I guess I could,' the plow driver said. 'What the hell you doing way up here, mister? Good way to kill your ass.'

'Urgent business.'

'Nothin is that urgent,' the plow driver said slowly and kindly, as if speaking to a mental defective. 'If you'd'a hit that post a leetle mite harder, nobody woulda got you out till All Fools' Day. Don't come from these parts, do you?'

'No. And I wouldn't be here unless my business was as urgent as I say.'

'That so?' The driver shifted his stance companionably as if they were having a desultory chat on the back steps instead of standing in a blizzard halfway between hoot and holler, with Hallorann's car balanced three hundred feet above the tops of the trees below.

'Where you headed? Estes?'

'No, a place called the Overlook Hotel,' Hallorann said. 'It's a little way above Sidewinder—'

But the driver was shaking his head dolefully.

'I guess I know well enough where that is,' he said. 'Mister, you'll never get up to the old Overlook. Roads between Estes Park and Sidewinder is bloody damn hell. It's driftin in right behind us no matter how hard we push. I come through drifts a few miles back that was damn near six feet through the middle. And even if you could make Sidewinder, why, the road's closed from there all the way across to Buckland, Utah. Nope.' He shook his head. 'Never make it, mister. Never make it at all.'

'I have to try,' Hallorann said, calling on his last reserves of patience to keep his voice normal. 'There's a boy up there —'

'*Boy?* Naw. The Overlook closes down at the last end of September. No percentage keepin it open longer. Too many shit-storms like this.'

'He's the son of the caretaker. He's in trouble.'

'How would you know that?'

His patience snapped.

'For Christ's sake are you going to stand there and flap y'jaw at me the rest of the day? *I know, I know!* Now are you going to pull me back on the road or not?'

'Kind of testy, aren't you?' the driver observed, not particularly perturbed. 'Sure, get back in there. I got a chain behind the seat.'

Hallorann got back behind the wheel, beginning to shake with delayed reaction now. His hands were numbed almost clear through. He had forgotten to bring gloves.

The plow backed up to the rear of the Buick, and he saw the driver get out with a long coil of chain. Hallorann opened the door and shouted: 'What can I do to help?'

'Stay out of the way, is all,' the driver shouted back. 'This ain't gonna take a blink.'

Which was true. A shudder ran through the Buick's frame as the chain pulled tight, and a second later it was back on the road, pointed more or less toward Estes Park. The plow driver walked up beside the window and knocked on the safety glass. Hallorann rolled down the window.

'Thanks,' he said. 'I'm sorry I shouted at you.'

'I been shouted at before,' the driver said with a grin. 'I guess you're sorta strung up. You take these.' A pair of bulky blue mittens dropped into Hallorann's lap. 'You'll need em when you go off the road again, I guess. Cold out. You wear em unless you want to spend the rest of your life pickin your nose with a crochetin hook. And you send em back. My wife knitted em and I'm partial to em. Name and address is sewed right into the linin. I'm Howard Cottrell, by the way. You just send em back when you don't need em anymore. And I don't want to have to go payin no postage due, mind.'

'All right,' Hallorann said. 'Thanks. One hell of a lot.'

'You be careful. I'd take you myself, but I'm busy as a cat in a mess of guitar strings.'

'That's okay. Thanks again.'

He started to roll up the window, but Cottrell stopped him.

'When you get to Sidewinder — *if* you get to Sidewinder — you go to Durkin's Conoco. It's right next to the li'brey. Can't miss it. You ask for Larry Durkin. Tell him Howie Cottrell sent you and you want to rent one of his snowmobiles. You mention my name and show those mittens, you'll get the cut rate.'

'Thanks again,' Hallorann said.

Cottrell nodded. 'It's funny. Ain't no way you could know someone's in trouble up there at the Overlook . . . the phone's out, sure as hell. But I believe you. Sometimes I get feelins.'

Hallorann nodded. 'Sometimes I do, too.'

'Yeah. I know you do. But you take care.'

'I will.'

Cottrell disappeared into the blowing dimness with a final wave, his engineer cap still mounted perkily on his head. Hallorann got going again, the chains flailing at the snowcover on the road, finally digging in enough to start the Buick moving. Behind him, Howard Cottrell gave a final good-luck blast on his plow's airhorn, although it was really unnecessary; Hallorann could feel him wishing him good luck.

That's two shines in one day, he thought, and that ought to be some kind of good omen. But he distrusted omens, good or bad. And meeting two people with the shine in one day (when he usually didn't run across more than four or five in the course of a year) might not mean anything. That feeling of finality, a feeling

(*like things are all wrapped up*)

he could not completely define was still very much with him. It was—

The Buick wanted to skid sideways around a tight curve and Hallorann jockeyed it carefully, hardly daring to breathe. He turned on the radio again and it was Aretha, and Aretha was just fine. He'd share his Hertz Buick with her any day.

Another gust of wind struck the car, making it rock and slip around. Hallorann cursed it and hunched more closely over the wheel. Aretha finished her song and then the jock was on again, telling him that driving today was a good way to get killed.

Hallorann snapped the radio off.

★★★

He did make it to Sidewinder, although he was four and half hours on the road between Estes Park and there. By the time he got to the Upland Highway it was full dark, but the snowstorm showed no sign of abating. Twice he'd had to stop in front of drifts that were as high as his car's hood and wait for the plows to come along and knock holes in them. At one of the drifts the plow had come up on his side of the road and there had been another close call. The driver had merely swung around his car, not getting out to chew the fat, but he did deliver one of the two finger gestures that all Americans above the age of ten recognize, and it was not the peace sign.

It seemed that as he drew closer to the Overlook, his need to hurry became more and more compulsive. He found himself glancing at his wristwatch almost constantly. The hands seemed to be flying along.

Ten minutes after he had turned onto the Upland, he passed two signs. The whooping wind had cleared both of their snow pack so he was able to read them. SIDEWINDER 10, the first said. The second: ROAD CLOSED 12 MILES AHEAD DURING WINTER MONTHS.

'Larry Durkin,' Hallorann muttered to himself. His dark face was strained and tense in the muted green glow of the dashboard instruments. It was ten after six. 'The Conoco by the library. Larry—'

And that was when it struck him full-force, the smell

of oranges and the thought-force, heavy and hateful, murderous:

(*GET OUT OF HERE YOU DIRTY NIGGER THIS IS NONE OF YOUR BUSINESS YOU NIGGER TURN AROUND TURN AROUND OR WE'LL KILL YOU HANG YOU UP FROM A TREE LIMB YOU FUCKING JUNGLE-BUNNY COON AND THEN BURN THE BODY THAT'S WHAT WE DO WITH NIGGERS SO TURN AROUND RIGHT NOW*)

Hallorann screamed in the close confines of the car. The message did not come to him in words but in a series of rebuslike images that were slammed into his head with terrific force. He took his hands from the steering wheel to blot the pictures out.

Then the car smashed broadside into one of the embankments, rebounded, slewed halfway around, and came to a stop. The rear wheels spun uselessly.

Hallorann snapped the gearshift into park, and then covered his face with his hands. He did not precisely cry; what escaped him was an uneven huh-huh-huh sound. His chest heaved. He knew that if that blast had taken him on a stretch of road with a dropoff on one side or the other, he might well be dead now. Maybe that had been the idea. And it might hit him again, at any time. He would have to protect against it. He was surrounded by a red force of immense power that might have been memory. He was drowning in instinct.

He took his hands away from his face and opened his eyes cautiously. Nothing. If there was something trying to scare him again, it wasn't getting through. He was closed off.

Had that happened to the boy? Dear God, had that happened to the little boy?

And of all the images, the one that bothered him the most was that dull whacking sound, like a hammer splatting into thick cheese. What did that mean?

(*Jesus, not that little boy. Jesus, please.*)

He dropped the gearshift lever into low range and fed the engine gas a little at a time. The wheels spun, caught, spun, and caught again. The Buick began to move, its headlights cutting weakly through the swirling snow. He looked at his watch. Almost six-thirty now. And he was beginning to feel that was very late indeed.

CHAPTER FIFTY
REDRUM

Wendy Torrance stood indecisive in the middle of the bedroom, looking at her son, who had fallen fast asleep.

Half an hour ago the sounds had ceased. All of them, all at once. The elevator, the party, the sound of room doors opening and closing. Instead of easing her mind it made the tension that had been building in her even worse; it was like a malefic hush before the storm's final brutal push. But Danny had dozed off almost at once; first into a light, twitching doze, and in the last ten minutes or so a heavier sleep. Even looking directly at him she could barely see the slow rise and fall of his narrow chest.

She wondered when he had last gotten a full night's sleep, one without tormenting dreams or long periods of dark wakefulness, listening to revels that had only become audible − and visible − to her in the last couple of days, as the Overlook's grip on the three of them tightened.

(Real psychic phenomena or group hypnosis?)

She didn't know, and didn't think it mattered. What had been happening was just as deadly either way. She looked at Danny and thought

(God grant he lie still)

that if he was undisturbed, he might sleep the rest of the night through. Whatever talent he had, he was still a small boy and he needed his rest.

It was Jack she had begun to worry about.

She grimaced with sudden pain, took her hand away from her mouth, and saw she had torn off one of her fingernails. And her nails were one thing she'd always tried to keep nice. They weren't long enough to be called hooks, but still nicely shaped and

435

(and what are you worrying about your fingernails for?)

She laughed a little, but it was a shaky sound, without amusement.

First Jack had stopped howling and battering at the door. Then the party had begun again.

(or did it ever stop? did it sometimes just drift into a slightly different angle of time where they weren't meant to hear it?)

counterpointed by the crashing, banging elevator. Then that had stopped. In that new silence, as Danny had been falling asleep, she had fancied she heard low, conspiratorial voices coming from the kitchen almost directly below them. At first she had dismissed it as the wind, which could mimic many different human vocal ranges, from a papery deathbed whisper around the doors and window frames to a full-out scream around the eaves ... the sound of a woman fleeing a murderer in a cheap melodrama. Yet, sitting stiffly beside Danny, the idea that it was indeed voices became more and more convincing.

Jack and someone else, discussing his escape from the pantry.

Discussing the murder of his wife and son.

It would be nothing new inside these walls; murder had been done here before.

She had gone to the heating vent and had placed her ear against it, but at that exact moment the furnace had come on, and any sound was lost in the rush of warm air coming up from the basement. When the furnace had kicked off again, five minutes ago, the place was completely silent except for the wind, the gritty spatter of snow against the building, and the occasional groan of a board.

She looked down at her ripped fingernail. Small beads of blood were oozing up from beneath it.

(Jack's gotten out.)

(Don't talk nonsense.)

(Yes, he's out. He's gotten a knife from the kitchen or maybe the meat cleaver. He's on his way up here right now, walking along the sides of the risers so the stairs won't creak.)

(! You're insane !)

Her lips were trembling, and for a moment it seemed

that she must have cried the words out loud. But the silence held.

She felt watched.

She whirled around and stared at the night-blackened window, and a hideous white face with circles of darkness for eyes was gibbering in at her, the face of a monstrous lunatic that had been hiding in these groaning walls all along—

It was only a pattern of frost on the outside of the glass.

She let her breath out in a long, susurrating whisper of fear, and it seemed to her that she heard, quite clearly this time, amused titters from somewhere.

(You're jumping at shadows. It's bad enough without that. By tomorrow morning, you'll be ready for the rubber room.)

There was only one way to allay those fears and she knew what it was.

She would have to go down and make sure Jack was still in the pantry.

Very simple. Go downstairs. Have a peek. Come back up. Oh, by the way, stop and grab the tray on the registration counter. The omelet would be a washout, but the soup could be reheated on the hotplate by Jack's typewriter.

(Oh yes and don't get killed if he's down there with a knife.)

She walked to the dresser, trying to shake off the mantle of fear that lay on her. Scattered across the dresser's top was a pile of change, a stack of gasoline chits for the hotel truck, the two pipes Jack brought with him everywhere but rarely smoked . . . and his keyring.

She picked it up, held it in her hand for a moment, and then put it back down. The idea of locking the bedroom door behind her had occurred, but it just didn't appeal. Danny was asleep. Vague thoughts of fire passed through her mind, and something else nibbled more strongly, but she let it go.

Wendy crossed the room, stood indecisively by the door for a moment, then took the knife from the pocket of her robe and curled her right hand around the wooden shaft.

She pulled the door open.

The short corridor leading to their quarters was bare. The electric wall flambeaux all shone brightly at their regular intervals, showing off the rug's blue background and sinuous, weaving pattern.

(*See? No boogies here.*)

(*No, of course not. They want you out. They want you to do something silly and womanish, and that is exactly what you are doing.*)

She hesitated again, miserably caught, not wanting to leave Danny and the safety of the apartment and at the same time needing badly to reassure herself that Jack *was* still . . . safely packed away.

(*Of course he is.*)

(*But the voices*)

(*There were no voices. It was your imagination. It was the wind.*)

'It wasn't the wind.'

The sound of her own voice made her jump. But the deadly certainty in it made her go forward. The knife swung by her side, catching angles of light and throwing them on the silk wallpaper. Her slippers whispered against the carpet's nap. Her nerves were singing like wires.

She reached the corner of the main corridor and peered around, her mind stiffened for whatever she might see there.

There was nothing to see.

After a moment's hesitation she rounded the corner and began down the main corridor. Each step toward the shadowy stairwell increased her dread and made her aware that she was leaving her sleeping son behind, alone and unprotected. The sound of her slippers against the carpet seemed louder and louder in her ears; twice she looked back over her shoulder to convince herself that someone wasn't creeping up behind her.

She reached the stairwell and put her hand on the cold newel post at the top of the railing. There were nineteen wide steps down to the lobby. She had counted them enough times to know. Nineteen carpeted stair risers, and nary a Jack crouching on any one of them. Of course not. Jack was locked in the pantry behind a hefty steel bolt and a thick wooden door.

But the lobby was dark and oh so full of shadows.

Her pulse thudded steadily and deeply in her throat.

Ahead and slightly to the left, the brass yaw of the elevator stood mockingly open, inviting her to step in and take the ride of her life.

(*No thank you*)

The inside of the car had been draped with pink and white crepe streamers. Confetti had burst from two tubular party favors. Lying in the rear left corner was an empty bottle of champagne.

She sensed movement above her and wheeled to look up the nineteen steps leading to the dark second-floor landing and saw nothing; yet there was a disturbing corner-of-the-eye sensation that things

(*things*)

had leaped back into the deeper darkness of the hallway up there just before her eyes could register them.

She looked down the stairs again.

Her right hand was sweating against the wooden handle of the knife; she switched it to her left, wiped her right palm against the pink terrycloth of her robe, and switched the knife back. Almost unaware that her mind had given her body the command to go forward, she began down the stairs, left foot then right, left foot then right, her free hand trailing lightly on the banister.

(*Where's the party? Don't let me scare you away, you bunch of moldy sheets! Not one scared woman with a knife! Let's have a little music around here! Let's heave a little life!*)

Ten steps down, a dozen, a baker's dozen.

The light from the first-floor hall filtered a dull yellow down here, and she remembered that she would have to turn on the lobby lights either beside the entrance to the dining room or inside the manager's office.

Yet there was light coming from somewhere else, white and muted.

The fluorescents, of course. In the kitchen.

She paused on the thirteenth step, trying to remember if she had turned them off or left them on when she and Danny left. She simply couldn't remember.

Below her, in the lobby, highbacked chairs hulked in pools

of shadow. The glass in the lobby doors was pressed white with a uniform blanket of drifted snow. Brass studs in the sofa cushions gleamed faintly like cat's eyes. There were a hundred places to hide.

Her legs stilted with fear, she continued down.

Now seventeen, now eighteen, now nineteen.

(*Lobby level, madam. Step out carefully.*)

The ballroom doors were thrown wide, only blackness spilling out. From within came a steady ticking, like a bomb. She stiffened, then remembered the clock on the mantel, the clock under glass. Jack or Danny must have wound it . . . or maybe it had wound itself up, like everything else in the Overlook.

She turned toward the reception desk, meaning to go through the gate and the manager's office and into the kitchen. Gleaming dull silver, she could see the intended lunch tray.

Then the clock began to strike, little tinkling notes.

Wendy stiffened, her tongue rising to the roof of her mouth. Then she relaxed. It was striking eight, that was all. Eight o'clock

. . . *five, six, seven* . . .

She counted the strokes. It suddenly seemed wrong to move again until the clock had stilled.

. . . *eight . . . nine* . . .

(?? *Nine* ??)

. . . *ten . . . eleven* . . .

Suddenly, belatedly, it came to her. She turned back clumsily for the stairs, knowing already she was too late. But how could she have known?

Twelve.

All the lights in the ballroom went on. There was a huge, shrieking flourish of brass. Wendy screamed aloud, the sound of her cry insignificant against the blare issuing from those brazen lungs.

'*Unmask!*' the cry echoed. '*Unmask! Unmask!*'

Then they faded, as if down a long corridor of time, leaving her alone again.

No, not alone.

She turned and he was coming for her.

It was Jack and yet not Jack. His eyes were lit with a vacant, murderous glow; his familiar mouth now wore a quivering, joyless grin.

He had the roque mallet in one hand.

'Thought you'd lock me in? Is that what you thought you'd do?'

The mallet whistled through the air. She stepped backward, tripped over a hassock, fell to the lobby rug.

'Jack—'

'You bitch,' he whispered. 'I know what you are.'

The mallet came down again with whistling, deadly velocity and buried itself in her soft stomach. She screamed, suddenly submerged in an ocean of pain. Dimly she saw the mallet rebound. It came to her with sudden numbing reality that he meant to beat her to death with the mallet he held in his hands.

She tried to cry out to him again, to beg him to stop for Danny's sake, but her breath had been knocked loose. She could only force out a weak whimper, hardly a sound at all.

'Now. Now, by Christ,' he said, grinning. He kicked the hassock out of his way. 'I guess you'll take your medicine now.'

The mallet whickered down. Wendy rolled to her left, her robe tangling above her knees. Jack's hold on the mallet was jarred loose when it hit the floor. He had to stoop and pick it up, and while he did she ran for the stairs, the breath at last sobbing back into her. Her stomach was a bruise of throbbing pain.

'Bitch,' he said through his grin, and began to come after her. 'You stinking bitch, I guess you'll get what's coming to you. I guess you will.'

She heard the mallet whistle through the air and then agony exploded on her right side as the mallet-head took her just below the line of her breasts, breaking two ribs. She fell forward on the steps and new agony ripped her as she struck on the wounded side. Yet instinct made her roll over, roll away, and the mallet whizzed past the side of her face, missing by a naked inch. It struck the deep pile of the stair carpeting with a muffled thud. That was when she saw the knife, which had been jarred out of her hand by her fall. It lay glittering on the fourth stair riser.

'Bitch,' he repeated. The mallet came down. She shoved herself upward and it landed just below her kneecap. Her lower leg was suddenly on fire. Blood began to trickle down her calf. And then the mallet was coming down again. She jerked her head away from it and it smashed into the stair riser in the hollow between her neck and shoulder, scraping away the flesh from her ear.

He brought the mallet down again and this time she rolled toward him, down the stairs, inside the arc of his swing. A shriek escaped her as her broken ribs thumped and grated. She struck his shins with her body while he was offbalance and he fell backward with a yell of anger and surprise, his feet jigging to keep their purchase on the stair riser. Then he thumped to the floor, the mallet flying from his hand. He sat up, staring at her for a moment with shocked eyes.

'I'll kill you for that,' he said.

He rolled over and stretched out for the handle of the mallet. Wendy forced herself to her feet. Her left leg sent bolt after bolt of pain all the way up to her hip. Her face was ashy pale but set. She leaped onto his back as his hand closed over the shaft of the roque mallet.

'*Oh dear God!*' she screamed to the Overlook's shadowy lobby, and buried the kitchen knife in his lower back up to the handle.

He stiffened beneath her and then shrieked. She thought she had never heard such an awful sound in her whole life; it was as if the very boards and windows and doors of the hotel had screamed. It seemed to go on and on while he remained board-stiff beneath her weight. They were like a parlor charade of horse and rider. Except that the back of his red-and-black-checked flannel shirt was growing darker, sodden, with spreading blood.

Then he collapsed forward on his face, bucking her off on her hurt side, making her groan.

She lay breathing harshly for a time, unable to move. She was an excruciating throb of pain from one end to the other. Every time she inhaled, something stabbed viciously at her, and her neck was wet with blood from her grazed ear.

There was only the sound of her struggle to breathe, the wind, and the ticking clock in the ballroom.

At last she forced herself to her feet and hobbled across to the stairway. When she got there she clung to the newel post, head down, waves of faintness washing over her. When it had passed a little, she began to climb, using her unhurt leg and pulling with her arms on the banister. Once she looked up, expecting to see Danny there, but the stairway was empty.

(*Thank God he slept through it thank God thank God*)

Six steps up she had to rest, her head down, her blond hair coiled on and over the banister. Air whistled painfully through her throat, as if it had grown barbs. Her right side was a swollen, hot mass.

(*Come on Wendy come on old girl get a locked door behind you and then look at the damage thirteen more to go not so bad. And when you get to the upstairs corridor you can crawl. I give my permission.*)

She drew in as much breath as her broken ribs would allow and half-pulled, half-fell up another riser. And another.

She was on the ninth, almost halfway up, when Jack's voice came from behind and below her. He said thickly: 'You bitch. You killed me.'

Terror as black as midnight swept through her. She looked over her shoulder and saw Jack getting slowly to his feet.

His back was bowed over, and she could see the handle of the kitchen knife sticking out of it. His eyes seemed to have contracted, almost to have lost themselves in the pale, sagging folds of the skin around them. He was grasping the roque mallet loosely in his left hand. The end of it was bloody. A scrap of her pink terrycloth robe stuck almost in the center.

'I'll give you your medicine,' he whispered, and began to stagger toward the stairs.

Whimpering with fear, she began to pull herself upward again. Ten steps, a dozen, a baker's dozen. But still the first-floor hallway looked as far above her as an unattainable mountain peak. She was panting now, her side shrieking in protest. Her hair swung wildly back and forth in front of her face. Sweat stung her eyes. The ticking of the domed clock in the ballroom seemed to fill her ears, and counterpointing it, Jack's panting, agonized gasps as he began to mount the stairs.

CHAPTER FIFTY-ONE
HALLORANN ARRIVES

Larry Durkin was a tall and skinny man with a morose face overtopped with a luxuriant mane of red hair. Hallorann had caught him just as he was leaving the Conoco station, the morose face buried deeply inside an army-issue parka. He was reluctant to do any more business that stormy day no matter how far Hallorann had come, and even more reluctant to rent one of his two snowmobiles out to this wild-eyed black man who insisted on going up to the old Overlook. Among people who had spent most of their lives in the little town of Sidewinder, the hotel had a smelly reputation. Murder had been done up there. A bunch of hoods had run the place for a while, and cut-throat businessmen had run it for a while, too. And things had been done up at the old Overlook that never made the papers, because money has a way of talking. But the people in Sidewinder had a pretty good idea. Most of the hotel's chambermaids came from here, and chambermaids see a lot.

But when Hallorann mentioned Howard Cottrell's name and showed Durkin the tag inside one of the blue mittens, the gas station owner thawed.

'Sent you here, did he?' Durkin asked, unlocking one of the garage bays and leading Hallorann inside. 'Good to know the old rip's got some sense left. I thought he was plumb out of it.' He flicked a switch and a bank of very old and very dirty fluorescents buzzed wearily into life. 'Now what in the tarnal creation would you want up at that place, fella?'

Hallorann's nerve had begun to crack. The last few miles into Sidewinder had been very bad. Once a gust of wind that must have been tooling along at better than sixty miles an hour had floated the Buick all the way around in a 360° turn. And there were still miles to travel with God alone knew what at the other end of them. He was terrified for the boy. Now it was almost ten minutes to seven and he had this whole song and dance to go through again.

'Somebody is in trouble up there,' he said very carefully. 'The son of the caretaker.'

'Who? Torrance's boy? Now what kind of trouble could he be in?'

'I don't know,' Hallorann muttered. He felt sick with the time this was taking. He was speaking with a country man, and he knew that all country men feel a similar need to approach their business obliquely, to smell around its corners and sides before plunging into the middle of dealing. But there was no time, because now he was one scared nigger and if this went on much longer he just might decide to cut and run.

'Look,' he said. 'Please. I need to go up there and I have to have a snowmobile to get there. I'll pay your price, but for God's sake let me get on with my business!'

'All right,' Durkin said, unperturbed. 'If Howard sent you, that's good enough. You take this ArcticCat. I'll put five gallons of gas in the can. Tank's full. She'll get you up and back down, I guess.'

'Thank you,' Hallorann said, not quite steadily.

'I'll take twenty dollars. That includes the ethyl.'

Hallorann fumbled a twenty out of his wallet and handed it over. Durkin tucked it into one of his shirt pockets with hardly a look.

'Guess maybe we better trade jackets, too,' Durkin said, pulling off his parka. 'That overcoat of yours ain't gonna be worth nothin tonight. You trade me back when you return the snow-sled.'

'Oh, hey, I couldn't—'

'Don't fuss with me,' Durkin interrupted, still mildly. 'I ain't sending you out to freeze. I only got to walk down two blocks and I'm at my own supper table. Give it over.'

Slightly dazed, Hallorann traded his overcoat for Durkin's fur-lined parka. Overhead the fluorescents buzzed faintly, reminding him of the lights in the Overlook's kitchen.

'Torrance's boy,' Durkin said, and shook his head. 'Good-lookin little tyke, ain't he? He n his dad was in here a lot before the snow really flew. Drivin the hotel truck, mostly. Looked to me like the two of em was just about as tight as they could get. That's one little boy that loves his daddy. Hope he's all right.'

'So do I.' Hallorann zipped the parka and tied the hood.

'Lemme help you push that out,' Durkin said. They rolled the snowmobile across the oil-stained concrete and toward the garage bay. 'You ever drove one of these before?'

'No.'

'Well, there's nothing to it. The instructions are pasted there on the dashboard, but all there really is, is to stop and go. Your throttle's here, just like a motorcycle throttle. Brake on the other side. Lean with it on the turns. This baby will do seventy on hardpack, but on this powder you'll get no more than fifty and that's pushing it.'

Now they were in the service station's snow-filled front lot, and Durkin had raised his voice to make himself heard over the battering of the wind. 'Stay on the road!' he shouted at Hallorann's ear. 'Keep your eye on the guardrail posts and the signs and you'll be all right, I guess. If you get off the road, you're going to be dead. Understand?'

Hallorann nodded.

'Wait a minute!' Durkin told him, and ran back into the garage bay.

While he was gone, Hallorann turned the key in the ignition and pumped the throttle a little. The snowmobile coughed into brash, choppy life.

Durkin came back with a red and black ski mask.

'Put this on under your hood!' he shouted.

Hallorann dragged it on. It was a tight fit, but it cut the last of the numbing wind off from his cheeks and forehead and chin.

Durkin leaned close to make himself heard.

'I guess you must know about things the same way Howie does sometimes,' he said. 'It don't matter, except that place has got a bad reputation around here. I'll give you a rifle if you want it.'

'I don't think it would do any good,' Hallorann shouted back.

'You're the boss. But if you get that boy, you bring him to Sixteen Peach Lane. The wife'll have some soup on.'

'Okay. Thanks for everything.'

'You watch out!' Durkin yelled. 'Stay on the road!'

Hallorann nodded and twisted the throttle slowly. The snowmobile purred forward, the headlamp cutting a clean cone of light through the thickly falling snow. He saw Durkin's upraised hand in the rearview mirror, and raised his own in return. Then he nudged the handlebars to the left and was traveling up Main Street, the snowmobile coursing smoothly through the white light thrown by the streetlamps. The speedometer stood at thirty miles an hour. It was ten past seven. At the Overlook, Wendy and Danny were sleeping and Jack Torrance was discussing matters of life and death with the previous caretaker.

Five blocks up Main, the streetlamps ended. For half a mile there were small houses, all buttoned tightly up against the storm, and then only wind-howling darkness. In the black again with no light but the thin spear of the snowmobile's headlamp, terror closed in on him again, a childlike fear, dismal and disheartening. He had never felt so alone. For several minutes, as the few lights of Sidewinder dwindled away and disappeared in the rearview, the urge to turn around and go back was almost insurmountable. He reflected that for all of Durkin's concern for Jack Torrance's boy, he had not offered to take the other snowmobile and come with him.

(*That place has got a bad reputation around here.*)

Clenching his teeth, he turned the throttle higher and watched the needle on the speedometer climb past forty and settle at forty-five. He seemed to be going horribly fast and yet he was afraid it wasn't fast enough. At this speed it would take him almost an hour to get to the Overlook. But at a higher speed he might not get there at all.

He kept his eyes glued to the passing guardrails and the dime-sized reflectors mounted on top of each one. Many of them were buried under drifts. Twice he saw the curve signs dangerously late and felt the snowmobile riding up the drifts that masked the dropoff before turning back onto where the road was in the summertime. The odometer counted off the miles at a maddeningly slow clip – five, ten, finally fifteen. Even behind the knitted ski mask his face was beginning to stiffen up and his legs were growing numb.

(*Guess I'd give a hundred bucks for a pair of ski pants.*)

As each mile turned over, his terror grew – as if the place had a poison atmosphere that thickened as you neared it. Had it ever been like this before? He had never really liked the Overlook, and there had been others who shared his feeling, but it had never been like this.

He could feel the voice that had almost wrecked him outside of Sidewinder still trying to get in, to get past his defenses to the soft meat inside. If it had been strong twenty-five miles back, how much stronger would it be now? He couldn't keep it out entirely. Some of it was slipping through, flooding his brain with sinister subliminal images. More and more he got the image of a badly hurt woman in a bathroom, holding her hands up uselessly to ward off a blow, and he felt more and more that the woman must be—

(*Jesus, watch out!*)

The embankment was looming up ahead of him like a freight train. Wool-gathering, he had missed a turn sign. He jerked the snowmobile's steering gear hard right and it swung around, tilting as it did so. From underneath came the harsh grating sound of the snowtread on rock. He thought the snowmobile was going to dump him, and it did totter on the knife-edge of balance before half-driving, half-skidding back down to the more or less level surface of the snow-buried road. Then the dropoff was ahead of him, the headlamp showing an abrupt end to the snowcover and darkness beyond that. He turned the snowmobile the other way, a pulse beating sickly in his throat.

(*Keep it on the road Dicky old chum.*)

He forced himself to turn the throttle up another notch. Now the speedometer needle was pegged just below fifty. The wind howled and roared. The headlamp probed the dark.

An unknown length of time later, he came around a drift-banked curve and saw a glimmering flash of light ahead. Just a glimpse, and then it was blotted out by a rising fold of land. The glimpse was so brief he was persuading himself it had been wishful thinking when another turn brought it in view again, slightly closer, for another few seconds. There was no question of its reality this time; he had seen it from just this angle too many times before. It was the Overlook. There were lights on the first floor and lobby levels, it looked like.

Some of his terror – the part that had to do with driving off the road or wrecking the snowmobile on an unseen curve – melted entirely away. The snowmobile swept surely into the first half of an S curve that he now remembered confidently foot for foot, and that was when the headlamp picked out the

(*oh dear jesus god what is it*)

in the road ahead of him. Limned in stark black and whites, Halloran first thought it was some hideously huge timberwolf that had been driven down from the high country by the storm. Then, as he closed on it, he recognized it and horror closed his throat.

Not a wolf but a lion. A hedge lion.

Its features were a mask of black shadow and powdered snow, its haunches wound tight to spring. And it did spring, snow billowing around its pistoning rear legs in a silent burst of crystal glitter.

Halloran screamed and twisted the handlebars hard right, ducking low at the same time. Scratching, ripping pain scrawled itself across his face, his neck, his shoulders. The ski mask was torn open down the back. He was hurled from the snowmobile. He hit the snow, plowed through it, rolled over.

He could feel it coming for him. In his nostrils there was a bitter smell of green leaves and holly. A huge hedge paw batted him in the small of the back and he flew ten feet through the air, splayed out like a rag doll. He saw the snowmobile, riderless, strike the embankment and rear up, its headlamp searching the sky. It fell over with a thump and stalled.

Then the hedge lion was on him. There was a crackling, rustling sound. Something raked across the front of the parka, shredding it. It might have been stiff twigs, but Halloran saw it was claws.

'You're not there!' Hallorann screamed at the circling, snarling hedge lion. '*You're not there at all!*' He struggled to his feet and made it halfway to the snowmobile before the lion lunged, batting him across the head with a needle-tipped paw. Hallorann saw silent, exploding lights.

'Not there,' he said again, but it was a fading mutter. His knees unhinged and dropped him into the snow. He crawled for the snowmobile, the right side of his face a scarf of blood. The lion struck him again, rolling him onto his back like a turtle. It roared playfully.

Hallorann struggled to reach the snowmobile. What he needed was there. And then the lion was on him again, ripping and clawing.

CHAPTER FIFTY-TWO
WENDY AND JACK

Wendy risked another glance over her shoulder. Jack was on the sixth riser, clinging to the banister much as she was doing herself. He was still grinning, and dark blood oozed slowly through the grin and slipped down the line of his jaw. He bared his teeth at her.

'I'm going to bash your brains in. Bash them right to fuck in.' He struggled up another riser.

Panic spurred her, and the ache in her side diminished a little. She pulled herself up as fast as she could regardless of the pain, yanking convulsively at the banister. She reached the top and threw a glance behind her.

He seemed to be gaining strength rather than losing it. He was only four risers from the top, measuring the distance with the roque mallet in his left hand as he pulled himself up with his right.

'Right behind you,' he panted through his bloody grin, as if reading her mind. 'Right behind you now, bitch. With your medicine.'

She fled stumblingly down the main corridor, hands pressed to her side.

The door to one of the rooms jerked open and a man with a green ghoulmask on popped out. '*Great party, isn't it?*' He screamed into her face, and pulled the waxed string of a party-favor. There was an echoing bang and suddenly crepe streamers were drifting all around her. The man in the ghoulmask cackled and slammed back into his room. She fell forward onto the carpet, full-length. Her right side seemed to explode with pain, and she fought off the blackness of unconsciousness desperately. Dimly she could hear the elevator running again, and beneath her splayed fingers she could see that the carpet pattern appeared to move, swaying and twining sinuously.

The mallet slammed down behind her and she threw herself forward, sobbing. Over her shoulder she saw Jack stumble forward, overbalance, and bring the mallet down just before he crashed to the carpet, expelling a bright splash of blood onto the nap.

The mallet head struck her squarely between the shoulder blades and for a moment the agony was so great that she could only writhe, hands opening and clenching. Something inside her had snapped – she had heard it clearly, and for a few moments she was aware only in a muted, muffled way, as if she were merely observing these things through a cloudy wrapping of gauze.

Then full consciousness came back, terror and pain with it. Jack was trying to get up so he could finish the job.

Wendy tried to stand and found it was impossible. Electric bolts seemed to course up and down her back at the effort. She began to crawl along in a sidestroke motion. Jack was crawling after her, using the roque mallet as a crutch or a cane.

She reached the corner and pulled herself around it, using her hands to yank at the angle of the wall. Her terror deepened – she would not have believed that possible, but it was. It was a hundred times worse not to be able to see him or know how close he was getting. She tore out fistfuls of the carpet napping pulling herself along, and she was halfway down this short hall before she noticed the bedroom door was standing wide open.

(*Danny! O Jesus*)

She forced herself to her knees and then clawed her way to her feet, fingers slipping over the silk wallpaper. Her nails pulled little strips of it loose. She ignored the pain and half-walked, half-shambled through the doorway as Jack came around the far corner and began to lunge his way down toward the open door, leaning on the roque mallet.

She caught the edge of the dresser, held herself up against it, and grabbed the doorframe.

Jack shouted at her: 'Don't you shut that door! Goddam you, don't you *dare* shut it!'

She slammed it closed and shot the bolt. Her left hand pawed wildly at the junk on the dresser, knocking loose coins onto the floor where they rolled in every direction. Her hand seized the key ring just as the mallet whistled down against the door, making it tremble in its frame. She got the key into the lock on the second stab and twisted it to the right. At the sound of the tumblers falling, Jack screamed. The mallet came down against the door in a volley of booming blows that made her flinch and step back. How could he be doing that with a knife in his back? Where was he finding the strength? She wanted to shriek *Why aren't you dead?* at the locked door.

Instead she turned around. She and Danny would have to go into the attached bathroom and lock that door, too, in case Jack actually could break through the bedroom door. The thought of escaping down the dumb-waiter shaft crossed her mind in a wild burst, and then she rejected it. Danny was small enough to fit into it, but she would be unable to control the rope pull. He might go crashing all the way to the bottom.

The bathroom it would have to be. And if Jack broke through into there—

But she wouldn't allow herself to think of it.

'Danny, honey, you'll have to wake up n—'

But the bed was empty.

When he had begun to sleep more soundly, she had thrown the blankets and one of the quilts over him. Now they were thrown back.

'I'll get you!' Jack howled. 'I'll get both of you!' Every other word was punctuated with a blow from the roque hammer, yet Wendy ignored both. All of her attention was focused on that empty bed.

'*Come out here! Unlock this goddam door!*'

'Danny?' she whispered.

Of course . . . when Jack had attacked her. It had come through to him, as violent emotions always seemed to. Perhaps he'd even seen the whole thing in a nightmare. He was hiding.

She fell clumsily to her knees, enduring another bolt of pain from her swollen and bleeding leg, and looked under the bed. Nothing there but dustballs and Jack's bedroom slippers.

Jack screamed her name, and this time when he swung the mallet, a long splinter of wood jumped from the door and clattered off the hardwood planking. The next blow brought a sickening, splintering crack, the sound of dry kindling under a hatchet. The bloody mallet head, now splintered and gouged in its own right, bashed through the new hole in the door, was withdrawn, and came down again, sending wooden shrapnel flying across the room.

Wendy pulled herself to her feet again using the foot of the bed, and hobbled across the room to the closet. Her broken ribs stabbed at her, making her groan.

'Danny?'

She brushed the hung garments aside frantically; some of them slipped their hangers and ballooned gracelessly to the floor. He was not in the closet.

She hobbled toward the bathroom and as she reached the door she glanced back over her shoulder. The mallet crashed through again, widening the hole, and then a hand appeared, groping for the bolt. She saw with horror that she had left Jack's keyring dangling from the lock.

The hand yanked the bolt back, and as it did so it struck the bunched keys. They jingled merrily. The hand clutched them victoriously.

With a sob, she pushed her way into the bathroom and slammed the door just as the bedroom door burst open and Jack charged through, bellowing.

Wendy ran the bolt and twisted the spring lock, looking around desperately. The bathroom was empty. Danny wasn't here, either. And as she caught sight of her own blood-smeared, horrified face in the medicine cabinet mirror, she was glad. She had never believed that children should be witness to the little quarrels of their parents. And perhaps the thing that was now raving through the bedroom, overturning things and smashing them, would finally collapse before it could go after her son. Perhaps, she thought, it might be possible for her to inflict even more damage on it . . . kill it, perhaps.

Her eyes skated quickly over the bathroom's machine-produced porcelain surfaces, looking for anything that might serve as a weapon. There was a bar of soap, but even wrapped in a towel she didn't think it would be lethal enough. Everything else was bolted down. God, was there nothing she could do?

Beyond the door, the animal sounds of destruction went on and on, accompanied by thick shouts that they would 'take their medicine' and 'pay for what they'd done to him'. He would 'show them who's boss'. They were 'worthless puppies', the both of them.

There was a thump as her record player was overturned, a hollow crash as the secondhand TV's picture tube was smashed, the tinkle of windowglass followed by a cold draft under the bathroom door. A dull thud as the mattresses were ripped from the twin beds where they had slept together, hip to hip. Boomings as Jack struck the walls indiscriminately with the mallet.

There was nothing of the real Jack in that howling, maundering, petulant voice, though. It alternately whined in tones of self-pity and rose in lurid screams; it reminded her chillingly of the screams that sometimes rose in the geriatrics ward of the hospital where she had worked summers as a high school kid. Senile dementia. Jack wasn't out there anymore. She was hearing the lunatic, raving voice of the Overlook itself.

The mallet smashed into the bathroom door, knocking out a huge chunk of the thin paneling. Half of a crazed and working face stared in at her. The mouth and cheeks and throat were lathered in blood, the single eye she could see was tiny and piggish and glittering.

'Nowhere left to run, you cunt,' it panted at her through its grin. The mallet descended again, knocking wood splinters into the tub and against the reflecting surface of the medicine cabinet—

(*!!The medicine cabinet!!*)

A desperate whining noise began to escape her as she whirled, pain temporarily forgotten, and threw the mirror door of the cabinet back. She began to paw through its contents. Behind her that hoarse voice bellowed: 'Here I come now! Here I come now, you pig!' It was demolishing the door in a machinelike frenzy.

Bottles and jars fell before her madly searching fingers – cough syrup, Vaseline, Clairol Herbal Essence shampoo, hydrogen peroxide, benzocaine – they fell into the sink and shattered.

Her hand closed over the dispenser of double-edged razor blades just as she heard the hand again, fumbling for the bolt and the spring lock.

She slipped one of the razor blades out, fumbling at it, her breath coming in harsh little gasps. She had cut the ball of her thumb. She whirled around and slashed at the hand, which had turned the lock and was now fumbling for the bolt.

Jack screamed. The hand was jerked back.

Panting, holding the razor blade between her thumb and index finger, she waited for him to try again. He did, and she slashed. He screamed again, trying to grab her hand, and she slashed at him again. The razor blade turned in her hand, cutting her again, and dropped to the tile floor by the toilet.

Wendy slipped another blade out of the dispenser and waited.

Movement in the other room—

(*?? Going away ??*)

And a sound coming through the bedroom window. A motor. A high, insectile buzzing sound.

A roar of anger from Jack and then – yes, yes, she was sure of it – he was leaving the caretaker's apartment, plowing through the wreckage and out into the hall.

(*?? Someone coming a ranger Dick Hallorann ??*)

'Oh God,' she muttered brokenly through a mouth that seemed filled with broken sticks and old sawdust. 'Oh God, oh please.'

She had to leave now, had to go find her son so they could face the rest of this nightmare side by side. She reached out and fumbled at the bolt. Her arm seemed to stretch for miles. At last she got it to come free. She pushed the door open, staggered out, and was suddenly overcome by the horrible certainty that Jack had only pretended to leave, that he was lying in wait for her.

Wendy looked around. The room was empty, the living room too. Jumbled, broken stuff everywhere.

The closet? Empty.

Then the soft shades of gray began to wash over her and she fell down on the mattress Jack had ripped from the bed, semiconscious.

CHAPTER FIFTY-THREE
HALLORANN LAID LOW

Hallorann reached the overturned snowmobile just as, a mile and a half away, Wendy was pulling herself around the corner and into the short hallway leading to the caretaker's apartment.

It wasn't the snowmobile he wanted but the gascan held onto the back by a pair of elastic straps. His hands, still clad in Howard Cottrell's blue mittens, seized the top strap and pulled it free as the hedge lion roared behind him – a sound that seemed to be more in his head than outside of it. A hard, brambly slap to his left leg, making the knee sing with pain as it was driven in a way the joint had never expected to bend. A groan escaped Hallorann's clenched teeth. It would come for the kill any time now, tired of playing with him.

He fumbled for the second strap. Sticky blood ran in his eyes.

(*Roar! Slap!*)

That one raked across his buttocks, almost tumbling him over and away from the snowmobile again. He held on – no exaggeration – for dear life.

Then he had freed the second strap. He clutched the gascan to him as the lion struck again, rolling him over on his back. He saw it again, only a shadow in the darkness and falling snow, as nightmarish as a moving gargoyle. Hallorann twisted the can's cap as the moving shadow stalked him, kicking up snowpuffs. As it moved in again the cap spun free, releasing the pungent smell of the gasoline.

Hallorann gained his knees and as it came at him, lowslung and incredibly quick, he splashed it with the gas.

There was a hissing, spitting sound and it drew back.

'Gas!' Hallorann cried, his voice shrill and breaking. 'Gonna burn you, baby! Dig on it awhile!'

The lion came at him again, still spitting angrily. Hallorann splashed it again but this time the lion didn't give. It charged ahead. Hallorann sensed rather than saw its head angling at his face and he threw himself backward, partially avoiding it. Yet the lion still hit his upper rib cage a glancing blow, and a flare of pain struck there. Gas gurgled out of the can, which he still held, and doused his right hand and arm, cold as death.

Now he lay on his back in a snow angel, to the right of the snowmobile by about ten paces. The hissing lion was a bulking presence to his left, closing in again. Hallorann thought he could see its tail twitching.

He yanked Cottrell's mitten off his right hand, tasting sodden wool and gasoline. He ripped up the hem of the parka and jammed his hand into his pants pocket. Down there, along with his keys and his change, was a very battered old Zippo lighter. He had bought it in Germany in 1954. Once the hinge had broken and he had returned it to the Zippo factory and they had repaired it without charge, just as advertised.

A nightmare flood of thoughts flooding through his mind in a split second.

(*Dear Zippo my lighter was swallowed by a crocodile dropped from an airplane lost in the Pacific trench saved me from a Kraut bullet in the Battle of the Bulge dear Zippo if this fucker doesn't go that lion is going to rip my head off*)

The lighter was out. He clicked the hood back. The lion, rushing at him, a growl like ripping cloth, his finger flicking the striker wheel, spark, *flame,*

(*my hand*)

his gasoline-soaked hand suddenly ablaze, the flames running up the sleeve of the parka, no pain, no pain yet, the lion shying from the torch suddenly blazing in front of it, a hideous flickering hedge sculpture with eyes and a mouth, shying away, too late.

Wincing at the pain, Hallorann drove his blazing arm into its stiff and scratchy side.

In an instant the whole creature was in flames, a prancing, writhing pyre on the snow. It bellowed in rage and pain, seeming to chase its flaming tail as it zigzagged away from Hallorann.

He thrust his own arm deep into the snow, killing the flames, unable to take his eyes from the hedge lion's death agonies for a moment. Then, gasping, he got to his feet. The arm of Durkin's parka was sooty but unburned, and that also described his hand. Thirty yards downhill from where he stood, the hedge lion had turned into a fireball. Sparks flew at the sky and were viciously snatched away by the wind. For a moment its ribs and skull were etched in orange flame and then it seemed to collapse, disintegrate, and fall into separate burning piles.

(*Never mind it. Get moving.*)

He picked up the gascan and struggled over to the snowmobile. His consciousness seemed to be flickering in and out, offering him cuttings and snippets of home movies but never the whole picture. In one of these he was aware of yanking the snowmobile back onto its tread and then sitting on it, out of breath and incapable of moving for a few moments. In another, he was reattaching the gascan, which was still half-full. His head was thumping horribly from the gasfumes (and in reaction to his battle with the hedge lion, he supposed), and he saw by the steaming hole in the snow beside him that he had vomited, but he was unable to remember when.

The snowmobile, the engine still warm, fired immediately. He twisted the throttle unevenly and started forward with a series of neck-snapping jerks that made his head ache even more fiercely. At first the snowmobile wove drunkenly from side to side, but by half-standing to get his face above the windscreen and into the sharp, needling blast of the wind, he drove some of the stupor out of himself. He opened the throttle wider.

(*Where are the rest of the hedge animals?*)

He didn't know, but at least he wouldn't be caught unaware again.

The Overlook loomed in front of him, the lighted first-floor windows throwing long yellow rectangles onto the snow. The gate at the foot of the drive was locked and he dismounted after a wary look around, praying he hadn't lost his keys when he pulled his lighter out of his pocket . . . no, they were there. He picked through them in the bright light thrown by the snowmobile head lamp. He found the right one and unsnapped the padlock, letting it drop into the snow. At first he didn't think he was going to be able to move the gate anyway; he pawed frantically at the snow surrounding it, disregarding the throbbing agony in his head and the fear that one of the other lions might be creeping up behind him. He managed to pull it a foot and a half away from the gatepost, squeezed into the gap, and pushed. He got it to move another two feet, enough room for the snowmobile, and threaded it through.

He became aware of movement ahead of him in the dark. The hedge animals, all of them, were clustered at the base of the Overlook's steps, guarding the way in, the way out. The lions prowled. The dog stood with its front paws on the first step.

Hallorann opened the throttle wide and the snowmobile leaped forward, puffing snow up behind it. In the caretaker's apartment, Jack Torrance's head jerked around at the high, wasplike buzz of the approaching engine, and suddenly began to move laboriously toward the hallway again. The bitch wasn't important now. The bitch could wait. Now it was this dirty nigger's turn. This dirty, interfering nigger with his nose in where it didn't belong. First him and then his son. He would show them. He would show them that . . . that he . . . that he was of *managerial timber*!

Outside, the snowmobile rocketed along faster and faster. The hotel seemed to surge toward it. Snow flew in Hallorann's face. The headlamp's oncoming glare spotlighted the hedge's shepherd's face, its blank and socketless eyes.

Then it shrank away, leaving an opening. Hallorann yanked at the snowmobile's steering gear with all his remaining strength, and it kicked around in a sharp semicircle, throwing up clouds of snow, threatening to tip over. The rear end struck the foot of the porch steps and rebounded. Hallorann was off in a flash and running up the steps. He stumbled, fell, picked himself up. The dog was growling – again in his head – close behind him. Something ripped at the shoulder of the parka and then he was on the porch, standing in the narrow corridor Jack had shoveled through the snow, and safe. They were too big to fit in here.

He reached the big double doors which gave on the lobby and dug for his keys again. While he was getting them he tried the knob and it turned freely. He pushed his way in.

'*Danny!*' He cried hoarsely. '*Danny, where are you?*'

Silence came back.

His eyes traveled across the lobby to the foot of the wide stairs and a harsh gasp escaped him. The rug was splashed and matted with blood. There was a scrap of pink terrycloth robe. The trail of blood led up the stairs. The banister was also splashed with it.

'Oh Jesus,' he muttered, and raised his voice again. '*Danny! DANNY!*'

The hotel's silence seemed to mock him with echoes which were almost there, sly and oblique.

(*Danny? Who's Danny? Anybody here know a Danny? Danny, Danny, who's got the Danny? Anybody for a game of spin the Danny? Pin the tail on the Danny? Get out of here, black boy. No one here knows Danny from Adam.*)

Jesus, had he come through everything just to be too late? Had it been done?

He ran up the stairs two at a time and stood at the top of the first floor. The blood led down toward the caretaker's apartment. Horror crept softly into his veins and into his brain as he began to walk toward the short hall. The hedge animals had been bad, but this was worse. In his heart he was already sure of what he was going to find when he got down there.

He was in no hurry to see it.

Jack had been hiding in the elevator when Hallorann came up the stairs. Now he crept up behind the figure in the snow-coated parka, a blood- and gore-streaked phantom with a smile upon its face. The roque mallet was lifted as high as the ugly, ripping pain in his back

(*?? did the bitch stick me can't remember ??*)

would allow.

'Black boy,' he whispered. 'I'll teach you to go sticking your nose in other people's business.'

Hallorann heard the whisper and began to turn, to duck, and the roque mallet whistled down. The hood of the parka matted the blow, but not enough. A rocket exploded in his head, leaving a contrail of stars . . . and then nothing.

He staggered against the silk wallpaper and Jack hit him again, the roque mallet slicing sideways this time, shattering Hallorann's cheekbone and most of the teeth on the left side of his jaw. He went down limply.

'Now,' Jack whispered. 'Now, by Christ.' Where was Danny? He had business with his trespassing son.

***

Three minutes later the elevator door banged open on the shadowed third floor. Jack Torrance was in it alone. The car had stopped only halfway into the doorway and he had to boost himself up onto the hall floor, wriggling painfully like a crippled thing. He dragged the splintered roque mallet after him. Outside the eaves, the wind howled and roared. Jack's eyes rolled wildly in their sockets. There was blood and confetti in his hair.

His son was up here, up here somewhere. He could feel it. Left to his own devices, he might do anything: scribble on the expensive silk wallpaper with his crayons, deface the furnishings, break the windows. He was a liar and a cheat and he would have to be chastised . . . harshly.

Jack Torrance struggled to his feet.

'Danny?' he called. 'Danny, come here a minute, will you? You've done something wrong and I want you to come and take your medicine like a man. Danny? *Danny!*'

CHAPTER FIFTY-FOUR
TONY

(*Danny . . .*)

(*Dannneee . . .*)

Darkness and hallways. He was wandering through darkness and hallways that were like those which lay within the body of the hotel but were somewhere different. The silk-papered walls stretched up and up, and even when he craned his neck, Danny could not see the ceiling. It was lost in dimness. All the doors were locked, and they also rose up to dimness. Below the peep-holes (in these giant doors they were the size of gunsights), tiny skulls and crossbones had been bolted to each door instead of room numbers.

And somewhere, Tony was calling him.

(*Dannneee . . .*)

There was a pounding noise, one he knew well, and hoarse shouts, faint with distance. He could not make out word for word, but he knew the text well enough by now. He had heard it before, in dreams and awake.

He paused, a little boy not yet three years out of diapers, and tried to decide where he was, where he might be. There was fear, but it was a fear he could live with. He had been afraid every day for two months now, to a degree that ranged from dull disquiet to outright, mind-bending terror. This he could live with. But he wanted to know why Tony had come, why he was making the sound of his name in this hall that was neither a part of real things nor of the dreamland where Tony sometimes showed him things. Why, where—

'Danny.'

Far down the giant hallway, almost as tiny as Danny himself, was a dark figure. Tony.

'Where am I?' he called softly to Tony.

'Sleeping,' Tony said. 'Sleeping in your mommy and daddy's bedroom.' There was sadness in Tony's voice.

'Danny,' Tony said. 'Your mother is going to be badly hurt. Perhaps killed. Mr Hallorann, too.'

'No!'

He cried it out in a distant grief, a terror that seemed damped by these dreamy, dreary surroundings. Nonetheless, death images came to him: dead frog plastered to the turnpike like a grisly stamp; Daddy's broken watch lying on top of a box of junk to be thrown out; gravestones with a dead person under every one; dead jay by the telephone pole; the cold junk Mommy scraped off the plates and down the dark maw of the garbage disposal.

Yet he could not equate these simple symbols with the shifting complex reality of his mother; she satisfied his childish definition of eternity. She had been when he was not. She would continue to be when he was not again. He could accept the possibility of his own death, he had dealt with that since the encounter in Room 217.

But not hers.

Not Daddy's.

Not ever.

He began to struggle, and the darkness and the hallway began to waver. Tony's form became chimerical, indistinct.

'Don't!' Tony called. 'Don't, Danny, don't do that!'

'She's not going to be dead! *She's not!*'

'Then you have to help her. Danny . . . you're in a place deep down in your own mind. The place where I am. I'm a part of you, Danny.'

'You're *Tony*. You're not me. I want my mommy . . . I want my mommy . . .'

'I didn't bring you here, Danny. You brought yourself. Because you knew.'

'No —'

'You've always known,' Tony continued, and he began to walk closer. For the first time, Tony began to walk closer. 'You're deep down in yourself in a place where nothing comes through. We're alone here for a little while, Danny. This is an

Overlook where no one can ever come. No clocks work here. None of the keys fit them and they can never be wound up. The doors have never been opened and no one has ever stayed in the rooms. But you can't stay long. Because it's coming.'

'It . . .' Danny whispered fearfully, and as he did so the irregular pounding noise seemed to grow closer, louder. His terror, cool and distant a moment ago, became a more immediate thing. Now the words could be made out. Hoarse, huckstering; they were uttered in a coarse imitation of his father's voice, but it wasn't Daddy. He knew that now. He knew

(*You brought yourself. Because you knew.*)

'Oh Tony, is it my daddy?' Danny screamed. '*Is it my daddy that's coming to get me?*'

Tony didn't answer. But Danny didn't need an answer. He knew. A long and nightmarish masquerade party went on here, and had gone on for years. Little by little a force had accrued, as secret and silent as interest in a bank account. Force, presence, shape, they were all only words and none of them mattered. It wore many masks, but it was all one. Now, somewhere, it was coming for him. It was hiding behind Daddy's face, it was imitating Daddy's voice, it was wearing Daddy's clothes.

But it was not his daddy.

It was not his daddy.

'I've got to help them!' he cried.

And now Tony stood directly in front of him, and looking at Tony was like looking into a magic mirror and seeing himself in ten years, the eyes widely spaced and very dark, the chin firm, the mouth handsomely molded. The hair was light blond like his mother's, and yet the stamp on his features was that of his father, as if Tony – as if the Daniel Anthony Torrance that would someday be – was a halfling caught between father and son, a ghost of both, a fusion.

'You have to try to help,' Tony said. 'But your father . . . he's with the hotel now, Danny. It's where he wants to be. It wants you too, because it's very greedy.'

Tony walked past him, into the shadows.

'Wait!' Danny cried. 'What can I—'

THE SHINING

'He's close now,' Tony said, still walking away. 'You'll have to run . . . hide . . . keep away from him. Keep away.'

'Tony, I can't!'

'But you've already started,' Tony said. 'You will remember what your father forgot.'

He was gone.

And from somewhere near his father's voice came, coldly wheedling: 'Danny? You can come out, doc. Just a little spanking, that's all. Take it like a man and it will be all over. We don't need her, doc. Just you and me, right? When we get this little . . . spanking . . . behind us, it will be just you and me.'

Danny ran.

Behind him, the thing's temper broke through the shambling charade of normality.

'*Come here, you little shit! Right now!*'

Down a long hall, panting and gasping. Around a corner. Up a flight of stairs. And as he went, the walls that had been so high and remote began to come down; the rug which had only been a blur beneath his feet took on the familiar black and blue pattern, sinuously woven together; the doors became numbered again and behind them the parties that were all one went on and on, populated by generations of guests. The air seemed to be shimmering around him, the blows of the mallet against the walls echoing and re-echoing. He seemed to be bursting through some thin placental womb from sleep to

★★★

the rug outside the Presidential Suite on the third floor, lying near him in a bloody heap were the bodies of two men dressed in suits and narrow ties. They had been taken out by shotgun blasts and now they began to stir in front of him and get up.

He drew in breath to scream but didn't.

(!!FALSE FACES!! NOT REAL!!)

They faded before his gaze like old photographs and were gone.

But below him, the faint sound of the mallet against the walls went on and on, drifting up through the elevator shaft and the stairwell. The controlling force of the Overlook, in the shape of his father, blundering around on the first floor.

A door opened with a thin screeing sound behind him.

A decayed woman in a rotten silk gown pranced out, her yellowed and splitting fingers dressed in verdigris-caked rings. Heavy-bodied wasps crawled sluggishly over her face.

'Come in,' she whispered to him, grinning with black lips. 'Come in and we will daance the taaaango . . .'

'False face!!' be hissed. 'Not real!' She drew back from him in alarm, and in the act of drawing back she faded and was gone.

'Where are you?' it screamed, but the face was still only in his head. He could still hear the thing that was wearing Jack's face down on the first floor . . . and something else.

The high, whining sound of an approaching motor.

Danny's breath stopped in his throat with a little gasp. Was it just another face of the hotel, another illusion? Or was it Dick? He wanted – wanted desperately – to believe it *was* Dick, but he didn't dare take the chance.

He retreated down the main corridor, and then took one of the offshoots, his feet whispering on the nap of the carpet. Locked doors frowned down at him as they had done in the dreams, the visions, only now he was in the world of real things, where the game was played for keeps.

He turned to the right and came to a halt, his heart thudding heavily in his chest. Heat was blowing around his ankles. From the registers, of course. This must have been Daddy's day to heat the west wing and

(*You will remember what your father forgot.*)

What was it? He almost knew. Something that might save him and Mommy? But Tony had said he would have to do it himself. What was it?

He sank down against the wall, trying desperately to think. It was so hard . . . the hotel kept trying to get into his head . . . the image of that dark and slumped form swinging the mallet from side to side, gouging the wallpaper . . . sending out puffs of plaster dust.

'Help me,' he muttered. 'Tony, help me.'

And suddenly he became aware that the hotel had grown deathly silent. The whining sound of the motor had stopped.

(must not have been real)

and the sounds of the party had stopped and there was only the wind, howling and whooping endlessly.

The elevator whirred into sudden life.

It was coming up.

And Danny knew who – *what* – was in it.

He bolted to his feet, eyes staring wildly. Panic clutched around his heart. Why had Tony sent him to the third floor? He was trapped up here. All the doors were locked.

The attic!

There was an attic, he knew. He had come up here with daddy the day he had salted the rattraps around up there. He hadn't allowed Danny to come up with him because of the rats. He was afraid Danny might be bitten. But the trapdoor which led to the attic was set into the ceiling of the last short corridor in this wing. There was a pole leaning against the wall. Daddy had pushed the trapdoor open with the pole, there had been a ratcheting whir of counterweights as the door went up and a ladder had swung down. If he could get up there and pull the ladder after him . . .

Somewhere in the maze of corridors behind him, the elevator came to a stop. There was a metallic, rattling crash as the gate was thrown back. And then a voice – not in his head now but terribly real – called out: 'Danny? Danny, come here a minute, will you? You've done something wrong and I want you to come and take your medicine like a man. Danny? *Danny!*'

Obedience was so strongly ingrained in him that he actually took two automatic steps toward the sound of that voice before stopping. His hands curled into fists at his sides.

(*Not real! False face! I know what you are! Take off your mask!*)

'*Danny!*' it roared. '*Come here, you pup! Come here and take it like a man!*' A loud, hollow boom as the mallet struck the wall. When the voice roared out his name again it had changed location. It had come closer.

In the world of real things, the hunt was beginning.

Danny ran. Feet silent on the heavy carpet, he ran past the

closed doors, past the silk figured wallpaper, past the fire extinguisher bolted to the corner of the wall. He hesitated, and then plunged down the final corridor. Nothing at the end but a bolted door, and nowhere left to run.

But the pole was still there, still leaning against the wall where Daddy had left it.

Danny snatched it up. He craned his neck to stare up at the trap door. There was a hook on the end of the pole and you had to catch it on a ring set into the trapdoor. You had to—

There was a brand-new Yale padlock dangling from the trap door. The lock Jack Torrance had clipped around the hasp after laying his traps, just in case his son should take the notion into his head to go exploring up there someday.

Locked. Terror swept him.

Behind him it was coming, blundering and staggering past the Presidential Suite, the mallet whistling viciously through the air.

Danny backed up against the last closed door and waited for it.

CHAPTER FIFTY-FIVE
THAT WHICH WAS FORGOTTEN

Wendy came to a little at a time, the grayness draining away, pain replacing it: her back, her leg, her side . . . she didn't think she would be able to move. Even her fingers hurt, and at first she didn't know why.

(*The razor blade, that's why.*)

Her blond hair, now dank and matted, hung in her eyes. She brushed it away and her ribs stabbed inside, making her groan. Now she saw a field of blue and white mattress, spotted with blood. Her blood, or maybe Jack's. Either way it was still fresh. She hadn't been out long. And that was important because—

(*?Why?*)

Because—

It was the insectile, buzzing sound of the motor that she remembered first. For a moment she fixed stupidly on the memory, and then in a single vertiginous and nauseating swoop, her mind seemed to pan back, showing her everything at once.

Hallorann. It must have been Hallorann. Why else would Jack have left so suddenly, without finishing it . . . without finishing *her*?

Because he was no longer at leisure. He had to find Danny quickly and . . . and do it before Hallorann could put a stop to it.

Or had it happened already?

She could hear the whine of the elevator rising up the shaft.

(*No God please no the blood the blood's still fresh don't let it have happened already*)

Somehow she was able to find her feet and stagger through the bedroom and across the ruins of the living room to the shattered front door. She pushed it open and made it out into the hall.

'Danny!' she cried, wincing at the pain in her chest. 'Mr Hallorann! Is anybody there? *Anybody?*'

The elevator had been running again and now it came to a stop. She heard the metallic crash of the gate being thrown back and then thought she heard a speaking voice. It might have been her imagination. The wind was too loud to really be able to tell.

Leaning against the wall, she made her way up to the corner of the short hallway. She was about to turn the corner when the scream froze her, floating down the stairwell and the elevator shaft:

'*Danny! Come here, you pup! Come here and take it like a man!*'

Jack. On the second or third floor. Looking for Danny.

She got around the corner, stumbled, almost fell. Her breath caught in her throat. Something.

(someone?)

huddled against the wall about a quarter of the way down from the stairwell. She began to hurry faster, wincing every time her weight came down on her hurt leg. It was a man, she saw, and as she drew closer, she understood the meaning of that buzzing motor.

It was Mr Hallorann. He had come after all.

She eased to her knees beside him, offering up an incoherent prayer that he was not dead. His nose was bleeding, and a terrible gout of blood had spilled out of his mouth. The side of his face was a puffed purple bruise. But he was breathing, thank God for that. It was coming in long, harsh draws that shook his whole frame.

Looking at him more closely, Wendy's eyes widened. One arm of the parka he was wearing was blackened and singed. One side of it had been ripped open. There was blood in his hair and a shallow but ugly scratch down the back of his neck.

(*My God, what's happened to him?*)

'Danny!' the hoarse, petulant voice roared from above them. '*Get out here, goddammit!*'

There was no time to wonder about it now. She began to

shake him, her face twisting at the flare of agony in her ribs. Her side felt hot and massive and swollen.

(*What if they're poking my lung whenever I move?*)

There was no help for that, either. If Jack found Danny, he would kill him, beat him to death with that mallet as he had tried to do to her.

So she shook Hallorann, and then began to slap the unbruised side of his face lightly.

'Wake up,' she said. 'Mr Hallorann, you've got to wake up. Please . . . please . . .'

From overhead, the restless booming sounds of the mallet as Jack Torrance looked for his son.

***

Danny stood with his back against the door, looking at the right angle where the hallways joined. The steady, irregular booming sound of the mallet against the walls grew louder. The thing that was after him screamed and howled and cursed. Dream and reality had joined together without a seam.

It came around the corner.

In a way, what Danny felt was relief. It was not his father. The mask of face and body had been ripped and shredded and made into a bad joke. It was not his daddy, not this Saturday Night Shock Show horror with its rolling eyes and hunched and hulking shoulders and blood-drenched shirt. It was not his daddy.

'Now, by God,' it breathed. It wiped its lips with a shaking hand. 'Now you'll find out who is the boss around here. You'll see. It's not you they want. It's me. *Me. Me!*'

It slashed out with the scarred hammer, its double head now shapeless and splintered with countless impacts. It struck the wall, cutting a circle in the silk paper. Plaster dust puffed out. It began to grin.

'Let's see you pull any of your fancy tricks now,' it muttered. 'I wasn't born yesterday, you know. Didn't just fall off the hay truck, by God. I'm going to do my fatherly duty by you, boy.'

Danny said: 'You're not my daddy.'

It stopped. For a moment it actually looked uncertain, as if not sure who or what it was. Then it began to walk again. The hammer whistled out, struck a door panel and made it boom hollowly.

'You're a liar,' it said. 'Who else would I be? I have the two birthmarks, I have the cupped navel, even the *pecker*, my boy. Ask your mother.'

'You're a mask,' Danny said. 'Just a false face. The only reason the hotel needs to use you is that you aren't as dead as the others. But when it's done with you, you won't be anything at all. You don't scare me.'

'I'll scare you!' it howled. The mallet whistled fiercely down, smashing into the rug between Danny's feet. Danny didn't flinch. 'You lied about me! You connived with her! You plotted against me! *And you cheated! You copied that final exam!*' The eyes glared out at him from beneath the furred brows. There was an expression of lunatic cunning in them. 'I'll find it, too. It's down in the basement somewhere. I'll find it. They promised me I could look all I want.' It raised the mallet again.

'Yes, they promise,' Danny said, 'but they lie.'

The mallet hesitated at the top of its swing.

***

Hallorann had begun to come around, but Wendy had stopped patting his cheeks. A moment ago the words *You cheated! You copied that final exam!* had floated down through the elevator shaft, dim, barely audible over the wind. From somewhere deep in the west wing. She was nearly convinced they were on the third floor and that Jack – whatever had taken possession of Jack – had found Danny. There was nothing she or Hallorann could do now.

'Oh doc,' she murmured. Tears blurred her eyes.

'Son of a bitch broke my jaw,' Hallorann muttered thickly, 'and my *head . . .*' He worked to sit up. His right eye was purpling rapidly and swelling shut. Still, he saw Wendy.

'Missus Torrance —'

'Shhhh,' she said.

'Where is the boy, Missus Torrance?'

'On the third floor,' she said. 'With his father.'

***

'They lie,' Danny said again. Something had gone through his mind, flashing like a meteor, too quick, too bright to catch and hold. Only the tail of the thought remained.

(it's down in the basement somewhere)

(you will remember what your father forgot)

'You ... you shouldn't speak that way to your father,' it said hoarsely. The mallet trembled, came down. 'You'll only make things worse for yourself. Your ... your punishment. Worse.' It staggered drunkenly and stared at him with maudlin selfpity that began to turn to hate. The mallet began to rise again.

'You're not my daddy,' Danny told it again. 'And if there's a little bit of my daddy left inside you, he knows they lie here. Everything is a lie and a cheat. Like the loaded dice my daddy got for my Christmas stocking last Christmas, like the presents they put in the store windows and my daddy says there's nothing in them, no presents, they're just empty boxes. Just for show, my daddy says. You're it, not my daddy. You're the hotel. And when you get what you want, you won't give my daddy anything because you're selfish. And my daddy knows that. You had to make him drink the Bad Stuff. That's the only way you could get him, you lying false face.'

'Liar! Liar!' The words came in a thin shriek. The mallet wavered wildly in the air.

'Go on and hit me. But you'll never get what you want from me.'

The face in front of him changed. It was hard to say how; there was no melting or merging of the features. The body trembled slightly, and then the bloody hands opened like broken claws. The mallet fell from them and thumped to the rug. That was all. But suddenly his daddy *was* there, looking at him in mortal agony, and a sorrow so great that Danny's heart flamed within his chest. The mouth drew down in a quivering bow.

'Doc,' Jack Torrance said. 'Run away. Quick. And remember how much I love you.'

'No,' Danny said.

'Oh Danny, for God's sake —'

'No.' Danny said. He took one of his father's bloody hands and kissed it. 'It's almost over.'

★★★

Hallorann got to his feet by propping his back against the wall and pushing himself up. He and Wendy stared at each other like nightmare survivors from a bombed hospital.

'We got to get up there,' he said. 'We have to help him.'

Her haunted eyes stared into his from her chalk-pale face. 'It's too late,' Wendy said. 'Now he can only help himself.'

A minute passed, then two. Three. And they heard it above them, screaming, not in anger or triumph now, but in mortal terror.

'Dear God,' Hallorann whispered. 'What's happening?'

'I don't know,' she said.

'Has it killed him?'

'I don't know.'

The elevator clashed into life and began to descend with the screaming, raving thing penned up inside.

★★★

Danny stood without moving. There was no place he could run where the Overlook was not. He recognized it suddenly, fully, painlessly. For the first time in his life he had an adult thought, an adult feeling, the essence of his experience in this bad place – a sorrowful distillation:

(Mommy and Daddy can't help me and I'm alone.)

'Go away,' he said to the bloody stranger in front of him. 'Go on. Get out of here.'

It bent over, exposing the knife handle in its back. Its hands closed around the mallet again, but instead of aiming at Danny, it reversed the handle, aiming the hard side of the roque mallet at its own face.

Understanding rushed through Danny.

Then the mallet began to rise and descend, destroying the last of Jack Torrance's image. The thing in the hall danced an eerie, shuffling polka, the beat counterpointed by the hideous sound of the mallet head striking again and again. Blood splattered across the wallpaper. Shards of bone leaped into the air like broken piano keys. It was impossible to say just how long it went on. But when it turned its attention back to Danny, his father was gone forever. What remained of the face became a strange, shifting composite, many faces mixed imperfectly into one. Danny saw the woman in 217; the dogman; the hungry boy-thing that had been in the concrete ring.

'Masks off, then,' it whispered. 'No more interruptions.'

The mallet rose for the final time. A ticking sound filled Danny's ears.

'Anything else to say?' it inquired. 'Are you sure you wouldn't like to run? A game of tag, perhaps? All we have is time, you know. An eternity of *time*. Or shall we end it? Might as well. After all, we're missing the party.'

It grinned with broken-toothed greed.

And it came to him. What his father had forgotten.

Sudden triumph filled his face; the thing saw it and hesitated, puzzled.

'*The boiler!*' Danny screamed. '*It hasn't been dumped since this morning! It's going up! It's going to explode!*'

An expression of grotesque terror and dawning realization swept across the broken features of the thing in front of him. The mallet dropped from its fisted hands and bounced harmlessly on the black and blue rug.

'The boiler!' it cried. 'Oh no! That can't be allowed! Certainly not! No! You goddamned little pup! Certainly not! Oh, oh, oh—'

'*It is!*' Danny cried back at it fiercely. He began to shuffle and shake his fists at the ruined thing before him. 'Any minute now! I know it! The boiler, Daddy forgot the boiler! *And you forgot it, too!*'

'No, oh no, it mustn't, it can't, you dirty little boy, I'll make you take your medicine, I'll make you take every drop, oh no, oh no—'

It suddenly turned tail and began to shamble away. For a moment its shadow bobbed on the wall, waxing and waning. It trailed cries behind itself like wornout party streamers.

Moments later the elevator crashed into life.

Suddenly the shining was on him.

(*mommy mr hallorann dick to my friends together alive they're alive got to get out it's going to blow going to blow sky-high*)

like a fierce and glaring sunrise and he ran. One foot kicked the bloody, misshapen roque mallet aside. He didn't notice.

Crying, he ran for the stairs.

They had to get out.

CHAPTER FIFTY-SIX
THE EXPLOSION

Hallorann could never be sure of the progression of things after that. He remembered that the elevator had gone down and past them without stopping, and something had been inside. But he made no attempt to try to see in through the small diamond-shaped window, because what was in there did not sound human. A moment later there were running footsteps on the stairs. Wendy Torrance at first shrank back against him and then began to stumble down the main corridor to the stairs as fast as she could.

'Danny! Danny! Oh, thank God! Thank God!'

She swept him into a hug, groaning with joy as well as her pain.

(*Danny.*)

Danny looked at him from his mother's arms, and Hallorann saw how the boy had changed. His face was pale and pinched, his eyes dark and fathomless. He looked as if he had lost weight. Looking at the two of them together, Hallorann thought it was the mother who looked younger, in spite of the terrible beating she had taken.

(*Dick – we have to go – run – the place – it's going to*)

Picture of the Overlook, flames leaping out of its roof. Bricks raining down on the snow. Clang of firebells . . . not that any fire truck would be able to get up here much before the end of March. Most of all what came through in Danny's thought was a sense of urgent immediacy, a feeling that it was going to happen *at any time*.

'All right,' Hallorann said. He began to move toward the two of them and at first it was like swimming through deep water. His sense of balance was screwed, and the eye on the right side of his face didn't want to focus. His jaw was sending giant throbbing bursts of pain up to his temple and down his neck, and his cheek felt as large as a cabbage. But the boy's urgency had gotten him going, and it got a little easier.

'All right?' Wendy asked. She looked from Hallorann to her son and back to Hallorann. 'What do you mean, all right?'

'We have to go,' Hallorann said.

'I'm not dressed . . . my clothes . . .'

Danny darted out of her arms then and raced down the corridor. She looked after him, and as he vanished around the corner, back at Hallorann. 'What if he comes back?'

'Your husband?'

'He's not Jack,' she muttered. 'Jack's dead. This place killed him. *This damned place.*' She struck at the wall with her fist and cried out at the pain in her cut fingers. 'It's the boiler, isn't it?'

'Yes, ma'am. Danny says it's going to explode.'

'Good.' The word was uttered with dead finality. 'I don't know if I can get down those stairs again. My ribs . . . he broke my ribs. And something in my back. It hurts.'

'You'll make it,' Hallorann said. 'We'll all make it.' But suddenly he remembered the hedge animals, and wondered what they would do if they were guarding the way out.

Then Danny was coming back. He had Wendy's boots and coat and gloves, also his own coat and gloves.

'Danny,' she said. 'Your boots.'

'It's too late,' he said. His eyes stared at them with a desperate kind of madness. He looked at Dick and suddenly Hallorann's mind was fixed with an image of a clock under a glass dome, the clock in the ballroom that had been donated by a Swiss diplomat in 1949. The hands of the clock were standing at a minute to midnight.

'Oh my God,' Hallorann said. 'Oh my dear God.'

He clapped an arm around Wendy and picked her up. He clapped his other arm around Danny. He ran for the stairs.

Wendy shrieked in pain as he squeezed the bad ribs, as something in her back ground together, but Hallorann did not slow. He plunged down the stairs with them in his arms. One eye wide and desperate, the other puffed shut to a slit. He looked like a one-eyed pirate abducting hostages to be ransomed later.

Suddenly the shine was on him, and he understood what Danny had meant when he said it was too late. He could feel the explosion getting ready to rumble up from the basement and tear the guts out of this horrid place.

He ran faster, bolting headlong across the lobby toward the double doors.

***

It hurried across the basement and into the feeble yellow glow of the furnace room's only light. It was slobbering with fear. It had been so close, so close to having the boy and the boy's remarkable power. It could not lose now. It must not happen. It would dump the boiler and then chastise the boy harshly.

'Mustn't happen!' it cried. 'Oh no, mustn't happen!'

It stumbled across the floor to the boiler, which glowed a dull red halfway up its long tubular body. It was huffing and rattling and hissing off plumes of steam in a hundred directions, like a monster calliope. The pressure needle stood at the far end of the dial.

'*No, it won't be allowed!*' the manager/caretaker cried.

It laid its Jack Torrance hands on the valve, unmindful of the burning smell which arose or the searing of the flesh as the red–hot wheel sank in, as if into a mudrut.

The wheel gave, and with a triumphant scream, the thing spun it wide open. A giant roar of escaping steam bellowed out of the boiler, a dozen dragons hissing in concert. But before the steam obscured the pressure needle entirely, the needle had visibly begun to swing back.

'*I WIN!*' it cried. It capered obscenely in the hot, rising mist, waving it's flaming hands over its head. '*NOT TOO LATE! I WIN! NOT TOO LATE! NOT TOO LATE! NOT—*'

Words turned into a shriek of triumph, and the shriek was swallowed in a shattering roar as the Overlook's boiler exploded.

***

Hallorann burst out through the double doors and carried the two of them through the trench in the big snowdrift on the porch. He saw the hedge animals clearly, more clearly than before, and even as he realized his worst fears were true, that they were between the porch and the snowmobile, the hotel exploded. It seemed to him that it happened all at once, although later he knew that couldn't have been the way it happened.

There was a flat explosion, a sound that seemed to exist on one low all-pervasive note

(*WHUMMMMMMMMMM*—)

and then there was a blast of warm air at their backs that seemed to push gently at them. They were thrown from the porch on its breath, the three of them, and a confused thought

(*this is what superman must feel like*)

slipped through Hallorann's mind as they flew through the air. He lost his hold on them and then he struck the snow in a soft billow. It was down his shirt and up his nose and he was dimly aware that it felt good on his hurt cheek.

Then he struggled to the top of it, for that moment not thinking about the hedge animals, or Wendy Torrance, or even the boy. He rolled over on his back so he could watch it die.

★★★

The Overlook's windows shattered. In the ballroom, the dome over the mantelpiece clock cracked, split in two pieces, and fell to the floor. The clock stopped ticking: cogs and gears and balance wheel all became motionless. There was a whispered, sighing noise, and a great billow of dust. In 217 the bathtub suddenly split in two, letting out a small flood of greenish, noxious-smelling water. In the Presidential Suite the wallpaper suddenly burst into flames. The batwing doors of the Colorado Lounge suddenly snapped their hinges and fell to the dining room floor. Beyond the basement arch, the great piles and stacks of old papers caught fire and went up with a blowtorch hiss. Boiling water rolled over the flames but did not quench them. Like burning autumn leaves below a wasps' nest, they whirled and blackened. The furnace exploded, shattering the basement's roofbeams, sending them crashing down like the bones of a dinosaur. The gasjet which had fed the furnace, unstoppered now, rose up in a bellowing pylon of flame through the riven floor of the lobby. The carpeting on the stair risers caught, racing up to the first-floor level as if to tell dreadful good news. A fusillade of explosions ripped the place. The chandelier in the dining room, a two-hundred-pound crystal bomb, fell with a splintering crash, knocking tables every which way. Flame belched out of the Overlook's five chimneys at the breaking clouds.

(*No! Mustn't! Mustn't! MUSTN'T!*)

It shrieked; it shrieked but now it was voiceless and it was only screaming panic and doom and damnation in its own ear, dissolving, losing thought and will, the webbing falling apart, searching, not finding, going out, going out to, fleeing, going out to emptiness, notness, crumbling.

The party was over.

CHAPTER FIFTY-SEVEN
EXIT

The roar shook the whole façade of the hotel. Glass belched out onto the snow and twinkled there like jagged diamonds. The hedge dog, which had been approaching Danny and his mother, recoiled away from it, its green and shadow-marbled ears flattening, its tail coming down between its legs as its haunches flattened abjectly. In his head, Hallorann heard it whine fearfully, and mixed with that sound was the fearful, confused yowling of the big cats. He struggled to his feet to go to the other two and help them, and as he did so he saw something more nightmarish than all the rest: the hedge rabbit, still coated with snow, was battering itself crazily at the chainlink fence at the far end of the playground, and the steel mesh was jingling with a kind of nightmare music, like a spectral zither. Even from here he could hear the sounds of the close-set twigs and branches which made up its body cracking and crunching like breaking bones.

'Dick! Dick!' Danny cried out. He was trying to support his mother, help her over to the snowmobile. The clothes he had carried out for the two of them were scattered between where they had fallen and where they now stood. Hallorann was suddenly aware that the woman was in her nightclothes, Danny jacketless, and it was no more than ten above zero.

(*my god she's in her bare feet*)

He struggled back through the snow, picking up her coat, her boots, Danny's coat, odd gloves. Then he ran back to them, plunging hip-deep in the snow from time to time, having to flounder his way out.

Wendy was horribly pale, the side of her neck coated with blood, blood that was now freezing.

'I can't,' she muttered. She was no more than semiconscious. 'No, I . . . can't. Sorry.'

484

Danny looked up at Hallorann pleadingly.

'Gonna be okay,' Hallorann said, and gripped her again. 'Come on.'

The three of them made it to where the snowmobile had slewed around and stalled out. Hallorann sat the woman down on the passenger seat and put her coat on. He lifted her feet up – they were very cold but not frozen yet – and rubbed them briskly with Danny's jacket before putting on her boots. Wendy's face was alabaster pale, her eyes half-lidded and dazed, but she had begun to shiver. Hallorann thought that was a good sign.

Behind them, a series of three explosions rocked the hotel. Orange flashes lit the snow.

Danny put his mouth close to Hallorann's ear and screamed something.

'What?'

'I said do you need that?'

The boy was pointing at the red gascan that leaned at an angle in the snow.

'I guess we do.'

He picked it up and sloshed it. Still gas in there, he couldn't tell how much. He attached the can to the back of the snow-mobile, fumbling the job several times before getting it right because his fingers were going numb. For the first time he became aware that he'd lost Howard Cottrell's mittens.

(*i get out of this i gonna have my sister knit you a dozen pair, howie*)

'Get on!' Hallorann shouted at the boy.

Danny shrank back. 'We'll freeze!'

'We have to go around to the equipment shed! There's stuff in there . . . blankets . . . stuff like that. Get on behind your mother!'

Danny got on, and Hallorann twisted his head so he could shout into Wendy's face.

'Missus Torrance! Hold onto me! You understand? *Hold on!*'

She put her arms around him and rested her cheek against his back. Hallorann started the snowmobile and turned the throttle delicately so they would start up without a jerk. The woman had the weakest sort of grip on him, and if she shifted backward, her weight would tumble both her and the boy off.

They began to move. He brought the snowmobile around in a circle and then they were traveling west parallel to the hotel. Hallorann cut in more to circle around behind it to the equipment shed.

They had a momentarily clear view into the Overlook's lobby. The gasflame coming up through the shattered floor was like a giant birthday candle, fierce yellow at its heart and blue around its flickering edges. In that moment it seemed only to be lighting, not destroying. They could see the registration desk with its silver bell, the credit card decals, the old-fashioned, scrolled cash register, the small figured throw rugs, the high-backed chairs, horsehair hassocks. Danny could see the small sofa by the fireplace where the three nuns had sat on the day they had come up – closing day. But this was the real closing day.

Then the drift on the porch blotted the view out. A moment later they were skirting the west side of the hotel. It was still light enough to see without the snowmobile's headlight. Both upper stories were flaming now, and pennants of flame shot out the windows. The gleaming white paint had begun to blacken and peel. The shutters which had covered the Presidential Suite's picture window – shutters Jack had carefully fastened as per instructions in mid-October – now hung in flaming brands, exposing the wide and shattered darkness behind them, like a toothless mouth yawing in a final, silent deathrattle.

Wendy had pressed her face against Hallorann's back to cut out the wind, and Danny had likewise pressed his face against his mother's back, and so it was only Hallorann who saw the final thing, and he never spoke of it. From the window of the Presidential Suite he thought he saw a huge dark shape issue, blotting out the snowfield behind it. For a moment it assumed the shape of a huge, obscene manta, and then the wind seemed to catch it, to tear it and shred it like old dark paper. It fragmented, was caught in a whirling eddy of smoke, and a moment later it was gone as if it had never been. But in those few seconds as it whirled blackly, dancing like negative motes of light, he remembered something from his childhood . . . fifty years ago, or more. He and his brother had come upon a huge nest of ground wasps just north of their farm. It had been tucked into a hollow between the earth and an old lightning-blasted tree. His brother had had a big old niggerchaser in the band of his hat, saved all the way from the Fourth of July. He had lighted it and tossed it at the nest. It had exploded with a loud bang, and an angry, rising hum – almost a low shriek – had risen from the blasted nest. They had run away as if demons had been at their heels. In a way, Hallorann supposed that demons had been. And looking back over his shoulder, as he was now, he had on that day seen a large dark cloud of hornets rising in the hot air, swirling together, breaking apart, looking for whatever enemy had done this to their home so that they – the single group intelligence – could sting it to death.

Then the thing in the sky was gone and it might only have been smoke or a great flapping swatch of wallpaper after all, and there was only the Overlook, a flaming pyre in the roaring throat of the night

★★★

There was a key to the equipment shed's padlock on his key ring, but Hallorann saw there would be no need to use it. The door was ajar, the padlock hanging open on its hasp.

'I can't go in there,' Danny whispered.

'That's okay. You stay with your mom. There used to be a pile of old horseblankets. Probably all moth-eaten by now, but better than freezin to death. Missus Torrance, you still with us?'

'I don't know,' the wan voice answered. 'I think so.'

'Good. I'll be just a second.'

'Come back as quick as you can,' Danny whispered. 'Please.'

Hallorann nodded. He had trained the headlamp on the door and now he floundered through the snow, casting a long shadow in front of himself. He pushed the equipment shed door open and stepped in. The horseblankets were still in the corner, by the roque set. He picked up four of them – they smelled musty and old and the moths certainly had been having a free lunch – and then he paused.

One of the roque mallets was gone.

(Was that what he hit me with?)

Well, it didn't matter what he'd been hit with, did it? Still, his fingers went to the side of his face and began to explore the huge lump there. Six hundred dollars' worth of dental work undone at a single blow. And after all

(maybe he didn't hit me with one of those. Maybe one got lost. Or stolen. Or took for a souvenir. After all)

it didn't really matter. No one was going to be playing roque here next summer. Or any summer in the foreseeable future.

No, it didn't really matter, except that looking at the racked mallets with the single missing member had a kind of fascination. He found himself thinking of the hard wooden *whack*! of the mallet head striking the round wooden ball. A nice summery sound. Watching it skitter across the

(bone. blood.)

gravel. It conjured up images of

(bone. blood.)

iced tea, porch swings, ladies in white straw hats, the hum of mosquitoes, and

(bad little boys who don't play by the rules.)

all that stuff. Sure. Nice game. Out of style now, but . . . nice.

'Dick?' The voice was thin, frantic, and, he thought, rather unpleasant. 'Are you all right, Dick? Come out now. *Please!*'

('Come on out now nigguh de massa callin youall.')

His hand closed tightly around one of the mallet handles, liking its feel.

(Spare the rod, spoil the child.)

His eyes went blank in the flickering, fire-shot darkness. Really, it would be doing them both a favor. She was messed up . . . in pain . . . and most of it

(all of it)

was that damn boy's fault. Sure. He had left his own daddy in there to burn. When you thought of it, it was damn close to murder. Patricide was what they called it. Pretty goddam low.

'Mr Hallorann?' Her voice was low, weak, querulous. He didn't much like the sound of it.

'*Dick!*' The boy was sobbing now, in terror.

Hallorann drew the mallet from the rack and turned toward the flood of white light from the snowmobile headlamp. His feet scratched unevenly over the boards of the equipment shed, like the feet of a clockwork toy that has been wound up and set in motion.

Suddenly he stopped, looked wonderingly at the mallet in his hands, and asked himself with rising horror what it was he had been thinking of doing. Murder? *Had he been thinking of murder?*

For a moment his entire mind seemed filled with an angry, weakly hectoring voice:

(*Do it! Do it, you weak-kneed no-balls nigger! Kill them! KILL THEM BOTH!*)

Then he flung the mallet behind him with a whispered, terrified cry. It clattered into the corner where the horseblankets had been, one of the two heads pointed toward him in an unspeakable invitation.

He fled.

Danny was sitting on the snowmobile seat and Wendy was holding him weakly. His face was shiny with tears, and he was shaking as if with ague. Between his clicking teeth he said: 'Where were you? We were *scared!*'

'It's a good place to be scared of,' Hallorann said slowly. 'Even if that place burns flat to the foundation, you'll never get me within a hundred miles of here again. Here, Missus Torrance, wrap these around you. I'll help. You too, Danny. Get yourself looking like an Arab.'

He swirled two of the blankets around Wendy, fashioning one of them into a hood to cover her head, and helped Danny tie his so they wouldn't fall off.

'Now hold on for dear life,' he said. 'We got a long way to go, but the worst is behind us now.'

He circled the equipment shed and then pointed the snow-mobile back along their trail. The Overlook was a torch now, flaming at the sky. Great holes had been eaten into its sides, and there was a red hell inside, waxing and waning. Snowmelt ran down the charred gutters in steaming waterfalls.

They purred down the front lawn, their way well lit. The snowdunes glowed scarlet.

'Look!' Danny shouted as Hallorann slowed for the front gate. He was pointing toward the playground.

The hedge creatures were all in their original positions, but they were denuded, blackened, seared. Their dead branches were a stark interlacing network in the fireglow, their small leaves scattered around their feet like fallen petals.

'They're dead!' Danny screamed in hysterical triumph. '*Dead! They're dead!*'

'Shhh,' Wendy said. 'All right, honey. It's all right.'

'Hey, doc,' Hallorann said. 'Let's get to someplace warm. You ready?'

'Yes,' Danny whispered. 'I've been ready for so long—'

Hallorann edged through the gap between gate and post. A moment later they were on the road, pointed back toward Sidewinder. The sound of the snowmobile's engine dwindled until it was lost in the ceaseless roar of the wind. It rattled through the denuded branches of the hedge animals with a low, beating, desolate sound. The fire waxed and waned. Sometime after the sound of the snowmobile's engine had disappeared, the Overlook's roof caved in – first the west wing, then the east, and seconds later the central roof. A huge spiraling gout of sparks and flaming debris rushed up into the howling winter night.

A bundle of flaming shingles and a wad of hot flashing were wafted in through the open equipment shed door by the wind.

After a while the shed began to burn, too.

★★★

They were still twenty miles from Sidewinder when Hallorann stopped to pour the rest of the gas into the snowmobile's tank. He was getting very worried about Wendy Torrance, who seemed to be drifting away from them. It was still so far to go.

'*Dick!*' Danny cried. He was standing up on the seat, pointing. '*Dick, look! Look there!*'

The snow had stopped and a silver-dollar moon had peeked out through the raftering clouds. Far down the road but coming toward them, coming upward through a series of S shaped switchbacks, was a pearly chain of lights. The wind dropped for a moment and Hallorann heard the faraway buzzing snarl of snowmobile engines.

Halloran and Danny and Wendy reached them fifteen minutes later. They had brought extra clothes and brandy and Dr Edmonds.

And the long darkness was over.

CHAPTER FIFTY-EIGHT
EPILOGUE/SUMMER

After he had finished checking over the salads his understudy had made and peeked in on the home-baked beans they were using as appetizers this week, Hallorann untied his apron, hung it on a hook, and slipped out the back door. He had maybe forty-five minutes before he had to crank up for dinner in earnest.

The name of this place was the Red Arrow Lodge, and it was buried in the western Maine mountains, thirty miles from the town of Rangely. It was a good gig, Halloran thought. The trade wasn't too heavy, it tipped well, and so far there hadn't been a single meal sent back. Not bad at all, considering the season was nearly half over.

He threaded his way between the outdoor bar and the swimming pool (although why anyone would want to use the pool with the lake so handy he would never know), crossed a greensward where a party of four was playing croquet and laughing, and crested a mild ridge. Pines took over here, and the wind soughed pleasantly in them, carrying the aroma of fir and sweet resin.

On the other side, a number of cabins with views of the lake were placed discreetly among the trees. The last one was the nicest, and Hallorann had reserved it for a party of two back in April when he had gotten this gig.

The woman was sitting on the porch in a rocking chair, a book in her hands. Hallorann was struck again by the change in her. Part of it was the stiff, almost formal way she sat, in spite of her informal surroundings – that was the back brace, of course. She'd had a shattered vertebra as well as three broken ribs and some internal injuries. The back was the slowest healing, and she was still in the brace . . . hence the formal posture. But the change was more than that. She looked older, and some of the laughter had gone out of her face. Now, as she sat reading her book, Hallorann saw a grave sort of beauty there that had been missing on the day he had first met her, some nine months ago. Then she had still been mostly girl. Now she was a woman, a human being who had been dragged around to the dark side of the moon and had come back able to put the pieces back together. But those pieces, Hallorann thought, they never fit just the same way again. Never in this world.

She heard his step and looked up, closing her book. 'Dick! Hi!' She started to rise, and a little grimace of pain crossed her face.

'Nope, don't get up,' he said. 'I don't stand on no ceremony unless it's white tie and tails.'

She smiled as he came up the steps and sat down next to her on the porch.

'How is it going?'

'Pretty fair,' he admitted. 'You try the shrimp creole tonight. You gonna like it.'

'That's a deal.'

'Where's Danny?'

'Right down there.' She pointed, and Halloran saw a small figure sitting at the end of the dock. He was wearing jeans rolled up to the knee and a red-striped shirt. Further out on the calm water, a bobber floated. Every now and then Danny would reel it in, examine the sinker and hook below it, and then toss it out again.

'He's gettin brown,' Hallorann said.

'Yes. Very brown.' She looked at him fondly.

He took out a cigarette, tamped it, lit it. The smoke raftered away lazily in the sunny afternoon. 'What about those dreams he's been havin?'

'Better,' Wendy said. 'Only one this week. It used to be every night, sometimes two and three times. The explosions. The hedges. And most of all . . . you know.'

'Yeah. He's going to be okay, Wendy.'

She looked at him. 'Will he? I wonder.'

Hallorann nodded. 'You and him, you're coming back.

Different, maybe, but okay. You ain't what you were, you two, but that isn't necessarily bad.'

They were silent for a while, Wendy moving the rocking chair back and forth a little, Hallorann with his feet up on the porch rail, smoking. A little breeze came up, pushing its secret way through the pines but barely ruffling Wendy's hair. She had cut it short.

'I've decided to take Al – Mr Shockley – up on his offer,' she said.

Hallorann nodded. 'It sounds like a good job. Something you could get interested in. When do you start?'

'Right after Labor Day. When Danny and I leave here, we'll be going right on to Maryland to look for a place. It was really the Chamber of Commerce brochure that convinced me, you know. It looks like a nice town to raise a kid in. And I'd like to be working again before we dig too deeply into the insurance money Jack left. There's still over forty thousand dollars. Enough to send Danny to college with enough left over to get him a start, if it's invested right.'

Hallorann nodded. 'Your mom?'

She looked at him and smiled wanly. 'I think Maryland is far enough.'

'You won't forget old friends, will you?'

'Danny wouldn't let me. Go on down and see him, he's been waiting all day.'

'Well, so have I.' He stood up and hitched his cook's whites at the hips. 'The two of you are going to be okay,' he repeated. 'Can't you feel it?'

She looked up at him and this time her smile was warmer. 'Yes,' she said. She took his hand and kissed it. 'Sometimes I think I can.'

'The shrimp creole,' he said, moving to the steps. 'Don't forget.'

'I won't.'

He walked down the sloping, graveled path that led to the dock and then out along the weather-beaten boards to the end, where Danny sat with his feet in the clear water. Beyond, the lake widened out, mirroring the pines along its verge. The terrain was mountainous around here, but the mountains were old, rounded and humbled by time. Hallorann liked them just fine.

'Catchin much?' Hallorann said, sitting down next to him. He took off one shoe, then the other. With a sigh, he let his hot feet down into the cool water.

'No. But I had a nibble a little while ago.'

'We'll take a boat out tomorrow morning. Got to get out in the middle if you want to catch an eatin fish, my boy. Out yonder is where the big ones lay.'

'How big?'

Hallorann shrugged. 'Oh . . . sharks, marlin, whales, that sort of thing.'

'There aren't any whales!'

'No *blue* whales, no. Of course not. These ones here run to no more than eighty feet. Pink whales.'

'How could they get here from the ocean?'

Hallorann put a hand on the boy's reddish-gold hair and rumpled it. 'They swim upstream, my boy. That's how.'

'Really?'

'Really.'

They were silent for a time, looking out over the stillness of the lake, Hallorann just thinking. When he looked back at Danny, he saw that his eyes had filled with tears.

Putting an arm around him, he said, 'What's this?'

'Nothing,' Danny whispered.

'You're missin your dad, aren't you?'

Danny nodded. 'You always know.' One of the tears spilled from the corner of his right eye and trickled slowly down his cheek.

'We can't have any secrets,' Hallorann agreed. 'That's just how it is.'

Looking at his pole, Danny said: 'Sometimes I wish it had been me. It was my fault. All my fault.'

Hallorann said, 'You don't like to talk about it around your mom, do you?'

'No. She wants to forget it ever happened. So do I, but—'

'But you can't.'

'No.'

'Do you need to cry?'

The boy tried to answer, but the words were swallowed in a sob. He leaned his head against Hallorann's shoulder and wept, the tears now flooding down his face. Hallorann held him and said nothing. The boy would have to shed his tears again and again, he knew, and it was Danny's luck that he was still young enough to be able to do that. The tears that heal are also the tears that scald and scourge.

When he had quieted a little, Hallorann said, 'You're gonna get over this. You don't think you are right now, but you will. You got the shi—'

'I wish I didn't!' Danny choked, his voice still thick with tears. 'I wish I didn't have it!'

'But you do,' Hallorann said quietly. 'For better or worse. You didn't get no say, little boy. But the worst is over. You can use it to talk to me when things get rough. And if they get too rough, you just call me and I'll come.'

'Even if I'm down in Maryland?'

'Even there.'

They were quiet, watching Danny's bobber drift around thirty feet out from the end of the dock. Then Danny said, almost too low to be heard, 'You'll be my friend?'

'As long as you want me.'

The boy held him tight and Hallorann hugged him.

'Danny? You listen to me. I'm going to talk to you about it this once and never again this same way. There's some things no six-year-old boy in the world should have to be told, but the way things should be and the way things are hardly ever get together. The world's a hard place, Danny. It don't care. It don't hate you and me, but it don't love us, either. Terrible things happen in the world, and they're things no one can explain. Good people die in bad, painful ways and leave the folks that love them all alone. Sometimes it seems like it's only the bad people who stay healthy and prosper. The world don't love you, but your momma does and so do I. You're a good boy. You grieve for your daddy, and when you feel you have to cry over what happened to him, you go into a closet or

THE SHINING

under your covers and cry until it's all out of you again. That's what a good son has to do. But see that you get on. That's your job in this hard world, to keep your love alive and see that you get on, no matter what. Pull your act together and just go on.'

'All right,' Danny whispered. 'I'll come see you again next summer if you want . . . if you don't mind. Next summer I'm going to be seven.'

'And I'll be sixty-two. And I'm gonna hug your brains out your ears. But let's finish one summer before we get on to the next.'

'Okay.' He looked at Hallorann. 'Dick?'

'Hmm?'

'You won't die for a long time, will you?'

'I'm sure not studyin on it. Are you?'

'No, *sir*. I—'

'You got a bite, sonny.' He pointed. The red and white bobber had ducked under. It came up again glistening, and then went under again.

'*Hey!*' Danny gulped.

Wendy had come down and now joined them, standing in back of Danny. 'What is it?' she asked. 'Pickerel?'

'No, ma'am,' Hallorann said, 'I believe that's a pink whale.'

The tip of the fishing rod bent. Danny pulled it back and a long fish, rainbow-colored, flashed up in a sunny, winking parabola, and disappeared again.

Danny reeled frantically, gulping.

'Help me, Dick! I got him! I got him! Help me!'

Hallorann laughed. 'You're doin fine all by yourself, little man. I don't know if it's a pink whale or a trout, but it'll do. It'll do just fine.'

He put an arm around Danny's shoulders and the boy reeled the fish in, little by little. Wendy sat down on Danny's other side and the three of them sat on the end of the dock in the afternoon sun.

Don't miss the following iconic chillers

To find out more about Stephen King please visit www.hodder.co.uk, www.stephenkingbooks.co.uk and www.facebook.com/stephenkingbooks